Sounding Line

Sounding Line

a novel

Anne DeGrace

McArthur & Company
Toronto

First published in 2009 by
McArthur & Company
322 King Street West, Suite 402
Toronto, Ontario
M5V 1J2
www.mcarthur-co.com

Library and Archives Canada Cataloguing in Publication

DeGrace, Anne
Sounding line : a novel / Anne DeGrace.

ISBN 978-1-55278-797-7

I. Title.

PS8607.E47S68 2009   C813'.6   C2009-903538-3

Design and composition by Tania Craan
Printed in Canada by Webcom

The publisher would like to acknowledge the financial support of the
Government of Canada through the Book Publishing Industry Development
Program (BPIDP) and the Canada Council for our publishing activities. The
publisher further wishes to acknowledge the financial support of the
Ontario Arts Council and the OMDC for our publishing program.

10 9 8 7 6 5 4 3 2 1

Preserving our environment
McArthur & Company Publishing chose Legacy TB Natural
100% post-consumer recycled paper for
the pages of this book printed by Webcom Inc.

Mixed Sources
Product group from well-managed
forests, controlled sources and
recycled wood or fiber
www.fsc.org Cert no. SW-COC-002358
© 1996 Forest Stewardship Council

To all who seek to understand the riddle of depth and space, if only to better understand our place in it.

Sounding line

n. A line marked at intervals of fathoms and weighted at one end, used to determine the depth of water.

Light

The tang of salt, diminished by the autumn chill, is so much a part of you that you scarcely notice it. But it's there just the same, like the coat on your back. Necessary; comforting. The sound of the foghorn travels across a still sea. When you first stepped outside, your hand pausing on the latch of the open door, you left behind lampglow, the clatter of teacup on saucer, and the creak of plank floors: past generations murmuring unfinished conversations. Now, in the remarkable dark of this night, you feel them following you, whispers you can't quite catch.

As you walk along the narrow road towards the government wharf, there is the general store—Coca-Cola and Orange Crush signs reflecting the light outside the firehall—and then the fish-packing plant. Farther along, outdoor drying racks loom like gallows under the single lamp swinging, ghostly, in the fog. Here and there along the dark road are houses, yellow light spilling out.

The fog squats above the water. Tongues of light from the Irish Moss Plant send beacons over the ink-black sea. You step onto the wharf, the sound of your boots accompanied by the soft roll of wave after wave on pebble beach.

At the end of the wharf you stand and watch as the fog retreats, as if it is being pulled by some hand you can't see. It surprises you, in its abruptness and in the sudden, startling clarity of stars on the dark plane of the sea.

That's when you see them. Lights, above the surface of the sea. It could be an aircraft, but it's flying awfully low. Someone in trouble, maybe. Peering, you see a third light, a fourth. The lights glow orange-red, not the red of an aircraft at all, something—different. They blink: one, then another, and another, in sequence. You can't tell if the lights you see are part of something larger, or are entities unto themselves, maybe farther in the distance than you'd first thought, and you squint, but the cold air makes your eyes tear up, and you can't be sure. You think about calling somebody. Who? What would you say?

And this is when you notice the sound: the sound of your breathing, of the waves. Behind you, on the highway, a car. Someone out late, maybe coming home from the Legion over on the Island. Someone who is a world away from you, standing as you are in the chill night air in the impossible dark, with the sea all around you.

There was something about sound, a thought you had. Something you hadn't quite figured out. It flutters around you like a moth, just out of reach.

There are the lights, closer now, floating low above the harbour's surface. Again, you peer, try to make out the dark shape to which they must be attached, strain to discern a wingtip. Something is missing; what? There is the sound of the car as it fades, the sound of your own breathing, the gentle wash of waves in the dark. The lights are closer, now. And then you realize. There is no sound of aircraft. No roar of engines.

No sound at all.

Wednesday, October 4, 1967

1 His tall frame hunched against harbour wind, feet wedged into too-small rubber boots, Pocket Snow was headed west: home. Too much too soon, that's what his father said about the size of his feet, and the short sleeves of his coat. At sixteen, Pocket was just over six feet, making mockery of the handle he'd earned as the newborn when his Uncle Scratch held him up in one broad flipper and pronounced him pocket-sized. Now, books under his arm, he felt conspicuous—due to both size and circumstance—as he made his way from where the schoolbus had dropped him. Half the guys he knew were no longer even in school.

Without turning around, Pocket knew the sound of the car as it rounded the corner: Cuff's '55 Fairlane, won on a bet and Cuff's pride after months of work to get the thing running and out of the cranberry bog it had been sitting in for years. For Cuff and Ernie, cruising down the road looking for someone to bait was a regular part of an afternoon between fishing seasons, this being October: the season over for Irish moss, lobster season not yet started. Neither much wanted to join their fathers out longlining, at least, not until they had to. Life was for living, after all.

The car slowed, revved for show, and Pocket heard the crank of the window as it rolled down. Cigarette smoke escaped, blue, from the car, and hung for an instant before being swept up on the bucking wind.

"Why it's wee little Pocket Snow, all hunched over like he's afraid he'll be blown away. Hey! Wanna ride, Pocket Snow?"

From behind the wheel, laughter. Pocket glanced up in spite of himself, blinking the fog droplets from his eyelashes. Cuff, leering, had one elbow hooked over the steering wheel. There was a day's reddish stubble on his chin. Ernie had his head down, looking for something on the floor of the passenger side. He straightened, the retrieved cigarette cupped into his palm, and caught Pocket's eye. The ballcap was low, but did Pocket see sympathy there? The sudden grin gave nothing away Pocket could decipher. Crooked teeth, laugh lines. He quickly looked away.

"No thanks."

"Hey, Ole Son, got a girl wants to meetcha…"

Pocket kept walking, the Fairlane drifting alongside.

"…she's what, Ern, seven, eight feet? You two get together, have kids, you could make a pack a kindling."

Pocket, close to his road, wondered if they'd follow him up to the house. He was pretty sure he could smell rum, even with his nose pointed dead ahead and that salt blow straight off the steel grey sea.

"Aw, c'mon Pocket. Time you figured out what yer dick's for, innit?"

Abruptly, Pocket cut across the scrubby grass over broken traps and hubcaps to shortcut his way to the lane. When he heard the Fairlane accelerate, he exhaled.

Pocket's Uncle Scratch had once told Pocket to give Cuthbert—meaning Cuff, of course—some leeway when it came to bad behaviour.

"It's a tough lot that crowd has," Scratch had told him at the time. "More riffs and rents in that family than in yer dad's Stanfields." He was hanging laundry as he said this, Pocket's mother in hospital for the first time. "Best stay clear."

Pocket had no problem with that. The thing was, the girls did not steer clear of Cuff Dodds and his square-jawed good looks. Even the guys liked him for the edge of danger he carried with him like a sharp object, ready for anything. As for Pocket, kids his age ignored him and even adults treated him differently. More like a lost dog, he reflected. When he looked at himself in the mirror he saw his mother's face: bow mouth, weak chin, the straight Lawrence nose, a widow's peak in thick brown hair. Nothing remarkable except his height, his shoulders stooping as if in embarrassment. He marvelled at the ones who dressed in the morning, ate breakfast, left the house, just like that. No apprehension. No apologies. What would it be like to take a lungful of air and own it? Shifting his books to his other arm, Pocket trudged the remainder of the path, eyes on the dry grass at his feet, while above, seagulls whirled.

The warmth hit him as soon as he opened the door. It always surprised him, even though he knew he should be expecting it: with his mother sick, the fire was always blasting. From the bed in the living room, his mother stirred, the roll of blankets almost too insubstantial to be human. He could hear his uncle in the kitchen, returned from Yarmouth this past week. He appeared now in the doorway, one hand absently scratching his head, sending salt-and-pepper tufts into a new dishevelment. Pocket nodded at him and then looked towards the figure in the bed.

"Slept most the day," said his uncle.

Pocket looked around. "Dad?"

"Cuttin firewood."

"When you goin back?"

"Not goin."

Pocket paused to let the import of this sink in. If Uncle Scratch was staying, there'd be a reason for it. He had the store in Yarmouth; he'd have to pay somebody in order to be here. Using the toe of one boot to hold down the heel of the other while he de-wedged his feet, Pocket lost his balance for a moment and dropped his books, *Math 10* falling open into boot drippings. Scratch picked it up and rubbed it against his pants.

"Gonna need that." From the pages had slipped the small, flat sketchbook Pocket carried everywhere. It was flipped open to one of Pocket's copious drawings. "Still at it, aintcha. 'Sgood." Scratch held the pencil drawing at arm's-length. The back of a ponytailed head, a girl at a desk, clearly an illustration of the student who sat ahead of Pocket. "Won't getcha pass, though."

Pocket coloured. "Nope," he said, stuffing the sketchbook into its usual place in his back pocket.

Pocket did want to pass. He hoped for a job at his uncle's store when he finished school. Or something. To be the next generation of Snows in Perry's Harbour was not his first choice. If you asked his mother she'd tell you she, herself, came from away. Which meant South Head, a few miles down the road. Whole different ball of wax, she used to say. Her people talk different, for one thing.

Even think different. You get a story from South Head, it means one thing; you get a story from Perry's Harbour, same story, different telling. Even the bullshit's different, you could say, although Merle Snow would never have used the word *bullshit*. Wilf Snow would. Either way, the point was that you read things differently depending on the speaker, and what part of the Shore they came from. And so marrying out to Perry's Harbour was marrying into a whole different culture.

Taking up life in the city was another thing altogether. People in Perry's talk about the ones who moved away like they'd moved to another planet. Uncle Scratch would have stayed in Perry's except for the accident, the one he doesn't talk about, and that Pocket knows enough not to ask about. All Pocket knows is that there was another brother, a boat and a squall. The Snows are diminishing, he thought now. Getting smaller and smaller, like snow in the spring. Seven kids in his grandfather's family, three in his dad's, and in this one, just Pocket. Uncle Scratch wasn't married.

"Sandwich?" Uncle Scratch said now. Pocket nodded; he was always hungry.

"They're saying '67's gonna be a bad winter." Pocket's father, Wilf, rocked backwards in his chair. He folded his hands across his belly, calloused fingers intertwined. The yellow light of the kitchen caught a worn look: two days' growth of beard, dark circles under blue eyes, thinning hair, but around his mouth, laugh lines from four decades of good humour.

Supper plates were pushed away, and the smell of salt

cod and potatoes hung in the air. Pocket was glad his uncle was there, that he knew how to make a good fish-cake, the result of a long, confirmed bachelorhood. In August, he'd made Pocket a blueberry grunt in honour of his sixteenth birthday. Not exactly a birthday cake, but you couldn't beat South Shore blueberries. His mother had been able to come to the table, then.

The lamp swung over the dirty dishes, throwing shadows. Outside, the wind rattled the siding.

"It's breezin up," Pocket offered. His father ignored him, but then, he was stating the obvious. Another gust hit the side wall like a fist.

"They're talkin hurricanes."

There was a rattle as a new gust hit the harbour side of the house, then a clap as if something airborne had hit the siding. From the other room, a stirring, his mother's voice calling out.

"You go, Pocket."

At his mother's bedside, Pocket stood awkwardly, keenly aware of his hands, unsure of where they should be. They hung at his sides, wooden. His mother's hand reached to find his, a cool pressure.

"Get us a bit of tea, wouldja, dear? And help me sit up. How long have I been sleepin?"

"Dunno. A while."

Pocket's hands, now gentle on her shoulders, seemed enormous. With care, he adjusted pillows. Even her head, with its sparse blond hair fading, seemed smaller.

"Get the kettle on, then. And get yer father. I want to use the commode."

In the kitchen, Scratch tossed Pocket a dishtowel while he stacked the dishes, the sink filling with steaming water. He did it jovially, but it felt false to Pocket. The howling weather was an odd counterpoint to the kitchen scene, Scratch whistling under his breath as he washed a plate. When the kettle sang, Pocket filled the teapot. From the living room he could hear, beneath the outside wind, his mother's soft noises of distress as she made the shuffling trip to the commode.

"Shouldn't we get someone in?" Pocket asked. The plate in his hand was hot and soapy, and he almost dropped it.

"Hands like those, ya'd think ya could hold onto a plate," Scratch remarked. "Yer dad doesn't want to. Don't know why, exactly."

"What about Mrs. Crosbey?"

Last week, Shirley Crosbey had come by with macaroni and cheese, brown bread, bakeapple crisp, a can of tinkers, and a jar of raspberry jam. Pocket had stood just inside the door while his father had thanked her in an embarrassed fashion, but it was the way around here, and to be expected. She had left, refusing his dad's offer of tea, and when the door had closed the two had fallen upon the food like they hadn't eaten for days. They both eyed the home-canned lobster until Wilf put it away for a future meal.

Later, when Pocket brought a small plate of Shirley's casserole to his mother, she'd smiled and asked if there was still chowder left. Meals seemed to tire her right out these days, as if the act of chewing took everything she had. After Pocket had helped her eat, he'd finished up her macaroni and cheese, now cold. Leaning over the side counter, he'd cleaned the plate in moments.

"'S a lot to ask," Uncle Scratch said now, thoughtfully. A neighbourly casserole was one thing.

"S'pose."

"You're right, though. I'll talk to him."

From the living room, a shout.

"Jesus, Merle, y'okay? I gotcha. Hold on." Wilf was beneath her, sitting on the bed, feet in his scabby socks sliding on the lino, his wife in his lap like a rag doll. He looked up at his son and brother, tears in his eyes. "Help me."

Pocket stood in the doorway. Gently, Uncle Scratch picked up his sister-in-law, nightgown dangling, damp spot on the back, and set her into bed while Wilf scrambled to pull the covers back in order to tuck in her feet. His mother's hands flapped. "Don't fuss," she snapped. "My legs just went out for a minute, that's all." In a moment she was asleep again, breathing audibly.

"She's herself all right," Scratch noted.

Pocket looked at his dad, saw the tears running down. He hadn't seen that before. He wanted to look away, but found that he couldn't.

"Got homework?" Scratch was already walking towards the kitchen. "You go on up. I'll finish in here."

At the foot of the stairs that rose by the front door, Pocket paused, his foot on the first step. Then he turned, pushed his feet into his boots, and plucked his coat from the hook. The bite of night air took his breath away.

2 Coming back from the Island in the dark, Cuff drove as if the road was liquid, and Ernie supposed that for Cuff, it was. It had that quality, for sure. They'd had a few to drink in the parking lot over at the Legion. Used to be, drinking happened on a weekend; these days, it happened any time, even on a Wednesday night.

"You wanna let me drive?"

"No way."

"C'mon. Yer pisseder than a—"

"Than a what?"

"I dunno—whoah, buddy, slow down."

The road ribboned, low trees on either side, now and then a slice of harbour. Here and there, houselight. Drift fog caught the headlights like a hand in your face, but above there were stars. The wind that had rocked the cove earlier had vanished. Cuff took the corner—"that was two wheels, Cuff," protested Ernie—and then the road straightened and the harbour lay before them.

Ernie looked at Cuff, recognized the narrowing of eyes: there was no point in arguing. Broad ginger sideburns and longer hair were Cuff's attempt to imitate the guys in the magazines at Crosbey's store, but the jacket, one of his brothers' hand-me-downs, was from an earlier decade. Nobody in Cuff's family cared what he did or how he looked, seven boys with Cuff coming in the middle. Nicknamed Cuff because he was always getting cuffed for *something*. When Ernie tried to grow his already-thinning hair past his ears, his mother sat him down at the kitchen table, scissors flashing—while his older sister killed herself laughing—and that was that.

Cuff pulled the Fairlane alongside the Moss Plant, gravel crunching under tires. He cut the motor before they'd come to a full stop. As the headlights swung in, Ernie saw the overturned crates where, during mossing season, they used to sit for a smoke break after dumping off the morning's load. He could still feel the blisters on his hands from raking all that moss, feel it slide under his boots in the boat. In the old days whole families would rake, the women and girls drying, turning; that's what his dad said, anyway. Now, they most times just sold it wet. They got less for it, but they didn't have to worry about a spell of bad weather, and anyway, times had changed, hadn't they? It was good money while it lasted, good to have some cash in pocket. Ernie wished he had a little more in his pocket these days. If he had, he'd take Edie to a movie. They spent a lot of time together, and she didn't ask for much. She deserved a night out, he figured. He thought of her, the soft curve of her jawline, gentle brown eyes.

"Good night, whannit?" Cuff lit a cigarette, sucked 'til it glowed up the dash, then exhaled noisily.

"Good for *you*."

"You look to be making out okay with that little Edie—where's she from?—from up Island, wherever."

"Bride's Neck."

Cuff leered. "She's from Bride's Neck? You watch yourself. Been seein her, what a month, now? Been seein a little too much of her, if ya ask *me*. Should be playin the field. Lotsa tail out there."

Ernie cringed inwardly. "Five months. Been seein her almost five months."

"Gotta play the field, Ole Son," Cuff said again.

"Yeah," Ernie said. He held out thumb and forefinger for Cuff's cigarette and lit his own. "So you've said," he added, heart speeding up. You didn't talk back to Cuff.

Cuff looked at him squarely, eyes glinting. "What's got into you, man? We've know each other since, what, since we learned to piss standin up, innit? Ya got something up yer ass, or what?"

Ernie, staring through the windshield across the harbour, watched the surface fog as it receded. It looked as if it was being pulled back off the water the way a magician would whip a cloth off a table. "Nothin," he said.

"Pass me another smoke," Cuff reached towards the dash, then: "Brenda. Mmmmm," he said, tilting his head back, eyes closed.

"So. You serious?"

"Serious as I ever am," Cuff said, and Ernie laughed. "Asked her to the Hallowe'en dance."

"That's not for a month!"

"That's just to keep her interested. So she knows my good intentions." Cuff started up the engine again.

"Good," said Ernie, thinking they'd be going home, now, but "just cold," Cuff said, and they sat, the car's interior warming.

They sat there for quite a while, lighting one cigarette from the butt of another, until the air in the car was thicker than winter fog, and then Cuff rolled the window down. The cold air came in on its own tide, and both boys shivered.

"Who's that on the wharf?" Cuff asked when the air had cleared. It was hard to see, the view partly obscured by the whitewashed siding of the building.

"That Pocket Snow?"

Ernie looked over. In the available light he could see Cuff's pale eyes glittering, from smoke or booze or evil intent, he didn't know. Cuff made Ernie nervous when he'd get like that. You just never knew.

"Leave him, Cuff. We got better things to do."

"Like what?"

"Hey, Cuff, you ever think about how you and Pocket are both parts of a coat? Hey, maybe you're cousins and you don' know it—" Ernie started to laugh. "Cuff, Pocket…who d'ya think should be Sleeve?"

Cuff wasn't laughing. "Like what better things we got to do?" He stubbed his cigarette out, one hand on the chrome door handle.

"Like let's drive back, see if there's anyone still hanging around at the hall. It's early, yet." Ernie didn't care to be back on the road with Cuff, but it seemed the safer alternative, given the mood Cuff was in. Ernie stubbed his own butt into the ashtray, sending one or two from the overflow onto the floor.

"Won't be anyone left by now," Cuff said, leering, eyes on the harbour. "'Cept maybe *Debbie*."

"What d'ya mean?"

"Meaning she'll be out back with her legs in the air." Cuff turned, lip curled.

"Fuck off."

"Only one in Perry's Harbour—only one on the whole South Shore—doesn't know that is you."

"I said fuck off."

"Fuck off yerself. You're the one with the sister can't keep her legs shut."

The ash of Cuff's cigarette glowed long and hot, and all at once fell, sending a shower of spark and ash down his front. He brushed wildly for a moment, sending one ember onto Ernie, burning his wrist. Ernie's fist clenched, anger rising in his throat. The air turned sharp.

But Ernie was just sober enough not to want to lose a fight. "Fuck off, Cuff," he said again, backing off but keeping the edge.

"You don't believe it? Well I should know. *First hand.*" The gesture Cuff made was more than Ernie could take. He lunged. Cuff held up his still-lit cigarette between them, a quarter-inch from his friend's lip, where it glowed malevolently. Neither boy breathed.

Before he knew what he would do, Ernie was out of the car. The slam of the door sounded feeble to his ears as he strode away.

Cuff's voice from the open window: "I did your sister, Ernie. *And* Edie Norris!"

On the highway, hands in pockets, head down, Ernie went over his last words, mouthing the things he should have said. Cuff was like that when he drank, but tonight was worse. He thought about where the conversation turned: he'd been trying to steer Cuff off Pocket, that's when everything changed. Ernie didn't dislike Pocket. There wasn't anything there to dislike—they had even played together when they were small—but now he just felt sorry for him. Besides being a pack of twigs walking around, everyone knew his mum was going to die. The baiting of Pocket Snow—just sport, really—had started before anyone knew about his mother, and then when she was first sick it continued on, because it had taken on a life of its own by then. And anyway, she was going to get better, right? And then she didn't, and it was— habit, that's all. They didn't mean anything by it. Ernie didn't even know for sure if the figure on the wharf had been Pocket, he couldn't really see, but if it *was* Pocket, then it was just sad, that's all, to be by yourself at night on the end of a wharf.

Ernie watched the squared-off toes of his boots as they rasped against the gravel shoulder. The salt-sour odour from the packing plant reached him before he looked up to see its bulk looming in the sharp air, back-lit by lights from the firehall and the parking lot at Crosbey's store. Walking its length on the highway side, his view of the harbour and the wharf was obscured, so he couldn't see if Pocket was still there; couldn't see anything it was so pitch dark. Ernie kept his eyes on his feet so he wouldn't trip, that's how dark it was. And he wasn't quite as sober as he'd thought, come to think of it.

There was a shift in light, and Ernie looked up to see what it was. He glimpsed something bright, an orange light that drifted slantways and then disappeared behind the packing plant. Someone setting off flares? he wondered briefly, but kept going, testing himself by walking as straight a line as he could on the road's edge. He was just past the plant on the harbour side when he heard the Fairlane start. He kept walking, head down. He wouldn't give Cuff the satisfaction of looking up.

When the car rounded the corner he saw the lights sweep the road ahead of him, and then it was on him, Cuff driving like a crazy man. Ernie whirled just in time to see the car bearing down on him, feel the nick of the sideview mirror on his arm before being flung into the gravel parking lot, and then it was past. He scrambled up as the taillights disappeared over the hill.

He was still cursing when he arrived, cold, at the door of his dark house. If his mother had been up waiting, no telling where he'd have told her to go if she'd started in on him the way she often did. The smell of onions, lingering in the kitchen, made him queasy as he passed. On his way to his room he paused to push open Debbie's bedroom door with the tips of two fingers. She was home, or at least something Debbie-shaped was under the quilt. When he heard her sigh and roll, he gently closed her door. Of course she was there.

The red welt on his arm where the mirror had struck appeared as angry as he felt. He tossed in the bed-clothes for a long time, imagining various fates for Cuff Dodds. The bruise, when it appeared, would extend from shoulder to elbow, shifting and seething in ugly shades for weeks.

At the phone booth under the light outside Crosbey's General Store, Cuff shouted into the receiver as if he was sure the listener was stone deaf.

"I've over to Perry's. At the store. I saw somethin, I think it was an airplane or somethin. Come right down into the harbour. Orange lights. Maybe they was blinkin, I dunno. They was flying, though, and then they hit the water, and then they floated there for, uh, 'bout five minutes. Yeah, 'bout that long. Then they went under, I guess, disappeared, anyway. What? I told you. Cuff Dodds. Yeah, Stanley's son. Yeah. What? No. No I haven't. Okay, maybe one, but that was ages ago. I'm not drunk, I swear to God, stack a Bibles. I told you what I saw. Yeah, okay, I'll hold on."

Cuff waited, shivering. He wasn't all that warmly dressed, something that didn't seem to matter when he was pressed up against Brenda Corbet behind the hall. Which was where he saw Ernie's sister Debbie with Joshua Smith, which ticked him off, because he'd had a thing for Debbie ever since fifth grade and now here she was with that stuck-up idiot from the Passage, the one with the new Chev and his father's lobster licence.

Ernie. What an idiot. Of course he wasn't really mad at Ernie, it was Josh he'd like to strangle, but Ernie was just so dim sometimes, well, he had it coming—

"Yes. Yeah, I'm still here. I haven't gone nowhere, stayed right here like you told me. Right. Orange lights, four a them, blinkin, came right down into the harbour. Couldn'ta gone anywhere else, nowhere else to go. Didn't I say blinkin? Well they were. I *told* you. I'm cold sober. Swear. Really? Yeah, okay."

Another call. So he wasn't the only one. Imagine Charlie Brannen suspecting alcohol, as if Cuff didn't know what he'd seen. The cop wasn't that much older than Cuff, graduated with Cuff's cousin Wally in '61, and here he was talking to Cuff like he was some kid who couldn't tell his ass from his elbow. Above the phone a shaky hand had scratched a girl's name and a phone number, not one he recognized. Reaching, he found the pen still attached to its cord dangling below the phone. Under the number he wrote: Debbie Morton For a Good Time 3-2662. He felt in the coin return for change, but found only a wad of chewing gum.

Where the fuck was Charlie? Cuff pranced from foot to foot for a couple of minutes before registering that, besides being cold, he needed to take a leak. As he pissed against a rock he kept one eye on the road in case Charlie had decided to drop everything and come, like he should've done in the first place instead of leaving him hanging around like this. When he'd zipped up he took a few quick strides towards the harbour, straining to see past the pilings of the lobster pound.

The phone rang, and Cuff sprinted back, catching the receiver up before the third ring. This time, Charlie was back right away, firing questions, all serious. Only one in the detachment, he told Cuff, he was doing what he could. Cuff felt his chest expand into the new attitude of seriousness, his role in it all. Still, he couldn't take his eyes off the harbour. There must be something out there. Something would have to come up from whatever went down.

"Don't ya think ya should just get over here? I mean, I can't see the place it went down from where I'm standin, here at the phone, could be anything going on out there. We need to get some boats out. You got to call, phone's out at our place. You know Donny Norris? Call Wilf Snow, or Donny Norris, or Tailgate, his boat's ready to go, saw him bring it in earlier…

27

"No, just me. I was with Ernie Morton, but he left before. And there was another guy on the wharf. Don't know. Maybe Pocket Snow. I just saw his back, that's all. Yeah? Yeah, okay."

Stay by the phone, Charlie had told him. The last thing Cuff wanted to do. He felt in his jacket for another dime, but who would he call? Maybe it was nothing. He wished Ernie was here, someone to joke around with. He walked a few steps and peered out over the black, still surface of Perry's Harbour. It's right strange, he thought, that's for sure.

3 It looked as if every light in the house was on when Pocket turned off the highway and up the lane, rubber boots slipping on gravel as he ran. To him, the windows with their glow looked like so many eyes watching his progress, which suddenly seemed remarkably, infuriatingly slow against the rapid beating of his heart.

At the wharf, he'd watched as the strange orange lights had come closer, waited for the explosion, some noise of impact. There was none. Whatever it was had appeared to float on the water, and then, after a few minutes, had disappeared. Were the lights extinguished, or did the thing sink? He'd watched for a few moments more, then left the wharf, walking at first, then running. He should tell someone.

It must have been past 11:30 when he turned up the path, but what should have been a sleeping house was, instead, ablaze with light. His breath caught, fear rising. Something must be wrong. His mother.

As he approached, he heard the unmistakable sound of hammering. Now?

"Pocket! Where was ya?" Wilf asked jovially, not looking around from where he stood halfway up a stepladder. He wrenched the crowbar, pulling the old plywood cupboard another inch from the wall.

Pocket stood in the doorway trying to make sense of

the scene. But: "saw something right strange," he said. Whatever was going on here could wait.

"Strange? I guess. Yer father's taken it into his head to start renovatin the kitchen," said Scratch from the kitchen table where he sat, barely visible behind stacks of dishes piled on the oilcloth cover. Around him crowded the Sobey's special offer china, and the gift mugs (*Over the hill!*: Pocket had given that one to his father last year for his fortieth birthday), with the two precious Maritime Rose dinner plates, still in their news-paper wrappings, perched at the top of the pile. In his uncle's hand was a coffee mug of rye whisky. Pocket could smell it from the doorway.

"Down t'the harbour. I saw—" Pocket tried again.

"Yer mother's always wanted a new kitchen." Wilf wrenched again, and the cupboard came away from the wall. Scratch caught the corner with a long arm in one fluid movement from his seat, toppling the wooden kitchen chair in the process. Pocket righted the chair and sat down on it. The other three chairs were stacked with dishes.

"Been askin for it for years," Wilf said, grunting. "Don't know why I didn't get around to it 'til now." Wilf had the crowbar under the far end, now, the nails squeaking loose from the wallboard. "Gonna build new ones," he said, grinning at his son. He'd been drinking too, Pocket could tell.

"Maybe you should have built 'em before you pulled off the old ones?" Pocket offered. "Place looks rim-wracked. Anyways, listen—"

Wilf and Scratch exchanged glances. "That's what

happens when you send 'em to school," Scratch said after a moment. "They get all logical on you." He turned to Pocket. "Hold this, wouldja?"

Pocket grabbed the loosened corner while his dad gave a final wrench. Together, they eased the cupboard to the floor. When Pocket straightened up, his uncle was handing him a mug. "Watered it down some," he said, more to Wilf than to Pocket. "He's lookin a little shaky tonight."

"Yer not listenin—" Pocket took a swallow and coughed when the fire hit his throat. "Hot," he choked, and both men laughed.

"Yer not listenin," he croaked, trying again. But the truth was, whatever he'd seen was starting to seem unreal. He'd thought it was a plane of some kind. But wouldn't there be a noise, an explosion? "There was—"

Wilf's eyes were back on his project. In some places the wrenching of the cupboards had pulled away the old wallboard. "Might need a new wall," he allowed. "Takin a break," he wheezed, moving a stack of dishes from the closest chair and setting them on the floor. Scratch followed suit, and both men sat heavily. "Cheers," Wilf said, then: "Ya do look kinda shaky. Wheredja say ya was, again?"

Pocket found his voice from under the whisky. "I *said*. Down to the wharf. Saw something."

"Saw what?"

"Dunno exactly. Lights, I guess. Something came down into the harbour. Maybe a plane, I dunno, but it didn't sound like one. Can't be the only one who saw it—"

"Crashed?"

"Yeah, must've, I—"

"You're sure?"

"Yeah, I—"

But Wilf was already pulling on his jacket, stepping into his boots. Scratch stood up, was in the hallway and pulling on his own boots almost as quickly.

"You goin out?" Pocket asked, surprised. Uncle Scratch didn't go out on the water anymore.

"A plane goes down, you go," Scratch replied. "That's all. Don't know why ya didn't tell us right away."

"I didn't say it was a plane, I—" Pocket remembered the absence of sound, and then his mind supplied the roar of engines. Had it been there or not?

Pushing an arm into a coat sleeve, Pocket's father turned to him. "You stay. There'll be a few down there already."

"Dad, wait—"

"No, you stay with yer mother. Someone has to stay with her."

When the door shut, Pocket sat with his mug of watered whisky in the wreckage of the kitchen. The flower-patterned curtains his mother had sewn for want of cupboard doors lay crumpled in the corner.

When he heard his mother stir, Pocket walked quietly into the living room. A sliver of wood from the demolition jabbed into his socked foot as he stepped and he winced, then leaned over to pull it out. When he righted himself, his mother was looking at him in that way she always used to, the way that always spooked him a little: entirely present, and seeing every cell of him.

"Where is everybody?" she demanded.

"Out in the boat. Something crashed into the harbour."

Merle struggled to pull herself up, thin hands pushing against the sheets with knuckles like chicken bones. Pocket put his own large hands under her armpits and together they raised her a little. Pocket adjusted the pillows.

"You need to, uh, go?" he asked, glancing towards the commode. He hoped she didn't. It seemed wrong for a son to help his mother to do something so private, but there was no one else. If only Mrs. Crosbey…

"No, not right now, dear," she folded her hands on the concave area of the blankets where her belly should have rounded them. "Make us a cup of tea?" She seemed to remember then, what Pocket had said a moment before. "You said they took the boat out? What time is it?"

"Yeah, Mum. I saw some lights, something come down into the harbour." Pocket remembered the sounds of voices on the road as he'd hurried home, the sound of pickup trucks turning down towards the wharf, the more distant startup of engines of Cape Island boats. How long ago was that? "Must be close to midnight."

"You smell like booze. Whatcha been getting into?"

"Dad and Uncle Scratch. They let me taste some whisky."

"Hmmph." She pursed her lips, looking like his mother again. "Now sit down and tell me what's going on, dear. Wait. Get the kettle on first."

In the kitchen, Pocket couldn't find the kettle. It should be on the stove, but it wasn't. The stove was piled with pots and pans from the lower cupboards, the ones still attached to the wall, and if the kettle was somewhere, Pocket couldn't see it in the jumble. It took him a while to move the pots onto the floor without making noise. It was a mercy his mother couldn't see the mess in the kitchen. He filled a small enamel pot with water and turned on the burner. No teapot in sight, either, and then he found it, several pieces lying in the sink. Making tea in a cup was something his mother soundly rejected, a method "for men and lazy folk," but there was nothing to be done. He'd just bring her a cup as if he'd left the pot in the kitchen, then. While he waited for the water to boil, he finished the whisky in his uncle Scratch's mug. Then, after a moment, he finished his father's too.

His mother's eyes were closed when he brought her the tea in a mug, and at first Pocket thought she'd gone back to sleep. She opened her eyes as he set the cup down, so he lifted it again and set it in her hand, keeping his own hand under it in case her wrist gave way like it had once before. But she looked—stronger, Pocket thought.

"Now tell me," she said, sounding like she used to. Sounding like his mother.

"I was down to the wharf—"

But she'd closed her eyes. When she opened them, she looked at him squarely and said: "Did they get the cannon out?"

"Cannon?"

"On Herring Island"

"Mum, that was in the summer."

"Tell me."

The cannon was known to everyone. It stood sentinel on Herring Island, and was a landmark for boats. In good weather, it was a good luck charm you nodded to as you passed, heading for the lobstering spots with a boat full of traps or longlines coiled and ready; a few days' food; a hot thermos. In bad weather, it told you where you were when every island looked about the same in thick fog, told you just how close you were to home. Nobody knew for sure who put it there, but the South Shore was full of old walls and foundations of forts built by some Frenchman or other who got called back home or maybe just didn't survive an Atlantic winter. It had been Pocket's father who first spread the word that the bank had eroded to the point that the old cannon was in danger of falling into the sea.

"They got it out. It's at the museum, on the front lawn."

"Must've been quite a job."

It was all they had talked about. How could she not remember? What month did she think this was?

"It was last summer, Mum. It's October, now."

"You don't have to tell me what month it is, Pocket."

She sipped her tea. Pocket waited, wishing his father and uncle would return. He looked at his mother's long fingers where they held the cup, then at his own, which fidgeted now on his knees. When he looked at his mother, she was looking at him.

"You been drawin?" she asked him.

"Some. Not so much these days."

"You always liked to draw. Soon as you could hold a pencil. If there wasn't a pencil, ya found somethin else.

Ya once drew the whole family in ketchup on the kitchen table before we caught ya. Did I ever tell you?"

"Yeah, Mum."

She was quiet for a bit. When the cup began to tilt, Pocket caught it and took it gently from her. She had drunk very little. She opened her eyes. "What for?" she asked him.

"What for, *what*?"

"What did they go out in the boat for?"

"To see if they could help."

"Help?"

"I told you, Mum. I saw these lights. Coming over the water, red—no, more orangey—and real low. And I thought they were a plane crashing, except there weren't any noise, it was right quiet. They came right down by Kettle Island, right in front, like, and then they went out and there was a yellow light on top, glowing there, floated for a bit and then sunk into the water. Too dark to see anything after that. So I just run home."

"Musta been an airplane come down. Someone lost, maybe? Someone should go out." Merle coughed a little.

Pocket passed the cup back and forth, hand to hand, cold tea sloshing. He tried to keep the exasperation from his voice. "They did. Uncle Scratch and Dad, they went out. And some others, I 'magin."

"Wasn't there wind earlier?"

"Yeah, but it's right calm, now. Not a breeze. And clear."

"Maybe blown off course earlier, then," she said, as if that summed it up.

"Didn't look like no airplane I ever saw."

But her eyes had closed. Pocket stood, staring down at his mother's slight form. He heard her shallow breathing. He thought of her singing to him, sitting at his bedside when he was small: "How Much is that Doggie in the Window?" He'd asked her where California was, the place where the person in the song was going away to, leaving his sweetheart alone. "Other side of the world, dear," his mother had said, and although he now knows it isn't, it might as well be. How far from Perry's Harbour had his mother even been in her life? He'd never asked.

Pocket reached over to pull the extra pillow from behind her head, but she opened her eyes and waved him away.

"No, leave it. I'll just doze here, like this, 'til they get back." She waved her hand again, this time in the general direction of the mug Pocket was holding. "And next time, make it in the pot, wouldja, dear?" Self-consciously and for no particular reason, Pocket hid the mug behind his back. "Sorry, Mum," but her breath had slowed, and she seemed to be asleep.

He had turned towards the kitchen when she spoke once more. "And by the way, what was all that commotion earlier? Sounded like yer dad was ripping the cupboards right off the walls, for mercy's sake."

4 The letter, written in his mother's fine, old-fashioned hand, was dated simply *August*. Pocket tried to remember August, which now seemed a long time ago; he believed that may have been when his mother stopped making her regular trips to Yarmouth, the significance of which had not been clear to him at the time. He'd thought she was getting better. He sat in bed, covers pulled up to his chin against the autumn chill, a circle of light falling on the paper's surface.

It was close to four in the morning; Pocket had waited for his father and uncle to return, and while he waited— while his mother slept, breathing shallowly, the bridge lamp in the corner softly glowing—he had idly opened the hinged cover on the oak writing desk.

Inside, four cubbyholes held various bundles of papers. In the first, bound by an elastic band, were Christmas cards. The dry elastic snapped when he pulled it off, the cards splaying out on the writing surface. Shirley's card from last year portrayed a winking Santa about to chow down on a plate of cookies. Inside, Shirley's note—don't let the fat guy eat them all—suggested that the card must have accompanied a tin of Shirley's Scotch shortbreads. But the older cards, a little yellowed and with a soft, often-opened feel to them, caused Pocket to run his finger across the front much as his mother would have done. Cheery messages from his English grandmother about "hoping to see you again soon"—something that was not to happen—inside a snowy countryside scene that was worlds away from Perry's Harbour.

The letter was in the second cubbyhole. He might have passed it by; the compartment looked like it held bills. But something made him pull out the envelope and remove the folded sheets of writing paper, and on them the first thing he saw was his name.

Dear John Wilfred,

Pocket so seldom saw his name written out that it made him pause. Even on report cards his teachers called him Pocket. The effect of his written name, in his mother's handwriting, was physical, a soft thud to the chest. He looked over at his mother, who slept on without eyelash flutter or movement of any kind. He watched until he was sure he saw her chest rise, waited until he heard her sighing exhale. He folded up the letter and put it in his pants pocket. Then he tidied the Christmas cards into their cubbyhole and shut the desk. It was then that he heard the sounds of his father and uncle approaching in the dark, and he moved to his mother's bedside chair to await their entrance.

"Whadja find?" he asked them when they had their boots off and coats hung and had come into the living room with the cold of the Sound still surrounding them.

Wilf looked at Merle. "How's she been?"

"Sleepin, mostly."

"Nothin," Scratch answered Pocket's question. "Nothin 't'all, 'cept some weird stuff on the water. Coast Guard and RCMP was out there, too."

"You talk to 'em?"

"Nope," said Scratch. "I think Turf did, but I dunno what they told him, he was still talkin when we left."

Wilf sat heavily on the chair beside Pocket's and rested a hand on Merle's arm where it lay, limp, atop the blankets.

"I don't mind sayin I was some nervous," Scratch said into the quiet. "I mean, we was lookin for bodies. Plane goes down, somethin comes up, ya'd think."

"Ya'd think," Wilf echoed.

"I'll get us some cocoa," Scratch said, leaving them. From the kitchen they heard: "Some cold out tonight. Warm us up before bed."

Sitting side by side in the living room, Pocket and his father watched Merle breathe. After a while, Wilf spoke.

"It's funny how stuff goin on out there doesn't matter right now," he said, eyes never leaving his wife's face. "Funny how small yer world can become."

"Uh-huh," Pocket answered quietly. He knew exactly what his father meant. All there was right now was the soft light, his father, his mother, and, in the kitchen, his uncle rattling around. Familiar, comforting sounds. Sometimes after sitting with his mother he'd go outside and feel he was in an alien world, its edges surreal. He would look at his hands, holding them out before him, to be sure he was still there, substantial.

"Out there on the wharf most of the talk was about the plane, about the crash. But some are thinkin it's something else. There's rumours of lights all up and down the shore. Some are thinkin we been visited from outer space." He shook his head. "'Scrazy."

Merle took a deep breath and exhaled, a long, shuddering sound. The room seemed to hold its own breath waiting for Merle's next one, and when it came after a long beat, Wilf and Pocket released theirs.

"Can you 'magin? The idea of something from way out there, and here we are, everything pared down to this one little place."

Pocket nodded. From the kitchen came the sound of a pot being placed on the stove.

"Don't think I'll go to school tomorrow," said Pocket. Wilf said nothing.

"She's, um—" Pocket didn't want to say the word. "Mum is—"

"I won't lie to you, Son. She come home because the docs at the hospital said that was the best thing for her. But I keep hopin. You hear about miracles all the time. There was that woman up t'wards Sheep Cove? Doctor gave her a week. Said she could go in hospital or go at home, no difference. Started playin cards, she did, an more than anything wanted to beat her brother I heard, who'd tormented her sumpin bad when they was growin up. Decided she wanted to play him 'til she beat him, and so he agreed. He was afraid she'd die once she won, so he did everything he could to make sure she'd lose so she'd keep goin, so he'd have her longer. By the time she finally won they musta played a hundred games, and by that time she was feelin better. Got up the next day. Lived two more years."

"Think that could happen with Mum?"

"Well, I never could beat her at crib anyways. So that don't make sense to do."

"I was thinking of a miracle. Like you said." Pocket

looked at his mother, thinking of their conversation earlier. "She was right interested in the lights goin down into the harbour, and everybody going out. Perked right up, like her ole self."

"Your mother was always one for the current events."

"She's not goin back to hospital, though, is she?"

"She don't want to. Says there's nothin for her there. Just wants to be home. I was s'posed to set somethin up with the public health nurse. S'pose it's gettin so's I better. I just wanted some time, like. Before a bunch of nurses start pokin and proddin."

Scratch stuck his head through the door. "They just come once a week, Wilf. That's what they said at the hospital. We maybe better take the doc's advice and get someone in, private." His head disappeared, and the sound of clinking china was heard.

"No money to pay someone."

Scratch came out with three mugs, two in one large hand. He set down the single carefully on the bedside table, then separated the two he clutched together.

"Couldn't find the tray," he said. "Or much of anything in that kitchen, for that matter. Hang on. I think there's still some of Vi Morton's cranberry loaf."

As Scratch disappeared again into the chaos of the kitchen, Pocket was surprised by the sudden presence of his father's hand on his shoulder. It lay there, warm, and as Pocket's eyes met his father's he recognized his own in their shape. He'd always been told he was the spitting image of his mother. But there was that slight downward tilt on the corners, making a waning moon of the grey-blue iris. He blinked, and realized his eyes were wet. "What?" he said.

Wilf removed his hand as Scratch came in with a plate of cranberry loaf. "Merle always did like a tea party," he said, "and I 'spect she's likin it now, even if she's sleepin through it."

Pocket wiped his eyes, saw his father do the same, a brief movement that could have been tiredness.

"'Spect she is," said Wilf. "Pocket, pass the loaf, wouldja?"

Sitting in bed, Pocket could hear the sound of his uncle snoring in the next room. His father, he knew, had pulled a blanket over himself on the couch. Pocket's knees made twin mountains under the red and black Hudson's Bay blanket, and on them lay the letter, the one that had burned in his pocket through a mug of cocoa and five slices of Vi Morton's cranberry loaf.

Dear John Wilfred,

I'm writing this to you now and I'll give it to your father to give to you when the time's right. Lately it's been getting so the least thing tires me out, and that makes me want to say some things to you.

Most kids don't listen to their parents at your age. It's just natural. But you've always been a good listener from the time you were small. You won't remember, but your dad used to take you down to the wharf and sit you on a pile of lobster traps. You'd sit there and listen while the men all talked about the catch and the price of lobster and I don't know what else.

Should have nicknamed him Ears, that's what your father said one day when he brought you home in time for dinner. You hardly didn't even talk yet and you were almost three.

You could walk early, though. Crawled at six months, walked at eight. People stared because you were just too small to be upright, and I thought you'd be bowlegged, walking before your bones were ready for it, and such long legs. And you were bowlegged for a time, before your legs straightened out. You used to play with Ernie Morton then who was right knock-kneed and Vi and me used to say that both of you standing side by side, you could spell the word ox.

Never saw a boy who liked to walk as much as you did, and you still do. Your Uncle Scratch maintained you'd go some far if you got the chance. Walk all the way to Timbuktu, he'd say. The first time we took you out to the Kettle Island light and you got to go all the way up those stairs and see the big lens and then look out and you were some excited all right. You were about eight years old I remember and you ran up all those stairs like you couldn't wait to get to the top. When we'd all climbed up behind you, you turned around from where you could see all down the shore and out to those big fishing trawlers from Spain or wherever and I'll never forget the look on your face. You said Mum, look. I'm the highest there is. Only thing higher is the stars.

I'd like for you to see other places. I never did that. And neither did your father since he couldn't serve overseas like so many other men. But you could. You could see England, where your grandmother came from. Or Spain, or Australia.

I'd like for you to go to university and learn things. You could go places, and then go to college. Or you could go to college and then go places. It doesn't matter what order you do things in as long as you do them. And then you could settle down and have a family. I like the idea of a bunch of grandkids running around. Oh how your father would like that. He did have fun with you when you were little, carting you around on his shoulder like a parrot on a pirate. We used to tease him some bad.

You were always drawing. Oh, your father worried some about you, that you wouldn't get any practical skills, but I remember my own mother, your grandmother, painting beautiful pictures. That one in the living room, the garden. She always painted what she remembered from England. She could paint right from her imagination, just like you. You're like her, Pocket, and you need to know I'm some proud of you.

One thing your grandfather told me was what I'm going to tell you now. He said Merlaine, the most important thing to be in this world is a good person. I suppose you can take that any way you want but I take that to mean the type of person who thinks about other people. And if you think about it, it makes sense, don't it? If everyone is always thinking about everybody else then you don't ever need to think about yourself because somebody else is already doing that.

If there's a need and you have something to fill it, then that's what you do. Simple as that.

Whatever you do in your life, if you do it with kindness that's all you need, because kindness comes back. You look around right here in Perry's, the ones who are kind, and you can see it right plain. That's the best advice I can give you.

I think I've said what I wanted to say to you, Pocket, and if you're reading this it's because I've gone to Heaven or wherever it is that we go. I've never quite held with the notion of heaven and all those angels and harps. But it's a good place *we go, I'm sure of that. I like to think it's somewhere up in the stars, the way you see them on a clear, calm night.*

 All my love, forever and ever,
 Mum

Pocket wiped his eyes on the sheet. Funny how if tears came once in a day, they came so easily the next time. His eyes, when they had cleared, rested once again on the last line, and he thought about *forever*, turning the word over in his mind, wondering why it suddenly looked so incomprehensible, a jumble of letters that made no sense.

He took a moment to listen to the sounds of the house around him: down the hall, the sound of his uncle's seesaw snores. From below, the creak of the couch springs as his father's weight shifted. The pops and clicks of the house as it settled, hunched against whatever wind the ocean sent this night into a clapboard embrace of a sleeping family.

He'd have to put the letter back, of course. Sometime when nobody was around, which would not be easy. There was always someone close by, always an ear cocked to divine from words, sighs, or murmurs the needs of his mother. For now, he slipped the envelope under his bed, turned off the light, and lay on his side with one ear to the floor below, one ear to the sound of the sea.

 Dark

It was as if you were there yourself. That's how clear it was when they described the way it was out on the Sound. Now, the house is asleep. You can close your eyes against the dark of your room and you can step aboard.

The boat's running lights cut through the dark, so black that without them you wouldn't be able to tell water from air, or see if Kettle Island is port, starboard, or right under your bow. Stars above, stars below, nothing to tell you where sky stops and sea starts. Other lights cut the water, Cape Island fishing boats converging on the spot where the thing went down, or near as anyone can tell, anyway. This is what you do when you live by the sea, the unspoken rule: someone needs help, everyone goes. It could be you, next time. Under all of that darkness.

At the dock, they said—untying ropes, priming engines— that "'t might be nothin, just those young hooligans from over't the Island settin off flares." Fun of an evening, that's all. There was a box of flares stolen not long ago from behind the firehall. Flares on the water, the colours, the reflection: could be confusing if you were near the water late at night. Maybe a prank is all it was, but when the call came, everyone out anyway. You just never know.

There's the taste of salt on your lips; you can feel your hair go stiff with it as the spray comes up from the bow. As motors are cut—one, another, another—the absence of sound roars.

On the deck, are cables and ropes, nets and winches, sliding with the sudden downshift in speed. The boats are all drifting, now, towards a compass point, dead quiet. That's when you hear an exclamation, not so much a shout as a loud exhale.

Jesus, mother!

You peer ahead, but there's nothing but black beyond the reach of the boat's light. And then you see it, on the water's surface: a swath of bright yellow foam, unlike any sea foam you've ever seen. Glowing, almost, although it may just be the effect of the light. You get strange effects sometimes, out on the water.

A call, now, from the closest boat: You see anything? Anything come up?

Further away, a call across the water: Anybody out there? *and you can sense the collective intake of breath as every ear strains for a cry for help. All you can hear is the slap of waves on the side of your boat.*

I'm goin closer! *someone calls, but nobody moves: nobody wants to put his boat through that foam.*

You'd think something would come up outta that.

Somebody has to make a move. You can't just sit there all night. So you start the motor, let the boat idle forward towards the foam, and when the stuff is right there at the bow you swing the wheel so it's the stern in the stuff, the boat's lowest point. Then you take the big net, the one with the longest handle, and you reach out with it as far as you can, chest against the gunwale, boots wedged against a rope coil. It's when you put your net into it, try to bring some of it up for a closer look, that the chill comes over you. There's nothing in the net at all.

From the black sea around you, voices: Ah, I'm goin in. Wait—we should wait, see if somethin comes up. There may yet be survivors. Wouldn't want to come up outta that to nobody.

But it's been half an hour since you got there, more than an hour since whatever it was went down. You watch as the Coast Guard trains a beam across the area, but there is nothing but yellow foam, drifting. Around you, motors are starting up. Already one or two boats are back at the wharf, pulling into their berths. There's nothing more to be done. You head back the way you came: towards lights, and home. The feeling of relief as you move away from that spot is palpable.

You think of the men who had gone out, now home and tossing, sleepless, in their own beds. You draw the blankets higher and shiver, knowing that if something fell into the dark waters of the Sound, it must be there still.

Thursday, October 5

1 Merle Snow was dreaming of the sea. She dreamed often of the sea these past weeks, the pull of the water she missed so great that it swept into her sleep state like a moon tide. Usually her dreams were of gentle floats on calm water. This morning's dream took on a stormy temperament.

She was on the boat, her father at the helm, and she was tossing lobster traps overboard every time he said "Now!" Each time he'd say it, he'd accompany the word with a stomp of his foot, but the stomps became more frequent, like a hammer, the rhythm growing faster and faster, and she couldn't keep up. Looking back, the line of buoys seemed to go on forever; she couldn't see land in any direction, just endless sea. Each time she looked down there were more traps, overflowing the boat. When she tried to grip them they slipped from her hands. "Now!" called her father again. "Now, now, now!"

"Stop!" cried Merle, fingers clutching at the blanket's edge.

Pocket was also dreaming. It had taken a long time for sleep to come, unsettled as he was from the night's events. Mostly it was the letter that kept Pocket awake, phrases repeating themselves in his mind. After a while he got up again, thinking to reread his mother's words, but instead he'd dug through the box in his closet, looking for a comic book he was sure was there somewhere.

The lights in the sky had reminded him; later, as he held the comic book, he felt the same sort of shiver as the one described within its pages when ordinary folks were faced with an extraterrestrial apparition.

On the comic's cover was a picture of two people running from their car, which was being zapped by a flying saucer. It was one of four discs in a sky that glowed orange-red. One zap—like a lightning bolt—had landed right beside the foot of the closer, older man, who wore a terrified look while a young man, frozen in flight, held a look that was closer to wonder. The comic promised ninety-six pages of true stories. When he was ten, Pocket had pored over it until the pages were dog-eared and creased. Now, resurrected, the comic lay on the floor beside his bed as he dreamed.

The strange orange lights were coming closer. They hovered above the harbour while he stood on the wharf, watching in wonder. In his dream, he felt chosen. But then the beam swung towards his left. There in the light his mother stood in her nightie, wind tugging at its edges, and as she raised her arms towards the strange object Pocket knew exactly what was about to happen. He opened his mouth to tell her not to go, but no sound came. There was only the hammering of his heart. He saw his mother open her mouth.

Pocket woke to the sound of his mother calling out. He lay there, heart thumping, in the semi-dawn of his own bedroom. Below, the sound of rapid footfalls, and his father's voice, soothing. When he came downstairs Pocket found his uncle standing in the middle of the kitchen, looking bleary-eyed. Scratch shook his head and spread his hands to take in the mess, which seemed even more chaotic in the morning light.

"He was up early pounding nails loud enough to wake the dead. Woke yer mum. You too, looks like. Get a bowl, Pocket, and try to find the cereal. I think I know where the fridge is. I'll get the milk."

The bowls were stacked on the floor. The cereal was in the pantry off the kitchen, so far untouched by his father's crowbar. Pocket grabbed the box and padded back into the kitchen. Scratch held up a bottle of milk, triumphant. After digging a spoon out of the cutlery drawer Pocket sat down, toes curled against the cold of the floor. His pyjama bottoms ended halfway up his calves.

The kettle whistled. "Seen the teapot, Pocket?" His uncle's eyes searched the dish piles, but Pocket pointed to the sink. "Oh, jeez."

Wilf came in, then. "Got her settled," he told them. "Bad dream."

"Probably all that bangin," Scratch said. Wilf gave him a look. "She was probably dreamin of pile drivers."

"Think she's ready for a cuppa. Did I hear the kettle?"

"Took me a while to *find* the kettle, but I did, and it's just off the boil," Scratch said. "Found the teapot, too."

"Ohh. Right."

"Maybe Crosbey's has one for sale. Or maybe someone's going in to Yarmouth," Pocket offered.

"We'll just make it in the cup. She won't know," Scratch moved towards the kettle, mug in hand.

"She'll know," Pocket and his father said, almost in unison.

"Maybe there'll be somethin in the jumble sale at the church. That's Saturday, I think, innit son?"

Which told Pocket that money was getting tight again. It always did before lobster season started. Pocket didn't want to ask about his dad's plans for the season, with his mother the way she was.

"Dunno," Pocket answered. He had already thought of checking Crosbey's. He still had some money left from summer mossing. "Jeez, I'm gonna be late."

In his bedroom, Pocket pulled on his longest pair of pants. They were pretty dirty, but he'd rather wear something dirty than something short. It didn't matter anyway: even while he went through the motions, he knew he wasn't going to school today.

The slant of October light fell across Ernie's face, waking him. He squinted, trying to guess: at this time of day, it was often hard to tell if you were seeing fog or cloud. Sitting up stiffly, he leaned towards the window. Fog. Might burn off when the sun got higher. A movement outside caused him to place his hands on the sill and lean, nose almost touching the glass. Two hundred feet away, ghostly, stood the house next door. Its yard was treeless, with two non-running pickups parked on the dead grass like lawn ornaments. Across the lawn came Neil Hitchens, toolbox in his hand, heading towards the newer of the two trucks.

Debbie's door was open when he passed, her bed empty. He recalled the night before, and felt his arm gingerly, anger swelling at the pain.

Goddamn Cuff.

Stupid asshole.

At the breakfast table, Ernie slid into a chair; a plate of toast and eggs slid in front of him at almost the same time. His mother turned back to the frying pan, breaking two more eggs into the hot fat for herself.

"Thanks, Mum," he said to her back. "Where's Dad?"

"Sleepin."

Debbie, hair still in rollers from setting it the night before, looked up from her plate, mouth full. "Izzee sick?"

"Nah, jes' tired. Phone rang 11:30—later, prob'ly—Mounties trying to get a bunch of boats to go out. There was a report of a crash, right in the harbour."

"Really?" Ernie had got home around then, must've fallen asleep as soon as his head hit the pillow. His mother always said Ernie could sleep through just about anything. He remembered the orange light he had glimpsed, and dismissed. "So did he go?"

"Where've you been, Son? 'Course not. He's got the engine all apart, gettin ready for the season. Be a fine day when he actually gets it back together and workin properly. Miracle we don't starve."

Ernie turned from the litany of complaints he knew was coming to see Debbie smirking at him. "Yeah, big brudder, where you been?"

She was still in her nightgown; Ernie could see her breasts outlined against the thin fabric. "Don't you ever wear a dressing gown?" he asked her.

She ignored him. "So what was it?" she asked their mother.

Their mother turned around and leaned against the

stove front, eggs sizzling behind her. She picked up her teacup and blew on it.

"Well, I called Crosbey's. I figured Shirley'd know before anybody. Some kinda plane, I guess. She said they waited, but nothing came up. Coast Guard's out there now, and the RCMP. Shirley said they're not lettin anyone go out. They closed the wharf."

"Closed the wharf?" Ernie couldn't believe it.

"Until they complete their investigation, they said."

"Gonna make people some mad."

"I 'spect. Don't make much difference to this family." She rolled her eyes.

Ernie craned his neck to see the patch of harbour usually visible from the kitchen window, but fog obscured the view. "If Dad didn't go out, why's he still sleepin?"

"Couldn't get back to sleep. You know yer dad. He starts worryin, he gets some agitated. Once that happens…"

Ernie did know. There had been a lot of pacing lately. The boat had been causing trouble, and new parts had been expensive. Things still weren't working right. His father blamed the manufacturers, the mail, the government, Ernie's mother and, when he was within cursing distance, Ernie.

Ernie wiped his mouth and got up, leaving his plate at the table.

"What, you born in a barn?" Debbie chided, and he picked up the dirty plate and put it beside the sink. His mother was flipping her eggs easy-over.

"Ernie, Donny Norris called yer father yesterday." Ernie froze. Why would Edie's father call? His mother set the flipper down and looked at him. "She's too young, Ernie. She's just gone fifteen. He doesn't want her getting serious."

Before Ernie could respond, Debbie spoke up. "Yeah, brudder, learn a thing or two from yer buddy Cuff. He appreciates more mature girls."

"Whattaryou sayin?"

"Debbie-girl, you're gonna be late for school, lookit the time," Ernie's mother waved the flipper at the clock on the wall. He left in the flurry of movement that follwed, Debbie's hands flying to her hair in its rollers, thinking of the time it would take to remove them. He never could fathom how she could sleep in those things.

"I'm outta here," he told nobody in particular.

Cuff had barely slept.

The night before he'd stood for a long time in the cold beside the phone booth, not sure if his shaking was due to temperature or the creepy feeling that seemed to walk up his spine at regular intervals. He'd faced the water, but could see nothing. For a moment he'd thought he glimpsed an orange light drifting on the water, in the sliver of harbour he could see between buildings from where he stood. When he'd looked again, there was nothing. His mind playing tricks, that's all.

When the cops finally did come, it was two cars instead of the single cruiser Cuff had expected. Charlie Brannen in one, and two cops he didn't know in the other. He felt important, escorting them to the spot where he'd been parked, describing what the light looked like, and the way whatever it was approached the water. He ran when it crashed, he told them, to call it in.

Do his duty as a citizen, he'd explained, hoping to buy himself points against some future indiscretion.

He thought he might have seen a light drifting on the surface, but he couldn't be absolutely sure. Might have been some sort of reflection he told them, he didn't have a clear view. But the thing hit the water. He was absolutely sure. Weird thing, he told them, though: no noise. Engine must've cut out.

They hadn't asked if Cuff was sober, the way Charlie had when he first called. He was stone sober now, anyway. There'd been a bunch of calls, Charlie told Cuff. All up and down the coast. Yarmouth, Bride's Neck, the Island.

After the cops had gone, he'd heard the boats starting up, and he'd headed back to the wharf to watch, maybe see if he could go out with one. By the time he got there they'd pretty much all pulled out. No sign of Pocket on the wharf, either. He'd stood for a long time watching the lights of the boats criss-crossing the area in the Sound where he'd seen the plane go down. The first boat back was Wilf Snow's. Cuff had approached, hands in his pockets, thoroughly chilled by now.

"Whadja find?" he'd asked, catching the rope to secure the boat.

"Nothin," Wilf had said.

"Whaddaya mean nothin?"

"Just what I said. Bit a foam, that's all. Out here for nothin." He sounded tired, and irritable. "Shouldn't you be home in bed? Either that, or out causin trouble?"

"Hey. I *saw* it. I called it in."

"Called *what* in?"

Cuff left, then, annoyed, feeling some respect was due. *Something.* At home, sleep had held itself back for what seemed like hours. When it came, it was fitful. He shared the room with his brothers Kyle, a year older, and Buddy, a year younger. At one point in his tossings and turnings, a crusty sock was flung across the room from Kyle's direction.

In the morning at the breakfast table he tried to tell them what had happened. At the best of times it was a challenge to be heard at the Dodds table. Eating in shifts made for the constant scrape of chairs, the push and reach for sugar or milk, a cacophony of food noises and truncated sentences and clatter of eating utensils and the movement in and out of the kitchen of Dodds offspring and affiliates in various states of dress and amiability. But when Cuff had, by slapping the table with the flat of his palm hard enough to make the dishes jump, got everyone's attention, it turned out that nobody had heard about the events of the night before. With the phone out they hadn't been called, and by the time Cuff had rolled in they'd all been asleep. Living up Perry's Lane, far from the water's edge and behind a scrub forest, nobody had heard any commotion. It took Cuff quite a while to get anyone to take him seriously.

"You drinkin, Cuff?" Kyle leaned over the kitchen table, pretending to take a whiff. He shook his head vigorously. "You do smell some rank this mornin."

"No, swear to God. Orange lights, four of 'em, blinkin. Some kinda aircraft, come right down into the water. Tide was goin out, figure it musta drifted with the current a ways, then they jus' disappeared—"

"What about dope? You get some hippie dope off a boat or somethin?"

"Jeezus, Kyle—"

"Not at the table," Cuff's mother admonished, coming up from the cellar. "You watch your mouth, Cuthbert."

"*You watch your mouth, Cuthbert*," mimicked Buddy.

"You called it in first, Cuff?" Pete asked. Six years younger than Cuff, Pete still held his older brother in awe.

Cuff looked at Pete gratefully, turning his back fully on Kyle. "Yeah, and they didn't believe me at first, but then all these other calls started comin in. I had to wait for them to show them where I was standin when I saw it go down."

"First time you been so close to a cop without bein a suspect for something, innit Ole Son?" Kyle smirked, shoving his brother's shoulder playfully.

"Beats sleepin with 'em." Cuff shoved back, harder, and a scuffle threatened.

Stanley Dodds stood in the doorway, filling it. "You givin yer mother trouble? And what's this I heard from Tip Morton about Cuff and the cops?"

At Crosbey's General Store, the little space at the back with the two wall benches and the one table—the Liar's Corner, as it was fondly called—was full, even though Shirley had unlocked the door just five minutes ago. For lack of chairs, some sat on boxes of canned food stacked two or three high.

The room opened out past a narrow aisle with counter on one side, four rows of shelves for dry goods on the other. The cooler was in front, by the door. From the back windows the harbour light flooded in, awash in dust motes, muted by last winter's saltspray still clinging to the glass. The smell was of damp wood, apples, and perked coffee. With the surprising arrival of so many, unusual on a Thursday morning, Shirley had to start a second pot of coffee percolating right away, and get more cream from the fridge. She caught herself in the reflection in the cooler's glass door and patted a wisp of curly blond hair back into place. As she filled the basket with fresh grounds, the door banged open and Neil Hitchens came in, dirty and, dressed as he was in grey workclothes, looking like an incoming fogbank.

"Can't get my truck goin. Can't figure it out. Stanley here?"

Shirley, hands on her broad hips and towel over her shoulder, nodded towards the back.

"Got a cup for me?"

"Be a few."

Neil moved on past the front counter, boots squeaking on the plank floor. He was still hunched inside his canvas coat from the morning cold, three days' stubble on his face. The crows' feet at the corners of his eyes multiplied when he saw no less than six men sitting around.

"Ho! Looks like Saturday afternoon 'stead of Thursday morning."

"Mornin, Neil," Turf Tyverson raised a cup his way.

Neil towered over Turf, so named for his proximity to the ground. "What," he said, grinning at the faces turned his way but speaking to Turf, "no fires to put out?"

Turf looked up and gestured in a circular motion with his cup. "Just the gossip's got everyone on fire, that's all."

"What gossip?"

That got a roar from those assembled. Tip Morton leaned forward conspiratorially, hand by his mouth, but whispered loudly enough to include everyone.

"Stanley's boy saw a flyin saucer last night."

"T'weren't no flyin saucer," Stanley Dodds objected. He ran his hands through hair the same ginger colour as his son's. "Plane went down in the harbour." He peered at Neil. "You didn't hear?"

"No," Neil said, scratching his head. "Plane, you say?" He looked at those assembled. Whatever it was didn't appear to be particularly urgent. "Hey, Shirl, coffee ready yet?"

"Thing is," Turf said, "I was talkin to Dale. You know, from the Coast Guard? They got confirmation when we was all still out there. No missing planes. So we're all out there lookin at this foam stuff and Sid puts 'is arm in and the stuff don't stick. Slides right off 'is arm like butter. Anyways, I asked Dale: so what're we lookin' for? Just shook 'is head. Somethin went down's all I know."

"Like what?" said Neil, then: "Shirl?"

Shirley came into sight, wiping her hands on a towel, and rested a hip on the counter's edge. "Hold yer pickle, Neil," she told him. "I'll let you know when it's ready."

Tip held his cup in the air for another when the time came, and Shirley nodded. She looked over her shoulder to check the coffee's progress, but stayed where she was to listen in. "Take a load off, Shirley," Tip suggested.

Neil put a hand up. "Whoa, Tip, we'll never get our coffee!"

"Oh, you—" she flipped her dishtowel at him.

"So what about this flyin saucer?"

Shirley kept the coffee coming, thinking to herself that this was the best morning she could remember, especially when Neil, in an uncharacteristic gesture, pulled a crumpled five from his pocket and told Shirley to put one of her apple pies on the table. She brought it over with a stack of plates and a fistful of forks, saying "keep this up, Neil, they'll think them little green men sucked ya up and spit ya back out different."

"Jus' feels like a party is all," he said sheepishly.

It was then that Cuff walked in. Tip stuck his cigarette in the side of his mouth to free his hands and started clapping. "Man a the hour!" he said around the butt. A smattering of applause joined him, and Stanley clapped his son on the back as he made his way to a vacant spot on the bench, bowing, hamming it up.

"Here comes Sunshine," Owen Corbet said under his breath, then: "You can sit here. I was just leavin." Owen never had much use for any of the Dodds, least of all Cuff, who he'd heard was interested in his daughter Brenda. "Thanks, Shirley," he said, pausing at the counter, setting a dollar by the till. "Keep the change."

Cuff had settled into Owen's seat, and was starting in on a piece of pie, one arm slung protectively around the plate, a necessary habit in the Dodds family. While he ate, his eyes lit on one face after another, waiting for someone to ask him to tell his part of the story. Neil obliged.

"So—"

Turf sat back in his chair, rocking it on two legs. "Let him come up for air first, or he'll choke to death."

"No, I'm done," Cuff wiped his mouth with the back of his hand.

"That was on Neil," Turf began, knowing Stanley would never tell his son to say thanks, but Neil waved him off.

"It was like I told Charlie Brannen. Four orange lights in the sky, like no airplane I ever seen, come right down in the water. Made no sound either. So I called it in."

"Plane?"

"Dunno, but Charlie was some interested once a bunch of other calls started comin in."

Shirley pulled a chair around from behind the counter to sit at the end, where she could hear the conversation better. "Yeah," she said, settling. "I heard someone saw it on the Island. And up shore."

"I was the first to call it in, though."

"Wasn't Ernie with you?" Tip asked. Tip was Ernie's uncle.

"Nope. He'd took off. Had to wait 'til Charlie and two other cops arrived. Told 'em to call and get the boats out, start a rescue mission."

"Who went out," Shirley asked, "besides Turf?"

"We did." Wilf Snow stood by the counter. He'd just come in, chill air wafting around him in the heat of the room. "Me and Scratch."

"Who stayed with Merle?" Shirley touched her hand to her breast.

"Pocket stayed."

But the men were more interested in Wilf. Several

moments of clamour and questions, and Wilf put up his hand. "If it was an airplane," he said, "it's just weird nothin came up, that's all."

Tip voiced the question in everyone's mind. "If it wasn't an airplane, what was it?"

"'S'all I know," Wilf said. He turned to Shirley to ask if she had a teapot for sale.

"Not much call for teapots," she said. "Maybe try the church sale on Saturday."

"Cuff here called it in first," Stanley told Wilf, to bring the subject back around. Cuff smiled and opened his mouth to speak.

"Heard that." Wilf was already turning away. "Heard they closed the wharf, too."

Neil grunted. "Better not be fer long."

There were murmurs of agreement around the tables, calls for government compensation for lost income, whether there had been any intention to go out or not. Nobody wanted to be told they couldn't.

"Stay fer coffee?" Tip asked Wilf, sure there was more to the story.

"Nah. Gotta get back, thanks." Wilf was halfway to the door when he heard Cuff start up his story again, heard the boast in his voice.

Cuff was just leaving when the phone rang five minutes later. Fred Crosbey, having just come in, waved Shirley to stay put and reached his arm across the counter to grab the receiver off the wall.

"Shirl?" he called after a minute. "Some fellow's lookin for a room to rent!" Which is what they were all talking about when Ernie turned up five minutes later.

2 Nobody seemed to have noticed or cared that Pocket hadn't gone to school. Both his father and Scratch had simply nodded when he came back downstairs without his schoolbooks. After breakfast, Wilf wandered off to Crosbey's to look for a teapot. When he came back, "they're all talking about aliens," he said, and shook his head before holding up both hands, empty. "No teapots," he said, then: "Call me if you need me. I'm goin out to the shed."

Pocket, on his way back to his room with a mid-morning sandwich and a glass of milk, had paused to see his uncle sitting beside his mother's bed, asking her opinion on this word or that as he filled in the boxes on the crossword puzzle in his lap, while beside him, Pocket's mother murmured possible answers. Scratch looked up.

"Yer mother's always been better at these than me," he said.

"That's because he doesn't read near enough," Merle told Pocket. "I hope yer goin up to study."

Sitting on his bed, Pocket took a bite of peanut butter and jam. He opened the comic he'd dug out the night before and read the words on the inside cover:

Face the facts!
Our radar has tracked them!
Our scientists have seen them!
Our airmen have fought them!

66

What is the truth?

What is the mystery behind the weird objects that streak through our skies?

The cartoons were silly: Pocket could see that, now. But as a kid he'd been fascinated. He remembered wishing he could see something like that. There were times, he knew, when he'd have welcomed an alien abduction to another planet. Anywhere but Perry's Harbour. He turned the page. In the first panel, a saucer-shaped object drifted above a city of skyscrapers.

Tucked inside the back cover was a drawing on lined schoolbook paper. Pocket had no recollection of it, but knew it to be his. He'd drawn himself waving from a flying saucer lifting off from the schoolyard. On the ground, three unrecognizable students and his teacher, Miss Zwicker, with tears splashing on the ground as she waved goodbye. He had loved Miss Zwicker, the only thing that had made school bearable. She had become quite round in the belly, he remembered, and was replaced before Christmas.

The drawing reminded Pocket of the sketchbook he'd had that year, the real art paper sketchbook Uncle Scratch had brought him from the city. He retrieved it from the closet and thumbed through idly, cringing at the clumsiness in the renderings of his ten-year-old hand, but intrigued by the memories his drawings conjured. Fantastic happenings in familiar settings. Their old dog, Biscuit, grown wings and a devil tail. A brontosaurus that reared its head between Cape Island fishing boats. He remembered his mother and father laughing over that one at the kitchen table. Happier times.

His drawings had been proudly displayed on the refrigerator, then. "When your father builds me some new cupboards," his mother had told him, "we'll put them up on the cupboard doors and have a real art show in here."

"Can we invite Miss Zwicker?" Pocket remembered asking the question, but he couldn't remember his mother's answer.

Of course, Pocket now knew the reason for Miss Zwicker's departure. What he really wanted to know was where she had gone. In a book, he thought, there was always an ending. In life it was not so clear. He closed the sketchbook and turned back to the comic book, propped himself on his bed, and read it as he finished his sandwich. Each story, he noticed, ended with a mystery.

...the case has never been put to rest.

...to this day, authorities wonder.

...no explanation has ever been found.

From the direction of the kitchen came a dull thump, then another. When he came downstairs, Pocket saw that Scratch had created some space on the Arborite table and was kneading bread dough. As he whumped the dough on the table, small clouds of flour rose. Pocket liked the store-bought bread better, but you couldn't say something like that to Scratch.

"Where's Dad?" Pocket asked, looking around the room at the chaos of his father's new project. On the stove, a pot of beans simmered.

"Out in the back shed. Doin what, I don't know. Came in for lunch and helped yer mum eat, helped her with her private stuff, went back out."

Pocket sat down on a kitchen chair. He pushed some of the loose flour into a small pile, then ran his finger through the centre.

"How is she, d'ya think?"

"Same."

"Is it hurtin her?"

Scratch stopped kneading and looked up. "Yeah, Son. I 'magin it does. Mostly, I 'magin it hurts her not to be gettin up and doin for you. Or jus doin the things she likes to do. Must be killin her not to be out walkin, like she does. She used to cover miles."

"Yeah."

"And rowin out on the bay."

"She hasn't done that for a long time."

"No, but she liked to row out to some spot with a picnic when you was small. Or just on her own sometimes, made yer dad some mad, though." Scratch went back to the bread dough, talking between the push and pull of it. "Said she liked to be out in the middle of the Sound. Like she was in another world, she said. No laundry, no cookin."

"Ya think she hates it so much? Cookin and stuff?"

"Nah. I think she'd give a lot to be in here doin this."

Scratch's muscles flexed in sinewy arms. On one forearm was a leaping tiger, but the fur on Scratch's arm, now dusted white with flour, almost obliterated the animal's striations.

"Didn't have so much hair there when I was twenty," Scratch had explained about the tattoo when Pocket had asked, once, curious. He'd have been nine or ten, he thought now, his uncle down for a visit, his mother

69

making finnan haddie for dinner. He loved it when his uncle came, loved the air of elsewhere he brought with him. And the joviality. After dinner, there would always be the slap of cards. Crazy eights with Scratch until Pocket's bedtime, then the sound of cribbage below while he lay in his bed listening: *fifteen two, fifteen four, double run makes twelve and one for the jack.*

"She's a strong woman, yer mother," Scratch said now. "Strong-willed, always has been. Hard to say no to. Yer dad thought she was a fragile wee thing when he met her, but she soon proved her mettle. Wasn't nothin she couldn't do 'bout as well as anyone. She could split wood like a lumberjack." He laughed. "Wouldn't want to have an argument with yer mother when she has an axe in her hand."

Pocket hated splitting wood. His aim was off, causing his mother to wonder if he needed glasses. As he watched Scratch work, he recalled the time—he was coming up to his twelfth birthday—when he'd sat in his usual spot on the second-from-top stair and heard his parents and Scratch talking in earnest tones. His mother's voice: *He's shyer'n hen's teeth. He doesn't play, just stays home drawin or readin;* his dad's voice: *Could be worse. Could be getting into trouble like some a those hooligans over t' the Island;* and then his uncle Scratch: *leave him be, Merle. He'll be himself, that's all.*

Roll, push, pound, flip. The motion of the bread as it was kneaded against the table's green-flecked surface mirrored the roll of Scratch's biceps. Pocket, mesmerized for a moment by the motion, shook himself back.

"Maybe Dad's buildin cupboards."

"Hmmph. That'd be something, wouldn't it?"

A noise from the living room, and Scratch nodded to Pocket to go. Merle opened her eyes when he pulled the chair up beside. Her thin hair was in disarray and her colour pale, but her eyes were bright. Pocket smiled.

"Hello, dear," she said. "My, that was a good sleep. I was dreaming...I was dreaming of...baking, I think. Do I smell yeast?"

"Uncle Scratch is making bread."

"Ah."

Pocket sat there for a while, unsure of what to say, as always. Finally, "did you sleep well, Mum?" he asked.

"Oh, I always sleep well. Always have, ever since I was a little girl. We lived behind the firehall in South Head, did I tell you?" Pocket nodded. Of course he knew where his mother grew up. "Slept through every siren. Could sleep through the end of the world, I could." Then: "Could you get your father? I need some freshening up, and then you come back and sit a while, wouldja, dear?"

In the shed, Wilf was swearing over a rusty T-square, chewed pencil gripped sideways in his teeth. He took it out and set it on the scarred bench. "My own dad always said I couldn't make a square drift," he said to Pocket. "S'pose he was right. Ya think, Son?"

Pocket looked at the half-assembled cupboard.

"Mum wants you," he said.

Wilf laughed. "Good answer." He put his cigarette out. "She okay?"

"Yeah, think so."

Pocket stood in the dim shed light feeling the cold

rise through the dirt floor. Along one wall was stacked salvaged boards and plywood sheets of various shapes and sizes, all deemed useful at one time or another. His father's workbench was cluttered with paint cans and stiff brushes, scattered tools and wires. The heavy glass ashtray was full of cigarette butts. A dark movement, accompanied by a sound like washing snapping on a line in a windstorm, and Pocket jumped and turned in time to see a barn swallow escape through a broken window into the fresh blue day.

His mother was propped up against several pillows when Pocket returned fifteen minutes later. He'd sat at the kitchen table peeling potatoes on his uncle's instructions, brown spirals falling into a bowl. Wilf, heading back through the kitchen to the back door, on his way to the shed, ran his calloused fingers through his son's hair.

"She wants you now, Son," he'd said, but didn't stop.

Merle smiled when Pocket returned; a smile Pocket remembered. How long had it been since she got up, got dressed? What was she wearing that last day? Pocket couldn't remember. But he could remember the day she told everyone she'd be staying in bed. "Pains in my legs," she said. "Just a day of rest, that's all I need. When I think of the miles these legs've walked I can't say's I blame 'em."

Maybe today she would get up again. He wondered if she remembered the night before. Apparently, she had.

"You been down t'the harbour?" she asked him. "They find anything?"

"They're not saying much, Mum. Boats are still out there, and RCMP and that coming and going, but they're not saying anything to anyone, that's what I hear. They even shut down the harbour, nobody can go out. Uncle Scratch says people are gonna get some angry if it goes on long."

They were both quiet for a bit.

"Some are talking flyin saucers," Pocket said, finally.

"Curious, ain't it?" Pocket's mother looked through the window and out towards the harbour, obscured mostly by seaside buildings, and waved towards the sea she knew was there. "Makes you wonder, don't it, that there could be something out there."

"Mum," Pocket leaned forward, feeling like a little kid. "Do you believe in flyin saucers? Alien spaceships?"

There was a pause. Merle closed her eyes for a moment. "I'd like to think there was more out there than just us," she said finally. "All those stars, all that space, seems like there should be. Wouldn't that be something? That there were worlds where everything was—better. Can you 'magin?"

Pocket could. "Like space cars."

"Everything touch-of-a-button."

"Flying suits."

"Robots to do your housework."

"Hey—you already got us." Pocket grinned. "We're even automatic. Look: you just snap your fingers and we hop to it!"

Merle was laughing quietly. "Not fast enough," she said. "Not nearly fast enough."

After Merle had closed her eyes and Pocket had smoothed his mother's blankets, he stood looking at her, thinking of a world where there'd be a pill or something to make her better. Just like that. As he stood by her bed, she opened one eye.

"A real robot would be rustling up my dinner," she told him.

"QZ-7, at your service." Pocket used his best robotic voice. "Right on it."

3 The paper in the typewriter had jammed. In a fit of frustration Rodney tore it from the carriage. He felt childish, but was too angry to care. Small pieces tore from the platen, settling on either side like snowflakes. All around him, the clatter of typewriters, the bustle of people in the busy newsroom. From across the aisle that ran between their desks, Lorelei was laughing.

"What?" he snapped, but she went back to work, head down. Rodney could see her smiling, see her long mascaraed lashes against her cheek. Her breasts pushed against her blouse, a phenomenon that usually made Rodney blush, but right now he was too frustrated to be flustered. And she was laughing at him. He stood up.

"I'm sick of this assignment. I'm sick of this office. And most of all, I'm sick of this goddamn piece of junk!"

Mr. Copeland opened his door, and Lorelei began shuffling papers.

"What's that you were saying, Rodney?"

"Typewriter jammed again."

"No, about being sick of this office."

There was no question in Rodney's mind: this was it. He'd finished his internship at the *Ottawa Journal* not three weeks ago; he'd only just started being paid as a reporter, a scoop of a job if there ever was one. Now, he was going to get the boot.

"Look, Rodney, you've been doing a good job…"

The roaring in Rodney's ears made it difficult to hear. Sure, he'd been given the lowest of story assignments—the ongoing feud between the ex-mayor and the mayor; the public school board's announcement of blackboard-writing training sessions for teachers; the cafeteria at Carleton University robbed—but he'd done his best to make them interesting, and he hadn't complained.

"…it's a quirky story, but Belton has a thing for these kind of stories, God knows why…"

The roaring abated; Rodney's mind scrambled to catch up.

"…so it's a bit of a perk, if you want to know the truth. I wouldn't waste the money. Train to Halifax tonight, then you'll rent a car. You'll have to call around, see if there's someplace you can stay. Fishing village, probably nothing. See if there's a store or a post office: they may have a lead on a room, and anyway you should get the local angle. There may be more of a public interest story there than hard news. RCMP is already on site, though. And the Coast Guard. Our taxes at work." Mr. Copeland shook his head.

"On site?"

"The crash site. If the Mounties are interested, it's gotta be more than just some cockeyed UFO story. Maybe the Russians. But most likely it'll just be a B-section piece, though; filler. Quirky Canadian news. But if Belton says to send someone, I have to send someone. Might as well be you."

"Um. Sure."

"Also, according to Belton someone at DND confirmed there were no aircraft in the area at that time.

See if you can track down someone there who'll go on record."

A distant phone rang, and Mr. Copeland turned back to his office. Rodney looked at Lorelei, who was leaning back in her chair, arms crossed under her breasts. With some effort he pulled his eyes upwards to her mouth, where he was met with a half-smile.

"Nice scoop, Nowland."

"DND?"

Lorelei rolled her eyes. "Department of National Defence."

"Okay...UFO?"

"Unidentified. Flying. Object."

"I *know* what a UFO is. What about it?"

"Where were you? UFO crash. Actually, I was listening when he took Belton's call. You know he's got that guy at the RCMP. So it's big enough, I guess. Sounds like that whole part of the province was full of strange stuff that night, all up the coast."

"What, um...province?"

"Jesus, *Rodney.*" She said his name, he thought, the way someone might say weasel, or slug. "Where *were* you?"

"Thinking about the typewriter?"

"Jesus," she said again. "I should be the one going. You're too lucky. *And* too male." Lorelei looked disgusted.

"Look, help me out, would you?" The feeling he had as he pleaded was the same feeling Rodney used to have, almost daily, back in grade five—woolgathering, as his teacher would say—missing instructions and then having to ask the girl in the seat next to him. Who, he recalled, also made him flustered as she batted her eyelashes at him and called him stupid. "You never get it, do you?" she'd say.

He didn't get Lorelei, either. The disdain with which she addressed him. It wasn't always like that: when she first arrived at the paper, fresh from college, she seemed interested in making friends. Rumour had it that she was from a rich family who had sent her off to boarding school. Over lunch at Bibby's, she had tried to tell him about it.

"It was—it wasn't a place to send a kid. Stuff happened—"

"What was it called, again?" Rodney interrupted. He'd been half listening, thinking hard to find something impressive to say. Now he grasped at a half-remembered connection.

"Scrimshaw College. Screw-you College, we called it. We learned pretty early how to…get what we wanted. I mean, as long as we were stuck there, we might as well get all the perks we could."

"Right!" cried Rodney, pleased with himself for the sudden recollection. "Scrimshaw! On Dundas? My mother's cousin taught there! Pauline Croftus."

"Right," Lorelei had echoed drily. "We had a name for her, too."

Rodney missed the cue. "So, how long did you go there?"

He'd asked her to lunch a few times after that, but she always had something else to do.

Now, "Perry's Harbour," Lorelei was saying. "Nova

Scotia." Then: "How can you be a reporter if you never listen? What planet are you from, anyway?"

In his room—bed, dresser, table, chair, sink, bathroom down the hall—Rodney stood, looking at the duffle bag on the bed. Five days. What do you pack for five days in a fishing village? And why such a long time, when Mr. Copeland had dismissed the story as tripe?

"Turn's out Belton's from that part of the world," Copeland had told him. "Though why he just doesn't go himself beats me, if it's that big a deal. Waste of a reporter." Rodney had felt, for a heady moment, as if he'd actually be missed. "Lorelei will cover your beat," Copeland said, "so we'll be fine. Won't we, Lorelei?" She'd gone into Copeland's office, then, for her new instructions.

Rodney had never been out of Southern Ontario. Ottawa was a big change from Guelph; he was still getting used to the pace. For Lorelei, who came from Toronto, Ottawa was positively rural. Maybe that explained why she seemed to know her way around, showed no hesitation when making cold calls as part of her research position. "You have to put yourself out to get what you want," she'd smugly tell him. When Rodney called National Defence, he'd been shuffled around, put on hold, and transferred again until his call was lost. The last person he spoke to said they had no information about a UFO crash anywhere in the country.

When he called Perry's Harbour post office the woman there had told him to call Crosbey's—the general store, he figured out eventually. "They got an extra room they let out sometimes. Call Shirley, dear. She'll likely help y'out." Accent so thick, he almost didn't make out the words. And had she called him dear? It sounded like dee-ah; perhaps he'd just misheard.

But he got the room, which, as it turned out, was the only room available, and his by luck.

"Had a call from some muckamuck just this morning, but I didn't like his attitude," Shirley told him. "Sent 'im to the Passage. There's rooms at the Victoria, I told 'im."

"Who was he?"

"Don't know exactly. Heard they was sending divers up. *Navy* divers, dear."

"Really?"

"Bessie, over at the Victoria, said CBC's sendin a film crew. And the Halifax paper's sendin a reporter down. And I—"

"Really?"

"I'll give you breakfast, but you're on your own after that. Fifteen dollars a night. Now, when can I expect you?"

He'd forgotten to ask about the weather. He looked at the contents of his duffle bag: four pairs of boxers, four pairs of socks, two pairs of pants, three shirts, and his tweed jacket. Should he pack a tie? He threw the plaid one in, took it out, replaced it with the blue. Then he took everything out, except the socks and underwear. Five days, he thought. Could even be longer, if there was any kind of story. What sort of "muckamucks" might there be? Who might he need to interview? For a politician, he might need a tie; for the locals, he supposed he'd better dress more like a local. So how did the locals dress? He envisioned sou'westers, big rubber boots.

From the bottom drawer of his dresser he pulled the rollneck sweater his aunt Bridey had given him for Christmas last year. He held it up and caught his reflection in the bureau mirror: he looked impossibly young and inexperienced. There it was: a round, almost baby-like face. High complexion. Like a schoolboy. He folded the sweater and put it in the bag. One pair of good pants, two pairs of cords. One good shirt, three casual. The tweed jacket, again. The plaid tie, after all.

He was standing there, wondering if October on the North Atlantic merited a parka or a windbreaker, when a knock at the door made him drop them both.

"Thought I'd come by and wish you well."

It took Rodney a moment to make sense of the apparition before him: Lorelei stood in the doorway in a short skirt and white go-go boots. Her jacket, open, was only just longer than the skirt. Her dark hair, usually ponytailed, wafted, loose, about her shoulders. Rodney felt the air grow warm.

"You came to wish me well?" he repeated. Could she have changed her mind about him?

"Sure. After all, I have your job, now."

Of course. She had been given his assignments. It must be a nice change from research and secretarial work, he thought, even if it was only temporary. There was a long pause while Rodney scrambled for words. It was then that he noticed the neck of a bottle protruding from an LCBO bag. Lorelei held it up.

"*Vino?*"

"I'm just, uh, packing," Rodney fumbled. He stood back, opening the door wider. Behind him, he knew, was a sink filled with dirty dishes, newspapers and magazines on every surface, and his duffle bag lying open on an unmade bed.

Lorelei drifted in, smiling, and set the liquor-store bag on the bedside table. She looked at his packing, hands on her hips. "You're taking this?" she asked, holding up the tie.

"You never know."

"It's a *fishing village*, Rodney." She appeared to check the edge in her voice, then: "Got a corkscrew?"

They sat on the bed drinking Chianti out of mugs. "They make great candle holders afterwards," Lorelei told him, holding up the half-empty bottle in its trademark basket. "How's your cup?"

"Um—" But she was already topping it up.

It never took much to get Rodney drunk. That was another embarrassment, one he'd felt keenly when out at the pub with the other journalism students. He'd learned to manage himself by pretending to drink more than he actually had. This bottle seemed to be three-quarters empty, he saw as he squinted, which, if he did the math correctly, meant he'd consumed most of it. How long had they been chatting? Lorelei, long legs crossed, sipped from her mug almost demurely.

"You know, it's probably just a hoax," she told him, mouth turning up at the corners. She rested her hand on his knee in a friendly way. Rodney tried not to look at her breasts. In his mind, he attempted to list the possible, plausible reasons for Lorelei's visit, but reasons eluded him. Perhaps it was the wine that clouded his ability to reason. Perhaps, as usual, he was just oblivious.

"You find out the real cause of those sightings, you'll save the paper a lot of embarrassment." Lorelei leaned forward conspiratorially. "Copeland will probably promote you."

"I thought..." the room was spinning ever so slightly. Rodney struggled to articulate his protest. "I thought Mr. Belton was really into this stuff. I thought he wanted an investigative piece, a series, even."

"You've got to learn to read between the lines, Rodney."

The look she gave him then was, to Rodney, enigmatic. That was the word. He felt proud of himself for thinking of it, considering the circumstances. He seemed to be having some difficulty with his vision. The walls tilted; with effort, he pulled himself back. What had she said about lines?

"Lines?" he said, not daring to move the leg where her hand still rested.

"Lines," she said, drawing a finger down the front of his shirt.

She leaned closer, inches from his face. Every eyelash was individually coated, Rodney could see, and perfectly separate. They almost touched her eyebrows as her eyes widened, then narrowed. "You have to know who's got the power."

I've got the power, thought Rodney. The wine bottle was empty, blood coursing through his veins. Lorelei unbuttoned the top button of his shirt.

"Wait," he said, mustering logic. "I don't get it."

"You never get it, do you?"

She was on the third button, now. Who had the

power? It occurred to him that he didn't get it, but that he didn't care.

"I'm going to get your job," she whispered, her lips at his ear.

"You mean you'll get my assignments while I'm away," Rodney managed. He took a last, long swallow of the Chianti in his mug. The warm red liquid flowed down his throat and then changed direction, washing into his head. The room softened. He was drunk; he must have misheard.

"By the time you come back," she whispered again, "I'll have your job."

He began to choke.

"Whoa, easy." Lorelei patted him on the back while he sputtered, red wine on the front of his white work shirt. She fingered the stain. "Guess that one's not going with you."

She was smiling, mischievous, while she undid the rest of the buttons of his shirt. The wine, this day: his mind was still trying to catch up. That feeling that he'd been temporarily absent, missed something really important. The familiar mental scramble to figure it out. Mrs. Jackson's grade five class swam before him.

His fingers fumbled at the bottom button of his shirt before her hands reached it. Perhaps she was just helping him change.

"These should really come off, too," she said, her hands at his belt buckle.

He got it, then.

They lay side by side, the duffle bag having slid onto the floor at some point, dislodging its contents. Rodney looked at the ceiling, which still swirled slightly. "I don't—I don't know what to say."

"Consider it a consolation prize." Lorelei leaned over the bed and dug in her bag for a package of du Mauriers, extracted a cigarette and lit it. The sulphur smell hung in the air like perfume. "Oh," she said after a noisy exhale, "want one?"

"Uh. Sure." It was to be a day of firsts, thought Rodney. But when he coughed for several moments after inhaling, "maybe not," he choked. He coloured when she laughed, but was too busy fighting back nausea—the wine, the cigarette—to say very much.

After several minutes of quiet, during which Rodney lay and looked at the ceiling, watching the smoke curl and gather in the corners, he managed to formulate a question.

"Why?"

Lorelei lifted herself on her elbow and looked at him. Her hair was in disarray, a tangled brown curtain. "I hate feeling guilty."

"Guilty?"

"Yeah. And—don't take this the wrong way—I guess I feel sorry for you."

This close, Rodney could see that her mascara had become smudged. There were tiny pimples on either side of her nose, and her teeth were a little crooked. Her breasts, though, now resting against one another with their nipples scant inches from his own left one, were everything he'd imagined. If this was the price he had to pay for her sympathy, he was all for it.

"I still don't understand," he said. "What do you feel guilty about?"

"Ah. Nothing, I suppose," she said, sitting up. "*Que sera, sera.*"

"Like in the movie? Doris Day?"

"Sure, I guess."

Rodney pushed himself up on an elbow as his mind segued, surging suddenly with optimism. She must surely like him to have come over at all. "Hey: when I get back, uh—" He could feel himself redden further, but he pushed on. "When I get back could we go to a movie or something?"

She started to laugh, head thrown back. After a moment Rodney started laughing, too, but he wasn't at all sure what the joke was. And then Lorelei was up and getting dressed, nylons over panties, skirt zipped up in front then twisted efficiently around, blouse slipped over her head, hair smoothed with two hands. Breasts out of sight, Rodney felt loss as well as bewilderment. She picked up her jacket.

"Guess I'll see you around," she told him, stepping into the white boots she'd abandoned in careless angles a scant half-hour earlier. She paused at the door, looking over her shoulder. "Send me a postcard, 'kay?"

After a bit Rodney rose and pulled on his boxers, stumbling slightly from the wine or the sex, he wasn't sure. He paused to look at his penis, marvelling that it would, forevermore, be an experienced penis. A penis that knew its way around. Whatever happened from this moment forward, Rodney Nowland was a changed man. Now, anything could happen.

He looked at the bed, scene of his deflowering. She'd forgotten her cigarettes, lost in the crumple of bedclothes.

A sign? What had he heard about the significance of leaving something behind? He tossed the red package into his bag.

The empty Chianti bottle stood on the dresser, iconic. Rodney was pretty sure he had a candle in the top drawer, tucked away in case of power outage in some earlier, entirely different lifetime. There it was, towards the back, behind the handkerchiefs.

When he pushed the candle into the neck of the bottle it fit perfectly, as if it had been waiting, its whole existence, for this bottle precisely.

4 From the church steeple on Chapel Hill, Pocket could see all three lighthouses of South Head, East Head, and Kettle Island. He could see Crosbey's store, the Moss Plant, the post office, the tiny scattering of houses that was Perry's Harbour. He took in the full breadth of the harbour itself, the circle of boats distinct. What were they doing?

He'd let himself in the small door at the back that was kept latched with a bent nail and climbed the rickety stairway that smelled of wood and undisturbed dust. He hadn't been up there for years; as a kid of nine or ten he'd come up here with Ernie Morton to smoke stolen cigarettes, but that was before Ernie and Cuff became buddies in an exclusive way that pushed Pocket into his own world when he wasn't being pushed into closets and doorways, or whatever was closest. Later, he'd come up just to see everything spread before him, like a meal on a table: variety, sustenance, but mostly distance, space.

He imagined himself at the end of the wharf, now a construction of Popsicle sticks below him. He traced the angle of his gaze from where he had been standing on the night whatever it was came down to the place where the boats were now, and thought about the point of impact, the current-borne drift he'd observed before it sank, and the angle the thing might have taken as it carried on to the ocean's floor. Were they sending divers down? He couldn't see. It seemed to him that they should be parked somewhere further west. Raising his eyes, he saw a ship sitting well past the harbour's mouth, indistinct against the fogbank. Military, he thought. He'd seen enough of them, the radar base being just around the head.

He went home, after a while, to find his uncle asleep in the chair beside his mother. In the kitchen, he could see the remains of the lunch she hadn't really eaten on the patch of counter that remained, more dirty dishes in the sink. From the shed came the sound of banging: things must be going well out there.

He'd eaten quietly and a little guiltily standing at the counter, adding his plate to the pile. The milk he'd drunk straight from the bottle, thinking about what his mother would say if she'd seen him. As he put the bottle to his lips for a second swig he tried to will her through the door, rebuking him. From the living room came his mother's laboured breathing, punctuated by Scratch's abrasive snores.

By late afternoon Pocket gave into the draw he felt, and found himself walking towards the wharf. He just wanted to look out from the same place as he'd been last night. He wanted to trace in his mind the trajectory he'd seen; even now, the memory was obscured, like something viewed through the murk of a tide pool. He'd just stop for a minute, he thought. Try to secure the memory as it had been when he'd closed his eyes in bed last night. Inhaling deeply, he imagined the lights, the orange-red glow of them. Remembered the certainty he'd felt that they were attached to something large. The way they went out, one by one, to be replaced by a glowing yellow dome, then nothing. The eeriness of it all. The absence of sound.

Cuff could hear the idle of engines across the water from where he stood at the wharf's end. He squinted at the three boats: Coast Guard, RCMP, and another, larger boat he couldn't identify. There were buoys, he saw, bobbing on the water; the area was out of bounds to non-officials. He felt cheated. After all, he'd been the one to call it in. And yet nobody seemed to want to talk to him since Charlie Brannen and those other two arrived at the phone booth last night. Nobody official, anyway. Even at Crosbey's the attention had turned else-where pretty quick, once the phone rang. Of course, a reporter coming from Ottawa—that was news. And, possibly, opportunity.

He stood in the chill air, the grease of salt-wet planks under his feet, thinking about the morning at Crosbey's. They'd been talking about the reporter coming the next day, speculating on what the story might be.

"They'll be calling it a hoax, I betcha," Tip Morton had said. "Nothin come up, did it? Nothin to prove any-thing went down. They'll be sayin it's one a those stories about the crazy things people believe down here. Hauntings. Wives' tales."

"Not with those boats out there already." Stanley shook his head, a slow side-to-side swaying. "No, they'll be takin this seriously. Russians, probably, a piece of some Russian rocket or somethin. Mounties close the wharf, there's somethin goin on."

That's when Ernie had come in. He'd stopped and

narrowed his eyes when he saw Cuff sitting over his cleaned plate. Cuff looked up and grinned broadly.

"Hey, you bugger, you missed it all! S'whatcha get for stompin off. Missed the whole goddam thing. Didja hear I called it in? Hadta wait for the cops an everything? Reporter's coming, I expect I'll be needed for an interview."

"Hmmph." Ernie leaned against the doorframe and crossed his arms.

"You *musta* seen it."

Ernie looked around the room, every face alert. "Cuff here'd been drinkin a fair bit," he said. "Coulda seen pink elephants for all anyone knows." He turned to Cuff. "That what you called in, Cuff? Pink Elephants?"

Cuff had half risen, but Ernie was already out the door.

"Relax, Son," said Stanley. "Jealous is all."

"Mad is all." Cuff had remarked, shrugging his shoulders. Who cared if Ernie couldn't take a joke?

Now, as he watched the circle of boats at the spot the thing had gone down, Cuff thought about the reporter, relishing the idea of a quote in the newspaper. Something to tell the girls, he figured. He should still be able to get some mileage out of it for sure. He decided he'd drop around the high school tomorrow, see if he could catch Brenda so he could tell her about it.

He looked out across the slate of water. From his jacket pocket he pulled a pack of smokes and lit one, inhaling deeply. What were they doing out there? And what was down there? Cuff imagined the murky wreckage of a plane, bodies floating inside. It would have to be miraculously intact for nothing to have come up, its speed so slow as to make the impact nothing more than a kiss of metal on water. Hadn't he seen it floating? Could an airplane float? Maybe if it was one of those float planes, but then it wouldn't have sunk at all, would it? But whatever it was had been bigger than any float plane he could imagine.

What if it *was* some piece of Russian space junk? Part of a satellite falling out of the sky? Another drag, as he watched the three boats jockey slightly in their positions on the water. He recalled the creepy feeling he felt when he saw the lights, thought of the comic books he'd read as a kid. There was one summer it seemed like that's all any of the kids were reading. Space aliens. Little green men.

The sound of footfalls and the accompanying lurch of the planks beneath him made him turn. Pocket Snow had stepped onto the wharf and was approaching, head down. Cuff took another drag and leaned against the end piling, watching. Around him, the moored boats creaked and swayed, their engines silent. Looking past the approaching figure, Cuff could see the squadron of unfamiliar cars parked at the wharf's end. They looked new; important.

When Pocket was halfway to Cuff he looked up, then stopped, startled. Clearly he did not expect to see someone at the end of the wharf. Or not Cuff, anyway. As he turned to retreat, Cuff called out.

"Hey, Pocket Snow. C'mere."

"Gotta be home for supper."

"No you don't. It's not gone three o'clock. C'mere. I didn't mean nothin by teasin you before. I was just havin some fun."

Pocket walked the length of the wharf, hunched, hands in pockets. Cuff watched him come, thinking: glad I'm not him. It was just painful to watch, that's all. He took another drag and continued to lean against the piling, recrossing his legs.

"Yeah?" Pocket's voice was wary as he drew up, keeping two feet between himself and Cuff.

"That you I saw out here last night?"

"Could be."

"Whadja see?"

Cuff watched as Pocket thought hard, weighing his answer. You could almost see the cogs moving. Jesus, he thought impatiently.

"Simple question, simple answer. Didja see lights?"

"Yeah," Pocket said, finally.

"Didja see it come down?" Cuff took a long draw on his cigarette, now almost to the filter.

"Yeah."

Cuff exhaled, then ground out the butt with his heel. "Good. Wasn't so hard was it? You tell anyone?"

"Dad. My uncle Scratch."

Of course, Cuff thought. They must've been one of the first boats out.

"Whadja think it was? Whadja *really* think it was?"

There was a long pause, long enough that Cuff didn't think Pocket would answer at all. Both boys watched the boats, immobile now, their lights taking on a greater glow as the autumn light faded.

"I gotta be home," Pocket said finally. "My mum's sick. I gotta go."

There was a moment when Cuff could have grabbed

Pocket's arm, could have held on until he got an answer, but all of a sudden it didn't matter what Pocket thought.

"Go home, then," Cuff said, and walked off the wharf briskly, as if he had immediate business to attend to, leaving Pocket to stand on the planks in the sway of his departure.

After the exchange with Cuff, Pocket hurried home again, unsettled. He hadn't expected to see anyone on the wharf, had hoped instead to recreate the event so that he could tell his mother about the lights again, if she was awake. Like telling her a story. She seemed to like the sound of his voice when he spoke. And she'd seemed more herself lately, more interested in the things going on around her.

It was with this thought that Pocket opened the door to his house, kicked off his boots, and put his head around the corner into the living room. Merle Snow lay on her back, eyes closed, hands folded on her chest. Pocket saw the jut of cheekbones, the sharp nose that had once been so much softer.

Pocket waited until he saw the rise of her chest before retreating to the kitchen. The smell of baking bread filled the room. Scratch, at the table, was back at the crossword puzzle. He looked up. "Where ya been?"

"Nowhere."

Pocket decided not to mention his brief encounter with Cuff Dodds. Cuff always made him uncomfortable. It had begun as kids: Cuff, a year older, sitting nonetheless a few rows behind him in the schoolroom. Sensing vulnerability, he'd honed in on Pocket right away. Mostly teasing, which was bad enough, but in grade two Cuff had convinced Pocket to taste the flagpole—in January. Oldest trick in the book, his dad had said disgustedly, once his tongue had been released from the flagpole with hot water and he'd been sent home. The pulpy mess that stuck to the metal had remained until thaw, causing renewed laughter from the boys each day, renewed disgust from the girls. Pocket kept his raw tongue to himself and said nothing, even after it had healed completely.

"Anything more about the crash?" he asked now.

"The crash? Nothin new, I don't think. Yer mum was askin about it, too. Seems quite taken with the notion. You seen the boats out there?"

"Uh huh."

"And here's news: there's a reporter coming from Ottawa, of all places. Owen told me, heard it somewheres. Gets in tomorrow, I think. He said the CBC's coming, even."

"Really?" The idea of television cameras in Perry's Harbour was more than a little exciting.

"Dunno. Just heard, that's all. 'Magin the *Herald*'ll send someone."

Pocket got up and opened the fridge. "What's to eat?"

Scratch jerked his chin in the general direction of the chaos that was once the counter. "Two heels left in the bag, somewhere over there. Baloney, maybe, in the door I think. Didn't you just eat?"

Pocket grinned. As he made himself a sandwich, he was grateful his mother wasn't there to tell him not to eat before supper. As soon as he thought it, though, he felt guilty, because of the reason his mother wasn't there.

"You eat, boy, and then you go sit with her for a while," Scratch said, as if in tune with his thoughts. "Peggy Corbet brought by a ham, all cooked; we'll have that tonight with the beans."

Before bed, Pocket, undressed, was about to pull on his pyjama bottoms when he caught his reflection in the window. He was not concerned about passersby seeing his nakedness: his window faced out back, a few acres of scrub forest without even his father's shed in view. And what would someone have seen if they had? A skinny kid in the warm light of a bedside lamp, all arms and legs and rib cage.

Pocket ran his hands down his own body, felt his own ribs like the ribs of a boat, felt the sharp edge of hip bone, the concave dip of abdomen with the pencil line of hair running upwards to his bellybutton, hair that hadn't been there a year ago. He placed both hands on his chest and inhaled, felt the swell of lungs. His stomach gurgled, and he put a hand there, realizing he was hungry again, the life in that. He felt the wonder of his body, the bloodflow, the organs, all working together to keep the spark of him here.

He paused for a moment more before he turned off the light, his reflection extinguished. Then he crawled under the covers, pyjamas puddled where they'd fallen on the bedside mat. He pulled the quilt around himself as tight as he could, the better to keep it all safe: pumping, breathing, flowing, working, protected from whatever harm might befall such an infinitely fragile thing as a human body.

Sound

When a lot of people are talking about something, the atmosphere shifts. It's not the same as the noise you hear in a crowded room. This sound is more subtle, and yet, it's everywhere. It's the accumulation of spoken words, all layered together. They colour the air, all these voices, and yet if you stopped someone on the road and asked: Do you hear something? They'd tell you it's nothing. It's just the wind off the harbour, they'd say, like any day.

Two people might be leaning across a kitchen table, speaking quietly. A half-dozen more are engaged in banter down at the store. In the schoolyard, the buzz of children. There might be several on the party line, some sharing information, others, hands across the mouthpiece, listening in. There will be chatter down at the wharf, men getting their boats ready for the season, swapping stories and opinions. Two men might trade theories leaning over the engine of a truck. Someone knows someone who was there, gets a new detail, and calls one, who calls another; someone else knows someone who was on the Coast Guard boat.

You might hear someone say that the Navy is sending divers; you might hear that the Department of National Defence in Ottawa is involved; that it was the Russians; that it was really the Americans, wanting everyone to think it was the Russians. You hear it was a couple of young goodfornothings setting off stolen flares, then concocting some cock-and-bull story that has *everyone fooled. This whole circus, you hear someone say, over a couple of boys who probably had too many beers and not enough to do.*

Standing by the Moss Plant, looking down along the shoreline at the scattering of houses, if you close your eyes you can almost hear the words sprinting along phone lines, blowing across steaming mugs, weaving around the pieces of a dismantled carburetor. It's as if the words grow legs and walk—no, run—from building to building, scurrying like squirrels across power lines, tailgating on the bumpers of cars. Like unruly children, these are words on the loose.

The words gather and disperse, forming intricate patterns in the air, while at home, it is sometimes as if all words had fled, there is so much quiet. As much quiet, you think, as there might be at the bottom of the Sound, where the strange visitor waits.

Friday, October 6

1 The sway of the club car, the rattle of the steel wheels on the rails, and the sway and rattle of the ice cubes in Rodney's glass of Scotch made for an odd sort of dance, and he was glad he was sitting down or, he felt quite sure, he'd be dancing as well. Across from him, the woman with the glass of red wine looked remarkably unaffected by the movement, reading a well-thumbed book with singular focus.

Rodney was grateful for the low light in the car and the darkness outside the windows, the occasional light from a trackside building flashing by. He had been watching the woman for some time, his glances as surreptitious as he could make them: subtle observation was, after all, necessary to the writer's craft. Glancing over his magazine, he watched as she licked her index finger with its red-polished nail to turn the page of her book. Unconsciously, he licked his own finger. It tasted like sweat and Scotch.

He'd ordered the Scotch because it seemed like the thing to do as a reporter on assignment; he wasn't sure he liked the stuff. Still, the second was going down smoother than the first. He nursed it now, a dated *Star Weekly* magazine open on his lap, while he studied the woman. Between the pages was the letter he was writing to Lorelei; he'd been at it for over an hour. *Dear Lorelei*, it read. *I...*

The rest of the paper expanded whitely before him. He looked up as, across from him, another page turned. The woman's book, when she lifted it high enough for him to see the cover, was entitled *Star People Among Us*.

"I see we're both reading about stars," he said, holding up the magazine. It sounded lame, he knew, but it was all he could think of. The cover of Rodney's magazine read: "Close-up of a Super-Hippie and Why He Matters to You." Rodney had already read the article, about hippie life in Toronto. It seemed to him impossibly free and a little immoral, and made him think of Lorelei and her go-go boots.

It was a moment before the woman with the book pulled her gaze from the page and looked at him over her reading glasses. Rodney was surprised; he had thought, with that halo of black curls, that she was much younger. But she was as old as his mother, Rodney could see now, although certainly not dressed like his mother. She wore great hooped earrings, a multitude of bangles, and several large silver rings. Around her neck, below a double chin, a tasselled scarf hung in generous swaths. She appeared to be wearing more than one skirt, the layers flouncing over the vinyl bench on which she sat, small feet in flat leather boots tucked neatly below. The glass of wine at her elbow was the same colour as her lips, which she pursed at him.

"Coincidence," he offered, faltering.

"Probably not," she drawled, the words sliding like honey into the air between them. "I find that most things are preordained."

"Preordained?"

"Everything leads us towards the One," she explained. She held up the book. "I'm reading about extraterrestrials in our midst."

"Aliens?"

"We're all part of God's Universe. There are no such things as Aliens." She took a sip of wine. "Just neighbours. What are you reading?"

Rodney glanced at the open page in front of him. It was an ad for the new 1968 Dodge Polara convertible, the "new generation." The car seemed ridiculously long, as did the legs of the model perched on the hood. He waved at the page vaguely.

"I just found it on the bench, here," he said. "It's from last month."

The woman rose and lifted her chin, indicating his table. "Join you." It might have been a question, but it came without the upward inflection, as if she was stating a fact. Before Rodney could muster a response she was seated across from him in the swivel chair, settling her skirts around her.

They exchanged names; hers was Wanda. She came from California, and had been travelling, she told him, almost since the moment she heard.

"Heard what?" asked Rodney, who had, in a moment of inspiration, introduced himself as Rod. It felt— stronger. More in charge. He was so delighted with this reinvention of himself, it took him a moment to catch up to what his table-mate was saying.

"I should explain," Wanda began, leaning her bosom on the table. "I belong to an organization called SEW. Society for Extraterrestrial Welcome. I'm also a member of the California Paranormal Investigation Psychic Society."

Rodney considered this for a moment.

"PIPS?"

"C-PIPS. There are twenty-three chapters in all, including three in Canada. I'm more active in C-PIPS, actually, but the two organizations are closely linked. Many of us belong to both. It's natural, since anecdotal evidence has repeatedly pointed to psychic and psychokinetic abilities in visiting extraterrestrials."

"It has?"

"Yes. If you read alien abduction reports—the ones the government hasn't managed to suppress—it comes up again and again. Some experience fear that their minds are being read, fear that something will be taken from them—memory, for example—but others experience a feeling of deep calm in the knowledge that they are, for the first time, connected to intergalactic collective consciousness."

"They are?"

"Yes. I know I would be. I'm a practising psychic, after all."

"You are?"

"Oh, yes. That's how I knew to come."

If Rodney had hoped that changing his name would affect some shift in his aural comprehension, he realized now he had been mistaken. He was definitely having trouble following.

"Knew to come...?"

"To Nova Scotia. This might be the biggest event since

Roswell. I have to be there." She sipped her wine again. "You've heard of Roswell." A statement, again.

"Um…"

"July 7, 1947. Roswell, New Mexico. My birthday, by the way. Well, twenty years later, but the same day. *Very* significant."

Rodney made a mental note. He could see his lead: "Not since the famous U.F.O. incident at Roswell, New Mexico, has such a significant event occurred…"

Wanda leaned closer, speaking in secretive tones, and Rodney found himself scant inches from her cleavage. She smelled spicy, and a little musty. He took a sip of Scotch and coughed involuntarily.

"They did their best to cover it up, but there's no doubt it was an alien spacecraft. The Air Force claimed it was a weather balloon. It still amazes me that some people seemed to buy that. Not our group, of course. We know it was a spacecraft that crashed, that there were alien bodies on board, and that they are being studied by scientists in secret laboratories in the desert."

It was dawning on Rodney, now, that Wanda might be on her way to the very same destination as himself. And then another thought struck him.

"Did you read about this—um, event—you're going to, in the papers?"

"Papers?"

"Newspapers. In California." Rodney had the sinking feeling he'd been sent off in pursuit of what was now old news. There would be no chance of an award-winning investigative report here. It would be dead in the water before he set foot off the train in Halifax.

"Oh, no. It just happened yesterday. I came as soon as I heard."

"Heard?"

"Well, saw. In a dream. I knew I had to come."

At this, Rodney sat back and drained his Scotch. They were, at this point, the only drinkers in the club car. Rodney's berth seemed to him lonely, and far away, and in any case, he knew he'd be unable to sleep. She's a nutcase, thought Rodney, but she's all I've got.

On the platform the next morning, Rodney tried to disembark quickly, intent upon exiting the station as quickly as possible. The night before in the club car, against his better judgment, he had eventually confessed to Wanda his assignment, and then immediately regretted it: his credibility was at stake, here, after all. He had imagined his by-line under the in-depth investigative report on Russian spy activity off the Nova Scotia coast; he'd seen the journalism award, the promotion. True, it was after a number of Scotches and before he'd staggered back to flop into his berth, where he'd spent the remaining scant hours of darkness trying not to throw up, but the dream's allure remained. He did not want to be seen with a charter member of the California Paranormal Investigation Psychic Society.

He hurried through the station with his shoulders hunched and his head down, trying to blend in. He chose the rental car booth at the far end of the station, putting crowds of passengers between himself and the gate through which Wanda would come. There were two people ahead of him; his foot tapped as if with a will of its own and he repeatedly buttoned and unbuttoned his coat while he waited. The man at the front seemed to be having some sort of argument with the girl with the bee-hive hair, her Pepsodent smile beginning to wilt.

A pressure at his elbow, and here was Wanda. In the light of day she looked pasty, her skin sallow and her eyes baggy.

"I thought I'd find you here. We're going the same way, after all. We might as well ride together."

"Um, I think it's against regulations. Company rental," he stuttered.

"How will they ever know?"

He was no match for Wanda, this much was clear. A half-hour later they were leaving downtown Halifax in a shiny new '67 Valiant, houses thinning until, on either side, there were nothing but stunted pines, all leaning inland away from the relentless sea winds.

In the yellow frame house behind the store, Shirley Crosbey snapped the sheets to ensure a good fit on the bed. She had forgotten to ask how long the reporter would be staying, but she hoped it would be a few days; she could use the extra money. She also hoped that she might get the inside scoop—that's what they called it—on whatever was going on out there. The Mounties, the Coast Guard: nobody was telling anyone in Perry's Harbour a single thing. Neil Hitchens heard over at the Passage that the radar base up shore had been watching a Russian sub sitting twenty miles off shore for the last week, that it must have something to do with that. It was a girl doing the janitorial there who told him, he said. She wasn't supposed to say, but she'd seen a memo on a desk when she was emptying the trash.

Shirley smoothed the blankets. If her boarder was renting a car from the train station, he'd have gotten in around lunchtime and would arrive in an hour, hour and a half from now. She had no obligation to feed him outside of breakfast, but she'd make him a sandwich just the same. She looked at her watch: Fred was looking after the store, but she knew he had things to do, and she'd promised to be back right quick. She gave the bed a pat.

Glancing out the spare room window on her way by, she caught sight of Pocket Snow, hands in pockets, hunched as always, walking down the road. Where would he be going, when other boys were out doing whatever it was teenaged boys did?

Shirley, without kids of her own, had seen the young people hanging in small packs around back of the Moss Plant, over by the community hall, smoking cigarettes when they thought their parents couldn't see, boys looking tough, girls flirting. It wasn't so different from her own teenage years in Perry's Harbour, and it made her smile. She'd been sweet on Fred Crosbey from grade seven, married him when she was barely seventeen, and had never regretted a day.

She watched Pocket turn to cut down to the shore. He was always alone, that boy. It occurred to her it was a school day; things must be getting worse if he was staying close to home. Her heart ached for that family, that was for sure. Poor Merle. The thought came to her then that Wilf had been looking for a teapot. She hadn't questioned why with all the hubbub that morning, but now she thought about it. It must be for Merle. She'd get Fred to pick up a nice one in Yarmouth.

The figure that was Pocket Snow became indistinct behind the afternoon fog. The fog bank had sat offshore, lying in wait all afternoon since slipping out mid-morning. She'd hoped for a little more sun to dry the washing on the line. Might as well bring it in.

On the shore, Pocket picked up a rock and threw it sideways into the waves. He never got tired of the fit of a rock in his hand, smooth as they all were from the relentless wash against one another. On a big surf day you could hear them from a great distance away, the roll and rattle of them, if you chose to pay attention, which most people didn't. Most didn't even hear it anymore, but to Pocket, it was a comforting sound, the sea smoothing the rocks until they were rounded like eggs, like the one in his hand now, soft grey granite flecked with mica and circled with a white band of quartz. A wishing stone.

He put it down and picked up another, this one almost perfectly round like a golf ball. He heaved it, and it travelled a satisfying distance. Pocket never threw rocks when there was anyone else around; when he did, they always fell short. It's why he never played baseball.

The next was oval, pale grey, perfectly formed. As a child he'd painted a sea scene for his father on such a rock, a paperweight in honour of his father's birthday. He'd painted their boat, a Cape Islander, and with a toothpick he'd tried to spell its name: *Merlaine II*. His mother's name, a combination of her own English mother's Elaine and her father's Mervin. It had been a First World War marriage, the girl from Devon journeying across the Atlantic to take up her wifely duties with the boy from Perry's Harbour, the good dancer with the disarming smile. His mother had told him this much later, of course. All he remembered now about painting that rock for his father was wishing the name of the boat was a great deal shorter, because even with a toothpick the letters had snaked past the bow of the boat and out into the watercolour sea. "It'll make a fine paperweight," his father had said, unwrapping it gently from the colour comics page. He had promptly placed it on top of the phone book as if to show how well it worked. Later, the rock migrated to the drawer-of-many-things, as Uncle Scratch called it, a kitchen catch-all for odds and ends.

Bending, Pocket picked up the wishing stone again. It was still warm from the heat of his hand a few moments before, surprising him. He hefted it, tossed it to his other hand, passed it back again. What would he wish for?

His mother, of course. But he'd thrown dozens of rocks, whispering: make her better. Please, make her better. He wasn't short of things to wish for, but they seemed selfish and petty, paling against the thought of his mother as she disappeared, becoming smaller daily beneath the blankets.

Turning, Pocket tucked the stone in his coat, hoping that, if he waited, inspiration would come. Because surely it was in the words you chose. If only you knew the right words, you could change anything.

2 Shirley lifted the lid of the Brown Betty teapot and looked inside. She couldn't imagine why Fred chose something so commonplace. Just like a man; why couldn't he have bought something pretty? Well, she'd bake up some ginger molasses cookies and take them over later with the teapot. Certainly the men wouldn't care what it looked like, and likely Merle wouldn't either. Still, if only Shirley had been there when the purchase was made…. Seems a sick person deserves something pretty, that's all.

When the store's door opened she knew at once that it was the reporter fellow, the one who had rented the spare room. He looked young to her, and vaguely uncomfortable, holding his bag before him like a shield. Behind him came a large woman who seemed to be wearing a lot of clothing, all of it the sort of flimsy stuff that would catch fire in an instant if she got too close to a woodstove. She carried a large flowered bag, which she deposited with a whump just inside the door.

"You must be Mr. Nowland," Shirley said, setting the teapot on the counter behind her. "It's just a single bed in the room. You didn't say anything about your—wife."

She saw now that the woman was old enough to be his mother, but the word was already out, and the young man was blushing fiercely.

"She's, um, she's—she, Miss—" Rodney realized he

only knew her first name. He tried again, after a breath. "This is Miss—"

"Kowalewicz. But call me Wanda," Wanda interjected.

"She caught a ride with me from Halifax," Rodney mustered, finally. He took a deep breath. He was a new man, he reminded himself. Nobody knows me here. I can be anyone I want. "Rod Nowland." He extended his hand, and Shirley took it.

"I'm just here to—absorb," Wanda explained. Shirley raised her eyebrows. "Although I will need a room," Wanda continued. "I expect to be here for several days."

"No places here I can think of," Shirley told her, lips pursed. "There's a hotel in the Passage. Maybe try there." But Wanda was already sweeping towards the back of the store, bangles jangling, to rest her puffy hands on the window ledge where she stood and looked out at the harbour, sighing deeply.

"I've made you a sandwich. Thought you'd be hungry after your drive." Shirley leaned over the counter and spoke pointedly to Rodney.

"That's very kind."

"First, why dontcha go over to the house—it's the yellow one right next door. Holler for Fred, he's around back, and tell him who you are. He'll show you the room. You can look around some after you eat." She laughed. "Don't s'pose it'll take ya long."

"How many people live here?" Rodney asked her. Surely there was more to it, he'd thought, when he was driving in with Wanda. There were two signs announcing Perry's Harbour, one at the east side and one at the west, about three minutes of highway between them;

Rodney knew, because they had driven from one to the other, looking for a village. As it turned out, Crosbey's General Store was not just the hub of commerce in Perry's, it was the only commerce.

"One hundred and forty-seven," Shirley told him. "A hundred forty-eight when Margie's baby comes. But then there's Merle—never mind. If ya don't get over t'the house and drop yer things, you'll starve to death before you get yer lunch."

Rodney glanced at Wanda, not wanting responsibility for her but feeling some nonetheless. She turned from the window and swept back towards the counter.

"Don't you give me another thought," she said as if reading Rodney's mind. She put her hand on his cheek, red nails against pallid skin, across which a flush was, once again, spreading. "I'm going down to the water. It's very strong, here; I can feel it. As for where I'll stay, an offer will come. And you and I will see each other again."

She was gone with a bang of the door.

"Well, I'll see her again for sure," Shirley said, looking after her. "She left her bag behind."

Pocket didn't know why he skirted the house to come in the back door. While most people used their kitchen doors as their usual points of entry and exit, the Snow family always used the front door. Uncle Scratch had explained to him once that, for Merle, it was what you grew up with, in this case an English mother. "She likes things done a certain way, that's all," he'd told Pocket. "Tea in a teapot. Coming in the front door. Right peculiar to some of us, always was. One thing for sure, she's been good for yer dad. When he was your age…geely crully, he was a bad'un." He'd shaken his head as if in disbelief that his brother Wilf could have been—whatever it was Pocket's father had been. But Pocket couldn't get him to say more.

Now, hand on the doorknob, Pocket heard his father and uncle at the kitchen table, his ears pricking at the sound of his own name. He leaned against the door quietly.

"Maybe Pocket could help out more," he heard his father venture, a response to some previous statement Pocket hadn't heard.

"No, Ole Son," Scratch was saying. "Not with the personal. It's too much to ask of the boy. She needs a woman to care for her. What about Shirley?"

"Shirley's all tied up in the store. And anyways, maybe we don't even need her. Merle's talkin more just these last two days. She's been right interested in the crash. It's given her spark. Maybe—" Pocket heard the shift of the kitchen chair, imagined his father leaning forward, "—maybe she's gettin better."

There was a long silence, and Pocket put his hand back on the doorknob, ready to make his entrance. Then he heard Scratch's voice, uncharacteristically gentle.

"Don't you remember? It was like that with Mum. Just before, she was up and makin *chowder*, for Jesus' sake—"

"I was, what, eight or something? Ya got four years on me. I don't remember. But Scratch, I grew up without a mother. We both of us did. Didn't want it for Pocket."

"He'll be okay, Wilf. He's a good kid. He's still got you. And me. An' folks here will look out for him."

"He's awkward as hell, Scratch. He's useless in the boat. Most things you set him to he just gets to day-dreamin. Or drawin in that book a his. Can't figure out what he's thinking half the time."

"She's been sick a long time, don't forget. Takes a toll on a kid. I remember, even if you don't."

"It's the waitin," Wilf said then, and Pocket felt the sound of his father's voice attach itself to his heart, and the grip of it took his breath away. He was halfway across the yard before he knew he was running.

He went back to the shore; it was the only place to go. At the wharf there was too much activity, people coming to watch the boats in the water, muse, speculate. He didn't want to see anybody, and he was sure to have to talk to someone. Worse, he might encounter Cuff Dodds again. And so he walked, further along the shore than was his habit, into the humps of kelp and eelgrass slumping over the chaotic tumble of shore rock that kept most people to the kinder part of the beach.

He turned his father's words over in his mind. *Awkward as Hell. Useless in the boat. Can't figure out what he's thinking half the time.* The words stung. Who was his father to say? There was more to life than fishing in a damn boat. That's the last thing he wanted. But what did he really want? He'd harboured vague ideas of working for Uncle Scratch at the store, but that was just a stepping stone out.

He remembered grade six, when the students were asked to write an essay about what they wanted to be. It was the only time Pocket had received a failing mark.

His teacher had waved the blank page in front of him after class. Behind him, chalked on the board, were various futures: fisherman fireman doctor nurse teacher lawyer policeman mechanic secretary pilot race car driver. The last suggestions had come from Cuff Dodds. They'd begun, after that, to lean towards the magnificent, the ridiculous, and the mundane: astronaut plumber prime minister road-line painter decoy-carver undertaker whirligig-maker. His teacher had indulgently noted them all. "None of these?" his teacher had asked him, waving at the board, and Pocket shook his head.

"Hand something in by tomorrow," Mr. Kendrick told him.

Brenda Morton, who sat in front of Pocket, had stayed after class was dismissed to help. "Television personality?" she suggested. "Champion fiddler? What about master chef?"

What he really wanted to be, but could not have articulated at ten years of age, was something at which he felt competent, and nowhere did he feel more competent than when he was reading, drawing, listening, or watching. One step removed, that's what suited him best. Pocket Snow was an observer, and observing was something Pocket knew he did very well. What he didn't know was of what use such a talent could ever be. It was certainly useless in a boat, unless it came to spotting an approaching storm, but any idiot could see that.

Tripping over the slide of angular rock, Pocket's eyes caught a glint of something wedged between boulders, half buried by seaweed tangle. When he pushed aside the weeds he could see a cable, metal-clad, flexible, snaking like a sea serpent washed ashore. Following the cable as it curved he saw it was attached to a metal cylinder the length of his arm. The thing, when he picked it up in both hands, was heavy, and warmer than the cold around it. He turned it over, examining its smoothness, looking for words or numbers: nothing. A chill came over him, and he set it down. He wiped the tears that had sprung to his eyes and looked over his shoulder, scanning the shoreline. No one. He pulled the sketchbook and pencil from his back pocket.

Afterwards, Pocket kicked at the seaweed until the thing was fully obscured. He couldn't say why he did this, just as he couldn't say why he'd gone to the back door earlier. He could not have explained any of it if he'd been asked. Tonight's tide, with the waning of the moon, wouldn't come so high. He'd have time to think what to do about it, and time was what he wanted. If only there was more time.

Heading back towards the pebble beach he slipped, foot sliding into a wedge in the rock, and went down. It took him by surprise: clumsy as he could be, he had always been sure-footed on the rocks he'd been scrambling over since he could walk. Maybe it was the water in his eyes.

When he looked up, a hand was reaching down to him: silver rings and bangles. Where had she come from?

"You look like you can use a hand," the woman told him, eyeing him. Pocket had the feeling she meant more than the hand up.

"Thanks, I'm okay," he mumbled, scrambling up on his own. "Rocks'r wet, that's all."

"I've just come," said the woman, as if that explained something.

Pocket was now upright, his shin smarting painfully, and he bent to rub it. The woman was obviously not from around here with those strange clothes and her accent, something Pocket didn't recognize. She stood, hands on her hips, waiting, and it dawned on Pocket after a few beats that she was waiting for him to speak.

"Where did you come *from*?" he asked, finally.

"Fresno," she said, and then, when she saw his blank expression, added: "California." The woman looked at Pocket for an extra beat, and Pocket felt his skin prickle just a little. "You live here," she said, a statement.

Pocket nodded.

"Then you can show me around," she said.

"I um, can't. I have to be home."

Pocket began to walk quickly, hoping to leave the woman behind, but she hurried beside him, skirts wafting in the harbour wind, boots slipping on the round beach rocks.

"My name is Wanda," she said. "I'm here about the incident. And your name is…?"

"Pocket Snow."

She stepped in front of him, stopping him in his tracks, and put out her hand. The heat of her palm was startling. Whatever chill Pocket had felt moments before was gone in an instant, and he met her eyes for the first time. Pocket had always felt awkward shaking hands, unsure of how it was done, but Wanda took his hand as if she had known him his whole life but had been away temporarily, an interrupted conversation now resumed. When Pocket withdrew his hand, the warmth remained, tingling.

"*Could* you show me around?"

"Guess so."

They stood facing the shore, harbour at their backs, and Pocket pointed out Crosbey's, the Moss Plant, the firehall. Turning, he pointed out the wharf and they began walking in its direction. Wanda kept looking at the harbour.

"Those boats," Pocket told her, "they're here because of the crash."

"The UFO."

"Whatever it was. It was some strange, anyway."

"You were there."

But Pocket didn't answer, so Wanda began telling Pocket about life on other planets, and as she spoke her voice, previously abrupt, became silky, as if sliding back and forth with the soft surf as they walked. Pocket was mesmerized.

"When you think of it, it's not really logical that we would be the only intelligent life in the universe, is it?"

Wanda gazed out at the harbour, and Pocket followed her gaze. "No," he murmured.

"There are so many things: the pyramids, Stonehenge, crop circles."

Pocket had studied the pyramids in school. He had no idea what these other things were, but he'd always found it hard to believe that slaves pushed those big rocks into place.

"Did you know they've found cave paintings of flying saucers?"

Pocket shook his head. They were approaching the wharf, heading up from the beach to the gravel parking area from which they could walk its length. They walked in silence until they reached the end, water on three sides. The hum of motors was audible from the small knot of vessels out towards the island.

"I was standin here when it came down," Pocket told her. "Right here. I saw it come down, at an angle, like, from over there." He pointed to the distant curve of shoreline.

Wanda didn't say anything for a moment, so Pocket turned to look at her. She was gazing in the direction he'd pointed, and she was smiling broadly. Pocket glimpsed a fleck of gold tooth.

"I knew it," she said, a little breathless. "I knew you saw it," and Pocket felt the swell of importance. "Tell me everything."

3 In the yellow room in the yellow house, Rodney unpacked. The clothes he brought all slid into the top drawer of the bureau. He set his toiletries in their case on the top, and beside them his aged Nikon, a stack of three crisp notebooks and a handful of ball-point pens. He had brought a tape recorder, but had neglected to bring the detachable cord. The batteries, he discovered, were dead. Sliding aside the plastic cover to the battery compartment, he felt their mute reproach. Maybe he could get some at the store.

He changed into Aunt Bridey's rollneck sweater, glad he'd brought it after all. His stomach growled, and he thought about the sandwich he'd been promised. As he zipped closed his bag he saw Lorelei's package of cigarettes in the corner and impulsively tucked them in the pocket of his windbreaker as if it was something he did all the time. Before closing the door he glanced around the room, taking in the iron bed-stead, the tufted cotton bedspread. It was so much like his grandmother's guestroom, it made him smile.

There was a young man sitting at one of the tables in the back of the store when he got there. He had ginger hair and long sideburns, and was holding a cigarette between his thumb and forefinger, which he raised at Rodney in a sort of salute.

"Cuff's been waitin for ya," Shirley explained. "Here,

I got yer sandwich ready. Thought you might like lobster, you bein from away. Coffee?"

Rodney nodded gratefully and took his sandwich over to where Cuff was sitting. To quell the growling of his stomach, he took a bite before he was halfway across the room. The sweet lobster salad in the soft white bread was unlike anything he'd ever encountered. He'd devoured most of one-half before he had even sat down. Shirley, beaming, placed a cup of coffee in front of him.

"Ya look right starved. I'll make you another."

"Shirley must like you," Cuff told him. "She don't usually offer seconds when it's on the house." He took a long drag and stubbed out his cigarette in the heavy glass ashtray. "You're the reporter, right?"

Rodney swallowed and set the remainder of his sandwich down, offering his hand after wiping it on his sweater. "Rod Nowland, *Ottawa Journal*," he told Cuff. The sound of his new, shorter name, and the ease with which he coupled it with the name of his newspaper, felt satisfying, a man reinvented.

"You lookin for interviews?"

Rodney remembered his tape recorder and his stack of empty notebooks sitting on the bureau in his second-floor room; might as well have been on another planet. Always be ready to seize the moment, that's what his instructor had taught. Instead, all Rodney had in his pocket were Lorelei's cigarettes. But "yes," he said through his sandwich.

Cuff leaned forward. "I saw it come down. I called it in. First one."

Rodney held up one finger, his mouth still full. After he swallowed he rose and approached Shirley, who in any case was leaning on the counter listening, and asked her for pen and paper. When he was seated with a stack of napkins and a red Bic pen, he nodded at Cuff as professionally as he could. "Tell me what you saw. First," he set a napkin in front of him, "tell me your name."

"Cuff Dodds," said Cuff.

"Cuthbert," said Shirley.

"Cuff," corrected Cuff. "Everybody calls me Cuff." Rodney wrote the name at the top of the napkin and underlined it. Cuff grinned.

"I was comin back from the Island, 'bout eleven. Parked at the Moss Plant just to take in the harbour, all pretty, like. It was right clear."

"You were alone in the car?" Rodney looked up from where he had written "right clear."

"My friend Ernie was with me, but he took off. I called it in. Ask Charlie Brannen. Calls from all up and down the Shore," Cuff leaned forward and tapped a yellow index finger on Rodney's napkin. "Charlie Brannen. RCMP."

Rodney wrote this down and underlined it three times. The pen tore through the napkin on the third underline and Rodney had to extract the nib from its folds.

"Here's something I forgot to tell Charlie," said Cuff, leaning forward. "Dunno why, just occurred to me now. But I'll tell you."

Rodney waited, pen poised.

"D'you, uh—don't newspapers pay fer information?"

Rodney tried to remember the *Journal*'s policy. "Sometimes," he said. "If it's exclusive."

Cuff looked blank.

"If you're only telling it to one newspaper," Rodney clarified. "That, and if it proves to be true."

Cuff leaned back in his chair and put his hands behind his head. "Well, I don't see no other reporters 'round here, d'you? So that's no problem. But provin it—"

Rodney felt himself growing impatient. "I'll see what I can do," he said.

Cuff withdrew his hands and placed them flat on the table. Rodney saw the deep tar stains on his right index finger, then looked up to see Cuff's face inches from his.

"After it went down," he said, "them four lights went out. And then it floated on the water—musta been sixty feet across—with a light on top, kinda like a ball. Like halfa ball. Musta stayed there, floating, five minutes 'fore it went under." He leaned back, smug. "That's gotta be worth a few bucks, innit?"

"If it's true," said Rodney.

"Ernie was there. He musta seen it, he wasn't a hundred feet down the road. I got a corroboratin witness."

"Why don't you just describe everything," Rodney said. "Everything you can remember, in detail."

Rodney looked up when Pocket and Wanda came in, at once irritated and relieved at Wanda's appearance. Cuff's testimony had become repetitive some minutes ago, and Rodney was already regretting his instruction regarding details. After a sideways tangent on Cuff's part about the

Legion and the girls in attendance, Rodney had begun looking for a way to extract himself, but was also waiting hopefully for the second sandwich Shirley had promised. He watched Shirley's expression while she took in Pocket with a motherly warmth, then Wanda, with something quite different.

Cuff, too, looked up and, seeing Pocket, said jovially: "Pocket, Ole Son! Hey, was that you on the wharf?" He turned to Rodney. "Pocket'll tell ya. Sure, it was him."

"Pocket'll have been home in bed," Shirley said. "He's not like you hooligans out gallivantin all hours."

"Well, somebody was," Cuff said. "Was some dark."

"Well, it was nighttime after all," said Shirley drily.

Cuff caught sight of Wanda. "Hey, Pocket, who's yer friend, anyways?"

Pocket hesitated, but Wanda turned, her eyes narrowing slightly as she took in Cuff, and then, as if making up her mind about him, turned back to Shirley.

"Thank you for looking after my bag," she said, and Shirley shrugged.

"Weren't a lot of work to look after," she said. "Just sat there the whole time not movin." Then: "Pocket, dear, how's yer mum?"

"Seems a little better," he said, then added, "Dad broke the teapot." Everyone knew about Merle and her tea.

"I heard," said Shirley, smiling.

"You wouldn't have one for sale?"

"No, hon, I don't have any teapots," she said, thinking to keep her present a surprise. "Though it seems I coulda sold about three the past twenty-four hours."

Wanda raised her eyebrows. "Me, I never travel without one," she said. She turned to Pocket. "Your mother is ill?"

"She has the cancer," Shirley told her abruptly. Her eye caught Pocket and her voice softened. "Good that yer uncle's here now, innit, dear?" Pocket shrugged his shoulders, his discomfort visible.

Wanda regarded Pocket thoughtfully, then turned to Rodney, who was folding his interview napkins and tucking them in his pocket. A small melancholy had settled over him as he thought of the second sandwich, the one he apparently thought wasn't going to appear. It took him a minute to focus on Wanda's words, so clear was the image of the missing sandwich.

"Pocket, here, saw the spaceship come down," Wanda told him. "Here's your key interview, Rod."

"Hey!" objected Cuff. "What about me?"

"I gotta be home," Pocket said. "I shoulda been home a while ago."

"You go on home, dear," Shirley told him. "And give my love to yer mum." She looked at Rodney. "I remember I promised to make this boy a sandwich; he looks right starved now if he weren't almost perished before. I'll bring him along later—" she looked over her shoulder at the Pepsi clock on the wall. "—Mercy, maybe tomorrow instead so's not to get in the way of supper. It's after four. Tomorrow, then, and you two can chat while I sit with Merle."

"I'll be talking to you," Cuff said to Rodney as he rose to leave. "Ya need proof? Y'just leave it to me. We'll be talkin again." He shot Rodney a meaningful look.

Wanda had been looking thoughtfully at Pocket for a few minutes. Now, "I believe I'm going your way," she said to him. "We can walk together." She picked up her bag and handed it to Pocket, who, looking bewildered, took it from her.

They were both out the door before Shirley could say: "Now, where do you suppose she was goin in the first place?"

It had been a remarkable evening. With Wanda's arrival, the addition of a female influence affected the Snows in a way that surprised all of them. Pocket had felt the shift with his uncle's arrival a week ago, and yet with Wanda's it was as if the earth beneath the house moved again, and then settled into something more comfortable. If the men were awkward at first, they relaxed soon enough. Pocket felt the whole house sigh with something like relief, and a new warmth descended. After Wanda had gone up to bed, Wilf, shaking out blankets to make a bed on the couch, stopped Pocket on his way upstairs to bed and pulled his son close.

"Huggin never did come natural to the Snow men." He laughed softly, holding Pocket at arm's-length, now. "Snowmen. Funny, ain't it? Don't s'pose we mean to be, it's just the way we are. Now, off to bed with ya, Son."

"D'ya think Mum looks better?" Pocket asked.

Wilf looked at his son. "I think it's a good thing we got some help, now," he said, instead of answering. "She's an interesting thing, in't she? Different, anyways."

As Pocket ascended the stairs, he could still feel the warmth of his father's hands on his shoulders. He would do anything for his mother's embrace, something he now realized had stopped at some point: when? He recalled crawling into her lap after tripping on the road and skinning his knee; he could remember hugging her legs the first day of school, afraid to go in. When had been the last time she'd hugged him? He resolved to embrace his mother in the morning, to the extent that he could.

In his room, Pocket undressed. Before slipping under the covers he retrieved his mother's letter from under his bed, but he didn't read it. Instead, he put the letter into the back pocket of the pants he had hung over the chair, knowing he'd put them on again in the morning, that the letter would be there, and that he'd find a moment to slip it back into the desk.

4 In the Crosbey kitchen, the smell of fish and onions lingered. Earlier, when Rodney had inquired about where one might buy dinner, Shirley had taken in his hangdog look and told him that, although the Victoria did serve meals, it was a half-hour to the Passage and if she was cooking for two, she might as well cook for three.

After cleaning up from dinner, followed by several games of solitaire on the kitchen table, Shirley had gone up to bed early, telling Rodney she was off to bed with Frank Yerby. When Rodney looked confused, Fred laughed.

"That's the fellow wrote this week's novel," he explained after she had climbed the stairs. "Shirley's always readin. Book a week, pretty much."

Fred poured Rodney a shot of rum in a glass bordered with spades, hearts, clubs and diamonds, and tilted back in his chair, feet on the kitchen table. "The missus would have a fit," he said, raising his glass in a toast to his feet, and Rodney returned the salute, happy for the company. It would have been a long evening in his room.

"Enough buzz around here for ya?" Fred asked, winking.

"A lot going on," Rodney admitted. "Guess I'll get started tomorrow. I'm expected to file a story by the end of the day."

"How'd'ya do that?"

"Phone it in. I read it out, and they write it down."

"Long distance?" Fred was incredulous. "Paper you work for must have some money."

"No other way."

"Must be an important story."

Rodney chose not to relate how Mr. Copeland had dismissed the story. He pictured his desk transformed into Lorelei's efficient world, his own space relocated to the janitor's closet. And yet the fantasy of her, waiting for him, lingered. He remembered her request for a postcard, and resolved to buy one tomorrow.

"Yes," he said eventually.

"Y'know, there was lights seen all up and down the Shore," Fred told him, warming to the story, and Rodney nodded. "Doin some strange things. Not actin like aircraft, none of em, I heard. Flyin sideways, takin off straight up. Dancin, even. That many sees something, you know it ain't coincidence."

"So what do you think it was?"

"Most think it's some sorta Russian thing. Or maybe a piece from a spaceship. It was a Russian that first went up, what, five, six years ago, eh? Before the Americans! No telling what they can do."

"I suppose not," Rodney agreed. It was the Gagarin story that had solidified Rodney's decision to become a journalist; that, and his mother's reverence for newspapers. He could remember clearly the 1961 article from the *Ottawa Journal*, the front-page story that reported the Russian space flight neatly folded in the bottom drawer of his mother's writing cabinet. She kept all the notable editions: the Queen's coronation, the Kennedy assassination, Yuri Gagarin's first space flight, and, later, Alan Shepard's and John Glenn's. "When they reach the moon, that one I'll have framed," she liked to declare. He would, he decided, some day be the by-line his mother collected.

What would it be like to interview an astronaut? To ask what it felt like, all that space. All that aloneness. When you're out there, he thought, alone means something different. It doesn't mean that people aren't interested, because out there, there *are* no people. Just you, and who you are is perfect.

Rodney brought himself back to the Crosbey kitchen table. It wasn't a moon landing, but the Perry's Harbour UFO crash was a start. "Is that what you think? That it was the Russians?"

"Makes sense. All that brass out there. Rumour is there's U.S. military out there, too."

"The Americans? That would be something."

"Yep. They'd be interested if it were the Russians, fer sure."

"My boss thinks it's something else. Like that crash that happened in New Mexico. You know, the space-ship." He felt on top of things, tossing this off as common knowledge, and mentally thanked Wanda, however annoying she may have been.

"Never heard of it," Fred shrugged. "But some do think it's a flying saucer. I hear 'em talkin in the backa the store. There's a group at South Head holdin some sort of vigil thing out on the point, there. To communi-cate, like."

"Really? When?"

Fred looked at the kitchen clock. "Over by now, I expect."

Rodney mentally kicked himself. Another missed opportunity; he needed to learn to ask more questions. He never seemed to be in the right place, at the right time. Today he'd just been getting his feet under him, he consoled himself. Tomorrow he'd be up early and meet the boats before they headed out, try to get some quotes from the Coast Guard. No other reporters were here yet as far as he knew; he could still scoop this story. He was surprised the Herald reporter hadn't yet arrived, at least, according to Shirley, who'd been on the phone to Bessie Parsons.

"Heard the CBC was sendin in a film crew." Fred refilled Rodney's glass. "Who knows who else'll be comin around. Good for business, that's fer sure."

Fred held the bottle up to the light, frowned comically at the level of liquid remaining, then set it down. They drank in silence for a few minutes.

"I talked to Cuff Dodds earlier," Rodney remarked after a bit.

"Hmmph." Fred shook his head. "You might want to take what Cuff says with a grain of salt."

"He seemed—sincere."

"He may be. Not many like Cuff Dodds, though. It ain't that he don't tell the truth necessarily, just that he'll stretch it to be useful to him in some way. Cuff's always been out for Cuff, which some might say is because nobody else is out for Cuff. But he ain't much liked," Fred said again.

"Well—"

"Ya didn't much like him, didja?"

"No," Rodney said honestly.

Fred, rocking again on the back legs of his chair, said: "Thing about a place like this, everyone knows everyone." In his glass, rum swirled and sloshed. "Where they came from. Who their family is. So you can give a little, when you know where someone's come from. Perry's being so small, we all know everyone's story all the way back. Can be a good thing or a bad thing. On the one hand, you know where the sore spots are. That's a good thing. On the other hand, you get a family with a rough history, people expect the worst, and then that bunch, they kinda rise to the occasion. Like Cuff. He's up against a lot of history, that boy. 'S a hard thing to step out of."

Rodney thought about the anonymity of the City. He'd hoped to reinvent himself there, but found himself followed by the person he was before he moved. He didn't know if, in a place like Perry's Harbour, he'd feel embraced or embarrassed. It took him a moment to catch up to Fred's words.

"For one thing," Fred explained, "Stanley Dodds has always got some scheme or other going. And Cuff's a chip off the old block that way. Like the time they was going to grow cranberries in that swamp behind their house. Boasted for weeks they had some big contract with a juice company. Drove everyone crazy with it, what they'd do with all that money. Course, there was no contract, and there never was a lot of cranberries, either. Still lotsa water out there, though."

"I suppose everyone dreams of getting rich," Rodney offered.

"Cuff's been tryin to get rich quick since he could count money," Fred told him. "Comes of laziness, I reckon. Why do any work when yer sure there's a pot a gold just on t'other side of the rock, y'know?"

Rodney nodded.

"But there's more to it than that, even. There's some dark stuff makes ya feel right sorry for that family. There's hope for Cuff, though. Always is."

Rodney sat with Fred's words for a moment, and then from upstairs came a thud.

"That'll be Frank fallin outta bed," remarked Fred, looking at the ceiling.

"Pardon?"

"Shirley always falls asleep when she's readin. How's yer glass, now, Boy?" Rodney pushed the near-empty tumbler forward.

"Things happen," Fred mused as he splashed rum into Rodney's glass. "Makes people see things a certain way after. Make 'em the way they are. There have to be some allowances for that."

"Yeah," Rodney murmured thoughtfully. By that time, Rodney was feeling the rum, much as he'd been feeling the wine the night Lorelei had come to see him.

"What about Pocket Snow?"

"S'tough on a kid, innit? You heard about Merle?"

Rodney nodded. "I wanted to talk to him. I heard he was there, and I'd like another perspective. But I wasn't sure—"

"Yeah. Know what yer thinking. Might not be the best time, and you might be right. But maybe it'll be good for the boy, give him somethin else to think about. I suppose this thing gives us all somethin else to think about. We'll all miss Merle, no doubt about that. If 't'weren't for the cancer she'd be down t'the wharf every day, chattin up them divers and whatnot. She could always make people wanna talk. Charm anybody, Merle could."

They listened to the wall clock tick.

"Some people, when they go, it's a big empty space they leave behind," Fred mused. "Merle's one a those."

Rodney nodded. "I think I know what you mean," he said. "When I was nine, my best friend was a girl named Daisy," Rodney began after a bit. He ran his thumb over the playing card symbols on his glass. Club, diamond, spade, heart. "Daisy Dorringer." Rodney said it reverently, looking skyward. "She was like that. When she'd come into the classroom it got suddenly brighter, somehow. She was a short girl, really, but something about her was—bigger than everyone else, somehow. I got teased at school about Daisy being my girlfriend—you know, Rodney and Daisy sitting in a tree, k-i-s-s-i-n-g…and when it first started I tried to avoid her, because it made me embarrassed. But Daisy cornered me in the boy's playground—she didn't care about getting in trouble or what anyone would say, she never did—and gave me an Indian burn and told me not to be stupid. She was so much tougher than me, and more—mature, I guess. But for some reason she wanted to be my friend. I never could quite figure that out. But it made me feel special."

"Maybe she saw something in you she liked."

Rodney looked up to see Fred smiling in a fatherly way, lines spreading like sunbursts from beside his eyes.

"Maybe. Maybe—I don't know. She had a bunch of

older brothers who were bad news. Maybe she saw a boy she could have some control over. She could tell me to do anything and I'd do it. I agreed with everything she said. If she said the moon was made of green cheese, I wouldn't disagree. Not because I was scared of her—although I suppose I was, a little—because she just had to be right. Because she was Daisy.

"We were just friends, though. Except this one day, it was a really hot day. We'd been at the playground and I found a dime by the gate. She said she saw it first, but I had it in my hand, so she said we had to share it. She said we should spend it on a Popsicle, so we could split it in half—which I was going to do anyway, but as soon as she said it, I—I don't know, suddenly I didn't want to. I mean, it was hot and she was being bossy and maybe I was growing up a little, maybe I was getting more confident. So I said I wouldn't. I just stood there with my hands behind my back and that dime in my fist. Do you know what she did?"

Fred shook his head and refilled his own glass.

"She told me she'd kiss me for it. I didn't know what to say. But I guess I nodded, because she did kiss me—right on the mouth—and her lips were the softest thing, softer than anything I'd ever imagined, and warm, and I felt this...electric current, kind of, running through me. Sounds crazy..."

Fred was grinning broadly. "Sounds like puppy love," he said, but Rodney went on.

"Then she was off and running, yelling for me to go one way, she'd go the other, and she'd race me to the store. Well, I didn't want her to get away, so I ran, too.

The store was six blocks away. From where we'd stood, it was the same distance to get there going either route, and in both cases it meant crossing Laurent Road, which was a busy thoroughfare that separated the row housing from the duplexes.

"I ran as fast as I could, and when I got there, I was thrilled to see I'd actually beaten her. I remember it surprised me, because she was usually faster than me. But it gave me a chance to catch my breath so I leaned against the iron railing and waited, trying to look cool, self-assured. I could still feel where she'd kissed me, you know?"

Fred nodded.

"I don't know how long I waited. A long time, longer than you'd think anyone would wait for someone who was coming from six blocks away. I started inventing excuses for her: she met up with someone from school, someone who invited her over or something, and she forgot about me. Or worse, she ran into Corby Brandt, who I thought she maybe liked, because I'd seen them talking at the painted line that separated the boys' yard from the girls' at school. Or she received an urgent message to go home right away. Something had happened to one of her brothers—they were always doing dumb things, getting into trouble, breaking an arm or a leg doing some stupid stunt. She'd have to go home and look after the younger ones while her folks took whoever it was to the hospital to get a cast put on.

"So when I heard the ambulance, that's what I thought it was. One of her brothers. And I walked home. I didn't even buy a Popsicle."

Fred's eyes were soft. He reached over and topped up Rodney's glass.

"When the car hit her she was running straight across the road. That's what they said. Why she didn't stop and look was anybody's guess. It happened so fast, she didn't know what hit her. What I couldn't get—what I still don't get—is how someone can be flesh and blood one minute, breathing, laughing, *kissing*, and the next just—gone. Like that. And there's that hole you were talking about."

"Makes you wonder," Fred said after a few moments of silence.

"Made me scared," Rodney admitted. "For a long time. I'd lie in bed at night, afraid of bad things happening without warning. Afraid an airplane would fall out of the sky and crash on our house. And I was afraid to go to school in case something happened to my parents while I was gone."

"You got over that, though."

"What was worse, though," Rodney continued, "was how guilty I felt, because I was alive, and she wasn't. I mean, we could've just walked together to the store, right?"

"Things happen the way they happen," Fred told him.

"Doesn't make it better," Rodney replied.

"Yeah."

Rodney could hear the rollers breaking down on the shore, the rattle of rocks as the waves sucked back. The sound brought him back, then, to where he was: a kitchen in a house on the sea, a village with a story. And out in the harbour, *something*.

"I don't know why I told you that story," Rodney said after a bit. "I haven't before now. Told anyone, I mean." Rodney stood up, swayed, and sat down again. The alcohol rushed to his head and made his tongue feel thick. "I better go to bed," he said.

"Looks like you better," Fred nodded, adding: "Don't let them little green men getcha in the night, then."

Rodney paused at the kitchen door, holding onto its frame for support. "You know the thing about Daisy?"

Fred shook his head. On the wall, the clock ticked audibly.

"She'll always be the potential of what she might have become. She'll never make a dumb mistake. She'll never disappoint anyone. She'll always be perfect."

Silence

The rocks on a seashore are myriad in size, shape and colour, each unique, and yet from a distance they merge into another thing altogether, a sum of parts. The magic happens when you bend and pick one up, smooth and round, fitting into your palm as if you were born to hold exactly this rock, in this place. You feel it warm with your body's heat, wonder at the journey it took over millennia to be here. Around you, thousands of rocks. In your hand, this one. What secrets would a warm rock tell, if it could?

This rock, this grey-flecked rock smooth as the skin of an apple, has been kissed by salt, nudged by fish, embraced by seaweed, kicked by shoes; it has sheltered beach spiders from the beaks of shorebirds. It had been tossed into the waves for the splash it makes, then rolled back ashore with the incoming tide. When you set it down with its thousand brothers, it is invisible.

It's quiet on the beach, but it is never silent. There is the lap of waves, the wash of stones; the distant hum of motors, carrying across the water; a Herring Gull's cry, and, closer, the reedy note of a Sandpiper, almost invisible at the water's edge. These sounds as common as the blood in your veins, folded into the day like the air you breathe, remarkable only when you stop to listen.

You breathe deeply, inhale the salt-sweet smell of the shore. Turning, you walk at the edge of the seaweed, deposited in a line that speaks of the tide's highest reach. Sand fleas jump ahead of your footfalls, making the sand look as if it is alive.

There is always flotsam on the beach. Amid the rocks are the broken bones of lobster traps; in the eelgrass, a woven bait bag. A rubber glove, an oil can, a child's sneaker. Broken free, washed overboard, left behind, lost. Sea-sanded planks from a boat that met its end some hurricane night last month, last year, a hundred years ago. These things carry stories, and with them, voices. If you listen you can hear the distant sound of children playing, or of men calling out across the seesaw of waves.

Some things wash up from a great distance. Some things don't appear recognizable at all. Unlike the ship plank or the rubber glove, the bait bag or the sneaker, sometimes a thing might be left as the tide recedes that speaks an unfamiliar language. Its stories are not our stories.

If you saw such a thing you would wonder: Whose stories are these? With what voice does it speak? You would wonder at its secrets, and yet, you might just leave it lie. Some secrets, you know, are better left.

Saturday, October 7

1 Pocket awoke from a night full of complicated dreams and lay clutching at them. In the one he could still half recall, his mother was sitting in a rocking chair he remembered but that no longer existed. She was rocking, and crooning at the bundle in her arms. In the dream, he thought he was in that bundle, but when his mother looked up and smiled at him, he realized he could not be. Proudly, she drew back the blanket to reveal a cylindrical silver object, wires protruding where a baby's head might be.

Pocket rose and dressed, not wanting to be seen in his pyjamas with a stranger in the house. As he passed the tiny room beside him that had once been his mother's sewing room he looked in, taking in the roll-away cot set up on one side, his mother's things shoved to the other. On the unmade bed Wanda's bag stood open, its contents spilling out. He peered, one foot inside the room, but all he could see was a jumble of clothes. A noise from downstairs made him step back.

He came down to find his uncle Scratch at the kitchen table, mug of tea in his hand and his feet up on the kitchen chair opposite his own. He was reading a tabloid newspaper, which he held up as Pocket entered.

"All true," he grinned, pointing to a headline about mutilated livestock in Arizona. "Aliens done it."

"Where'd you get that?"

Scratch grinned again and nodded towards the living

room. "Yer mum's taken a real shine to her. She's a strange one, in't she?"

"Dad seems to like her well enough."

"Yer dad's happy to have someone who wants to pitch in. Room and board is a cheap enough price to pay. She's a talker, too, charmed yer dad right off too, give him something else to think about. *And* she can play crib." Pocket saw his uncle had been charmed, too. After complimenting Scratch on the dinner, she'd done up the dinner dishes in no time, a job that normally fell to Pocket. "She's been up since Merle woke up, crack a dawn. Gave her a sponge bath already."

"Where's Dad?"

"Somethin at the church. Rummage sale. Seemed right happy to leave, with the woman here. Wanda." he drained his mug. "Furthest yer dad's been from home for a while."

In the living room, Wanda sat close beside Merle's bed. Pocket could see that his mother was sitting almost upright, propped on pillows, and held in her hand a teacup—not a mug, but an actual teacup with a saucer, one of the few Maritime Rose cups she kept for special occasions. She was smiling, and Pocket, catching her eye, found himself smiling back. She looked better than he'd seen her for weeks.

"Wanda's going to read my tea leaves," she announced, her voice clear. "She's going to tell me about my future."

"Come. Sit," said Wanda.

To Pocket, Wanda appeared larger than she had before. A presence. Perhaps it was just in contrast to his mother's diminutive form under the covers. He pulled a ladderback chair up to the other side of his mother's bed. On the high bedside table stood a round-bellied teapot painted in rows of intricate designs, its colours a tapestry of blues, greens, maroons, and deep gold. Pocket thought it looked like something from far away, and he wondered about it.

"My mother's. From Poland," Wanda told him without looking at him, and Pocket shivered. "I take it with me everywhere."

Merle sipped her tea and, with her free hand, reached for Pocket's where it rested on his knee. She nodded towards Wanda's teapot.

"Isn't it lovely?"

Pocket looked at his mother's narrow hand on his, then at the other hand holding the teacup. She was holding the cup with one hand, and steadily. No shaking.

"Y'know, I always say: use the good china now. You just never know."

Pocket couldn't remember them ever using the Maritime Rose plates. "Where's Dad?" he asked, forgetting he'd just asked Scratch the same thing. Thinking his father should see this.

"He went out early. Something at the church, I think. There," she pronounced, tilting the last of the tea into her mouth. "I'm ready."

Wanda leaned forward across the bed and gently placed her hand under the saucer. "Turn the cup over slowly," she instructed, "and turn it counterclockwise three times."

Merle did this, glancing at Pocket with a complicit smile. *Isn't this fun*, her expression said, and Pocket smiled back slightly, still fascinated by his mother's renewed energy.

Wanda took the cup and saucer from Merle and set them both carefully on the bedside table. Before turning over the teacup, she began to speak, her voice dusky.

"The art of tea-leaf reading is called Tasseography," Wanda explained. "In the Middle East, coffee grounds are read, and in some countries, wine sediments. It's an old, old art. A very ancient practice." Wanda's voice had become noticeably deeper. "As far back as the days of ancient Greece. Farther."

Merle's eyes were closed now, but she was nodding and smiling, entirely present. Pocket felt calmed by Wanda's voice, as if a warm hand was stroking his brow. He looked up when Uncle Scratch came to the doorway and then leaned against it, arms folded.

"Wanda's going to read Mum's tea leaves," Pocket whispered, and Scratch nodded as if this sort of thing happened all the time in the Snow household.

Wanda looked up, taking in Merle, still with a smile playing at her lips, wide-eyed Pocket, and Scratch, who she looked at for a long moment before turning back to the cup. "Everyone in this room is drawn here for a reason," she said. "It's part of the Grand Design."

As Wanda turned the cup over and gazed into it in silence, Pocket thought about the words *Grand Design*. Grand was a word his English grandmother had used, the only time Pocket met her. After his grandfather had passed away—before Pocket was even born—his grandmother had gone home to England, returning to Perry's Harbour just once. "It's a spare life you have,

Merlaine," she'd said. "And not one I envy. But you do have a grand boy, here." Pocket could remember the feeling of his grandmother's warm hand on his head as she said these words, and Pocket had, for years afterwards, consoled himself with the word *Grand* when feeling inept—which, as he grew into a gangly teenager, was most of the time. Watching Wanda's eyes, unmoving beneath a veil of eyelashes, he thought about Grand Design, and what that might mean. It seemed a positive thing, cheerful words in an optimist's world. Now, as Wanda tilted the cup, Pocket could see the wash of tea leaf stuck to the inside, and on the saucer's surface the same scattering, creating patterns. Was this the grand design she'd meant?

"Mmmm," said Wanda, and Merle leaned forward.

"Let me see," she said.

Wanda tilted the cup towards her, and Merle peered inside. "Looks like seaweed," she remarked, "when it washes up after a storm."

Wanda tilted the cup back towards herself, closed her eyes, and exhaled. When she opened them and began to speak, her voice was lower still.

"There are messages in the leaves," she began, "and there are messages in the spaces where there are no leaves. Here," she pointed to a smudge of leaves that, to Pocket, looked like a lobster.

"Ah," Wanda said. "A bird. Now, a crow or a raven, that's not so good. But there's another side to it: a bird or a feather, that's ascension. There are two sides to everything. Nothing is ever as simple as it seems." She looked at Pocket. "And even the things that seem hard, well, there's good that comes out of them. Ascension is good."

"That's what they say in church," Merle quipped.

"You're a religious woman?" Wanda asked her.

"Been wonderin about that lately," Merle answered after a moment. Pocket thought about the letter, about the doubts his mother had expressed. Although not forced to go himself, his mother had gone to church every Sunday until she could go no longer. For Pocket, the dusty wood smell of the church, the filtered light with its swirling motes, the dreary, sometimes discordant notes of the old organ were a part of the fabric that was his mother. "There's a comfort there, I suppose. But when I think of heaven, of all them angels, I can't fathom it. 'Though I do like to think of it. 'Specially the ones I miss, waitin for me somewhere up there, if there is an Up There. Wouldn't that be somethin?"

"Looking at the leaves, I can tell you there are people waiting to see you. Ancestors." Wanda peered deeper. "A chain of people..." she tilted the cup. "You are a link in the chain. I can see it in the leaves."

Pocket saw, in his mind's eye, the chainlink fence around the sports field at the high school in the Passage. In gym class, he'd always felt caged by those links. Imprisoned. But: "It's a comfort, it is," his mother repeated.

"We are, all of us, linked," Wanda continued. "In some way. In this world, in other worlds."

Pocket knew she was talking about aliens, because Wanda had talked all about them on the way from Crosbey's store. She'd told him about SEW and C-PIPS, and explained to him about psychic abilities. "When you know something you couldn't know about through conventional means," she'd said, and Pocket remembered the dream he'd had about his mother, and wondered if it meant she would be abducted by the aliens. If she was, he thought just for a moment, he'd like to go, too. So she wouldn't be alone. The thought of his mother out there, in all that space. He'd told her about his mother, then, and how his uncle Scratch was staying, and how his father was building kitchen cupboards instead of getting ready for lobster season, never mind going out after haddock. Last week he'd seen the other boats come in from longlining, fish boxes full to bursting. Tip Morton came in with three swordfish, one of them a hundred-and-fifty pounder.

"This time last year he'd go out week at a time," he'd told her at the time.

"Don't you go?"

"Well, I got school. But I'm not so good in a boat," he'd said sheepishly.

Coming in, then, he'd introduced her to his uncle and father, and then when his mother had called from the living room to ask if the visitor would be staying, Pocket surprised all of them by saying, firmly: *yes*.

Now, Wanda tilted the cup again and looked over its rim at the people in the room. "We're all part of the same cosmic neighbourhood," she said.

From the doorway Scratch grunted, himself thinking of the front-page story of the newspaper Wanda had brought. She tossed him an irritated glance, then softened when she saw that his look contained humour rather than derision. She smiled, then set the cup down and picked up the saucer.

"I see a bird with a large beak, like a crow."

Pocket remembered his uncle talking about how one crow means bad luck, two mean good. Whenever Pocket would see one, he'd look for another. When he didn't find one, he'd look over his shoulder for Cuff Dodds. He also remembered something else Uncle Scratch had told him. Something better.

"Crows are smart," Pocket said, leaning forward. "Really smart. That's good, right?"

"Actually," said Merle, "I always liked crows. They talk like people, if ya listen. Always wondered what they was talkin about."

Wanda cleared her throat and waited for silence. "The dead speak to us through birds," said Wanda. "Birds are messengers. It may mean—yes, I believe it does—that this ancestral link I'm feeling in this reading means that your loved ones are trying to communicate with you."

"Well, they're usually nattering on at me about *somethin*," said Merle.

"Those who have already passed," explained Wanda gently.

Pocket shivered again. The fire was low; he should have brought a sweater from his room. Scratch moved from the doorway and put another piece of wood on, leaving the door ajar so it would catch more quickly. There was a petit-point stool near the stove, one of the things Merle's mother had left behind when she'd returned home to her own line of ancestors. Scratch pulled it forward and sat on it, his long legs making him look, himself, like a squatting bird. He rested his elbows on his knees and folded his hands, then nodded as if to say: get on with it, then.

"Now, if you turn it this way, that bird looks more like an airplane," Wanda continued. "That means a journey. But remember, it's not just the tea leaves that tell the story; it's the places *between* the leaves. Like here," she let Merle see the saucer. Pocket leaned forward to see, as well. "That's a rabbit. It's important to be brave." Wanda looked at Pocket again, as if the statement was meant for him.

Merle smiled. "Always liked rabbits, too. Had one, when I was a girl. Stu, we called him, my father's joke." Nobody spoke, the comment hanging. "Stu the Rabbit," Merle explained, chuckling. "Dad always threatened that's what we'd do with him. Never did, of course. Some ol' dog got him."

"Now, a hammer," Wanda continued, "means hard work is needed—"

"Hmmph," Merle snorted. "I guess it must."

A knock, and the front door opened immediately.

"Brought some cookies, Merle," Shirley said from the hallway, "and a—" she stopped when she saw Wanda, taking in the colourful teapot on the side table between them. She looked down at the Brown Betty she held in her hand, "—teapot."

"She's reading Mum's tea leaves," Pocket offered.

"Here," Scratch stood up. "Let me take those, Shirl." He took the tin of cookies from where it had been wedged under her arm. "That's right kind a you. Come in, now. I'll put the kettle on, we'll make some fresh."

Shirley took a step into the room, still holding the teapot, frowning. "Didn't expect to see you here, Miss—"

"Wanda," reminded Pocket, thinking Shirley must have forgotten. "She's stayin in the spare. To help out, like."

"We generally look after our own." Shirley looked at Wanda, who was still holding Merle's teacup. Wanda glanced at her, then turned her attention back to the cup in her hands.

"She's been helping—" Pocket's voice was firmer this time, but he didn't finish because Wanda, ignoring Shirley, continued.

"An apple, here—" she tipped the cup towards Merle, "That's a gift."

Merle, looking at Shirley, put her hands together. "A teapot for me? Do you know, I had one just like that—I do love a Brown Betty—got broke just recently. Shirley, dear, how'd ya know?"

"Little bird told me," Shirley smiled.

"Or maybe you're psychic," Pocket suggested. "Like Wanda. She came for the UFO." Everyone looked at Pocket, who was speaking more than he usually did.

Shirley's eyes settled on the elaborate teapot, and her hands moved protectively around the Brown Betty. "My mother's teapot," explained Wanda, following her gaze.

"From Poland," Pocket interjected.

"From Poland," affirmed Wanda, nodding. "I take it everywhere with me. For readings." When she saw Shirley's hands relax, "Would you like me to read your leaves?" she asked.

"No, thank you." Shirley's voice was clipped. Then,

"Merle, you look real good today," she said, and, moving to Pocket's side of the bed, gave her friend a peck on the cheek, ignoring Wanda. She turned to Scratch. "It's crazy out there, all sorts showing up, television cameras, bunch a Navy people, I don't know who all. Sure, Scratch, a cuppa would be fine. Wouldja like me to put summa those on a plate? We can make a fresh pot in this." She held the Brown Betty out.

In the commotion nobody heard Wilf enter from the hallway. In his large hands he held something delicate and white. When he held it aloft, its flamboyant roses almost glowed.

"Just a small chip," he said sheepishly. "Got it at the church sale. Nice one, eh, Merle?"

Fifteen minutes later, every kitchen chair had been dis-lodged of its stacks of plates and pulled into the living room around Merle's bed. In the party atmosphere, Merle looked as if she were holding court. On the side table, three teapots steamed, while the plate of ginger cookies was passed around.

"Was gonna bring that reporter fellow along," Shirley told them. "Couldn't find 'im when it was time to go, once Fred showed up to take over. Left him a note and told 'im where to come, we might see 'im yet."

"Reporter?" Merle asked.

"Yep. Came with this one, in fact," Shirley told her, jerking her head in Wanda's direction. "He's writin about the UFO."

"CBC's come with a film crew," said Wilf. "Saw 'em on my way back from church. Interviewin Cuff Dodds."

"Hmmph," Shirley grunted.

"Hung around listenin for a bit. Story gets wilder every time that boy tells it. Next, it'll be little green men comin out sayin take me to your leader."

"S'pose Cuff'd tell 'em 'that's me,'" laughed Shirley.

"Then 'magin what they'd think of mankind," Scratch offered, laughing with her. "Scare 'em back home fer sure."

"Been more traffic on the road, though," commented Shirley. "More in the store. Good for business, all these people: RCMP, Coast Guard, television people, and a bunch a bigwigs I dunno *who* they are. Whatever it is came down, it's a good thing all around."

"Hear the Base is real interested. You hear about that memo? Neil told Stanley that Selma—what's her name? Owen Corbet's cousin, must be a Corbet—saw it when she was cleanin there. Heard there's a Russian sub been sitting there all last week, just outside the boundary. Could be it's a Russian spyship come down, and now they're communicatin."

Wanda had been sitting quietly, having pushed her chair a little back from the circle of chairs. Now, she spoke.

"It's not of this world," she said, catching the gaze of everyone in the room. "I promise you."

"That'd go for most 'round here," Scratch broke the spell. "We're an odd lot, that's fer sure."

"Speak for yerself," Shirley laughed.

"It's fascinatin, though, ain't it?" Merle said quietly. Wilf reached forward and put a hand on his wife's. Pocket looked at the two hands. It was a tender moment;

those gathered in the room felt they should look away. Teaspoons tinkled in teacups, stirring.

After a moment Merle withdrew her hand gently and, sipping her tea, smiled, her mouth taking the funny downturn of amusement when she was warming to a story, something Pocket realized he had not seen for a long time.

"Speakin of tea," she said, although they hadn't been, "I told you 'bout how my dad loved his tea, didn't I? Well, Wanda ain't heard this anyways." She turned her head slightly to catch Wanda's eye, who smiled back. Then she closed her eyes and continued. "We used to drink cup after cup and play cribbage. Did I ever tell you, Pocket, about how, on the day I married yer father, my dad and I drank tea and played cards while we were waitin 'til it was time for him to take me down the aisle?" Pocket nodded; of course she had. "Mum would always laugh about my dad and his tea. Always had to have his tea…" her voice drifted, soft with memory. Shirley looked at Wilf, who was looking at Merle. The room was quiet; nobody wanted to interrupt the flow of words. Then Merle laughed, a girlish sound. "She'd always say: that man and his tea! If I was on my deathbed and he was told to come quick he'd say: tell that woman to hang on 'til I'm finished my damn tea!"

In the room, nobody spoke, but listening to Merle's soft laugh, each thinking about the future. Merle took a sip and, noticing the silence, looked around at them all. She set her teacup down and tilted her head up. That amused downturn of her mouth, again.

"And what do you think yer father would say, Pocket?"

"I'd say: tell her to hang on 'til I'm finished her damn kitchen!" Wilf, grinning, spoke before Pocket could.

"Just what I was going to say," Merle smiled, meeting his eyes.

"You know about the kitchen?" Pocket asked.

"'Course I do," she told him. "Mercy, I'm not dead yet."

2 Saturday started badly. Rodney rose, bleary from the long and boozy night of before, with a queasy stomach, certain he couldn't possibly eat breakfast. He'd slept in, but dressed quickly nonetheless, picked up his camera, and headed for the wharf, hoping the fresh air would clear his head and calm his stomach and that, as a bonus, he'd get a photograph. As he skirted around the house, avoiding the kitchen and the smell of cooking bacon, he could see the boats well out in the Sound. Still, perhaps from the end of the wharf he'd be able to get a good enough image for the *Journal*, something to run alongside an image of a local witness or military spokesman.

As he stepped onto the wharf Rodney looked up to see that the circle of boats seemed to have vanished, as if it had never been there, and he stopped abruptly, only to see the fog shift again and the vessels return to view. He quickened his pace, hoping for an unobscured view from the wharf's end before the fog descended altogether. As he hurried along the damp planks he was mentally framing the shot with a picturesque Cape Islander in the right foreground, already composing the cutline, while at the same time watching the drift of surface cloud, teasing him. He began to run.

All at once, Rodney's hard-soled shoes on the wet wood slipped from beneath him. He hit the planks like the slap of a tuna on a boat deck, the whoosh of his breath as it left his body mimicking the trajectory of the camera as it left his hands. Unable to breathe, he watched, sure he was dying, as his camera arched towards the water. He heard the splash before the first wheezy gasp assaulted his flattened lungs.

Later, standing behind the store out of sight of the back windows, Rodney struck a match in the fourth attempt to light one of Lorelei's cigarettes. At twenty-four years old he figured it was time he learned to smoke, but the wind off the water was making things difficult. He was still hung over. And then there was the lost camera. The list of indignities was growing, and he felt disgusted with himself.

Rodney struck the last match, the cigarette clutched damply between his lips, but the harbour wind snatched the flame away. A grunt, a laugh of sorts, and Rodney turned to see a young man of about eighteen leaning against the siding. When their eyes met, the young man pushed himself off and came forward, a lighter in his hand.

"Ya cup yer hands, like this," he explained to Rodney. The cigarette lit, "du Maurier," he remarked. "'S'a girl's brand. That's what Cuff says, anyways."

"Cuff Dodds?" Rodney asked, choking slightly on the smoke. He looked at the red package with the woman on the cover.

The young man inhaled, his own blue and white pack poking manfully out of the breast pocket of his jean jacket. "Yep. S'pose you've been talkin to him."

"Yesterday."

"Ernie Morton." Ernie waved his cigarette in a circle that ended near his chest. "Hard to say how much Cuff saw. Got himself some jagged up over to the Legion before."

"Jagged up?"

"Drunk. I was there, out walkin. Nobody believes what comes outa the mouth of Cuff Dodds. You just ask anyone. He's just hopin to get on the TV. Just wants to be a celebrity. The big man around town. Always been like that."

Rodney thought about Fred's comments from the night before.

"So what did you see?"

"I saw a light come down. Orange-coloured. When I think on it now it was right strange, but my mind was somewheres else at the time. It woulda come into the harbour at an angle, like a Shag landin—" Rodney must have looked blank. "—A Cormorant. Like a duck, ya know? The way they land, real smooth. And then out on the water, later on, this yellow foam—"

"Did you go out?"

"No, but my dad did, an he told me. Tip. Tip Morton. You come see us, he'll tell you. We live just up the way, past Snows."

Rodney didn't know where anything was, and he told Ernie that.

"You need a guide?" Ernie asked. "I'm yer man." Cigarette finished, he ground it under his boot into the cracked asphalt. Rodney did the same.

"What's it like where you live?" Ernie asked. "There lotsa work?"

Rodney was just mustering a reply when Fred came around the side of the store.

"There you are," he boomed. "Shirl's gone over to Snows. Looked for you, but you were hidin out, I guess. You want to head on over, you'd be welcome. Merle Snow hasn't been doin so well, but she's taken a turn for the better, I heard. You want to get some interviews, that's the place to go, an now's the time to do it."

Rodney thought wistfully about the Coast Guard, the RCMP, the interviews he'd hoped to conduct at the wharf. But he'd slept in anyway; it was too late for this morning. He'd try to catch them later, when they came in from their day out on the Sound.

"I'm goin right by there," Ernie said. "I'll take ya. 'S'no trouble."

Scratch shooed everyone out of the house when Merle appeared, quite suddenly, tired. Her lips still smiled, but "her brow looks weary," Shirley agreed. She shot Wanda a look. "Too much excitement," she said. "Tea-leaf reading and whatnot."

There was the sound of the door closing, and Scratch's gentle tone as he suggested Wanda help with something in the kitchen, after which, he said, they'd go to Yarmouth. Merle had a prescription for morphine that had so far not been filled. "In case we need it," he said. "It'll be good to have it handy."

The living room emptied, Pocket and Wilf exchanged a glance, and then Wilf looked at the rose teapot.

"Guess we didn't need another."

"'S'a nice one, though," Pocket said, and Merle opened one eye.

"'S'lovely," she said. "I do believe I got the best friends and the best family."

Wilf cleared his throat.

"Oh, go on with ya both," Merle said, eyes closed again. She flapped a hand vaguely. "Let me sleep, now."

Pocket, leaving the house, saw the reporter wave goodbye to Ernie Morton and then turn up the drive. He was tempted to duck around back before he was seen. He wanted to mull over what just happened, his mother's remarkable change. He needed time. But instead, Pocket took a breath and approached the reporter, who looked up and smiled.

"Pocket Snow?" Rodney reached a hand forward. "Rod Nowland, *Ottawa Journal*. We met yesterday."

"I remember." Pocket dropped the hand he'd shaken briefly—an unfamiliar gesture—and now shuffled his boots, kicking at the clamshell pieces and shore rock in the driveway.

"I was hoping to ask you some questions," Rodney continued, sounding professional to his own ears. "About what you saw. And your dad, too. He went out that night in the boat, didn't he? With your uncle?"

"He did."

Rodney looked at the house, which appeared oddly unapproachable. It looked like a house that held its breath.

"My uncle's gone to Yarmouth," Pocket continued, "to get something for her. That lady who came with you? She went, too. She's stayin with us."

"Wanda is staying with you?" Rodney had assumed she was at the Victoria.

159

Pocket nodded. "She's helpin with Mum. My uncle Scratch said it's a miracle she came, too. She's been lookin after her—personal stuff. Good timin fer sure."

"Are you on your way somewhere?"

Pocket couldn't think of where he was on his way to. Important business? The lie wouldn't form. "Not really."

"Maybe I could buy you a soda," Rodney suggested, wondering if this was a claimable expense.

"I like to walk," Pocket said, looking into the chill of the day. "S'pose I get it from my mum."

Rodney thought of Aunt Bridey's sweater, tossed on the chair in the corner of his room. His jacket felt like tissue paper against the sea wind. "So do I," he said.

They walked together along the shore. Rodney peered at the sky, wishing the sun would break through.

"You lived here all your life?" he asked Pocket.

"Uh huh."

They walked, and Rodney began to relax a little. Pocket's awkwardness was familiar, making it easy for Rodney to rise above his own. He recognized that with Pocket, a slower approach was best. The afternoon stretched, flat, before them, the light even. The high clouds in a mackerel sky removed any trace of shadows, and it seemed as if even their footfalls left no sound nor impression. Except for being cold, Rodney felt he could amble along for hours. It was like walking with himself. He glanced at Pocket, took in the shock of hair under the peak of a ballcap, the long lashes, the soft adolescent down on his chin and upper lip. Pocket kept his eyes fixed on the middle distance as they walked, apparently lost in thought.

"You said your mother's not well?" Rodney ventured.

Pocket scuffed the packed grey sand between beach rocks. "My dad told my uncle she's gettin better," he said. "I heard 'em talkin."

"Is she?"

Pocket didn't say anything at first, but began adjusting the direction they were walking, angling towards the Marram grass above the beach. He couldn't say why he felt the need to keep away from the thing he had found. Rodney let him lead, unconcerned about where they were headed. They walked until they reached a large rock, big enough for two to sit, and Pocket climbed aboard, his long limbs like the legs of grasshoppers. When they had settled, facing the harbour and the boats that sat offshore, "All this talk about the crash?" he said. "It seems to have perked her up some."

"Uh—" Rodney never knew what to say in the face of illness or tragedy. He thought of Daisy, remembered how his friends had avoided him afterwards, as if they might somehow catch his loss. The snatch of whispered words when he'd walk down the hall.

"She has the cancer," Pocket continued. "She was goin to Yarmouth every two weeks for a long time, but she stopped goin."

Rodney's eyes were watering; he wondered if they might be tears. He didn't think so. He didn't *feel* as if he was crying. He cleared his throat to speak, hoping something would occur to him by the time a word was formed, while Pocket wiped at his own eyes with his sleeve and gazed towards a spot further down the beach. Rodney looked but could see nothing but rocks and seaweed.

Rodney felt the interview was slipping from his grasp. He cleared his throat and looked out at the boats, hoping to steer the conversation towards his reason for being in Perry's Harbour. But as he opened his mouth to speak, Pocket filled the salty air with his own words.

"Makes you wonder, don't it?" He held his fingers over the closed lids of his eyes, rubbed them, then put his hands in his jacket and blinked. "If it's better to know yer dyin, so everyone can say goodbye. So you can say what you want to everyone. And then after a while, it's all said, an everyone's just waitin. Waitin and feeling bad, you know, because it's not right to be waitin for someone to die. Yer not supposed to want it to happen."

Rodney opened his mouth again, but no sound came out.

"An ya don't want it, ya really don't, it's just—"

"I—" Rodney began, but Pocket continued, eyes straight ahead.

"Like, maybe it's better to just get hit by a car or something. Sudden, like. No waitin. Yer just here one minute, gone the next."

Rodney coughed.

"Nobody's waitin," Pocket went on, "because everyone's taken by surprise. And they're all sad and that, but they'd be sad anyway, even if they were waitin for it. Knowing doesn't make it better."

Pocket pushed himself up off the rock. Rodney followed, and the two began to walk back the way they had come, both watching their feet on the uneven ground. Under their boots, a steady grind of rock against rock; above, a gull's cry.

"But then I s'pose ya'd spend yer whole life wishing you'd had a chance to say something you never got to," Pocket said. He stopped to pick up a beach rock with a double ring, then set it down again.

"I think," said Rodney, "I think it's just hard no matter how it happens."

"Yeah," agreed Pocket, his eyes on the harbour. "Makes you feel right small, though, don't it?"

Shirley looked up from the magazine she was reading when Pocket and Rodney came into the store. Pocket, she thought, looked a little better than when she'd seen him a short while ago.

"Ya both look chilled to the bone," she said. "You, 'specially," she nodded to Rodney. "Here, I've got the coffee on. And I suppose ya'd like somethin to eat. You too, Pocket. How's yer mum, doin, now she's got some quiet?"

"Haven't been home since," Pocket told her. He nodded at Rodney. "He wants to ask me about the crash. I'll go home after."

"Who's there?"

"Jus' Dad. Uncle Scratch and Wanda are out somewheres."

Shirley grunted. Then she looked at Pocket and her face softened. "Let me make you a sandwich, warm yerself up. I'll pack up some food to take home while yer eatin." She glanced at Rodney, who was hugging himself and looking, to Shirley, decidedly blue. Silly city folks, never dress warm enough. "Well, go on, sit down," she told them. "Talk about spaceships or whatever ya like. 'S'what everyone else is talking about. I'll be along with something shortly."

Rodney felt as if he'd never be warm again but before long they were sipping hot chocolate from a mix that, to Rodney, tasted exquisite. His skin tingled; warm light flooded the room, a sharp contrast to the grey day. He felt for his notebook, but came up short a pen. "Here," said Shirley, handing him the red Bic.

While they waited for their food Pocket told Rodney about the aircraft—if it was an aircraft—about the lights, the angle, the sound.

"What sound?"

"Well, no sound, really. It was right strange. No sound at all, nothin. I mean, until it hit the water. Funny, now I can't even remember, but it must've made right some splash. I suppose the engine maybe cut out, that's why it crashed."

"Has anything come up?"

"Come up?" Pocket thought of the thing in the seaweed.

"Out of the water. Floated to the surface."

"Ya didn't talk to the Coast Guard? Or the RCMP?"

Rodney fumbled. "Um. Not yet."

"Missed the boat, didja?" Shirley called from behind the counter, reminding Rodney that she was listening to every word. She laughed at her own joke. "They'll be comin in around five. You go on down to the wharf, you'll catch 'em then. If they'll talk to you, that is."

"What do you mean?" Rodney looked up from the notebook.

"They're not talkin to any of *us*. Fred was down there this morning tryin to find out somethin. Stanley's been down, and Tip. They're hushed up tighter'n a clam."

Rodney took that for information. If they weren't talking to the locals, would they talk to the press?

"CBC crew should be here any time, now. Heard they booked all the rooms at the Victoria. Bessie Parson's gotta be havin a field day."

"Who?"

"Gal runs the Victoria."

Rodney wrote her name down as a possible source. He looked up, glancing between Shirley, as she approached with sandwiches, and Pocket, whose eyes were fixed on Shirley. "Nothing came up then, that anybody knows of?" Rodney asked again. "Nothing washed ashore?"

"Nope," said Shirley, setting down the plates. "You want pickle with that?"

Pocket nodded. He didn't look at Rodney, but bit into his sandwich enthusiastically, as if he hadn't eaten for days.

Shirley watched him for a moment. "Don't eat that too quick," she told him. "Slow down, give me a minute to pack you up a box."

After Pocket had left, Shirley joined Rodney at the table. With a full stomach, a warm fuzziness had crept over him, an odd belonging. The *Ottawa Journal* seemed a very long way away. He wanted to ask Shirley what she'd heard about the crash, and more importantly, who she thought he should talk to—she seemed to be the one person who knew everything—but Shirley spoke first.

"I heard you and Fred talking in the kitchen. Stayed up late dintcha?"

"I'm sorry if we kept you awake."

"Oh, nothin keeps me awake. I was reading, could hear yer voices, that's all. It was nice to hear a coupla men talkin in my kitchen. I 'magined it'd be like that if our boy were to come back and visit."

"Where's your son now?" Rodney asked, imagining him away, working.

When Shirley spoke, her answer seemed, to Rodney, unrelated to the question.

"You know, Merle and I both grew up in South Head. Always been like sisters." She leaned back in her chair. "She was always one for rescuin animals, runt piglets, orphaned bunnies, you name it. A mother through and through, and when Pocket came along you never saw nobody happier. Saddest thing there never was no more, but one's good enough, and yet she never once spoiled 'im. But you could watch her eyes follow 'im around a room jus' the same. She gave up collectin animals about the time he was born, cometa think on it. Guess she figured she had enough. There never was a boy more loved than Pocket, nor worried over."

"He's lucky, then," said Rodney. "I mean, I don't mean—"

"Oh, I know you didn't mean he's lucky to be losin his mother," Shirley said. "It's hard on him, and hard on

Wilf, too. They was a match, those two. Before Pocket was born Merle used to go out with Wilf on the boat. Oh, but she loved the water. They'd go out for days sometimes longlinin. Sometimes she'd just row out into the middle of the Sound and just drift there a bit. Wilf would call it her thinkin time. Y'know how they met?"

Rodney shook his head.

"It was durin the Halifax riots," Shirley began. "The war was over, and thousands of servicemen on leave. And what did the City of Halifax do? Gave everyone a holiday. So the shops all closed, the theatres. You couldn't get a cup of coffee, and you sure couldn't get a beer. You get that many sailors and soldiers, everyone wantin to have a party and there was nothin for 'em 'cept a little parade, and then what were they gonna do? By the second day they were fed up and somebody musta thrown a rock in a liquor store window and that was the beginning. They even looted the brewery. Stanley, Cuff's dad, was there, heard he stayed blind drunk for a week.

"Wilf was there, too. Wilf never served, had some heart thing, though he's still tickin all these years later. He'd gone up to Halifax to meet Scratch, who was comin in on his boat for a leave. Wilf didn't know the war in Europe was over when he started out—nobody did. And Merle was up there, too, gone up to visit an aunt and get a bit of the city. It'd been a long war."

Shirley paused, clearly in the time, and Rodney waited.

"We did good here, there was always fish and we had some good dances I'll tell ya, but there were lotsa things we couldn't get and all that worry over the men who's gone, and sadness over the ones didn't come back."

The door swung open with a squeak and a rattle and a girl of about seven came in, face ruddy. Shirley got up and went around back of the till and leaned on the counter, grinning.

"What have we here?"

"I come for some Lucky Elephant popcorn," the girl replied, her small voice serious.

"And whose boy em ya?"

"I'm not a boy! It's me—Lucy."

"Lucy! Well I musta not recognized ya. And what didja say ya wanted? An elephant?"

Lucy pointed to the boxes behind the counter.

"Whatcha hopin for, then?" Shirley asked, reaching for the box. *Prize Inside!* read the words in the corner.

"Marnie got a ring last time," Lucy said as she released a small collection of palm-warmed nickels onto the counter. "With a real ruby."

"Really," said Shirley, raising her eyebrows. "Well then I hope you do, too. Everyone should get their wish once in a while, dontcha think?"

Lucy nodded and left, the thud of the door behind her a soft punctuation.

"She's a good one, that one," Shirley said into the air as she clattered about behind the counter. "Gonna be a heartbreaker when she grows up. Meanwhile, I better order some more of that popcorn. If Marnie Hicks got a ring, s'gonna be a lot of girls in here hopin." She turned and smiled. "Best part about havin a store. Ya see 'em grow up, it's almost like havin yer own."

When Shirley had returned to the table, "Anyways, where was I?" she said. "Oh, right. Story is, the end of the day there weren't a single window downtown not smashed to bits," she said. "'Course, I wasn't there, just heard about it. But Merle was."

"She was there in the riot?"

"Yep. Merle was in Halifax visitin family, like I said. Her aunt and uncle told her to stay put, I guess, but she snuck out to join the fun. Started out as a parade and a bit of a party, you recall. Trams weren't supposed to be runnin but I guess nobody told the tram drivers that because they were still runnin from the North end and by the time Merle got off she was right in the thick of it.

"Poor Merle was just a young thing from South Head, she'd never been in a crowd at all, never mind a crowd like that. Anyway, there was this one drunk sailor who just picked her up and threw her over his shoulder. I dunno, maybe he was just goin on guff, harmless, y'know? But she was some scared, screamin and cryin and I guess nobody heard her with all the noise or they just thought she was part a the fun, just foolin around. An then there was Wilf, grabbed her 'round the waist and gave the sailor a shove sent him reelin, about three blocks—not hard, he was just that drunk, Wilf said—and Merle out of her mind, cryin and hittin Wilf, hysterical. She told me Wilf just held her there until she gave up and then made her look at him, sayin: Merlaine Lawrence, yer a long way from South Head, aintcha?

"He got her outta there somehow and he walked her back to her aunt's house an that was the start of things. It wasn't until much later Wilf remembered Scratch—

he'd forgotten all about him. Scratch was some mad, too, lookin for Wilf for hours, but he forgave him in the end, seein as it was a buddin romance and all. Scratch never did have a girl of his own far as I know."

"Where were you then?"

"Oh, I was here. Some girls joined the Wrens, but some stayed home to help look after the young ones, especially if the men in the family were joined up."

"You didn't join the Wrens?"

"No, I was married by then, and then Fred went and joined up in September '44. Looked like conscription was comin and he didn't want to be *told* to go, an you know he'd've gone before except he was the only man left in his own house with his father gone, pneumonia it was. By the time Fred did sign up his sisters had married…. But that's not what you asked, was it?"

"Um—" Rodney couldn't remember what he'd asked.

"I was pregnant, almost nine months along when VE day came. Fred due back any time. As it happened he was home a week after."

"In time for the baby."

"Not quite. Baby came early. Stillborn," she said, matter-of-factly. Rodney's face must have betrayed the sympathy he felt. He realized that, in a remarkably short time, he'd grown to like Shirley a great deal. "Oh, it's been years," she said, seeing his look. "He'd have been a little older than Pocket now. My soul, he'd be twenty-two, come to think on it. Where do the years go?" She shook her head. "It's funny: some have eight, ten, twelve kids, and some of us—Merle and me—are lucky to have even one. I was lucky enough to almost have one, I guess. In the old days, people would have a dozen kids just so's they could see six of 'em grow up. Things have changed, that's for sure.

"But everythin's a blessin if you look at it right. Your heart goes through a sadness, it's stronger for it. There's more to give, and that's the blessin."

Shirley got up and cleared away Rodney's cup and plate. As the afternoon light waned, the store felt, to Rodney, like an island in a storm. He felt he could sit there listening to Shirley for days. When she was seated back at the table, she continued.

"What about you? You got a sweetheart?"

Rodney thought of Lorelei. The scene before he left Ottawa, once cast in a rosy glow and limned with hope, now seemed flat, colourless. "No," he said.

"Well don't worry, dear, you will. Nice boy like you."

As he walked home, Shirley's box tucked under his arm, Pocket's eyes scanned the harbour. He felt his own presence acutely: the tension of his skin around his body, the person he was, looking out through his eyes. What was this thing inside him that made him think, see, hear, feel? He'd never thought about such a thing before, merely taken it for granted. It seemed to him his body had always been something he wore like a shirt, just there, not requiring thought. He'd never considered what was inside the shirt: not just stomach and lungs and heart beating away, but that other thing.

What happens to the thing that is you when your heart stops beating? He imagined flight, the beating of wings. Himself, spiralling upwards towards the sun, and then, whatever lay beyond. He laid a hand upon his heart.

He saw, with sudden clarity, concentric circles spreading before him. There was himself, the beating of his heart beneath his palm. His home, the orange house, and inside, the beating hearts of his family. He could hear them, the lub-lub of them, and he shook his head, but was unable to stop the next thought: the people of Perry's, Fred and Shirley, Cuff, Ernie, the kids in his class, the guys at the docks, all the hearts beating inside workshirts and overalls, and the sound merged in a great percussive beat and he had to resist the urge to put his hands over his ears.

Looking again towards the Sound, he imagined the men in the vessels, their own hearts beating. They lived in distant places, and he wondered what that would be like. In Yarmouth, in Halifax, Toronto, New York, beating hearts. If you could put them all together, the sound they would make. He could barely fathom such numbers, such sound.

He thought of the thing on the beach, of whatever was below the water. Where did they come from? Could Wanda be right? What life pulsed out there, beyond his own imagination?

It was too much, and he shut the thought away. He opened Shirley's box and removed a sandwich wrapped in wax paper and bit into it. Egg salad.

Sandwich in hand, box beneath his arm, he began walking towards his house, where his mother's heart beat still.

3 Rodney walked back along the length of the wharf, frustrated. The wind blew his hair into his eyes while overhead a tern circled and dived at him.

"Classified," the RCMP officer had told him bluntly when the boat had pulled in and been tied up. The man was all business, barely looking at Rodney who stood, pad and pen in hand. "No comment."

The Coast Guard had been somewhat friendlier. "Sorry, buddy. We've been asked not to speak to anybody. Been getting calls from all over. Fellow from the *Halifax Herald*'s on his way, but he won't get anything either. We have orders not to comment."

"From who?" Rodney had asked, but the Coast Guard officer had shaken his head.

A tall cameraman from the CBC had been more enlightening.

"Department of National Defence. We did find someone there who confirmed there were no missing aircraft, but then wouldn't go on record." He began coiling cables. "So we've got footage of the boats, of the divers going over, that's about it. That, and a voiceover, basically saying *something's* happening." The cameraman spent a few moments tucking things into compartments, then straightened up. "The Canadian audience will be interested in the military presence."

Rodney wrote this down, but the cameraman shook his head.

"We're hoping someone in Ottawa will eventually make some sort of statement once the piece runs." The cameraman paused, hoisting his equipment onto his shoulder. "I'll give you this, though," he said. "There are two submarines off the coast. One may be Russian. But the other is definitely U.S. Navy."

Earlier, Rodney had called the Victoria Hotel.

"You can come 'round if ya like," Bessie Parsons had told him. "But nobody's sayin anythin to anyone far as I can tell. Shut up tight as a clam. I been expectin a fella from the *Herald*, but he hasn't shown up. Call back later, maybe you two can trade notes or somethin."

He should have a story in by Monday if he wanted any points at all with his boss. Sooner would be better; he didn't want to be scooped by the Halifax paper. His return ticket was for Tuesday morning. He supposed he could still cobble something together from eyewitness reports—Cuff's, anyway. But it sounded like locals didn't put a lot of faith in Cuff's words, generally. He needed something concrete.

When he returned to Crosbey's for a cup of coffee to warm up, Shirley was unpacking boxes of canned goods, ticking the order off against a list. She held up a can of clam chowder. "Ordered beef barley," she said, "an' this is what I get."

"Like coals to Newcastle," Rodney offered, but Shirley was busy circling the offending items on the invoice. When she had finished, she set aside the paper.

"Saw you comin up from the wharf," she told him. "Thought you looked right chilled. Down in the dumps, too. Nobody talkin, right?" She turned to the coffeepot.

"'Magin you could clean the inside of an oven with this," she said, but poured him a cup anyway.

Rodney shook his head. "Thanks," he said, curling his hands around the cup, warming them. His eyes scanned the wall behind the cash register. Clothespinned to strings strung behind the counter were various packages: potato chips and peanuts, rubber gloves, playing cards and car deodorizers in the shape of pine trees. "Say, Shirley," he asked, "do you sell postcards?"

After a bit of rummaging, Shirley pulled a box from beneath the counter. "I keep 'em out durin the summer, but there's no point in having 'em clutter up the place the rest of the time."

Rodney flipped through the cards, looking for Perry's Harbour. The images of churches, lighthouses, oxen and a ferryboat didn't look particularly local, and he said so.

"Well, that's Yarmouth," Shirley pointed to the ferry. "That's about the closest, I guess. And the Kettle Island lighthouse is a little smaller than this one at Peggy's Cove, but one lighthouse is the same as the next, pretty much. Looks the same, anyways, if you cut out the tourists. And we got oxen, here. Ever been to an ox pull?"

Rodney shook his head.

"Sandy Hudson's win every year, pretty much. Logs with 'em. My father always kept oxen for ploughing and hauling, and sometimes for show—" Shirley pointed to the two big animals on the postcard, their foreheads sporting fancy leather triangles with brass embellishments, "—two of them: we called one This and one That, and when I was small I thought that was the name for oxen in general: thisanthat. I once asked my mother if daddy was out workin with our thisanthat. Made my mum laugh for 'bout five minutes. Anyways, beautiful creatures they were, all red and white, just about glowed on a sunny day, but stubborn? I can still hear my dad calling 'gee-over'—"

"I'll take this one." Rodney didn't know what postcard Lorelei would like, but somehow the oxen, with their massive shoulders, dangerous-looking horns, and inscrutable eyes seemed like the best choice. He could see from the photograph that the horns were capped with brass knobs. He wished all dangerous things could be so easily mitigated.

He sat at the table he'd begun to think of as his own and sipped his coffee. His pen was in his breast pocket, where he'd placed it in hopes of interviews at the wharf—the one time he actually had his tools of the trade readily at hand. Now, pen poised above the postcard, Rodney reflected that having the tools in hand didn't help when the words wouldn't come. His evening with Lorelei seemed impossibly far away. Not only was he not sure what it meant, he was becoming increasingly unsure it had happened at all. He tapped the pen on the table's surface, turned it over, tapped again. After a while Shirley slipped a cinnamon roll onto a plate and brought it over.

"Yer too skinny," she told him, and he looked at her gratefully. She peered at the postcard. "Who you writin to?"

Rodney, who hadn't written a word, not even *Dear Lorelei*, blushed.

"Ah," said Shirley, smiling.

"Actually, um. Actually, I wonder if I could use the phone. It's a long distance call. I'll pay you, of course."

"Well it's against company policy," Shirley smiled, "but since you're such a good tenant…"

It felt odd to be on Shirley's side of the counter. Rodney could smell the pine scent of the car deodorizers through the cellophane. He hunched over the receiver, turning his back to the room. Shirley wandered over to the far side of the store and began straightening already-straight shelves, one ear cocked. The operator connected his call after she'd looked up Lorelei's home number, this being Saturday. To his surprise, her roommate told him Lorelei was working overtime.

"Lorelei?" Rodney stuttered into the mouthpiece when he reached her at the newspaper. "What's going on?"

"Roddie-boy! Forgot all about you down there with the codfish. How's it going?"

"It's, uh. It's going well."

"Really? Because Copeland's grumbling about not having gotten anything yet."

"I only got here Friday morning." Rodney gripped the receiver more tightly.

"Well, you should have filed something Friday evening," Lorelei scolded.

"What are you doing in the office?"

"Special assignment. Most of us are working overtime. Scandal brewing on the Hill. It could be big. Too bad you're missing it all."

Rodney could think of nothing to say.

"Don't worry." Lorelei's voice took on a consoling

tone, "I've got it covered. Meanwhile, get *something* in. That's my advice. Maybe you could use the crop circle angle."

"*Crop* circles?"

"That's what I said. Don't you read your own newspaper? Last month, those things that farmer in Alberta found in his field."

"But that's five thousand miles away!"

"No, listen. First there were a bunch of lights that kept showing up at night and nobody could figure out what they were. Then one night his cows didn't come back from the pasture, so he went out to check on them. And found these four huge circles pressed into the grass."

"Helicopter?"

"No, they sent experts out. It wasn't made by a helicopter, or anything else they could identify. This UFO thing could be like that. Maybe it's all part of a big alien invasion. There's your lead. You won't get the DND to go on record there, either, but the farmer had lots to say."

"Wait. I thought you said my angle was that it was the Russians." There was static on the line. "Was Copeland really grumbling? Because—"

"Well, not since the scandal story broke. That's all anyone's talking about right now. I don't think—"

More static.

"Bad connection, Rodney. It's crazy here anyway. I gotta go."

Rodney listened to the dial tone for a moment, then set the receiver back on the wall phone before removing it again to wipe off the sweat with his sleeve. His eyes

met Shirley's across the room where she stood, a box of
Red River cereal in her hand.

"Everything okay?" she asked.

4 Pocket, sitting with his mother as the day's light faded, noted that the days were becoming shorter with the approaching winter. He felt as if everything was that way, time truncated so that its passage came as a surprise, no matter how commonplace its markers. As a small child waiting for Christmas, or even now, waiting for summer vacation to start, how long those days were, how slow the hours crawled. Here, too, as he sat with his mother, time crawled, and yet darkness could still take him by surprise.

They'd had an early supper, Merle surprising everybody by requesting seconds. Now, she slept. Pocket considered turning on a light but felt the dusk gather around him in a way that was almost comforting.

A memory surfaced, both surprising and embarrassing him. As a small boy, he had woken in the night and come into his parents' room only to find his mother and father locked in a sweaty embrace. The light always left on in the bathroom down the hall offered a dim illumination and in that, his mother's face in the dark as she looked at him across the bedclothes while he stood, frozen, in the doorway. At the time he was confused by both the disturbing intimacy of their nakedness and the embarrassed reproach in her look, even as he did not understand the scene before him. What he'd felt was betrayed: his mother was in a place he wasn't allowed to go. A personal place that excluded him. He must have pushed the memory away, as he did again, now, confused by the emotions that surfaced. There was something of that in this: a place he shouldn't be, and in any case could not follow her into.

Pocket heard the back door open, and from the kitchen, his father's voice.

"Scratch, help me a minute, wouldja?"

A few moments later there was a series of bumps and scrapes at the back of the house. Pocket put his head inside the kitchen.

"First one. Got just enough wood fer the others. Whatcha think?" Wilf asked as he and Scratch stood a two-door cupboard on the floor. Pocket could smell sawdust.

"Where'dja get the wood? It's new wood, innit?"

"Bone-box."

"Nice of 'im," Scratch commented. "S'pose he keeps a stockpile."

"Who's Bone-box?" Wanda, at the kitchen sink, asked over her shoulder.

"Fella makes coffins," Pocket told her. Then to his father, he asked: "How'd he know you needed wood?"

"Shirley, prob'ly. I'll replace it by an by."

Scratch opened and closed the hinged doors. They had been hastily painted swimming-pool turquoise, a colour Pocket recognized from Tip Morton's storage shed. He could see places where his father's paintbrush had missed a drip. Scratch held the cupboard against the bare wall, muscles flexing in his sinewy arms. "We better slap a coat of paint on the wall first."

"Right. Got some yellow in the shed. Think there's enough."

"They'll look right smart, Wilf," said Scratch, nodding.

"Well, I want to get it up quick for Merle, get everything squared away before she comes in and sees this mess. Won't she be pleased? She's been wantin new cupboards forever."

Pocket, standing in the doorway between kitchen and living room, looked over to his mother's form in the bed. She hadn't left her bed since Tuesday. Wanda had been helping with Merl's personal care these past two days, all the while keeping up a brassy chatter that seemed to animate his mother when she was awake.

After a moment, "we'll bring her in to see them when it's all done, then," said Wanda.

"Right," agreed Scratch. "Push her bed inta the kitchen if we hafta, set her up with a nice cuppa so she can admire them proper."

Wilf beamed. "Yep. That we will, Ole Son. Now, gimme a hand you two, let's get this one up temporary, just to see how she looks. Wanda can sit with Merle. Pocket, get the whisky. Might need a little lubrication to get this done."

Four mugs of whisky stood on the cluttered kitchen table, beside them the dead soldier that was close to full at the start of things. Wilf remarked that Wanda could drink like a man, and Scratch had looked at her approvingly and nodded. Wanda had borrowed one of Scratch's work shirts, rolled up the sleeves, and was covering more wallspace with yellow paint than any of them. "Didn't know it was a contest," Pocket protested when Wanda bumped him with her shoulder, sending him into Scratch, who pushed back. They painted right over the holes and gouges, Wilf rationalizing that "the cupboards'll cover most of it up anyways."

"It's a happy colour," Scratch commented when the wall was finished. "I think Merle's gonna like it."

"Yellow means renewal. It means hope," Wanda said. "For the Indians it symbolizes the east, where the sun rises. A new day."

"Well, it's pretty, anyway," Pocket offered.

There was yellow paint under Pocket's fingernails and in his hair. "You always been a messy one, ain'tcha." Scratch laughed. "I'd say ya got more'n the wall."

Pocket, who was feeling the whisky, took his brush and ran it down the front of his uncle's paint-spattered shirt, a yellow skunk-stripe. "Hey!" he yelled, then turned as Wilf painted the other side, teeth glinting white through a face streaked with paint.

"Don't lie down, Scratch," he said. "They'll think yer the centre line on the highway."

"An' yer the passin lane," Scratch countered, but Wilf ducked the brush, laughing.

All at once Pocket leaned against the doorframe. The hand that held the brush fell to his side.

"Ain't this enough?" he said. He looked towards the living room.

"What, Son?"

"I just think—" Pocket's words faltered.

"Boy looks tuckered out," Scratch said. He put the brush down. "I 'magin we all are."

Wilf sat down. The hilarity of a moment before had

dissipated as though it had never existed. He looked at Wanda, who had gone to check on Merle and now stood at the kitchen door. "How is she?" His voice sounded small.

"Sleeping. Peaceful, which is a miracle considering the racket we've been making."

Scratch turned to Wilf. "You haven't really slept in days, have ya?"

Wilf lowered his eyes. "I can't. I'm afraid she'll wake up an' need me, an' I'll just sleep on through."

Pocket couldn't bear to see this side of his father, the beaten, sad side. He preferred the dad that built wonky cupboards and goofed around with a paintbrush.

"I'll sleep on the couch tonight," Scratch said. "No arguin. You stay upstairs, get a good night's sleep."

Later, Scratch stood with a blanket and pillow in hand, ready to bed down on the couch. He watched as Wilf kissed Merle's forehead.

"You'll call if she needs—"

Wanda, on the stairs, cut in. "Scratch will call me, won't you, Scratch. I'll help if the need arises."

"Dunno if I'll be able to sleep upstairs." Wilf, so animated earlier in the kitchen, looked diminished to Pocket from where he had paused at the foot of the stairs. "I mean, s'good a you to offer, Scratch, but I just as soon stay down here."

"Wilf, ya need one good night's rest."

"You do your best to try," Wanda agreed, and to Pocket's surprise, she kissed his father on the cheek.

As Pocket placed his foot on the bottom stair, Wanda stopped him.

"Everything becomes clear in time," she said. "What you're not sure of now will fall into place, and you'll know what to do. You just have to trust," she told him.

He had no idea what she meant.

Pocket slept, then woke after a while for no reason he could immediately discern. He could hear his father's deep breathing in the room next door, the heavy sighs of sleep. It was comforting to have him there: the room had been empty at night for quite a while, his father sleeping on the couch downstairs. He strained to hear stirring from his mother's sewing room, where Wanda was sleeping, but heard none. Instead, he heard quiet voices from below. As he crept to the top of the stairs he heard Scratch's voice, soft as flour.

"Sleepin the sleep of the dead he was, when I looked in. Good thing, too. He needs it."

From his perch, Pocket could see a slice of living-room light and the figures of Uncle Scratch and Wanda on either side of his mother's bed. Scratch was dressed in the clothes he had worn all day and was clearly planning to sleep in. Wanda wore a nightgown, and, over it, a large woolly sweater Pocket recognized as his mother's. His uncle must have found it for her, and it made Pocket uneasy, and yet in the next thought was his mother's voice offering, as she had to guests a hundred times, a sweater or a pair of slippers to keep the chill off, and the thought comforted him.

Only the corner lamp was turned on, and so the light was soft, the scene like an illustration in a story-book, edges framed by the doorway. Pocket felt like a small boy, sitting on the stairs in his pyjamas as he was, his long legs tucked up, arms around his knees. He shivered, but didn't want to go back to his room for something warmer.

"Well, I sure couldn't sleep," Wanda told him. "I figured I might as well keep you company, seeing as you don't seem to be sleeping either."

Scratch shook his head. "Don't think she'll be with us much longer," he said, then: "Do ya think I should be talking out loud with her right here?"

"Well, I don't think you're saying anything she doesn't already know. But yes, I think she can hear, in some way." Pocket saw Wanda's hand reach out and brush his mother's cheek in a gesture so tender, he felt awkward: Wanda wasn't family, after all. But then, what tender gestures had his own awkward hands performed? His mother didn't move, but he saw her chest rise in a deep breath, then fall.

"She may wake up again," Scratch mused, "when the morphine wears off. You were right, y'know. I think she was sufferin some but didn't want to say. Good to let her sleep easy for a bit."

"She didn't protest when Wilf suggested it, did she?"

"Nope. She did not. S'pose that tells ya something."

Five minutes passed. The room seemed to breathe quietly, its occupants calm as a morning tide. Pocket thought about the harbour, the Coast Guard cutter and the RCMP, the presence of the Navy, while below— what? How his mother would love the gossip and buzz, the speculation of it all. Given half a chance she'd be sneaking out in the dory to get a closer look. He leaned against the wall, absorbing the quiet, feeling himself slide into sleep.

"Merle'd love this whole UFO thing," Scratch said, as if voicing Pocket's thoughts of a moment before. "She loves a good mystery, that's fer sure. She gets her hands on a Agatha Christie, sometimes Wilf and Pocket haveta fend for themselves in the kitchen 'til she finds out who-dunit," he chuckled.

"It's no mystery," Wanda said firmly. "They're visitors from another planet. And I will make contact. Tonight—"

"Tonight what?"

"Nothing. It's closer, that's all. I will make contact," she repeated.

"And say what?"

"Tell them they are welcome. Put them in touch with people who will foster exchanges of ideas, of knowledge. They have great gifts to share with us. You don't think the pyramids happened by themselves, do you?"

"Can't say as I ever thought about it."

Merle stirred, and Scratch changed the subject. "She was right talkative today when you was givin the tea-leaf readin. That was some interestin, by the way. How'd ya come to be doin such a thing?"

Wanda angled her chair so she could put her feet on the petit-point stool she'd pulled close. She patted Merle's hand, then left her own there, resting gently.

"My mother was superstitious," she began.

"Huh. Mine, too," Scratch snorted. "If the fog rolled in and stayed for too long—it's a cold, damp, fog that sometimes settles in like it's fixin to never leave—she'd get us kids to catch one of the cats. Tell us to put that cat under a big ol' tub at the northwest corner of the house, just at sundown. That's so's the wind would shift and come from that corner, blow the fog right back out. Always worked, too. But the cat was some mad when we let it out in the morning."

Pocket heard Wanda's laugh, a tinkling sound like the sound of the bangles on her wrist, and alongside of that, Scratch's deeper chuckle. He was clearly enjoying the audience.

"But you were sayin—"

"We had a few superstitions like that, too, although our cat was safer than yours," Wanda said. "Don't buy your man a pair of shoes or he'll walk out of your life forever, for example. I'm sure she never did buy my father shoes, but he left just the same." Wanda's voice was serious, now. "I remember when my mother broke a mirror once, in the upstairs hallway just under the attic stairs. She was bringing it up there to store it, I think. And I seem to remember—but I could be remembering two different events—it was in the mirror she'd seen the ghost of her own mother, one time when the power was out and she walked by with a candle. You should *never* look into a mirror by candlelight unless you want to see a soul from the spirit world. Anyway, she knocked it, I guess, and it shattered, and the pieces fell together at the bottom of the attic stairs. I wasn't allowed to touch the pieces for seven years, just leave them exactly where they lay, so as not to trigger the seven years' bad luck."

The low lamplight was almost like candlelight, and Pocket thought of the oval mirror on the wall above his mother's writing desk. He was glad he couldn't see it from where he sat on the top step.

"Ya didn't touch the pieces for seven years?"

"Wasn't allowed to go near the stairs at all. And as far as I know, nothing went into, or came out of, that attic. That happened when I was about six, I guess. So it must have been when I was twelve that my father left—just moved out one weekend when my mother and I had gone to visit my aunt Ruby—and I never told my mother, but I always thought I was the cause. Because the week before I'd gone up into the attic when they were fighting about something, so as to get as far away as possible. I thought I could make a place for myself up there, someplace just mine. I carefully stepped around the glass, pulled down the trap door, and up I went. And I loved it. I made a hiding place behind some old dresses hanging there. Behind them was an attic window in the shape of a half-moon, and through the dusty glass I felt like I could see for miles. I made myself a little nest there, and I guess I fell asleep. When I woke up the light was fading and I couldn't hear my parents' voices, and I was afraid they'd left me alone, or might even be searching for me, so I jumped up and ran down the stairs—and straight into the broken mirror, scattering the pieces across the hallway floor.

"I felt this pall of dread descend—it really was like that—and I did my best to rearrange the shards as they had been. But it was too late."

"Do you really believe that?"

"There are things in the world we can't explain."

"Well, sure. Every time someone whistles on a boat, for example, a squall comes up. Every time."

Pocket held his breath, waiting for more. He knew there was something about his uncle and a boat, something that happened, but he had not been able to discover more. But after a beat, "lots of things like that," Scratch continued. "Red sky at night, sailor's delight, red sky in th'mornin…'course, that's just basic weather sense. If you say a toast to a new boat the first time out and raise a glass, you always throw some over the side for luck. Keeps y'out of Davy Jones' locker, and there's another one for ya. We got more ghost stories 'round here than you could tell in yer whole life. One a my earliest memories was my mum tellin us one, and I still remember how she described how the ghost sounded: like somethin soft knockin on nothin." He chuckled. "Lost some sleep tryin to listen for that one, I'll tell ya."

Merle stirred, and they both looked at her, but she slept on.

"And then there's those things ya see before somethin bad happens," Scratch continued. "Forerunners."

"Forerunners? Like omens? Harbingers?"

"Yep. 'Cept these things walk around. Ya can see 'em. It's not like walkin under a ladder or seein a black cat, or the shiver ya get when ya say someone walked over yer grave. Saw one once when I was out duckin in the fall, I musta been seventeen or so. Dark thing ran right through the brush ahead a me, too big for a bear, wrong shape for a deer or moose."

"Bigfoot?"

"Heard a them things. Jeez, I dunno, but it gave me

the creeps. But right after that I heard a shot and ran like hell. My huntin buddy Pinch had accidentally shot hisself in the foot."

Wanda was laughing. "Pinch and Scratch?"

"Long story. We got a lot a nicknames, here. Pinch was always a scrapper, guess that's why he got the name. Now he's a lawyer over in Yarmouth. His real name is Dan. Got hisself a new nickname, now." Scratch grinned. "They call 'im Suitcase Dan."

"Okay. I'll bite. Why do they call him Suitcase Dan?"

There was a pregnant pause. Pocket leaned forward. He knew the answer, but he wanted to hear Scratch say it anyway, and to hear Wanda's laugh when he did.

"If he's defendin you in court, you better have yer suitcase packed, 'cause yer goin to jail."

"Go *on*."

Pocket leaned back against the wall, smiling to himself at Wanda's laughter. He wasn't as cold as he had been at first, perhaps because his body had adjusted to the temperature, or perhaps from the warmth of the conversation below. He heard the foghorn blow out on Kettle Island, a long, mournful two-note with a minor fall at the end.

"I saw a harbinger once, too," said Wanda quietly. "I was coming in the back door of the house—I would have been sixteen by then—coming home from school, I think. As I came in the kitchen I saw something dark duck around the corner and into the pantry. It sent a shiver right up my spine, but I went and peered into the pantry and flicked on the light, sure someone was hiding there, my heart in my throat the whole time." Pocket heard Wanda's intake of breath, imagined her hand on her breast. "Nothing, just cans of soup. Then I heard a knock on the door."

There was a clatter, then, the sound of something hitting the floor, followed by Scratch's apologetic laugh. "Sorry, just the empty bedpan. Knocked it with my elbow."

"There was a man at the door asking for my mother. Said he was an old friend of her brother's, come to look her up. Her brother, my uncle, died in the war. I never met him."

"Was he an old friend of yer uncle?"

"He might have been. But he looked like the devil to me."

"And yer Mum?"

"Well, within six weeks he'd moved in. He had a very persuasive way about him. He could be charming, and I expect my mother was lonely. Do you know, I can't even say his name. Can't now. Couldn't then. I felt as if something horrible would befall me if I said it.

"At first he laughed at my mother's superstitions, but then they started to make him angry. Like if we ate boiled eggs, we'd make a hole in the bottom so the witches couldn't use the eggshell to sail across the sea. We *always* did that. But it made him furious: he threw the eggshells across the room, and my mother had to clean up the mess.

"It seemed like the angrier he got, the less able she was to stop herself from doing the things she felt she needed to do to avoid bad luck. For instance, if she'd leave the house and have to go back for something she'd forgot, it was important to sit on a chair before going back out the door, or bad luck would befall the house. Or if she saw a penny, she *had* to pick it up. Once, he stepped on her hand in the street to stop her. Broke a finger."

"No call for that. Seems like a harmless sort of habit."

"Not harmless for my mother. By this time, my own psychic abilities were developing rapidly. I could see the future, and it didn't look good. I always thought that my mother's superstitions meant she also saw things coming. That they were her way of dealing with psychic abilities she never explored. But I never got to find out."

Wanda's voice grew quiet. On the top stair, Pocket leaned forward to catch her words. He closed his eyes so as to hear them better.

"There was always a Bible on the hall table, set there to keep the devil out. Not that it kept *him* out. He came in one day with a gun catalogue and dumped it right on top. I was just coming into the hallway and without even thinking reached to grab it, to move it. It's terrible luck to place something on top of a Bible.

"He grabbed my wrist and held it, hard, then wrenched it 'til it hurt. 'We'll have none of that witchery,' he hissed at me. I fled to my room and he—"

Pocket almost didn't hear the last word.

"—followed."

They were quiet for several moments.

"Bad luck?" Scratch asked.

"I took off the next day," she said. "I left a note for my mother where I thought only she would find it—in the Bible—and hitchhiked to the next town where I knew I could get a job at a restaurant the aunt of a friend owned. I'd left my mother the phone number, but she never called. After a couple of months I summoned up my courage to call the house, but the line was disconnected. When I called a neighbour, I was told they had moved."

"That's a sad story, that is."

"Never had much use for men after that," Wanda said quietly. "But I did learn to trust my intuition. If I had a strong feeling about something, I paid attention after that. It was a while before I learned that my talent was more than simply intuition." Pocket heard the shift of a chair, then Wanda's voice again. "Anyway, that's how I got started in divination. Trying to find my mother, at first, and then later, other things. Reading tea leaves is just one of the things I do. I can see the future, I can find lost things, but I never found my mother. She'd be old, now, of course. If she's still alive. It's an awful thing, to lose someone. More than that, not to know what happened to them."

Very quietly, Pocket moved down two stairs so that, if he jackknifed his torso, he could more clearly see the living room scene. Scratch had reached his hand across Merle's bed and taken Wanda's in his.

"I know what you mean. Lost my brother, Yabut, when he was about the same age you were then," Scratch said.

Wanda pulled her hand away and leaned back. She shook her head. "Yabut?"

"You want me to tell you why he was called Yabut?"

"Well, you're going to anyway."

Scratch chuckled. "He was a contrary fella, my baby brother. You'd tell him somethin, anythin, like ain't the sky blue or that's a nice red shirt ya got on, didn't matter

what ya'd say, and he'd say 'yeah, but—' and then go off
about why it wasn't so blue or so red. Drove us some
crazy."

"What happened to him?"

Pocket moved down another step.

"We was out lobster fishin. First time out without our
Dad. He'd broke his ankle the week before trippin down
the step, drunk as a skunk, so he was laid up. Wilf was
somewhere else, can't recall where. So it was just us, and
we were right proud to be out on our own. But it was
wicked fog, so thick ya couldn't see past the bow. And
still dark. We'd left long 'fore dawn to haul in the traps,
then somehow got confused between the light buoy and
the bell buoy and we thought we were well clear of any
rocks until we were right on 'em. Didn't even know
where we was near fer sure, and here was the boat
smashing up around us. Not much point in stayin with
it. So we each grabbed a coupla lobster buoys, tucked
one under each arm, and got ready to step over into the
water. Black as ink, it was.

"Before we went over the side my brother asked me
'Can ya swim?' 'Course he knew I couldn't. Not many
could. 'Yep,' I said. 'You?' He nodded. 'Beatcha to shore,
then,' I said, and he said 'Yeah, but—' I was already over
by then, headin for the water feet first.

"I never seen water so black. It was cold as hell and
wanted to suck the clothes offa me. It was all I could do
to hang onto those buoys and I lost one of 'em. I called
out to Yabut and I didn't hear no answer but I figured if
I was okay he was okay. The waves took me away from
the boat and I could see it was smashed up bad on a

bunch of rocks sharp as teeth but also that we were still a ways from shore, so I just started kickin fer all I was worth. Here's where it gets right spooky."

Pocket, on the stairs, shivered and hugged his arms around himself. Below him, Wanda sat with her elbows on her knees, leaning forward. Scratch, on the opposite side of the bed, pulled a handkerchief from his pocket and blew. From out on Kettle Island, the foghorn sounded again, the two noises comically similar. Nobody laughed.

"There was a tug on my right foot. Just like someone had my foot in both hands and wanted to pull me under. I gasped and kicked and then looked towards the shore to see how far I was, and I saw this city, risin up outa the fog. Like it was magic. Somethin out of a fairy tale. Beautiful, like some kinda paradise. So I just kicked off that hand and swum with every bit a strength I could muster. If it was heaven I was swimmin to, if it meant I'd died, that was okay with me right then.

"An then before long I felt smooth rocks under my feet and scrambled up on shore an dropped my one remaining buoy and turned around and called. Just called into the fog that closed all up around me, and waited and waited for an answer."

There was such a long silence that Pocket thought his uncle might not continue. As if on cue, the Kettle Island foghorn sounded again. Somewhere close by, a dog barked.

"There was no city, of course. I'd heard about the fog playin tricks like that, I just never seen it before. Heard also it can be a forerunner, tellin ya somethin's gonna happen. Or pointin the way. Hard to know sometimes what's God and what's the other fella.

"After a while it started to lift and I saw a fishin shed over t'other side a the cove and I made my way there. Coupla guys still sleepin inside, had holed up there overnight. Been out huntin, I guess. Turned out we'd smashed up around back of Northwest Point. So they warmed me up some an we all went out lookin, but didn't find nothing."

"Did he ever turn up?" Wanda asked quietly.

"Nope. And that's the hardest thing. I can still see his grin before we went over the side. And then there was the water. And whatever it was wantin to pull me under. Sometimes I dream about all that black water."

Pocket, on the third step down, was thinking about heading for bed when his mother's voice surprised him.

"Sometimes I dream about the water, too," she said hoarsely.

Scratch leaned forward. "Merle? You been awake?"

Pocket moved down two more steps, no longer caring if his presence was detected. His mother was indeed awake, her eyes remarkably bright after her long sleep, in spite of the morphine.

"You want the bedpan?"

"No, I want water."

Wanda took the cup from the bedside table and put it to her lips. She drank, coughed, and drank some more. Pocket thought to get up, then decided to stay put. He wanted to hear his mother's voice a while more in that storybook setting. He wished he could keep the scene pressed between covers, open the pages whenever he chose.

"Thank you," Merle said, and Wanda set the cup down. "I been asleep a long time?"

"Yeah. A while," Scratch told her. "You want me to wake up Wilf?"

"What time is it?"

"Oh, gone two, I think."

"Can't seem to keep track of time. Nor days. I was dreamin—"

"'Bout the water?"

"Dream about it all the time. I miss it some bad, bein out on it, a calm day and all that sky around you. I musta been dreamin about it..." Merle's voice trailed off as if she were trying to remember. "Then I heard ya talkin. I remember Yabut, even though I weren't more than ten years old when it happened. He could be some comical." Merle lifted her arm and let it drop as punctuation.

Scratch nodded, smiling a little. "Yep. He surely could."

"It was God's plan, I guess ya could say. It's not for us to say."

"Well, I like to think he's arguin up there about it."

"Sure he is." Merle patted Scratch's hand with her own thin one. She looked at Wanda. "You're still here, dear. Shouldn't ya be sleepin?"

"Yes," Wanda agreed. "I think maybe I'll head to bed. Need anything?"

"No, dear. Not a thing. Just a little more rest is all. Now you just go to sleep, both of you. I'll be right as rain in the morning."

Wanda gave Merle's hand a squeeze, then met Scratch's eyes.

"You go on up," he whispered. "That couch is lookin right comfortable just now."

"Yes," Merle murmured. "You go on up. And see that Pocket gets back into bed, too. He'll need his sleep if he's gonna grow up at all. "

High

In your dream, you watch a Great Black-backed Gull soar above you, a strong wing against a steel grey sky. What does it see from such a lofty perspective?

You close your eyes and, in the manner of dreams, you become the gull: feel wind in pinfeathers; smell salt, and the tang of a storm brewing out at sea. Looking down through the eyes of the gull, the shore spreads out like a child's toy village.

Circling shoreward, you see the cluster of houses. Amid a graveyard of trucks, a man tries to breathe life into one less rusty than the rest: you hear the engine turn over, whimper, turn again. Nearby, a woman hurries to the door of a plank-sided house, a parcel held carefully in her hands. From inside the house, with your keen avian ears you hear voices: several creatures are gathered there. The sound swells from the open door, and then the woman is inside, the door closed, the sound dampened.

Riding an updraft you tilt and circle, catch sight of more two-legged creatures behind the yellow building, where, sometimes, garbage can be found in a silver container with a loose lid. Gulls here do well by fish, but a bit of leftover this and that is always a nice change. But there is no garbage today, just two people blowing smoke from their mouths and talking the way they do, and looking at the harbour, where a knot of boats sways with the waves.

There are strange things about. There is the object you spied washed up on shore, obscured as it was by seaweed but clear to your sharp avian vision. That thing looked similar to the things humans put their garbage in, but after you went closer you quickly determined that it contained nothing edible; that it was something you wanted to stay away from.

On the Sound, the boats ride the waves like oversized gulls. You circle, see the beam of light from the radar station as it arcs across the sky, reaching. This far, the beam says; no farther. Out past the Sound, well beyond the arc of light and just below the surface of the sea, a long, black boat. Waiting.

In your bed you sigh and roll, pull the blankets closer, and as you do, your dream is broken. You try to catch the details before they slip away, but what you're left with is more essence than story.

You wake, and stretch, rise and pad to the window in time to see a distant gull flying home to Kettle Island. You watch until the bird is too small to see, and as you do you wish for height, distance, perspective.

Sunday, October 8

It was well past midnight, the wee hours of Sunday. The patrol vessel HMCS *Barrington* loomed large at the end of the dock, dwarfing the Cape Islanders and the Coast Guard vessel nearby. Cuff whistled to himself. It had to be what, two hundred feet? It looked bigger up close. Why had they brought it in instead of anchoring out in the Sound? His dad said he'd heard they brought something up from the bottom, but nobody had seen it unloaded; it was Tip Morton's second cousin on the Coast Guard cutter who told Tip who told Stanley who told Cuff. Cuff would've liked to ask Ernie to get the real story, but Ernie still had a crab up his arse about the other night, stupid bugger. Too bad for him. This was the second time Ernie had missed out on something big, and Cuff figured it served him right.

Made sense, though, that they should be in dock after a couple of days' diving, that is, if they'd got what they came for. If they *had* got something, they might've gone off celebrating in Yarmouth. Even Navy guys need a night off once in a while, he reasoned. And, he reasoned further, what they'd found might still be on board.

Cuff stood at the end of the wharf, secure in the remarkable dark of this particular night. The heavy blanket of cloud that squatted low over the Sound seemed to absorb what light there was. The *Barrington* looked deserted. With those guns mounted on the foredeck and all that radar stuff, Cuff figured it would be imposing enough all on its own to keep the curious off, but it didn't make sense that it should be unguarded. He shook his head; man, it was a beautiful boat. He'd heard they could turn on a dime, these things. Running his hand through his hair, he imagined himself as part of the crew. Joining the Navy would be one ticket out of Perry's, if only he could get in. He knew sciences and maths were important if he wanted to get anywhere beyond ordinary seaman. It was tempting anyway, but this, if he was right, would be a much quicker ticket out. Leverage, that's what this would be.

The deck felt solid beneath is feet, almost as if he was on firm ground; this was no wooden-hulled fishing boat. The smell of iron surrounded him like a great weight. He had never realized a smell could be tangible like this. It had become dark quickly, like a hand across your face. Cuff blinked into it, averting his eyes from the fore and aft spotlights that cast circles of light on the deck, so as to better see into the shadows. He listened, head cocked: nothing.

He'd search the deck first. He could see a light towards the bow, could imagine a crewman dozing in front of an unlit navigational panel. No way they'd leave a boat like this unguarded. He felt his way along the bulkhead, stepping carefully. Diving equipment hung from hooks: drysuits, coils of cable. He couldn't see the oxygen tanks, figured they were stored securely some-where. You could get some money for this stuff if you could figure out where to sell it. He shook himself from the thought. It's not why he was here.

He moved aft towards the quarterdeck. If they found something, how big would it be? Would they keep it abovedecks, or below? If he did find it—whatever it was—he had no clear picture of what he would do with it. He hoped it was a piece of something, some evidence small enough to carry away. He was sure the government would pay to get it back, or at least to keep it concealed from the public.

It grew darker, and Cuff felt the bite of wind coming from the west: some weather coming. The air took a chill turn, and he shivered but pressed on. He could barely see his feet, now, as he skirted to the windward side, the light from the wharf and the foredeck absent, here.

He made out the dark shape of something, light glancing off the dull surface of the tarp that covered it. And then his eyes began to water.

There was that wind again, and the sound of the fishing boats, restless, in their berths, the clanging of line against wood and metal. He knew that, at home, his dog Lou would be under the bed, whimpering, as she always did when the wind came up. Right now, strangely, he wanted more than anything to be there with her, although if you asked him he could not have accounted for the feeling that had come over him.

A noise from the foredeck stopped Cuff in his tracks. The click of a door swung shut, the sound of footfalls. He was up and leaping deck to dock, a blind sprint. When he hit the planks something in his left knee gave, a sickening lurch he felt in his stomach, but from behind him "Hey!" and he tore down the length of the dock, zigzagging, his compromised leg giving him a rabbit's gait. His car waited for him down behind the Moss Plant. He leaned against it, panting.

Quietly, he opened his car door and eased himself into the back seat. He'd rest his leg, get some shuteye, be out of the wind. In that hour before dawn, he'd try one more time. Now, he knew exactly where to go.

The point of light danced into Pocket's room, mothlike. It came through the window, slipped across the sill. Pocket realized he must have left his window open, but then, that didn't make sense; it was October, after all, and cold at night. And yet the air was warm, a balmy temperature that felt delicious on his skin. He watched as the moth-light fluttered around his room, its flight describing playful circles around the model airplane suspended from the ceiling, over his collection of bottle caps in their Mi'kmaq basket, alighting upon the tower of books stacked on his desk. Its journey made him sleepy, and he felt his eyes closing, only to open them with a start when he felt a touch on his cheek, an airy caress, sweet as the butterfly kiss his mother would playfully give him as a baby, when she would flutter her eyelashes against his cheek.

He opened his eyes for real then, and the dream faded. He struggled to hold onto the feelings it evoked, but it was like pulling in a snagged net, fish spilling back into the sea. In a moment, there was nothing.

He lay in the darkness, then rose and padded to his window, feet curling against the cold floor. The obsidian sea stretched into the night. His eyes scanned the sky for lights; he'd welcome a visit now, the thought of something reaching to him from far away a comfort rather than a fear.

Looking out towards the Sound, he thought he could see the search vessels in dock, looming shapes that could not be Cape Island boats. What would it be like, he wondered, to be a mate on one of these. From away, just passing through, no stake in anything. To come with clear purpose, and when that purpose was concluded, to leave as if Perry's Harbour never existed at all.

Rodney awoke to a light in the room. Or so he thought; when he looked there was nothing there, and he marvelled at the quality of dark. People who think it's dark in the city have no idea, he decided. He tried to catch the receding end of the dream that must have wakened him. Nothing, just a wisp of memory that slipped, catlike, away.

He rolled over and tried to return to sleep, but sleep wouldn't come. His conversation with Lorelei had rattled him. He should have tried harder to reach his boss. He couldn't shake the feeling that the world was swirling about him while he stood, oblivious, in the still eye of the storm. He would need to get a story in as soon as possible. He should have filed right away, he knew, filed whatever he had. By now, he should be on his third update. What had happened, since he'd arrived? He felt he had slowed to the speed of Perry's Harbour, the shifts of tide and fog.

After an hour he knew he wouldn't be getting back to sleep. He rose, pulling his jeans over his shorts and the rollneck sweater over his t-shirt. The floor was cold, and he hurried to pull on socks, stumbling. Grimacing, because he didn't want to wake Fred and Shirley. With uncharacteristic stealth he crept down the stairs and out the back door into the small, dark hours.

At the beach he stood at looked out across the Sound. To his left was the wharf, where the dark shape of the Navy vessel loomed. It was almost worth waiting for the first stirrings of the boat, try to catch someone who would say something, but even as he thought it he knew that true dawn was an hour away at least, and the bite of air was already numbing his toes in his boots. He knew with certainty he'd be back in bed before the Eastern sky turned pink.

Standing there, he reflected on the situation: something had crashed into the harbour. It was enough to bring out the brass, as well as the media, and it had to mean something. There was a story in that, at the very least. *If only I had the right words*, he thought. He recalled the story of his great-uncle Basil, who had been a First World War correspondent. He had never met his British relative, who had died when Rodney was small. But the legend was there: how his great-uncle, as a clandestine war correspondent at the outbreak of the war, had evaded authorities to roam the front lines in France at a time when journalists were not allowed in the war zone. Later, when they were, he moved freely everywhere, with bravery and passion for the printed word, filing stories alive with action with the *Daily Mail*. It occurred to Rodney now, as he stood in the dark by a remote fishing village where the biggest threat was a local bully, that had there been a war to report on, he'd have had a crack at his father's respect. As it was, stories about errant priests and politicians were hardly the stuff of admiration, let alone stories about unidentified flying objects. He gazed at the water's edge, wishing something tentacled would crawl up out of the ocean, preferably wearing a space-suit.

A sound from the direction of the wharf startled him. He turned and saw the shape of a man running, a hunched body in silhouette against the first dawn light.

Pocket understood, as he turned from his window, that he would not be going back to sleep. Crossing the floor, he placed his feet carefully so as not to creak the floorboards. He could hear Scratch breathing heavily in sleep, snores threatening to surface. From his mother's sewing room, he heard Wanda shift and roll, her heavy sigh. He had no idea what time it was. He turned to his clothes, draped across his chair.

The wharf, in the middle of the night, was eerily familiar, and yet it wasn't. Pocket had been here only a few hours before with Cuff, but now it felt as if a lifetime had passed, and the wharf, the rocky shore, the ocean inexpressibly altered. The Kettle Island light described its arc, its beam reflecting from against fog that waited offshore. The gentle nudging of surf against the pebble beach washed in a strangely minor key.

The planks were slick with frost: it was a colder night than it had been this fall, the stars sharp in the sky. It was just bright enough to see the rocks on the shore. Walking back on the slippery surface, he followed the pull of the thing in the sand. He'd tell Rodney about it tomorrow, but now he wanted to see it himself, one more time.

There is something about walking along the sea in the dark, Pocket thought as he placed foot after foot on the rounded rocks. The ocean feels bigger, even, than it does by day, and Pocket felt its enormity, a living creature of awesome presence.

For when I'm far away, on the briny ocean tossed
Will you ever heave a sigh and a wish for me

There was the sea and there was the land, and in between—what? Slipping on a piece of slimy driftwood, Pocket caught his balance and then stood for a moment, one boot in the water, one against a curve of barnacled rock. There he paused between elements and tilted his head back and looked at the stars until his head swam.

Will you ever heave a sigh and a wish for me

After a moment he straightened and looked down the beach. It had become darker, or seemed to, and all at once the walk to where he knew the thing lay seemed long and treacherous, the night cold. The distance, too, between where he stood now and his mother where she lay seemed unfathomable, as if vast seas lay between them. He'd come back tomorrow, he decided, in the light of day.

A sound in the night caught his attention. Looking towards the wharf, he thought he saw a movement, a dark shape running. *A forerunner?* he thought, then shook himself. Of course not. Probably just his imagination.

Returning to his house, he let himself quietly in the back door, removed his boots, and, still wearing his coat, moved as silently as he could through the sleeping house. As he passed the living room, he stopped. On the couch, the dark shape that was Scratch snored, oblivious. The room was in darkness, but a light had been left on in the kitchen. It cast a yellow rectangle through the kitchen doorway and across his mother's bed. Framed in its light, Merle lay in bed as she had hours before, hands folded on the bedclothes. Curled around her was his father, still dressed, his arm laid gently across her shoulders as if to keep her there, just like that, forever.

2 Cuff waited until near dawn before creeping onboard the Navy vessel again. Still no guard posted, at least none that he could see, and he reasoned that a big vessel like· this in a little place like Perry's, they'd see no reason to be on any sort of alert. If he'd been at all sleepy from his night of dozing in the car, once his feet found the deck he felt more awake than he'd felt in his life. Every now and then he felt a twinge in his knee so he kept himself weighted to his good leg, moving quietly across the iron deck.

The thing under the tarp squatted black in the slimmest shimmer of pre-dawn light, so black it seemed to absorb what little light there was. It was made of some sort of metal, Cuff thought, yet looked like nothing he'd seen before. He could see no rivets of any kind, no seams, but this cylindrical object about the size of a Cape Island boat engine must surely be fitted together in some fashion rather than formed of a piece. A piece of seaweed was stuck along one edge: the meeting of two worlds. He tried to lift the thing but it was far heavier than its size suggested; there was no way he could get it off the boat. Now on his knees, between glances over his shoulder, he searched with his hands for some part he could pry loose. His left knee protested vehemently, and he shifted his weight again. It was hard to see anything with his eyes tearing up like that. He wiped at them and felt again, and then there it was: a sliding plate the size of a deck of cards. It slid easily towards him, like butter on a hot knife, and into his palm. Holding it, he felt its alarming weight. Somewhere in the ship, a door closed. There was no time to reach inside, to see what the plate concealed. In an instant, he was running, unaware of the pain until he stopped and leaned, panting, on the Fairlane's hood.

He'd driven around for a while after that, eventually parking in his own driveway.

Sitting in the car, Cuff held the thing in his hands. He'd never seen anything so black, without shine or reflection. Slightly curved, it was perhaps a half-inch thick. On the underside were textured patterns much like the patterns left by insects in wormy wood, just under the bark, except these were more regular, more sharply angled. Tracing his thumb along one of these small roadways, he felt a tingle run up into his hand and pulled abruptly away. It felt impossibly cold, cradled in his hands, yet at the same time its presence burned like a hot coal.

Behind him in the early light, home: the flat, almost featureless expanse of peeling grey siding, small windows facing the sea. Around the house, a rusty jumble of junked cars, a kitchen stove, a rusted oil furnace, along with broken traps and tangles of rope and netting. Pete's bicycle—the envy of his older brothers, who felt the baby of the family got everything—lay on its side amid the refuse, one tire flat. He remembered how jealous he'd felt about that bike. None of that mattered, now.

Before the house began to stir he wrapped the thing in a piece of newspaper and tucked it under the seat of the car, then crept inside and into bed. His brothers didn't wake, clutching at every last moment of sleep, subconsciously knowing they'd be awoken soon enough. He lay there, unable to sleep himself, until his brothers should wake and witness his presence. They would be his alibi. The fewer who knew, the better.

First thing after he got up, he'd go find Ernie. Whatever Ernie was pissed off about, it couldn't have lasted this long. It never had before. While it would make sense to keep this to himself while he figured out how best to use this, neither could he be alone with it. Ernie was his friend. He could trust Ernie, bounce some ideas off him. Cuff wasn't sure: should he sell it to a newspaper? Or straight to the Department of National Defence—although he couldn't imagine how he'd go about making contact, or that they wouldn't double-cross him. A newspaper, then. He heard they'd pay big bucks for an inside scoop, enough to get him to Toronto for sure. They had budgets for this kind of thing. Once he made it to the city he knew the world would open like an oyster for a young man like himself.

When Rodney woke for the second time it was to light flooding his room. He picked up his watch from the bedside table: past nine o'clock. Through the floorboards he could hear movement downstairs, the click of the back door: Shirley gone to open the store. He hoped she'd left him breakfast.

He lay, looking at the ceiling, for a moment more. By the time he got to the wharf the boats would be out in the Sound if they weren't there already. That's what comes of midnight beach rambles, he thought, and on the heels of that came the memory of the figure running down the wharf towards the shore.

Ernie was sitting on his front steps smoking when Cuff pulled onto the shoulder, Ernie's house being so close to the road as to be easy shouting distance. As Cuff rolled down the window, the sounds of the Bobby Fuller Four poured out from the 8-track Cuff had installed with his moss earnings, the only person in Perry's who had one of the new players. Cuff swung an elbow out the window, singing along with a mocking country twang, "...fought the law and the law won..." He stopped singing and grinned. "Stop playin with yerself and c'mon."

"C'mon where?" Ernie stubbed out his cigarette on the step and tossed it into the dirt, but didn't get up.

"Just c'mon. Got somethin to show ya."

Ernie rose slowly, as if he had better things to do but was humouring Cuff as a personal favour. "What, we're gonna go chase some aliens or somethin?" he said as he climbed in. He could see Cuff's agitation in the way his knee jiggled, the way he tapped his hand against the steering wheel.

"Ha ha." Cuff pulled back onto the road while Bobby Fuller sang about doing time in jail. Gravel spun out behind the Fairlane's wheels.

"Whatcha got to show me, then?" Ernie asked, but if he was impatient before, Cuff wasn't telling, now. It was just like Cuff. Like playing with a fish, Ernie, thought resentfully.

"Been some busy," Cuff said conversationally. "Givin interviews. Been interviewed by that reporter guy for the paper up in Ottawa."

"Ottawa. From way up there. It's surprisin, ain't it? I talked to him, too. He took notes, wrote it all down."

Cuff ignored this. "Been thinking that's the place for me. Ontario."

Ernie grunted. "'Magin that interview's the closest ya'll ever get."

"Whatcha bet? I'll be in Toronna before you know it."

"To do what?" Ernie didn't bring up the unlikelihood of Cuff and his dad making much money this season. Last season was poor, and this year his dad seemed even more disinclined to get ready. Worse, he wouldn't let Cuff near the boat except to drop traps, which was crazy because Cuff was the better mechanic. It would be a miracle if the *Seven Brothers* even made it out on the water.

"Find a job. Live, some. There's nothin here. Hear the girls are hot in Toronna. Hotter'n Brenda. Way hotter'n Debbie." Cuff leered for a moment, then moved on. "Never mind Edie. You still messin with her? Yer hard to find these days, Ole Son."

Ernie didn't answer. His hand shot out to steady himself on the dash as Cuff rounded a corner on what felt like two wheels.

"Eh?" Cuff asked again.

"Yeah," Ernie said. "You could say that."

But Cuff had moved on. "Maybe I'll get on somewheres fixin cars."

"Not without mechanic's papers."

"Whadda *you* know? Besides, maybe I don't even need a job.".

"'Course ya need a job. How're ya gonna live?"

"Got some ideas."

"Jeezus, Cuff, if it's not one thing, it's another," Ernie said. If he pissed Cuff off, he just didn't care anymore. "Yer always schemin somethin, aintcha? Remember when you shellacked them sculpins? Mounted 'em on plywood?"

"Sold four, didn't I?"

"Tourists'll buy anything side a the road. Bet they didn't get fifty miles before their cars started to stink like a fish plant."

Cuff pulled sharply into the wharf road, scattering rocks. The car's nose was pointed towards the beach that ran along the south side of the wharf. From where they parked they could see the full length of the wharf, the Sound spread out beyond. The pilot vessel, RCMP and Coast Guard boats were gone.

Ernie peered through the windshield. "Hey—where's the boats?"

Cuff shrugged. "Maybe they found what they were lookin for."

"Or maybe they jus' gave up."

"Nah. Ya blind? They're just in dock. Anyways, they didn't give up." Cuff reached under the seat and pulled the thing out. He'd wrapped it in newspaper which, opened, provided a kind of nest for the slightly convex object that lay like an egg of sorts. It looked bizarrely as if it were about to hatch, and Ernie recoiled involuntarily.

"Jeezus. What *is* that thing?"

"That," Cuff answered, "is my ticket outta here. Maybe yers, too, Ole Son, if you behave yerself."

"Lemme—"

"It was some kinda slidin cover on this thing, heavy thing 'bout the size of a engine, looked like nothin I ever seen—"

"Lemme—"

"Wait. Who's that?" Cuff wrapped the paper back around the object and stuffed it under the car seat.

Ernie peered through the windshield. Wanda looked out of place on the beach, clearly a foreigner even as she wore, over a long skirt and leather boots, an oilskin coat that Cuff recognized as Scratch's, a relic of a jacket if there ever was one.

Cuff leaned forward. "Look. It's the crazy lady. Man, she gives me the heebies."

They watched while Wanda walked back and forth across the pebbled beach, fingers touching her temples. Her hair wafted around her head, curls corkscrewed from the damp climate. She stopped suddenly and swayed, foot to foot, as a mother might do with a small baby. After a moment she stilled, then reached her arms towards the sea, palms out, and held them there.

"Whatthe—?" Cuff started to laugh.

Ernie felt the familiar chill descend, portent of something nasty. "C'mon, let's go," he suggested. "Whaddar we gonna do with this thing, anyway?"

"Whadda ya suppose she's doin? Talkin to aliens?"

In the rearview mirror, Ernie caught a glimpse of Pocket on the road, heading towards the wharf. His uneasiness increased. "It's from the boat, ain't it? It's from the thing that crashed. You think it's from some Russian spacecraft? We don't know what kinda stuff they got."

"Ho! Lookit her *now*. She some kinda hippie gypsy freak or what?"

"C'mon, Cuff," Ernie said again.

"C'mon where? Just *Lookit* her. This is some comical, if she weren't so dangerous."

They watched while Pocket approached Wanda, watched them talk.

"Whadda ya mean, dangerous?"

"She knows something, man. I can just tell. Maybe she's workin for DND. Or the Russians. What'd I hear was her last name? Karloff or somethin?"

"More likely she's workin for the aliens," Ernie joked. Better to lighten things up, he figured. "Forget about her. What about that—thing?"

"Nah, we're gettin outta here." Cuff said, putting the car in gear. "I dunno, maybe it's nothin. But she creeps me out, that's fer damn sure. This thing's too valuable to lose to some Russian spy posin as a wingnut."

3 When Pocket woke late that morning to the flat morning light he lay in bed for a while, eyes reluctant to open properly. He could hear Wanda downstairs helping with his mother's personal care. He heard their voices, Wanda's gentle, his mother's firm. At one point, as Wanda must have been adjusting the pillows, "careful, now, that's the only neck I've got," his mother joked. Pocket, reassured, rose then, and came down to find his mother sitting up in bed, her hair brushed, a cup of tea cooling beside her.

"I just don't feel much like eatin anything," she was saying to Wanda.

Pocket's father came in from the kitchen. "Merle, ya gotta eat somethin. See, here's Pocket." He gave Pocket a nod as he stepped from the bottom stair. "Tell her, Pocket."

But Pocket didn't answer, just crossed the floor and took his mother's outstretched hand. She curled her fingers around his, then let them go and gave his hand a pat, releasing it. She smiled at him, almost her old smile, and Pocket returned it, heart lifting.

"Now, dear," she said, "tell me what you're goin to do today."

Wanda left the house soon afterwards, shooed out by Scratch, who told her to take a walk, get some air. After Wanda had left, Pocket stayed by his mother's bed, lulled into shared quiet, until a knock at the door startled him.

It was the pastor, fresh from the morning service. Although there was a church service every Sunday, the Baptist minister came through just monthly, the services rotating between Baptist, Presbyterian, Anglican and Lutheran in the little chapel on the hill. Pocket had opened the door to the jowly, neatly groomed man.

"I only just heard," he told Pocket, both hands on the Bible held flat against his belly. "May I come in?"

"Well, she's only just taken a turn this past week," Pocket told him. He opened the door to let the man step inside. "Dad?" he called.

He slipped out, then. He never really liked Pastor Gould, and he wasn't sure his mother did, either. It was in the way the pastor held his head when he talked, always slightly inclined, bulbous eyes looking up past his pale eyebrows, fishlike. He often had the feeling that, at any moment, the pastor would begin speaking in bubbles, as if underwater. He knew it was bad to think this way, but there it was.

Would his mother talk to Pastor Gould about him? It was clear that the pastor's presence—he didn't want to think about it. In his mind were the words from his mother's letter, still resting under his bed. He'd return the letter to the desk today, he told himself.

The morning was fine, the air crisp, sea calm as glass. As Pocket walked towards the shore he gazed out into the Sound. The boats he'd come to expect out there were absent, and then he saw them, docked: the RCMP cutter and a larger boat he now knew to belong to the Canadian Navy's Fleet Diving Unit, thanks to information Scratch had picked up at the store. With nobody talking to the people of Perry's, snippets of information that surfaced were clutched at, examined, passed along. He wondered what they might be finding out there, and thought about the thing in the sand. He knew he should tell someone, but couldn't say why he hadn't. In a way, he figured, it served them right. They weren't telling anyone anything; why should he? For now, it was something he had that nobody else had. That was enough.

He kicked a rock off the road as he crossed and watched it tumble to rest on the shoulder. Catching up to it, he kicked it again as he left the main road to take the lane to the wharf. On the third kick, it skittered sideways, and giving up he raised his eyes to see the figure of Wanda on the pebble beach beside the wharf.

As Pocket drew near he saw that Wanda's head was tilted backwards, her eyes closed. Facing the Sound, she stood with her arms in the air. Like the pastor, Pocket thought as he looked on, when he raised his arms to God and entreated his parishioners to pray for salvation. Coming closer, he heard a humming, almost unearthly. With the sound of the waves on the shore and the cries of seagulls, it made for an odd sort of music. He stood and watched her for a while, standing back so as not to disturb the scene.

It was quiet at the wharf. These last few days it had been as if Perry's held its breath, he thought, waiting for—something. Or maybe that was just his perception, the emergence from the intensity of home carried over into the light of day. Again, he felt the strangeness of the air, wondered when things might return to normal. He tried to remember what normal felt like, the memory of the day-to-day of even half a year ago now indistinct. Wanda swayed, and the hum reached his ears again. It made him vaguely uneasy; she didn't fit. And yet, standing there, hands in his pockets, he reflected that he had never felt as if he fit, either. Why not? Five generations of Snows in Perry's Harbour. He thought of his father's words: *He's useless in the boat.*

Wanda turned when she heard Pocket's boots on the round beach rocks and let her arms fall to her sides.

"You're out early after a late night," she said.

"You, too. Pastor came to see Mum, so I left." He looked around. There was nobody else on the beach that he could see, which was a relief. "What're you doin?"

"Trying to communicate."

"With who?"

"The aliens. I know they're out there. I'm sure they want to communicate. I can sense it. But with all these boats…"

Pocket thought about the *UFO Mysteries* comic, still under his bed. "If they wanted to communicate, I mean, wouldn't they just do it?"

"They might. They have. Maybe the time's not right. But I can feel a—presence. It's an energy flow coming from the Sound, especially now that there's nobody diving. It's quite pure. I don't know why I can't get more."

"Is that why you came? To talk with the aliens?"

"That's exactly why I came. To tell them they are welcome—at least by some of us. To try to protect them, to warn them that there are humans who would do them harm." She sighed. "But so far, nothing."

"You disappointed?"

"Something will happen." She looked in the direction of Pocket's house, although it could not be seen from where they stood. She looked back out to sea, then smiled at Pocket. It was then that Pocket noticed Cuff's Fairlane sitting in the gravel lot at the end of the wharf. It reminded him of a sleek black cormorant, neck outstretched, its headlights a pair of beady eyes.

"You wanna go?" he asked. "Maybe get somethin warm to drink or somethin?"

They started up the beach towards the store. As they walked, Wanda spoke into the quiet air. "Sometimes, when we're drawn to something," she said, "it's for a reason that hasn't yet been revealed."

Rodney was on his third cup of coffee when Wanda and Pocket walked in. There was a sudden chill in the air, not from the temperature, but from Shirley's reception.

"Ain't you supposed to be lookin after Merle?" she said to Wanda, her voice a knife edge.

Pocket stepped from foot to foot, uncomfortable with the climate at hand. He spoke before Wanda could answer. "Pastor's visiting right now," he said.

Shirley spoke to Wanda. "You've made yerself right at home, haven't ya?" she said. "Look, I don't know what yer after…"

Wanda gave Shirley a long look. Shirley returned it, and then faltered, her hands straightening tillside items on the countertop.

"You lost a sister to cancer, didn't you?" Wanda said.

"Who told you that?"

"I'm sorry. I know it was hard for you. It must be terribly hard to lose a friend, too."

Wanda turned and pulled a chair out at Rodney's table. She took off the oilskin jacket and lay it across a vacant chair, then settled herself on the chair across from Rodney like a hen on a nest. Pocket, at the counter, told Shirley in almost a whisper that they would like coffee. Shirley looked at Pocket as if not recognizing him for half a beat, but then, collecting herself, said: "Seems like all I ever do some days is pour coffee."

When Pocket reached the table Wanda was answering a question from Rodney. "Crop circles?" She took the coffee from Pocket and blew on it. "Yes, they are related. But this incident your colleague is referring to happened a long way from here. Still," she mused, "there's no doubt these are alien communications. There's also evidence of scientific experimentation." She leaned forward. "Livestock mutilations."

Pocket, who had been adding the third teaspoon of sugar to his cup, stopped and stared. "What?" he asked.

"This event Rod's talking about was a couple of months ago in Alberta. The farmer went out to investigate when his cows didn't come home."

"And they were—*mutilated*?" Rodney asked. Pocket hung on to her answer. This was weirder than whatever was going on out in the Sound.

"Well, not these cows. At least, none that came back home, eventually. But when the farmer went out to look for them, he found four circular impressions in his field, about thirty feet across, all the grass pressed flat in a geometric design. No other marks around them.

Your Department of National Defence can't explain it. But we can."

At the counter, Shirley snorted. "What, d'ya think a bunch a aliens come down to mutilate our lobsters?"

Wanda ignored this. "Two of our members went up right away. The circles were still there. The cows wouldn't go near that field. You know," she said, turning to Rodney, "you may have something there. Crop circles are a common form of extraterrestrial visitations. And these two events occurred relatively close together in time. It could be significant."

Shirley snorted again, her back to all of them as she worked at the long back counter, slapping butter onto an assembly line of bread slices. "Significant, my fanny," she said over her shoulder. "What, ya'll be readin the seaweed next."

The door opened then and Stanley Dodds came in, his clothes oil-stained. He was unshaven, with a ballcap on his head that read *Atlantic Fisheries*. Stanley helped himself to a bottle of Fanta from the cooler as, behind him, Neil Hitchens pushed through the door. Neil found a Coke for himself and paid for both drinks, counting dimes from a blackened palm. "Been workin on the truck all morning," he told Shirley. "Both of us. Still can't get it to run worth a damn. Manual's useless as tits on a bull." Both men took in the group at the table, and Neil nodded.

Shirley rained the change into the till. "Dontcha got yer boat to work on, Stanley?" she asked him.

She was thinking of Irene Dodds, all those boys to feed. She could never fathom how Stanley would work on other people's projects but never his own. She knew of carpenters whose own houses were never finished. And there was Sally Peters who cut hair in her kitchen for the ladies of Perry's—their kids, too—but never her own kids' hair. They walked around shaggy as winter ponies. But *still*.

"Lotsa time," Stanley said, tipping the bottle back and swallowing half of it.

The door opened again and Cuff, limping slightly, walked in with Ernie, the two bringing with them a short blast of cold air.

"Look who's here," Stanley grinned. He turned to the group at the table and looked at Rodney. "Ya here to talk to my boy 'bout what he seen?"

"We've talked already," Rodney told him.

"Ya hear he was the first to call it in? You'll put that in the paper, right?"

"I haven't written anything yet. But uh, yes. Cuff was one of the people I interviewed." His leg was jiggling, he realized, and he stopped it.

Cuff spoke up, leaning back against the counter as he faced the table. "Don't believe everythin you hear, now. Some'll spin a yarn just for entertainment. Some of us got *proof*." He paused for emphasis, his face displaying a knowing smile. He looked at Rodney. "Maybe you an me should talk some more."

Cuff's tone evoked memories of schoolyard bullies. "Sure," Rodney said, mustering a confident tone. "We can talk here."

"Nah. Somewheres else," he said, his gaze taking in Wanda and Pocket. "Not around this bunch." He remained leaning, back against the counter. "Coffee, Shirley?"

"You look at me when ya talk to me, Cuff Dodds," she said, folding her arms.

"People round here'll bullshit ya soon as tell the truth," Cuff continued, speaking directly to Rodney.

"Language," said Shirley, not pouring any coffee.

"Ya gotta know who yer talking to."

"My boy's right," Stanley said. He put his empty bottle on the table. "People talk bullshit around here all the time." He laughed. "Ain't that right, Shirley?" But he looked sideways at Cuff, a question.

"'Course, it ain't just people 'round here who're full of shit." Cuff looked pointedly at Wanda.

Shirley crossed her arms. "What're you two playin at?" she said. By the door, Ernie studied the items in the cooler as if he were considering a long-contemplated purchase. From the corner of his eye he could see the sneer that curled Cuff's lip.

"Ah, he's just goin on guff," Neil said, but his words fell flat. Cuff said nothing.

Wanda narrowed her eyes and levelled them at Cuff, unwilling to be intimidated. Then, as if coming to a sudden realization, "It's not yours to keep," she said.

For the slightest moment Cuff felt an icy sliver of unease slide down his spine. He shivered involuntarily, then straightened and looked around the room.

"What's she talking 'bout, Boy?" Stanley set his drink down on the counter.

"She don't have a fuckin clue 'bout anythin," Cuff said. "You see her down to the shore? She's a fuckin nutcase."

"Shirley, could use a packa smokes," Ernie ventured into the thick air.

"Wavin her arms around like she was doin some kinda rain dance. You an injun?" he asked her, "Or just escaped from the nut-house? Or maybe yer an alien yerself. Hey, what planet are ya from? The Planet of the Crazy Old Broads?"

"Hey—" said Rodney, but further words wouldn't come. His heart raced the way it always had in the schoolyard, making any retort—smart or otherwise— impossible. He glanced sideways at Wanda, whose face was a mask.

"Cuff, you go on, now," Shirley warned. She picked up the phone to call the house, then remembered Fred was in Yarmouth. "Go make trouble somewheres else."

"Ah, he don't mean no harm," Stanley said.

Neil set his bottle down and nodded to Shirley. "Let's go, Stanley. Bring that boy of yers."

"Bet she's a witch. Castin spells, bring them little green men up outta the water."

"When the aliens show themselves, they won't have much use for humans like you," said Wanda.

"Ya don't know what yer talking about. First thing them aliens'll do is get ridda all the crazies, startin with you. Beam ya right up for fertilizer, you bein so full a shit. Not that they'd even wantcha fer that. Nobody'd ever want you, would they? Yer *mother* wouldn't even want you. Fuckin idjit." He waited a beat before spitting out the last words: "Useless *cunt*."

Pocket stood up. He felt a roaring in his ears, a crashing of waves. Inside his chest, a hurricane wind.

"She's not an— idjit. She's *helpin* us. She's helpin my mum. *You're* the one who's useless. You should just *shut up* for once."

229

The entire room was silent: Shirley stood, mouth open. Stanley, still at the counter, stood with one hand on the Fanta bottle, one hand on his son's shoulder, unmoving. Neil, one step towards the door, halted midway. Ernie, at the cooler, stood, head swivelled. Rodney and Wanda at the table sat transfixed. Cuff's derisive smile froze on his face like a parody of itself.

Pocket remained standing, fists clenched by his sides. All at once he released his breath.

The phone rang, jarring the silence. Shirley picked it up.

"Pocket, Wanda. It's Scratch. He says Merle's fallen. You'd better get on home. He's on his own, there, says fer you to find yer father, Pocket."

4 The wharf was the logical place for Pocket's father to have gone if he wasn't at home or in the workshop. It seemed plausible that his father, needing to keep busy, might have gone to set things right in the *Merlaine II*. Still, why wouldn't he tell Scratch where he was going? As he ran, Pocket was struck by the clarity of the day, everything hard-edged. He began to run harder, his running shoes hitting the dirt shoulder with the rhythm of his heart.

He paused by the last telephone pole before the wharf, leaning, breathing hard, the stitch in his side making it difficult to move. Resting his head against the smooth wood, he looked skyward. A gull reeled, keening. He stifled the urge to echo the sound, his chest tightening against it. A car passed; he felt faces turned towards him. He stared ahead, feeling his breathing slow. Pushing himself off, he continued at a half-run towards the wharf, holding his side.

Pocket had hoped to find his father on the boat. But at the wharf's end he recognized Wilf by his green workshirt, his stooped back, as he sat on a bollard facing the sea, hands on his knees. His father wasn't wearing a jacket, and the air was cold.

Wilf looked up when Pocket neared and nodded towards an overturned bait box. Then he tilted his chin towards the Sound. "Think they've found anything?" he asked.

"Don't matter." Pocket sat down beside his father, still holding his side. "You need to come on home." At the seriousness of Pocket's tone, Wilf's countenance changed. Pocket had no reference point for such a look. "Mum fell," he said. "I think she's okay, but Uncle Scratch said to come home."

"She fell?" Wilf scrambled up. Pocket stood as well.

"Uncle Scratch called Crosbey's lookin for us. Wanda went home, and I came to find you. What're ya *doin* out here?"

"I dunno I can. I jus—" Wilf's look was bewildered, a small animal in a desperate situation. "I know it's cowardly. I jus—it's here." His hand, fisted, found the centre of his chest. "When I'm there it just—"

"I know."

"Christ, what'm I sayin," Wilf said. "I shoulda been home."

"C'mon, Dad."

"I just—"

"I know, Dad."

"You're a good boy, Pocket."

"*C'mon*, Dad."

"Jeesuz—"

They began to run, father and son, through the knife-sharp air.

"She tried get to the commode herself," Scratch said in the hallway when Pocket and Wilf pushed in through the front door. "She said she was feelin so much better, she figured she could. I was in the kitchen."

"S'my fault," Wilf said. In two steps he was by the bedside. Merle's eyes were closed, her breathing ragged.

Scratch ran his hands through his hair. "She was more mad at herself than anything."

"For trying?" Wanda asked.

"For being so weak. Frustrated's more the word, I think."

"Nothing's broken," Wanda said. "Just a scare, and a bruise I'm sure. But it scared her, and it tired her right out."

"Scared me, too," Scratch said. "Thought you was with her, Wilf."

Wilf, standing at the bedside, took his wife's hand. "Sorry, Merle," he whispered.

Scratch made a sound. "Ya can't just take off like that."

"Sorry," Wilf said again, not looking up. "I—"

"Look, we gotta get some help in. I called Cindy Morton at home, you know, Tip's cousin in Yarmouth? Even though it's Sunday an all. It's all I could think of to do." Scratch said, looking up at Wanda. "She's a public health nurse, though she says she's not doin the actual nursin anymore, more the paperwork. Gave me an earful that we hadn't set somethin up a long time ago." He shook his head. "Anyways she's comin round herself tomorrow, as a favour. We been too long without help."

"We got Wanda," Pocket said. He'd been standing just inside the doorway from the front hall, watching.

"I'll do whatever I can," Wanda said, "but I'm not a nurse. I *can* ease the transition to the spirit world. In a metaphysical sense."

The words hung there. Wilf was clearly trying to make sense of them, while Scratch cleared his throat. On the road, a car without a muffler went by, its engine roar at odds with the quiet in the room.

"Or I can just help," Wanda said.

Scratch looked relieved. "Thanks," he said. "You have been, actually. It's not like we're not grateful."

"Yeah," Wilf agreed.

"Rollers," Merle said in her sleep, distinctly.

"Hair?" Wanda asked.

"Waves, more likely," Scratch said. "Big ones."

"West," she mumbled.

"Sounds like she's out rowin," Wilf said. "Where do you suppose she's goin?"

Within moments the store was empty save for Rodney and Shirley. Pocket and Wanda had left first, Wanda brushing by Cuff who stood back with his hands in the air in mock alarm. "Better get a move on, then," Neil had said, and Stanley followed him out after a quizzical glance at his son. "Don'tcha got chores to do at home, Boy?" he'd said, prompting Cuff and Ernie to head for the Fairlane and off in the opposite direction of the Dodds home.

"We'll be talkin." Cuff nodded towards Rodney as he left.

"Uh, sure," Rodney answered.

In the settling air, Rodney and Shirley looked at one another, and then Shirley came around the counter and joined Rodney at the table, pushing half-empty coffee cups into the centre.

"I better make a casserole," she sighed. To Rodney, the comment seemed apropos of nothing. "Maybe tuna. It's a good comforting casserole, that one. I'll take it over later. Oh, those poor dears. I'll get Fred to come look after things here soon as he gets back."

"A casserole?"

"It's what we do," Shirley told him, and Rodney took this to mean more than something done in Perry's, but rather something done throughout all humanity, and he felt chastened for not knowing such a thing.

"Why don't I stay and look after the store?" he offered. "I'll write my article, and you can go home and cook. It seems pretty quiet."

"Oh, aren't you a dear? Here. I'll show you how to work the till."

On her way out the door, Shirley paused. "Look on Cuff's face—" she laughed. Rodney could hear her chuckling as she crossed the parking lot.

Sitting at the table, Rodney wrote in longhand, forming the letters in an echo of Mrs. Brison's grade four lessons. He seemed to recall grade four was the last time he'd ever liked school. Mrs. Brison read his stories aloud to the class, extolling his creativity. He remembered one in particular. "Rodney is a natural storyteller," she'd told his mother and father at Parents Day. "The story he wrote about your dog, when he saved Rodney's baby sister, was exceptional."

His father had been dismissive. "We don't have a dog. Or a baby," he'd said, missing the point. On the way home, "Why don't you write about real things?" he'd asked Rodney. He'd been pleased, in his way, when

235

Rodney chose journalism, which was, at least, a saleable skill. His mother, in any case, hoped for the headline she'd add to her collection, this time with her son's by-line. Now, Rodney wondered if writing about possible alien crash-landings would qualify as writing about real things.

He'd better get down to work. He'd finish this now and call it in as soon as Shirley returned and he knew he wouldn't be interrupted on the phone by a customer coming into the store for bread or cigarettes. His return ticket was for Tuesday; he might still get something more from one of the divers, maybe, but he'd write that as a followup. He wondered, not for the first time, about the *Herald* reporter. Why hadn't he seen the guy around? Shirley had said nothing. Could it be that folks were holding out on him? Was somebody else getting the scoop? For a brief moment he saw the residents of Perry's Harbour as a sinister lot, holding their cards close to the chest in order to—what? Rodney could think of no pos-sible motivation for such a thing.

The thought led him to Lorelei. It's true, he could be dim when it came to the motives of others. And yet she seemed genuinely to like him, or else why would she have come over to see him off—and in such a memorable way? He felt himself stir at the thought. To distract him-self, he pulled the pack of du Mauriers from his pocket, extracted the last cigarette, and lit it. On the adjacent table was a quahog shell that held a few cigarette ends, and he reached for it. Inhaling shallowly, he resisted the urge to cough and exhaled smoothly, pleased with himself. He seemed to be getting the hang of it. He looked around the empty store as if for an audience and, finding none, settled back to the task at hand: searching for a lead, pen point tapping on the paper.

Residents of Perry's Harbour, Nova Scotia, gather daily in the local store to talk about the unidentified flying object that crashed into the Sound last Wednesday night.

Time and place were clear, but readers might stop there, assuming rural ignorance and superstition. He looked around the empty store, glad they weren't gathering at this moment, although he supposed if they were, he might learn something new. He decided to try a different lead.

Local fisherman Cuff Dodds is sure that the thing that crashed into the waters of Perry's Harbour, Nova Scotia, last Wednesday night was no plane.

Good to start with a mystery to pique reader's curiosity, but the truth was that Cuff's testimony had been full of his own bravado, but short on details. And he may have been drunk. He'd rather not make Cuff the focus of the piece. But writing about Cuff got him thinking about Cuff, and Cuff's family. The "darker place" Fred had hinted at. And Shirley had told him about Merle and Wilf and the Halifax riots. It would be more interesting to write about these things. He thought about his dog story, and he wondered briefly if he'd missed some calling for a different kind of writing. He shook himself back to the moment.

Could the unidentified flying object that crashed into the waters near a remote fishing village last week be an alien visitation?

Too much like the *Ripley's Believe It or Not!* comics

he'd read as a kid. Not that Wanda would say such a thing. He knew what her take would be, and the thought of leagues of wacky UFO-chasers smugly vindicated by his story made him squeamish. He wanted to be taken seriously. Even if—and he pushed the thought away, even as it came flooding in—he was beginning to think such a thing himself. The fog of secrecy was thicker than ever. Something was up, for sure. Cold War or not, wouldn't someone official say *something* if it was the Russians?

Near a remote fishing village in Nova Scotia, the Navy's Fleet Diving Unit has been on site since Friday searching Perry's Harbour for an unidentified flying object.

That wasn't bad. The Navy lent credibility; it was good to get that clear in the first sentence. Whatever Mr. Copeland had said, he didn't want his story to be buried as a quirky news piece on some back page. Better to play down any alien connection. Just state it's a UFO, just as the Department of National Defence had done. Nothing more, nothing less; an open-ended question pending further investigation.

At approximately 11:20 p.m. something crashed into the dark waters...

It was sounding like a comic book again. But then, it did sound like a comic book, didn't it? The urge towards purple prose was overwhelming. He tried again.

Eyewitness reports...

If Lorelei were writing the story, what would she say? He dismissed the thought: Lorelei was a researcher, not a reporter. She wouldn't be trying to find a good lead, if Lorelei were here she'd be getting him some solid background to work with. He tried to imagine Lorelei's white go-go boots against the raw plank floor of Crosbey's General Store. He turned back to the paper in front of him. If only he had something concrete.

It was then that Rodney noticed, left on the seat of the fourth chair at the table, a book. It must have fallen out of Wanda's pocket when she placed her jacket there. The book, variously notated in what was probably Wanda's hand, was well thumbed, but obviously new, with its shiny black and green cover. He picked it up and began to read.

> *Many skeptics would be surprised to learn that evidence of flying saucers and extraterrestrial visitations can be found in the Bible. And yet, the passages are indisputable. Consider Exodus 3:2–5: "And the angel of the Lord appeared to him in a flame of fire out of the midst of a bush: and he looked, and behold, the bush burned with fire, and the bush was not consumed."*
>
> *The forcefield around a spaceship would most certainly have made the bush appear to Moses as if it were on fire.*

Rodney, rapt, read through three pages of biblical evidence, his own article temporarily forgotten. The words, crisp on the page, seemed to rebuke any skepticism. The 1917 miracle at Fatima in Portugal was described, and even to Rodney the "lady of the light" seemed quite obviously to be an extraterrestrial appearance, interpreted by small children in a manner they could understand. From there, the book went on to relate eyewitness accounts by commercial and military pilots, clearly people of professionalism and integrity, many corroborating the same sighting. Large power failures were attributed to UFO interference, and, in the absence of better explanations, these seemed almost to make sense. He shook himself mentally. Where was his journalistic balance? He read on about first-person meetings with spacemen, interactions that sounded like comic-book plots.

He was much smaller than me—about a foot—and seemed considerably younger, his face very smooth. And yet I felt like a little child in the presence of someone much older and wiser. He had a very high forehead and eyes that were slightly slanted, his mouth small. He smiled at me, and held up his hand palm out in front of his chest in a gesture of greeting, and I responded in kind, even though the gesture was unfamiliar. His clothing appeared like something one would wear for a ski holiday, which made little sense to me considering the Arizona heat. There were no zippers or buckles on his outfit that I could see. I asked him where he came from. When he didn't appear to understand, I pointed towards the sky, to which he replied with a smile that I took to mean yes.

Rodney could only imagine a meeting between an alien and someone less than likely as an earth ambassador. Cuff Dodds, for example, might just ask for a smoke, having exhausted all of the local possibilities. Wanda would be trying to telepathically communicate, or some such thing. And Rodney himself? Well, he'd want the visitor to go on record, of course. For sure he'd have left the tape recorder where it is now, on the dresser in his room at Shirley's, no camera on hand to record the momentous event. Rodney looked at the Fanta clock behind the counter. The whole afternoon was gone, and what had he written?

Looking around self-consciously, Rodney placed his hand, palm out, in front of his chest. "Greetings," he said into the empty room. Then, whispering: "Take me with you," he said.

He'd meant it as a joke, of course, even if it was a joke without an audience. But Rodney recognized, in the reverberation of his own words as they fell into the still air of the empty store, the sound of longing.

In the kitchen of the yellow house, the onions in the frying pan simmered softly, while on the wall, the round clock ticked. Shirley stopped cutting haddock into chunks, her hand stilled as she thought of Merle. *It just washes over you sometimes*, she thought. *It's the everyday things keeping you busy and then there it is, like it's been waiting all day.* Laying down the knife, Shirley placed both hands on the counter's edge, bent her head and wept.

5 Pocket sat on the front step of his house with a sandwich. He could have eaten in the kitchen or in his room, but somehow the step allowed him both distance and proximity. The air had warmed a little, but the wood beneath him was cold.

Occasionally, a car would pass and he would look away from the faces that would inevitably turn his way. Everyone knew what was happening at the Snow house, the Perry's Harbour telegraph having been active all morning. News of Merle's fall spread quickly, and in any case, there was hardly a soul who didn't know that Merle Snow had stopped getting up. The food dropped off at the back door had been coming all week, more than they could ever eat, delivered with murmurs of "if there's anything I can do…"

Pocket should have been hungry; it was late afternoon, after all. It occurred to Pocket that he'd never gone so long without thinking about food, at least not that he could remember. Even Scratch had noted that "s'hard to keep much of a routine in times like these." Pocket supposed that was why the women of Perry's made casseroles when anyone was sick, or having a baby.

The bread in Pocket's mouth tasted flat, textureless. Bologna was usually his favourite, but today it stuck to the roof of his mouth like a second pink skin. He put the sandwich down and looked towards the road, the sound of footfalls on gravel reaching his ears before he actually made out the figure as that of the Ottawa reporter. He had a casserole dish in his hand.

"Shirley sent me over with this," Rodney told Pocket as he reached the step. He set the dish down gently. "She said to call if you need anything. She didn't come herself because Fred's still not back. Don't think she trusted me with the store any longer," he grinned weakly. "What are you doing out here?"

"Just a change, I guess. Sometimes it feels—sometimes the room feels small. I can't explain, really."

"No, I think I get it." For Rodney, rooms were always contracting. Like they had this afternoon, the scene at the store. "Good for you. You know, this afternoon," he said.

Pocket looked at Rodney quizzically.

"I mean, saying your piece. Standing up to Cuff."

Pocket shrugged his shoulders.

"I get mad," Rodney told him, "but I never have the words I want."

Pocket looked over at Rodney. "Me neither, usually." He grinned a half-grin, sheepish. There was a shared moment between them, then:

"How are you getting on?" Rodney asked. "Is there anything I can do?"

"Nah. People keep askin that. I dunno why they do."

Rodney sat down beside Pocket as the misery of Pocket's voice reached inside him and tugged at something remembered. "People just want to help," he said.

"Yeah, well they can't," said Pocket. He raised his hands and scratched both sides of his head vigorously, as if trying to dislodge some thought. When he'd finished, he looked like his uncle, Rodney thought, and for a moment he envied the closeness of these families, here in this place. Rich or poor, there was a familial tightness echoed in the bond of community. It hadn't been there in his own family. It wasn't there in his upper-middle-class Ottawa neighbourhood. It was certainly not there at the *Journal*. He felt like an island. Pocket, even in his misery, had his family, his community.

"Talk about something else," Pocket said abruptly. "Talk about the UFO."

Rodney laughed, a short bark. "Not much to tell. They've been out there, what, two days? Nobody's talking about anything. The CBC left, and I don't know what they'll file since Shirley and Fred's TV is out, so I can't even check. There's supposed to be someone from the *Halifax Herald* here, but I haven't seen him. Maybe he's been and gone, I don't know," he paused in case Pocket wanted to offer insight, then when nothing came, asked: "Doesn't anyone get the Halifax paper? I haven't seen one since I've been here."

"Not enough people here to warrant sendin 'em, I guess. People generally get 'em in Yarmouth if they get 'em at all."

Rodney shook his head. "People don't care about the news?"

"Well, my mum sure does. Listens to the news on CBC every night. Or did, anyways."

Rodney resolved to get to a radio or a television, but of course, none of this helped him find out if there was print coverage anywhere. But how could there be? Except for the CBC, he seemed to be the only one here.

"I talked to someone from my office," Rodney said,

"and she said to file something, anything, so I just spent the last two hours writing up an article about—well, about nothing. But I wrote it." He paused, and Pocket could sense there was more.

"And?"

"And I then called the office again. I figured I'd better check in with the boss before dictating the story. But he's out. There's some scandal at Parliament Hill. So I talked to an assistant, not even a name I knew, must've just got hired. Funny, that was my co-worker's job, she must've been given something else. The message the new assistant gave me was not to bother. *Not to bother.* She read my boss's message out loud. I guess he'd tried to call me, but he must've called the house, and nobody was there."

In an unconscious parody of Pocket a few minutes earlier, Rodney scratched his head, eyes screwed shut, surprised at the satisfaction it gave. He didn't feel any better about the story, but any measure of physical touch—even his own—was good right now. He smoothed his hair and went on.

"He said not to bother, unless I interviewed an actual alien. No little green men, no story."

"That's too bad."

"Gets worse. He said he needed me back for research. He wants all the background dirt on certain politicians. Research. That's a demotion. I don't always get it," he told Pocket, shaking his head, "but it's pretty plain to me. Writing's on the wall."

"Better than in the garbage," Pocket offered.

"Not much." Rodney rubbed both hands over his face.

For a moment, Pocket had forgotten about his mother. His heart lifted with the distraction, and he felt profoundly grateful to Rodney for the relief in even those brief moments. "I got something to show you," he began.

They were interrupted by the swinging open of the front door, Wanda's head poking out.

"Pocket? Your mother's awake. She's asking for you."

After Pocket went in, Rodney and Wanda sat in silence on the front step for some time, Shirley's casserole beside them, before Rodney remembered the book in his pocket.

"Thank you," she said, settling the book on her knees. "I haven't quite finished reading it."

"It was interesting about the Bible stuff," Rodney ventured. "I mean, you could take that stuff that way, if you wanted to."

"You read it?"

"Well, bits of it. I mean, just out of journalistic curiosity."

"Uh huh." Wanda smiled at Rodney sideways.

Rodney looked over his shoulder towards the door. "How is she?"

"She's getting ready to make the journey," Wanda said.

"You know this because...?"

"Honestly, Rod, it doesn't take a psychic." Wanda turned back towards the book. "The question is, what will Merle see when she arrives? Will she understand what the rest of us struggle to understand? Will everything become clear?"

"I'd go for anything being halfway clear right about now."

"You know, human beings have always explained unexplainable things using religion. Like Moses and the burning bush, or God appearing in a pillar of cloud, or the appearance of angels. Do you believe in God?"

"I don't know," Rodney answered honestly. "Do you?"

Wanda didn't answer, but instead opened the book on her lap. "Did you read the chapter on the Nazca lines?"

Rodney shook his head.

"Enormous geoglyphs in Peru. Massive drawings made by removing rocks, created around the same time Jesus was supposed to have been alive. Some are geometric designs, but there are also monkeys, spiders, hummingbirds…hundreds of feet wide. Some archeologists think they were prayers to the Gods, but there's a researcher in Switzerland with a pretty good argument for spaceship navigation."

"What, aliens made them?"

"No, probably people. But they were told to do it by aliens. Like the pyramids, or the Easter Island heads."

Rodney shook his head.

"Huge things. Why would people build them, over great periods of time, if there wasn't a good reason for it?"

"I don't know," Rodney said. "Seems like an awful lot of people believing the wrong thing if it's not God. If it's really just all about space aliens."

"Maybe," Wanda swivelled to look at Rodney full on. "Maybe it's just what they want us to believe."

A car drove by, and Rodney recognized Cuff Dodds behind the wheel. Music blared from the open window, and he winced. It seemed disrespectful, such sharp contrast to the quiet drama within the house.

"Life goes on," Wanda commented.

There was no more traffic, and Rodney took in the remarkable quiet compared to his room near the ByWard Market. The walk-up apartment, surrounded as it was with sounds of vehicles, sirens, and shouts from the street, as well as the noises and cooking smells that came through the walls, seemed a long way away, now. Another world. He inhaled the dryleaf smell of the air mingled with Wanda's patchouli, and the savoury scent of Shirley's casserole as it cooled.

"What do you do?" Rodney asked. "I mean, for a living?"

"You mean, do I make my living as a psychic?"

"Do you?"

Wanda smiled, a little sadly, Rodney thought. "Partly," she said. "Partly, I clean houses. And look after old people."

Rodney considered this.

"It helps, actually," Wanda told him. "Being able to see what might happen to people."

"Can you see—" Rodney paused, embarrassed.

"Can I see what? Cuff Dodds heading for Debbie Morton's?"

"Who's Debbie Morton?"

"Ernie Morton's sister. But I'm just teasing." Wanda gave Rodney a playful bump on his shoulder with her own. "You want to know if I can see what's going to happen to you."

Rodney didn't answer, but his look was clear.

"Yes," Wanda said finally. "Yes, I can."

6 "So?" Shirley leaned on the counter as Rodney entered the store. "How is she?"

"I didn't go in. I don't really know."

"Well, ya missed the rush."

Rodney looked around the empty store. The tables were clean, but he could see the sink in the corner was full of soapy water, coffee cups draining alongside.

"Most a the men been out duckin, seems like. Those jokers out there in the Sound, and the wharf closed, I guess they gotta have somethin to keep 'em occupied. They're treatin the whole thing like some sorta holiday, now, which I s'pose is better than sittin around grumblin. They were right full of their stories, I'll tell ya, about all their great shots. Been drinkin some too, I'd say, came in to sober up before headin home." Shirley laughed. "Not that they'll be foolin anyone."

"Fred back, yet?"

"There's the funny thing. Thought he went to Yarmouth, you recall? Seems he ran into Tip on the way to the truck, went duckin instead! I was some mad I'll tell ya. I got plenty around here for him to do. He got two ducks and guess who'll be getting 'em ready? I told Fred he could deal with the things. Get 'em plucked and ready, maybe I'll cook 'em if the mood strikes me."

Shirley sat back in her chair. Her voice grew serious. "Since they left, I've been thinking about Merle. I want things to be real nice for her—after. The pastor will look after the service, but it's the ladies of Perry's Harbour who'll take care of the afterwards. It's not easy to think about, but there it is, and plannin a funeral's a blessing in a way. People think funerals are for the dead, but the thing is, they're really there for the livin. For the ones left behind. To come together, like. And to make everyone busy, kinda gets y'over the hump. But oh, there'll be a lot who'll want to be there. For the family, sure, but also to remember Merle."

"So you're not holding out for a miracle."

"Just the fact of Merle, here on this earth with the rest of us for as long as she has been, is miracle enough. Now the Lord wants her, and I can't say's I blame him."

"You believe she's going to heaven, then. That she's been called by—by God."

"I do."

Fred came in, then. With him came the chill of the evening. Behind him, Rodney could see a wash of lilac in a deepening sky.

"All naked, and pretty, too," he told Shirley. He looked at Rodney. "Ducks, I mean. Ya been down to the wharf?"

Rodney looked at the clock. It was past four o'clock. "We've been talking," he said.

"They didn't come in at all, looks like they're stayin out. Not that it woulda helped. They're still not talking to anyone. Turf was down this mornin, tryin to get some information about when they'll open up the wharf again. He was right roiled, I'll tell ya. So's everyone."

"Don't s'pose there's a newspaper story in that?" Shirley asked.

Fred snorted. "Nobody cares if a buncha Nova Scotia

fisherman got work, do they? S'been what, now, four days?"

"Actually, they do. Or they should. Even if I can't get information, there's a story in the fact that they're not talking."

"There ya go, then," Shirley told him, pushing herself up from the table. She patted him on the shoulder. "Now, I suppose I got some ducks to see to."

Cuff Dodds found Pocket Snow sitting at his usual spot at the end of the wharf. First, he'd tried to find Ernie. He couldn't explain it, but he didn't want to be alone, the presence of the thing in his car weighing on him. He had resisted the urge to unwrap it and look at it again, the feeling of uneasiness outweighing the curiosity he felt.

It pissed him off that Ernie had taken off after the incident at the store, and now he had the uneasy feeling that he'd told Ernie too much. Sure, he'd known Ernie since they were in diapers, but Ernie had been different lately. Cuff realized he wasn't sure if he could trust his friend— all the more reason to find him. But Ernie was not at home, and Debbie couldn't tell him where Ernie was. Which was okay, after all: Debbie had been cool towards him, but he knew she liked him, so he took the opportunity. "Ya come with me t'the Legion Sat'day night, I'll show you a good time," he'd said to her, and she'd gone inside, then, but not before she'd given him a look that could only mean yes. He was sure of it.

From there he'd been going to find the reporter when he saw Pocket. The truth was, Cuff wasn't altogether sure that talking to the reporter was the way to go. Maybe he should call the Navy or something, or—what was it called?—National Defence. He could place a call to someone in the morning, soon as he figured out who. There had to be a lot more potential than just in some dumb paper, and the reporter didn't look like the kind of guy with the clout to offer up any kind of money. He had to figure out a way to sell the thing he'd taken from the diving vessel. He parked the car on the gravel shoulder and sat for a minute watching the figure that was Pocket before getting out.

Pocket didn't turn around as Cuff approached and stood for a moment behind him, then eased himself onto the same bollard Wilf had sat on the day before.

"Hi," Cuff said. He took his pack of cigarettes from his pocket, extracted one of the two remaining, and lit it, blowing the smoke away from Pocket, who gazed across the Sound. On Pocket's knee was his battered sketchbook, closed.

"Hi," Pocket replied after a moment.

Cuff sat, not knowing what to say next. He'd been surprised at Pocket's words earlier, surprised into silence, his usual ready retort momentarily paralyzed. The conflicting emotions he'd felt were unfamiliar feelings, small, gnawing things he couldn't quite get a grip on. He couldn't say why he felt drawn to Pocket, but it must, he figured, have something to do with the scene at the store.

"Ya drawin?"

"Nope."

"Can I see?" Cuff reached for the sketchbook, but Pocket tucked it back in his jacket. "Didn't wanna see yer stupid drawings anyways," he said, and immediately regretted it. After a beat, he tried for a more conversational tone. "Water's flatass calm today," he ventured.

"Uh huh."

"Y'think they'll find something?"

Pocket, his eyes fixed firmly on the water, said nothing. Maybe he should talk to the reporter after all, Cuff thought to himself. He'd hint at what he found, feel him out. The guy must have *some* connections. It would take some finessing, but Cuff was confident he could pull it off. He felt like a double agent, selling Russian secrets.

"Seen that reporter guy around?"

"Uh huh."

Suddenly irritated by Pocket's monosyllabic answers, "Ya got more than two words inside that stupid head a yours?" he snapped, the habit of abuse too comfortable a groove.

"What do you want?" Pocket asked, turning.

Cuff looked for even the slightest edge of challenge in the question and found none. It was a question, nothing more or less. What he really wanted, he realized, was to ask Pocket what he should do, and this surprised him. He lit the last cigarette and tossed the package into the water, then began carefully, weighing his words.

"If ya found something," he began, "something of interest—"

Pocket startled. "Whaddaya mean?"

In the face of Pocket's sudden intensity, Cuff back-pedalled. "Nothin. I don't mean nothing. Just if ya did, that's all. Ferget it."

Cuff inhaled deeply, shaking his head. "Ferget it," he

said again, exhaling. The smoke hung suspended in the calm, cold air.

"How's yer mum?" he said after a while.

"Dyin," Pocket told him. As he said it, he knew it to be true, whatever miracles he'd been hoping for. The words hung between them like the smoke, almost tangible.

"Oh. Right. Sorry 'bout that." He offered Pocket a drag from his cigarette, but Pocket shook his head.

"I better go back."

Cuff nodded. "I'm goin yer way. Ya wanna lift?"

Pocket shook his head again. Cuff watched as he walked the length of the wharf, a lonely stick figure against a deepening sky.

In the car, it took Cuff a moment to realize what was different. He put his key into the ignition and jiggled it into place. You could probably start the thing with a screwdriver, he figured, but there was no danger of anyone stealing the car around here. You couldn't get far before someone would recognize it. That's when he realized what had changed: his eyes weren't watering. At first, he'd dismissed the tears as something unrelated. Later, it had occurred to him that the thing he'd taken somehow caused his eyes to water, something like the hay fever he got in the spring. Now, the thing under the seat appeared to be having no effect. He must be getting used to it, he reasoned, or whatever it was he was allergic to was wearing off.

He paused, hand on the gearshift. Maybe he should take another look at it before he went to find the reporter. It was already becoming indistinct in his memory; it was such a small thing, after all, no bigger than his palm. When he'd looked at it last he'd imagined that its lustre had faded, then convinced himself he was wrong.

Of course he was wrong. He'd find the reporter and arrange a meeting as soon as possible. He might not pay for hearsay, but this was solid evidence: there'd be no denying its value. He put the car in gear.

7 It was evening, after dinner, when a knock at the door interrupted the quiet. Wanda and Scratch sat in the two wingback chairs that had been pushed away to make room for Merle's bed, their placement oddly domestic in the scene. Wilf, who had spent an hour in the workshop, had come in and was paused beside the bed in which Merle slept. Pocket was upstairs, but had heard footfalls on the walk and was halfway down the stairs when a second knock sounded. This time, the door opened immediately.

"Tried to call," Turf said, his head inside. "Ya got yer phone off the hook or somethin?"

They all looked at the phone handle, which had been knocked from its cradle.

"What's goin on, Turf?" Scratch asked.

"Big meetin at the store. What to do about the wharf bein closed. People want to know when they can go out. Not many's able to lose days out, and there's no telling when it'll open. Least, nobody's tellin us anything. S'pose that's the worst part."

"When? Now?" Wilf was already reaching for his coat by the back door. "Scratch, you comin?"

"I'm not fishin anyways," Scratch began. "What're you thinking, Wilf? There's Merle—"

"Wilf, everyone's gonna understand if you don't come. Just, Tip thought you folks should know, that's all."

"It's just—" Wilf began. "She's sleepin peaceful."

"You go," Wanda said. "We all need a break sometime. Pocket and I will stay. Merle's been doing well today. Wilf could use your company, I think, Scratch."

Scratch looked at Wilf, then at Wanda and Pocket. "Arright," he said. "S'pose it can't hurt. Won't be gone long. You'll call if there's anything—"

After a short flurry of boots and coats the door closed, pushing a final blast of cold air into the house.

"You go sit with your mother," Wanda told Pocket. "I'll clean up in the kitchen."

Pocket sat, watching his mother sleep, listening to Wanda as she put things to rights in the next room. His hands lay on his knees, his breathing slow, his own body a mimic of his mother's in its stillness. He wished she'd wake up and talk to him. He gazed at her hands folded on the blanket and tried to list in his mind all of the things those hands had done. He could remember watching, when he was small, his mother making sandwiches for a picnic on Kettle Island, spreading peanut butter, cutting on the diagonal because that's how he liked it best, and then, later, her hands gripping the oars of the dory. He would sit on her lap sometimes, her hands over his as she taught him to row.

One fall, his mother had put up fifty-seven quarts of tomatoes. He could remember the scene, her hands on her hips as she surveyed the fruit of her labours, the jars lined up on the kitchen table illuminated in the afternoon light. As he'd come into the kitchen she'd held her hands palm out as if to say: *Look. Aren't we lucky?*

He thought about his mother's hand resting reassuringly on his back when he threw up with the stomach bug that had been going around school, remembered the comfort in that touch. He imagined her hands adjusting his collar as they'd done so many times, before school or on Sundays before church. He could see them, clear as day, shuffling a deck of cards and dealing, fanning them, deftly slipping out two for the crib. He remembered the way, when her peg would land in the winning hole, his mother would clap both hands together under her chin, grinning.

The television hadn't been on in days. Pocket crossed the room to where the console stood in the corner and turned the knob. There was a beat during which the screen remained black, Pocket listening as the tubes sparked to life inside. The picture began with a white horizontal line before expanding into an image of television personality Fred Davis. Pocket turned the sound down, but not off. His mother, a lover of current events, adored *Front Page Challenge*. She thought the moderator was "a lovely lookin' man," as was panelist Pierre Berton, but she didn't like his know-it-all attitude. Gordon Sinclair she liked because "you can always trust a man without a chin." But her hero was Betty Kennedy, who she said was "some smart, but still a lady." Mostly, Merle loved to tell the panelists what questions to ask the mystery guest, the identity of which was known to the audience, who received a clip of the news story in question at the beginning of the show. Once the panel, by asking yes or no questions, had guessed or given up, an interview ensued, and Merle would rock in her chair, hands gripping the arms as she leaned forward, fascinated.

"Is it a happy story?" Betty Kennedy was asking now, and Pocket hoped that his sleeping mother could hear it, and was inwardly approving. It's the sort of question his mother would have asked. Pocket had always believed his mother should have been on the show; she would have asked all the right questions.

Pocket reached over and turned down the sound. For a while, he listened to the diminished voices of the panelists as they attempted to extract the newsmaker's identity. He could hear Wanda singing in the yellow kitchen. It is a happy colour, he thought, echoing his Uncle Scratch and Betty Kennedy. The lilting song, its words indiscernible, wafted into the living room. The song stopped, and Wanda appeared in the doorway, wiping her hands on a towel.

"How is she?"

"She's good, I think. She's sleepin peaceful, anyways."

Wanda crossed the room and looked at Merle where she slept, mouth slightly ajar. "She looks like she's got some colour," Wanda said.

At this, Merle stirred and opened her eyes. On the television, the theme music signalling the end of *Front Page Challenge* began.

"Turn that up, wouldja, Pocket?" Merle said, turning her head towards the sound. "That's my show, innit?"

"S'over," Pocket told his mother. "You been asleep. You wanna watch something?"

"No. No, let's talk," she told him. Pocket reached over

and turned the television off. "Help me sit up. My Lord, what a good sleep I had. Pocket, push the commode over, wouldja? And then go away, I can do this on my own, I don't need ya."

"I'll help you," Wanda offered, but Merle looked at her and shook her head.

"Let Wanda help, Mum," Pocket said. "What if ya fall again?"

"I won't. Promise. I feel stronger. Maybe because I had such a good sleep. Besides, I just slipped a little is all. Don't know what all the fuss was about. No, really. Go on, now." She shooed them away with her hand.

In the kitchen, Wanda nodded at Pocket. "Dignity is important," she said, but Pocket fidgeted, ear cocked, until his mother called them back in.

"You go," Wanda said. "It's good for you two to spend some time. I'll be in here if you need me."

When Pocket pushed through the kitchen door, Merle was not lying in bed, as he expected, but sitting on its edge. He felt confused by this, at once alarmed and heartened. There was a glint in her eye that Pocket couldn't quite read. "Where is everybody?" she demanded. Her intake of breath after she spoke came with a wheezy gasp, and Pocket saw her close her lips against it.

"Meetin at the store," he said, watching her. "About the wharf bein closed on account of the Navy bein here, investigatin the UFO."

"They closed the wharf?"

"Yeah. Thought I said. Folks are gettin mad, that's why the meetin. Navy, Coast Guard, nobody's talkin. Won't tell us how long, even."

"I'd love to be a fly on the wall," mused Merle.

Pocket nodded. "Yeah. Bet them Navy guys' ears'll be burnin."

"Meltin, more like."

"You want me to help you get back into bed? Call Wanda?"

Merle shook her head. "Pocket, get me some clothes," she said.

"What?"

"There's no need to be repeatin myself."

"You wanna get dressed?"

"Yes, Son. I'm goin out."

"Mum—"

"Pocket, Son," she had said. Her grip was remarkably strong, a clutch of bones. "I'm feelin good right now, better than I have in days. I need yer help, though."

Wanda came through the kitchen door, then, and Pocket could see she had been listening. "Maybe it's time for a change," Wanda suggested. "You could sit in the wing chair for a while. I could make a pot of tea."

"A tea party, Mum," Pocket agreed, his voice sounding desperate to his own ears. The idea of walking in to the meeting with his mother—however they would get her there—the shock of those assembled and the anger of his father and uncle...the thought made his stomach sink.

But his mother's determined tone brought back memories. He'd heard that voice before: when she told him he would be going back to school after the flagpole incident, that when you hit a bump you just had to climb over it, that's all; or when she told his father that her time alone on the water was not negotiable. Pocket remembered his father's sheepish grin, the acquiescent shake of his head, when he admitted to his son: "Yer mother ain't one to demand much, and Lord knows she puts up with enough from me. Least I can do is listen when she means business."

"No," she said now, looking from one to the other. "No, I'm goin out."

"It may just be the morphine," Wanda said. "Just enough still working to make you feel stronger."

Merle's lips were set. "You can help me or not, it's up to you."

"She means it," Pocket said.

Wanda and Merle exchanged a look that lasted several beats, while Pocket looked from one to the other. Wanda surprised them both. "She deserves it," she said, finally. "She deserves to do what she wants to do."

Pocket followed his mother's direction as he retrieved clothes from his parents' room: the heavy pants his mother used to wear when she'd row out on the Sound, the knitted sweater. He had never before opened her underwear drawer, but he took out her things quickly without thinking too much. When he brought her clothes she shooed him off again and he stayed in the kitchen for what seemed like far too long listening to the movement of fabric and the soft grunts of her laboured breathing, quiet direction exchanged with Wanda. He could not stop his heart from pounding.

When they called him back in, she was lying down, angled on top of the bed, exhausted.

"Look—" he began. He was going to tell his mother that he would not help with this, with whatever it was

she wanted him to do. He looked at Wanda, and his con-
viction faltered. His voice, when it emerged, was almost
pleading. "I been thinkin in the kitchen. What about we
wait 'til Dad and Uncle Scratch get back, maybe in the
morning we could all go down to Crosbey's if yer feelin
so much better, you could get out some—"

He looked at Wanda, who shrugged in a manner
Pocket felt was un-Wanda-like, as if she, too, was uncom-
fortable with all of this. But: "It's what your mother wants,
Pocket," she told him. "It's what we should give her."

Merle interrupted him. "My kitchen! All that bangin.
Almost fergot 'til you mentioned it just now. I want to
see what's been goin on."

"Oh, Mum." There were still dishes stacked everywhere. "Maybe in a few days."

"Wouldja get my boots, dear?" Merle's breathing was
laboured, but her eyes were bright.

"D'ya wanta rest?" Pocket asked her once the boots
were on her feet. His hands still held the shape of her
small ankles.

"No, I'm feelin better, I was just restin for a minute,
that's all. Now, I'll see my kitchen, then we'll go."

Merle stood at the kitchen door, Pocket behind her,
while Wanda turned on the overhead light.

"My," she said, when the room was illuminated.

"He's buildin cupboards, Mum," Pocket said, his
voice a croak. He cleared his throat. "He's buildin the
cupboards you wanted. T'was s'posed to be a surprise.
It's a bit of a mess, innit?"

"It's wonderful," she said. She took a step towards the
kitchen table and Wanda reached out to cup her elbow,

but Merle steadied herself with the back of a chair, bony knuckles white against the painted wood. She took one hand and ran it across the plate on the top of a stack that had been placed on the chair. One of her coveted plates, its wrapping had fallen open. "My mother's," she said. "Spode. When the pattern first come out, musta been before the first war, my grandmother fell in love with it. Started collectin it for my mother's trousseau. Now let me think, my mother was born in 1901, so she'd have been nine or ten when her own mother bought the first piece. It says something, don't it? That my grandmother could imagine the time when my mother would be a young woman. 'Course, she never 'magined her comin all the way here." Merle's voice was wistful. "Maritime Rose. Funny when ya think on it, innit? That she wanted the pattern for her daughter, and then my mother met my father at the end of the war and of all places she'd end up, it'd be here?"

It was a long speech for Merle, and Wanda and Pocket had listened, rapt. Wanda spoke quietly. "It's prophetic."

"It's some spooky, anyways. And lovely, too. An' now here I am with 'em, and no daughter for 'em. Ye'll make sure yer wife gets 'em, wontcha, Pocket."

"S'pose, Mum," Pocket said, blushing.

Merle ran her hand over the plate, stroking the raised flower pattern on its edge as if petting a small animal. Pocket followed the movement, mesmerized.

"'Course, most of what my mother brought with her from England didn't survive the trip. And then Dad started buyin her a piece a year, but we lost some of that in some hurricane or other—in 'forty, I think it was. After

Mum moved back, after Dad died, yer father took to buyin me a piece a year, when he could. And then a bunch more pieces broke durin Hurricane Ginny a few years back. Ya get a good blow on, this house always shakes somethin awful." She looked around the wreck of the kitchen. "Won't be losin anymore, now I'm gettin cupboards."

"Nope," Pocket told her.

"Funny, we're always losin and gainin, losin and gainin. You make sure you buy yer wife a piece every year, wontcha Pocket?"

"I don't have a wife, Mum," he said, but his mother turned to him, her wistful tone absent when she spoke again.

"Now, we'd best be goin right quick, now, if we're gonna go at all," she said. "Get the wheelbarrow, you can line it with a blanket an we'll be good t'go."

"A wheelbarrow? We're goin to the meetin with you in a wheelbarrow?"

"Oh, it's not the meetin I want to go to. Yer goin to take me out on the Sound."

"What?" Pocket looked at Wanda again, who was regarding Merle.

"I want to see what's happening out there. See for myself. It's not every day a flyin saucer crashes into Perry's Harbour, now is it?" She turned to Wanda, who stood slightly behind where she still sat on the bed. "I want to go out," she repeated.

"To see where the UFO went down?" Pocket's voice was incredulous.

"I think," Wanda said slowly, "I think it's more about

the water. All those dreams about the water. Is that why, Merle?"

"I want to go out," Merle said again, and Pocket heard his own desperation echoed there. The words wrapped themselves inside Pocket's chest and coiled there.

"They'll be gone a bit, yet," he offered, looking at Wanda. "We'd haveta hurry, though." Even as he said the words he wanted to take them back.

"But in the wheelbarrow?" Wanda asked.

"You don't think I'm gonna walk all the way down there myself, do ya?" Merle replied.

Out by the woodpile, Pocket paused, mittened hands on the metal handles of the wheelbarrow. He couldn't believe they were *doing* this. But neither could he see himself going back in, telling his mother this would not be happening. He gripped the handles tighter, resolved, and pushed the barrow towards the kitchen door, then changed his mind and pushed it around to the front. Merle always insisted on using the front door, after all, and he didn't think she'd be changing her ways now.

To Pocket's surprise, Merle walked to the front door on her own power, one thin hand holding walls and doorframes for support, Wanda close behind her. Pocket helped her into her coat, and while she pulled a toque over her head, said, "Wait a minute, Mum." He ran up the stairs two at a time to retrieve the old quilt from his bed. When he returned she was sitting on the stairs, eyes closed.

"Does it hurt?" Wanda was asking, but Merle shook her head.

"Just catchin my breath is all," she said, and to Pocket it was a voice shot with holes.

"You can go back to bed," he said. "We don't haveta."

"Yes," she said, "we do."

When they pushed off, Merle sat in the wheelbarrow wrapped in her winter coat and Pocket's quilt. She faced Pocket, her back in the wheelbarrow's pointed end, feet tucked up in the square end. Pocket, who had often bemoaned the size of the large wheelbarrow when it was full of split firewood, could see how it fit his mother's own diminished size perfectly. She clasped each side in a mittened hand, her sparse hair beneath the toque sticking out in wild directions. Pocket could see every cord of her thin neck above the folds of the quilt, but her eyes shone. She looked, in the light cast by the window with the starry sky all around her, like a young girl.

"Dad'll kill me," Pocket said.

"He won't know. Shush. Push me. I think we better hurry, now, don't you?"

They each took a handle, and Wanda whispered to Pocket: "Are you okay?" Pocket shook his head. There was no answer for that. "It'll be all right," Wanda told him. "It's supposed to happen like this." Her voice, to Pocket, sounded less sure than it had earlier.

At the shore end of the wharf, Pocket stopped and looked at the *Merlaine II* where she bobbed in the dim light cast by the Moss Plant. He heard the creak of the Cape Islander in her berth, the squeak and groan against the wharf's sides reproachful.

"S'a beautiful boat, innit?" Merle said, and Pocket, to his surprise, saw it for the first time basked in the glow of his mother's words. "How I loved goin out. Felt like the water was rockin me, keepin me safe. Funny, considerin."

"Considerin what?" Pocket asked, resuming the push across the hard, packed ground.

"Used to go out with my dad. And before you was born, I used to go out with yer dad, too. Always thought, I'd been a man you'da been hard-pressed to keep me on shore." She cocked her head slightly as she looked at Pocket through the dark. "Never told no one that before. It'll be good to be on the boat again."

"Wharf's closed, remember?" he said.

"So it is," Merle agreed, her voice a hoarse whisper.

Wanda looked out across the Sound, as if momentarily transported elsewhere. "It's stronger than it's ever been," she murmered. "The signal."

Pocket glanced at Wanda, then looked at his mother folded in the wheelbarrow, a bundle of twigs wrapped in blankets. The glint in her eye seemed brighter, somehow. "And anyways," he said, "I'm useless in a boat. Dad says so."

"He said that?"

"He did."

"Well, we can't prove 'im otherwise, I s'pose, and we ain't goin back, now," Merle said, as if mustering energy by force of will. "Where's the dory?"

8 At Crosbey's store the air was thick with smoke and words. Some forty men and women were gathered, sitting on chairs, boxes; some standing, leaning on coolers and shelves. Shirley, sitting on the counter beside the till, had never seen so many people in the store at one time. When Wilf and Scratch had come in, among the last, Shirley had leaned close. "I'm surprised to see you two. How is Merle?"

"Wanda and Pocket are there, an' she's sleepin peaceful. Thanks fer askin, Shirley. That Wanda's a godsend, true enough. Dunno where we'd be without her."

"Hmmph," Shirley had said. "She's only been here a coupla days. Worked her way in some good, ain't she?"

But Stanley was standing towards the front, addressing the room. "They're tellin us nothin," Stanley said. "We got our rights."

"They can't deny us earnin a livin," agreed Tip. "What, they think we're gonna scare away the aliens or something?"

"I asked Charlie Brannen to come," said Turf. "Ya'd think the Mountie's'd have somethin to say. Where is he?"

"Oh, shit, I was s'posed to tell ya, sorry. I was in there, springin Danny from the tank—" There was laughter throughout the store. "He said they'd be sendin someone around to talk to us. A 'dedicated spokesperson.' *Next week*, he said."

269

"Next *week*?" Neil was furious. "We already lost four days!"

Discussion ensued as those assembled compared general inconvenience and lost incomes. But the prevailing attitude was outrage at the heavy-handedness on the part of what Rodney said was really the Department of National Defence.

"It's coming down from Ottawa," he explained. "They won't talk to me, either."

"Who're you?" asked someone from the back.

"Reporter from Ottawa," Fred offered. "He's boardin with us. Thought everyone knew by now, Skid."

"Been up to Halifax all week," came the answer from the large man with a week's stubble. He waved a hand, which was missing a finger. "So what, they really are lookin for aliens?"

"That or the Russians. More likely the Russians, I 'magin," said Fred.

"I was countin on goin out Monday," said Skid. "Got a few debts racked up."

"I 'magin, you havin been up to Halifax all week. Whatcha been doin?" Turf, sitting beside Skid, elbowed him slightly.

"Never you mind."

"We all of us got debts. It's our right to go out. Closin the wharf makes no sense," Stanley told them, voice rising.

Tip Morton spoke up, then. "What if we all went out? All of us, at the same time? Can't go after just one of us if we all go."

"What if they start shootin at us? Like in Winnipeg,

or what was that one up in Ontario a few years ago?" said Skid.

"We're not strikin,' Neil weighed in. "We're anti-strikin. We just wanna work."

"Okay. So Monday, then, we go. All of us, meet here at 7 a.m.," said Skid. "Okay, Shirley?"

"S'pose you'll want coffee," said Shirley, eyes rolling.

Skid looked at Rodney. "And you'll be there, wontcha, Mister Reporter-from-Ottawa."

"Wouldn't miss it," returned Rodney. In his mind the headlines, at last, were forming.

Wanda pushed Merle in the wheelbarrow while Pocket ran down the shore to the sheds where his father had the dory pulled up high on the pebble beach. He could see his breath and he focused on that, and on keeping his balance on the slick shore rocks. The dory was heavy and hard to flip onto its bottom, his boots sliding with the effort. The oars were leaned against the outside of the shed. As he dragged the boat to the water and fitted the oars into the oarlocks, he felt like he'd been gone a very long time. The short pull, dragging against rock and water, to where his mother waited at the sandy edge of the water beside the wharf seemed to take forever.

Wanda and Pocket helped Merle into the boat, "You was pulling some hard, there, like you was racin to the finish line, Pocket," Merle said between breaths. "Who said you was useless in a boat?"

Pocket took the quilt from the wheelbarrow and wrapped it around her shoulders.

"We'll just go out an come back, okay, Mum?" Pocket

pushed the dory, rubber boots slipping in the sand. He turned to Wanda. "I'll just show her where, and then we'll come back," he said again. "We'll be right quick." He looked in the direction of the store. He could not keep the nervousness from his voice. Once they were adrift he climbed in, trying to keep the icy sea water from his mother's legs.

"I'll be here," Wanda said to them both. "I'll be waiting."

Merle reached over and placed her hand on his knee. "Thank you, Son," she said.

It was calm on the water, and cold. The harbour beneath them was so black it seemed to absorb the light from around them, while above the sky was awash in stars. Pocket's mother sat straight, quilt around her, hands gripping the seat for stability, while Pocket rowed. Looking back he could make out, on the shore, the dark figure of Wanda, arms outstretched. He hoped she would, also, get what she wanted.

"There's the boats. The Coast Guard, RCMP and the Navy," he said, pointing. "They been comin in at night, but looks like tonight they're stayin out for some reason." He kept his voice low, imagining his words snaking across the water's surface to be picked up by the three huddled vessels.

"I can see 'em." She held a mitten up flat, and Pocket stopped rowing. "Where'd it go down?"

"Right thereabouts," Pocket told her. "They're sittin on it, more or less."

"Shoulda drifted, though. There's a current. Take me a little closer."

"Don't wanna be seen, Mum."

"Just a little closer, Pocket."

After a few more minutes of rowing, Pocket rested the oars on the gunwales. He had been sweating, and immediately began to chill. He looked closely at his mother, but she appeared warm enough. Instead of looking at the boats as he'd expected, she was looking at the sky.

"Beautiful. Stars always seem bigger this time a year, don't they? Can't say why that is. Ya get a night like this, so calm you could hear a star whisper just before it falls…. It's like the whole world's holding its breath. Takes yer own breath away, don't it?"

Pocket tilted his head back, felt the breadth and depth of space. When he brought it back down, a little dizzy, his mother, mittens on the gunwales for support, was looking into the water. Pocket could see points of light reflected there, and for a moment he imagined that the night sky and the sea were one continuous entity.

"'Magin, something down there," she said. She looked at Pocket, smiling slightly.

"Maybe."

"They been divin, you say?"

"Uh huh. Wonder how deep it is right here." Pocket knew he was humouring his mother, and then felt bad for that. He looked back at the shore. He could see Wanda and then, farther along, the light spilling out from the back windows of Crosbey's.

"Need a sounding line to tell. Yer grandfather used one."

Pocket knew his grandfather had died in a fishing mishap before he was born. It was funny, his mother had never really talked about it. He wasn't sure, sitting here now, why she hadn't or even how he knew, and yet there were some things you knew not to ask.

"You seen 'em, aintcha, Pocket? Sounding lines?"

Pocket nodded. He'd seen the older men uncoiling the long rope, its fathoms marked off, a lead weight at the end. They both looked over the boat's side now, Pocket thinking about the water beneath them, the distance to the bottom.

"That's how—" Merle said, voice so low Pocket almost missed her words.

"How what?"

"How he died. Foot tangled." Pocket let the truth of this settle on him.

Around them, and against the sides of the dory, the water lapped.

"Yer grandfather would put some grease on the weight, so he could tell what the bottom was like, sandy or what," she continued. "So he could be where he knew the fish would want to be."

Pocket imagined a sounding line, its weight descending. Merle began coughing, a dry sound that went on too long. Pocket gripped the oars, ready to get off the water, get his mother home safe into bed, but she continued, and he paused.

"You're named for him. John. You know that, dontcha?" Merle told him. Pocket did, but he let the weight of her words pull him under for a moment. "It's strange, innit?" she continued. "How much I love the water, considerin. It gives and takes, don't it? It's part of us, I s'pose." She continued to look over the side, hands gripping the gunwhales for balance. "It's the size of it. So big, so deep, ya can't fathom it, can you? The way ya can't fathom God, least I can't. So big a notion it just don't fit in your head. But the sea, you can reach down and touch it."

She did, then, reach down, and Pocket experienced a leap in his heart as he imagined his mother tipping out to be swallowed up by the black water.

"Cold," she said, smiling slightly, as she withdrew her hand. Pocket could see droplets of water sparkling in a light he couldn't source.

Pocket looked down. For him, the sea had always been an alien thing.

"It's not fer you, though," she said as if she could tell his thoughts. "I could tell it weren't. D'you know, I'd just found out I'd be havin a baby when it happened." It took Pocket a moment to realize she was talking about his grandfather, the accident with the sounding line. "I hadn't told anyone yet, not even yer father. I wished I'd a got to tell yer grandfather."

Pocket looked at his mother. On the shore, he heard a door open and close, voices.

"S'pose he knows, wherever he is," she said, looking at the water. She raised her head and looked at Pocket. "Yer dad would like you to go out with him. He'd like to pass his licence on to you someday."

"I know."

"Ya don't have to. There's no shame in knowin it's not for you."

Pocket looked across the sound, and the lights of the vessels squatting on the water.

"He'll come to see that, if he hasn't done already. You need to do what you love, Pocket. There's a letter—"

From the shore they heard the sound of a distant door opening, laughter escaping, the sound skating across the water. Pocket gripped the oars again. "We better go back," he said.

"The ocean floor's like the land," Merle continued as if Pocket hadn't spoken. "Mountains and valleys. Nobody really knows how far down is all the way." She looked up at the dome of stars. "Just like no one really knows what's up there." Beneath them, the boat gently rocked. "Some are afraid of it, but I never was, not even with all the souls it's taken." Pocket could see his mother's eyes shining in the dark. "Such a beautiful night," she said. "I could die out here."

Her words fell into the air between them.

"We gotta go back now." Pocket began to row, putting everything he had into the pull. It was difficult to see his mother, where she sat facing him and so close their knees almost touched, through the water in his eyes.

As they neared the shore, "Did they ever find Grandad's body?" he asked her. He wasn't sure if he should, and when she didn't answer at first he wasn't even sure she'd heard him, and was relieved. But after a moment, she spoke.

"They didn't," she said, and in Pocket's mind, the sounding line went down, endlessly. He tried, but he couldn't see it touch bottom.

They did not speak again. Wanda was waiting for them when they felt the scrape of wood against rock. She looked both anxious and, to Pocket, oddly animated.

"Are you all right?" Wanda asked Merle.

Merle, whose eyes had been closed, opened them. "Just a—just a little tired," she said. She looked back at the water as Pocket lifted her, astonished again at how light she was, and placed her gently in the wheelbarrow. With his ear close to her mouth as he settled her, he could hear her breathing, the airy rattle in each short breath.

"You're a good boy, Pocket," she said.

Pocket heard voices, a man's and a woman's, but then heard nothing further. He hoped the meeting was still in progress. It was harder pushing the wheelbarrow up the incline towards the road. He could hear Wanda's quiet grunts with the effort. When they hit a bump, soft cries of distress came from the bundle in the wheelbarrow.

"Maybe I was wrong," Wanda said under her breath. "Maybe this *was* too crazy."

"No," Pocket told her. He caught her eyes in the darkness. "It was good."

They reached the paved road and pushed across it, panting. There had been no more traffic, to Pocket's relief. The sounds he'd heard must have been someone leaving early, that's all.

"We just need to get her into bed," Pocket said. He imagined her there, sleeping peacefully as if all of this had never happened. They were on the path to the house, now, a slight downward slope. Pocket thought he saw, for an instant, a shadow slip around the side of the house ahead of them, and his skin prickled. He shook it off; nothing. A little farther and they would be home.

Wanda took one hand from the wheelbarrow handle

and laid it gently on Merle's shoulder. Merle extracted her own from the blanket's folds and patted it once.

"Thank you, dear," she said, her voice almost inaudible.

"I should thank you," replied Wanda. "I believe I made contact, at last."

Getting Merle out of the wheelbarrow, into the house and into bed was the hardest thing Pocket had ever done. His mother's limbs were like those of a ragdoll. "Just plain tired out, I guess," she said. "My get up and go got up and went," she joked, but appeared not to have the energy to chuckle. Her eyes were heavy, and her face was pale.

"Aw, jeez, Mum," Pocket whimpered in spite of himself as he half carried her through the doorway. She weighed almost nothing, he thought. He was looking at her, lying across the bed still fully clothed, her boots dripping where they hung over the side, when he heard the door open. His panic quelled when he heard Wanda's voice, back from putting away the wheelbarrow. "She's fast asleep," he said, his voice sounding helpless.

"Well, we'd better hurry up and get her undressed," Wanda said. "I expect she'll sleep like the dead after all that." She laid a hand across her mouth, then, aware of her words, but Pocket hadn't noticed. Gently and without trace of awkwardness, he slipped the boot from his mother's foot.

By the time Wilf and Scratch came in fifteen minutes later, the wheelbarrow was back by the woodpile,

Wanda and Pocket were sipping tea, and Merle was tucked into bed and sleeping deeply. The dory, hastily pulled ashore some fifty feet from its normal spot, and with its oars left to float away with the next tide, would not be noticed for days.

Lou

If you were to drop a shiny penny into the water somewhere in the middle of the Sound—the day is fine, blue sky cloudless, water so bright you have to squint—it would waltz downwards in a dance of coppery light until you could see it no more, but you'd know it's there. You can imagine its journey, down a dozen metres to the sandy bottom, there to lie, as if slumbering, on a bed of kelp. Out of sight, it winks in your mind's eye. Find me, it says.

There are always things to find on the ocean floor, especially in a bay frequented by fishing boats, where odds and ends wash overboard daily. A wave could take your workgloves, the bait bag you'd set down for a moment, your thermos of hot tea. It's as if the sea reaches up and whispers: mine.

The sea claims what it will; flotsam of all description finds land on a full moon tide, embraces rock or sandy shore, holds on for a breathy respite as the water recedes, until claimed again when the waves return. Things lost sometime drift to the bottom and lie waiting, joined as time passes by new treasure, that left glove, or the penny tossed, Neptune's magpie collection.

There are bones, too, on the bottom of the sea. There is disarticulation of hand from wrist, knee from leg, prodded by currents and rock snags and things that swim in the sea. So it can be that a body isn't found by an idle seashell gatherer some low tide. It may never be found at all.

How deep is deep? How far the bottom? If you had a sound-ing line, how many fathoms might you count before the lead weight finds bottom, and you know the truth of depth?

In your pocket, there is a penny, warm from your hand where you've held it while the dory drifts, oars pulled from the water and resting on the gunwales. You take it out and look at it in your palm, turn it so the penny catches the light. You can feel the pull of the sea, now: mine.

Above, the sun; below, dark. Not yet, you say. You put the penny back into your pocket, grasp the oars and begin the long pull towards home.

Monday, October 9

1 "It started sudden," Wilf said from Merle's bedside. It was just past seven o'clock in the morning. The blankets from the couch where he had been sleeping had slipped to the floor; he had knocked over a water glass. "It was the breathin that woke me up. Not loud or nothing, just—different."

Pocket, Scratch and Wanda, awakened by Wilf's cry, stood close. Merle didn't stir, and for a moment appeared as if she didn't breathe. She took several shallow breaths, followed by another long pause. Then a deep, shuddering breath, followed by two more. Wilf listened, then continued.

"Maybe it was the *not* breathin that woke me up, ya know? Then she started takin these deep breaths, like now. Then a bunch a little ones, close together. I can't wake her up." He looked imploringly at Wanda, who stood, the quilt from her bed wrapped around her, hair wild from sleep. "I can't wake her up," he said again.

Pocket stood in his pyjamas, not noticing the cold floor under his bare feet. Scratch was dressed only in a pair of longjohns, a mat of greying fur crawling up from their tops.

"She's in another world," Wanda said quietly. "I saw it in my aunt Ruby."

"Cindy Morton said she'd be by first thing," Scratch said. Scratch's eyes were on Merle's face. "Funny, she asked about Merle's breathin. Said to listen for—what did she say? Sounded like chain stokin. I think that's what she said. Never heard of it before."

"Like what?" Pocket asked.

"She said it's the breathin they do at—the end."

Pocket felt the walls crumble around him, a strange disintegration of the room at the edges of his vision. His eyes didn't leave his mother's face. There was no doubt in his mind that he was responsible. That he'd killed her. His throat and chest constricted. He felt dizzy.

Scratch looked at Pocket. "Y'okay, Boy?"

Looking at the woman in the bed, mouth slack, face long and thin and without colour, she did not look like his mother. Not the mother of a year ago or even a month ago. Not the mother of last night, telling him things, her eyes bright in the dark.

"You're not to blame," Wanda said, later. She and Pocket sat by Merle's bed; Wanda had earlier sent Wilf off for a bath and shave, telling him "It'll make you feel better," and Wilf had seemed grateful to be told what to do. Scratch was in the kitchen making another pot of tea.

"But I—"

"Each person's time is preordained. Things happen the way they are meant to happen. You couldn't have said no to her if you wanted to."

Pocket thought about this. "Yes," he said. "I could've."

"You need to see it for the gift that it was."

"Some gift. She's—" But even as he protested, he knew it to be true.

"She's where she needs to be right now. And she was where she needed to be last night. That was her gift to you, and your gift to her. It's something you'll never forget, right?"

"Don't s'pose."

Wanda's voice was soft. "The gift," she said, "also, is that we are here for this. It changes your life. I know that might sound funny, that death changes life, but it does. We become closer to something inside ourselves."

"Closer to what?" Pocket couldn't keep the bitterness from his voice. He was suddenly angry. "What do you know about us, anyways? Yer just goin to go back to California…" His voice trailed off. He felt tired, every cell weary.

"There are windows everywhere; they open when the time's right," Wanda said. She reached over and put her hand on Pocket's arm. Pocket shook it off.

Wanda had opened the curtains, and light entered the room, highlighting the dust on surfaces. Merle would never have let dust gather like that, and Pocket, who would never have noticed such a thing before, felt absurdly as if someone should clean things up before his mother awoke.

Wilf, looking fresher for the bath, pulled up a chair on the opposite side of the bed. Wanda began to hum softly, and Scratch, coming in from the kitchen, set down the teapot and picked up the tune. The hair stood up on Pocket's arms as their voices, awkward at first, rose together.

"Toora loora loora…"

It was a song Pocket's mother had sung to him, one he'd forgotten about completely. An Irish lullaby, as sweet as a warm bed on a cold night. The moment swept over

Pocket, and he felt as if he could willingly drown in it, and that drowning would be a relief. He felt he should join them, but he couldn't make his throat work.

"Toora loora ligh…"

Dust motes hung in the light that reached through the windows. Outside, distant jays called to one another.

"Hush now, don't you cry…"

Tendrils of sound wrapped around Pocket, until the notes faded.

"One of her favourites," Wilf said from the doorway. "Merle used to sing it to Pocket. How'd ya know?"

"Think we could—sing her back?" Pocket asked, his voice a croak. It sounded ridiculous, the words out of his mouth before he knew he would say them.

Nobody spoke.

"Sometimes," Wanda said carefully, "it's best to give a dying person permission to go. Not to hang on because of the pull of loved ones."

"Please," said Wilf.

Merle was swimming. The first sensation was that of softness, a gentle brushing against her arms as they swept forward in breaststroke motion. Her vision came as if dawn were breaking, and as the sun crested there lay before her a sea of marram grass undulating in a warm wind. In the distance, the impossible, aching white of sand dunes. Beyond these, a flat sea beneath a cloudless sky. Merle had never seen such blue.

As she swam, she became aware that she could dive into the marram green world, grass stroking her face, and then surface, dolphinlike. She seemed to be covering great distance, and yet, the dunes drew no closer.

From somewhere deep came sound. It coursed through her, travelling the length of her spine, to emerge at her mouth and from there, come forth in colours, painting the landscape with joy. It was a moment in which she knew she could exist forever.

Merle awoke, her own throat making a sound that was neither beautiful nor intelligible. When her eyes focused she saw familiar faces bending, concerned, and she closed them again. She reached for the grass, the dunes, the distant blue but the vision hovered just out of reach. As she opened her eyes again to the faces she knew, from the eye nearest the window there slipped a single tear.

When Pocket's mother returned to the living room in her house near the sea, it was as if she had swum up from some great depth, and needed to blink away the saltwater in order to see him clearly. In her eyes was a great sadness, as if she had lost something dear to her.

"Pocket," she murmured. "You're here."

"'Course I am, Mum," he said.

Merle had closed her eyes. "Good," she'd said. "Good."

Later, Cindy Morton had come by, taken his mother's pulse and listened to her breathing. She told them she'd be calling the doctor, the one who'd looked after Merle in Yarmouth. She couldn't believe the doctor hadn't been back in touch, shaking her head. "You been doing good, considering," she told them. Wilf had nodded gratefully.

After the nurse had left, Wilf had sat for a long time, eyes fixed to his wife's face, hoping for some movement. Pocket was also quiet, from time to time studying his father as his father studied Merle. "I'm sorry. I'm just not ready to let you go," Wilf whispered once into the still air.

Pocket felt a fist tighten in his chest.

The house was so quiet through the morning that those keeping vigil could hear the movement of hands of the big round wall clock in the kitchen, or the sigh of the wind outside. Merle slept on, her breathing shallow but regular, without the slightest flutter of an eyelash.

It was suprising, in that quiet, that no one heard the approach of Turf Tyverson, who arrived with a pan of meatloaf and fresh news, until his knock at the door.

"From the missus," he said, holding the heavy glass dish. Scratch took it and asked him to step inside, but Turf shook his head.

"Just wanted to bring that fer ya, and to tell ya that the boats've gone. Every one of 'em."

"Gone?" Wanda had come into the hallway and stood behind Scratch.

"Yep. Loaded somethin in a van, that's what Owen said. Then they all pulled up and lit out 'round the point, real early this morning."

Wilf joined them. "So I guess we didn't need to meet last night. Waste of time, gettin everybody out to the store."

"I thought I felt a shift, this morning," Wanda said.

Everyone looked at her. "I thought it was—never mind. Everything happens for a reason."

Turf shook his head. "Uh. Well, anyways, I wanted to tell you. I better get on. Thelma sends 'er best."

Pocket, who had come down from upstairs and stood a few steps above them, listened, head racing. If the meeting hadn't been called, if his father and uncle hadn't gone out...

In the living room, Merle dreamed. The air was warm, the surface of the water calm. The oars in her hands were comfortable, like old friends, as she rowed steadily towards a distant point.

2 As Pocket approached the wharf, the absence of foreign boats on the Sound or in dock was notable. In a few short days he'd grown used to the trio, poised like hens above the alien egg below. Among the fishing boats, activity appeared to have resumed as if no interruption had ever occurred. He heard the sound of one motor, then another, and the shouts of men as they readied to go out for a few days' longlining first thing in the morning. It was as if a spell had been broken and now, with the strange boats gone, life had returned to normal.

Pocket lowered himself and sat on the wharf on the cold wood, feet hanging over the edge. He felt guilty, being away from the house, and yet, as the morning wore on, Scratch had insisted he go, get some air. Pocket had been reluctant, but: "Go on," Wanda had encouraged. "She'll still be with us when you get back," and Pocket had believed her.

Below, the sea shifted and moved in an edgy manner, as if aspiring to be patient but not quite succeeding. Pocket, too, felt at odds with himself, new feelings he could not articulate. On his lap lay his sketchbook, the page blank. He had not even removed his pencil from his coat. He heard the sound of footfalls behind him, but he didn't turn.

"So they've all gone," Rodney said, lowering himself to sit beside Pocket. He winced at the cold beneath him, but didn't get up again. "Fred told me first. Had to look for myself, I guess."

"S'pose you missed yer story."

"Doesn't matter," Rodney said, and told Pocket, then, about the message he'd been left at the office. "I never did get to talk to my boss. But I suppose it doesn't matter," he said again. When he looked at Pocket the smallness of his own problems became suddenly clear. "I don't think I've properly said I'm sorry," he said.

"Everybody says that. Ya didn't do anything to apologize for."

"No, I mean, I'm sorry that it's happening. That's all. It's just—it's just what we say."

"Well, don't."

"Sorry."

"See what I mean? Anyways, if anyone's sayin sorry, should be me."

"Why you?"

Pocket didn't answer. To Rodney, Pocket looked like an island, shores surrounded by reefs. There was no way in. But there was that sameness, again, for Rodney the curious feeling that, regardless of the difference in their lives, he was looking at himself.

"I never know what to say," Rodney said. "I don't mean now. I mean all the time."

Pocket raised his head slightly and looked at Rodney.

"It's always seemed like everyone else had the words, but not me. I guess that's why I decided I'd go into journalism. Because when you write the words you can sit with them for a while, get comfortable with them. You can adjust them until they really say what you want.

There's this luxury of time. So when they're right, that's when you're done. When you talk—"

"I know." Pocket's voice surprised Rodney, who had almost forgotten about Pocket while he sat talking and looking across the Sound. "It's like that with drawing fer me. You put a line on a piece of paper, you don't like it, you can just—erase it, y'know? You say something, you don't get to take it back. You can't say it better afterwards."

Rodney looked at his hands, turning blue in his lap. He put them in his pockets. "Even when you write something down, though" he said, "it's never right. It's never perfect. When something is just left to memory? Then you can hold it, perfectly. Maybe not the details of it. But, uh—" his voice softened, and he felt his face grow warm in the chill air. He was thinking of Daisy. "The heart of it."

Pocket thought of his mother's letter. There were the words, and then there was the heart of it. The feeling that came over Pocket at that moment was not one he could have described. He thought of his mother's hand, as if it now lay on his forehead, a gentle touch smoothing away illness, pain, worry. The balm he felt was so palpable that he touched his own hand to his forehead as if to find something resting there. He stared out across the water. In the daylight, the Sound looked benign. The memory of the night before on the water had taken on a dream-like quality.

Pocket held up his sketchbook, its blank page. "I thought maybe I'd make a drawing of the Sound, the boats. Fer Mum. I thought maybe she'd like that."

"But the boats are gone. Can you remember what they looked like?"

"Yeah. Maybe. I just—I dunno. Guess I was sittin here before you came, wonderin if they were ever really there. Like maybe we all dreamed it."

"I hope not," Rodney laughed. "I can see the story: *Fishing Village Dreams UFO.*"

"All of us dreamin it at once, though, that'd be some strange. Like a *Ripley's Believe It or Not!* comic book."

"I loved those when I was a kid," Rodney said. "All those things that couldn't be explained. Used to give me shivers."

"Yeah. Me, too." Pocket wondered if, some day, the Perry's harbour UFO might turn up in the pages of a comic book, to be read about by some kid in the future. "Mum's some interested in the UFO."

"Too bad she couldn't have seen all the action."

Pocket didn't comment. Eventually, "There's somethin I wanted to show you," he said. "Don't know why I didn't before now."

A few minutes later they were skirting the Moss Plant. "Maybe it's nothin, though. Maybe just something offa ship," Pocket said as the angled down towards the water. "Lotsa international trawlers, come in real close. It's a twelve-mile limit, ya get a good blow…"

The sun had not succeeded in burning through the fog, but the light was bright enough to make Rodney squint—brighter, it seemed, than a sunny day would be. He peered ahead, but saw nothing but a curving pebble beach striated by seaweed. Here and there, flotsam: broken traps, tangled net, sea-rounded planks, odds and ends. They were almost upon the silver cylinder, in its blanket of seaweed, before Rodney saw it.

"When I first came across it, it made my eyes water some bad," Pocket commented, blinking, "but not so much, now. Maybe whatever done it is wearing off. Whaddaya think it is?"

"Jesus, I don't know." Rodney bent and brushed the seaweed away, careful not to touch the thing itself. He couldn't explain this reluctance, but it felt far greater than any curiosity he might have. He straightened and walked around the thing twice. "Have you moved it? Picked it up?"

"Don't want to. Can't say why, I just—don't. Don't look like nothing I ever seen before. It's just weird, that's what it is. Right weird."

Rodney whistled under his breath. A real reporter would be all over this. It was quite the opportunity. He hoped he was up to the challenge.

"Whaddaya think?" Pocket asked again.

"I think I better call someone," Rodney answered. He *had* to be up for this. "I'll demand an exclusive." His voice sounded firm, and this gave him courage. "I'll show them, but it won't come free." He looked at Pocket. "Nobody else knows? What about that reporter, the one from the *Herald*?"

"Ya didn't hear?"

"No—"

"Accident. Bessie Parsons at the Victoria told Shirley, and Shirley told Scratch. Swerved to miss a porcupine, wound up in the ditch, went right through the windshield."

"That's horrible."

"He'll live, I hear, just ain't making much sense right now. In hospital up in Halifax."

"I hadn't heard."

Rodney looked at the thing in the sand, felt the glow emanating there. How could something that seemed so malevolent be so beneficial? He shivered, and looked at Pocket gratefully. "Thank you. You don't know how you've helped me. Thank you," he said again.

Pocket kicked the seaweed back over their find.

"Sounds better'n sorry, anyway."

"You'll need to be getting home, I suppose," Rodney said.

Pocket thought of Wanda's voice, her gentle insistence that he go out, and her assurance that nothing would happen while he was gone. Still, the pull was strong. "Yeah," he said. "I better."

Rodney headed for the store, where he planned to ask Shirley for use of the phone at the house, away from the bustle of the store. When he entered, Shirley was sitting with another lady.

"Thelma and I was just goin to see Merle," Shirley told him. "But thought I'd call, first. In case she was sleepin or somethin. Got that Wanda woman on the line. She said not to come right now! 'Magin. Said it's not a good time."

"Shirley," Thelma patted her hand, "s'pose it's just family, now."

"*I'm* family," Shirley's eyes brimmed. "*She's* not family."

Rodney looked on sympathetically. By tomorrow

afternoon he would be long gone, he realized now, on the train and heading home. Things would go on without him as if he'd never been there at all. Haltingly, he told Shirley he'd like to make a long distance call from the house. She seemed grateful for the distraction.

"You go on, then," Shirley dismissed him with a wave. "Just get the charge from the operator. I'll add it to your bill."

He slipped out and over to the house, which he found blessedly, happily empty. He needed to be alone to collect his words, figure out how to say what he needed to say when he made the call. He paused, hand on the heavy black receiver, and drew a deep breath. He wished he could draw into his lungs the breadth and depth of this day, this place, these people, while on the other end of the ringing phone lay a different world altogether.

3 Pocket started towards home. Gone was the burden of the thing in the sand, and he supposed that was something. He hadn't realized it held any weight for him until now, the secret shared. It was the uneasiness he felt whenever he thought of the thing, although it wasn't something he could easily articulate. Like finding an egg in a rockpile, symmetry and fragility against something sharp, hard, heavy. Or perhaps the other way around: a rock in an eggpile. The implied threat. The lurking potential for damage.

And then there the night with his mother on the Sound. Wanda had said it wasn't his fault, that it was all part of something bigger. *Things happen the way they are meant to happen*, Wanda had said. *You couldn't have said no to her if you wanted to.* Although he recognized the truth in that, he wondered if the weight of guilt would always be with him.

Ahead lay the pull of home, of his mother. He'd been gone long enough. Pocket put his hand in his jacket and withdrew the wishing stone. He put it back inside and held it there, warm, in his palm. He turned as the Fairlane pulled up beside him.

"Ya wanna lift?"

"Don't have far ta go."

"I know that. Get in anyways."

But instead of pulling away they sat on the shoulder.

"I might be takin off," Cuff told Pocket. "I might be headin for Toronna. Soon."

As far as Pocket knew, the Dodds were like the Snows: always had been in Perry's, always would be. But more and more young guys were leaving, it was true. There were all kinds of new oil wells in Alberta. Budge Hitchens had gone, and Sorry Peterson. Those twins over in South Head, Joe and Jerry Sidney, both had gone, near breaking their mother's heart, or so she told everyone. But Toronto?

"What'll ya do there?"

"Well, I'll be comin into some money. So maybe nothin for a while, just see the sights." The corner of his lips turned up. "Hear there's lotsa pretty women there. City girls. I'll have so much money I can take 'em to the good places." He waited for Pocket to ask him where the money was coming from. Pocket didn't. They sat for a bit, and Pocket put his hand on the door handle.

"I should be..."

But: "When I was a kid, ya know, Ernie and I had this game," Cuff began. Pocket waited. "I had this bow an' arrow set, ya know? We'd tape a pen lid onto the arrow, and then we'd find a bug and stick it in the lid, then stuff some grass or something in the end to keep it in. You know, like Sputnik?"

"Sputnik?"

"Yeah, you know. The Russian satellite. They sent dogs up. We shot the arrows in the air, like Sputnik, then checked when they came down to see if the bug survived." He looked at Pocket. "And they did, every one. Not like that dog. The dog they sent up died. And it really bugged me, you know? I musta been nine or something. And I really wanted a dog and my folks said it was enough to feed us never mind some mutt, and my dad said if it ain't a workin dog it ain't a dog at all so I never got to have one, though now he's got one for huntin that nobody can get near for fear of losin a finger, hasn't even got a name but Dog. More cats than ya could fry up fer dinner in a month of Sundays, but what good're they?

"So anyways we'd dump the bug out and then we'd step on it." He paused, eyes on the road through the dirty windshield. "I can't say why we did that."

Cuff put the car in gear but kept his foot on the brake. "Ernie doesn't really wanna hang around any more. Doesn't wanna do nothin. He's been seein that girl Edie, ya know? In Bride's Neck? Ya hardly see the bugger anymore. Kinda crept up on me, but cometa think on it—"

Pocket fumbled with the rock in his coat. "Ya know, I gotta get back," he said.

Cuff regarded him, coming back to the moment. "I suppose ya do. Sorry 'bout that. Here, I'll getcha right there. Hey, sorry about yer mum and all. Jeez, and here I was talking away about Sputnik an whatnot."

Pocket gave Cuff a sidelong glance, surprised at the genuine regret in his tone. It was almost like respect.

They were at Pocket's driveway in less than five minutes. Pocket reflected that he'd have arrived five minutes earlier if he'd walked, but it didn't matter all that much. There was a familiar car at the house, he could see, belonging to Pastor Gould. Suddenly, he wasn't in such a hurry to get home, or to get out of Cuff's car. Cuff, however, was looking at his watch.

"Jesus, lookit the time," he said. "Got an appointment." He said this with an air of importance, and Pocket glanced at him.

"Hey, y'know what I'll do?" Cuff drummed his fingers on the steering wheel, clearly anxious to get going. "I'll send you a postcard from Toronna when I get there. Hey, ya might even wanna come yerself someday."

After leaving Pocket, Rodney had run back to Shirley's and called the office, but could not reach Copeland. He wasn't even sure Copeland was who he wanted to reach. He felt there was leverage here, but wasn't quite sure how best to use it; he was out of his depth. He tried Lorelei at home; she had the smarts to know what to do, and by the time he called it was well past quitting time with the time change. A man answered.

"Lorelei? She's—" the mouthpiece took on a muffled sound "she's busy. Sorry, man."

"Could you ask her to call me? It's Rodney. I'm calling from Nova Scotia."

"Sure, man. I'll give her the message."

Rodney had listened to the dial tone for a half-minute before hanging up. Looking at the clock, he saw it was close to the time Cuff had mentioned earlier when he'd pulled up beside Rodney as he walked back to the store, startling him. What ensued had been a remarkably non-linear speech peppered with cryptic comments, followed by a wink and a demand that was not quite a threat: "Come alone," Cuff had said. "You'll be sorry if ya don't show up."

Now, Rodney paced the wharf waiting for Cuff. The

kid was bad news, but Rodney felt compelled to be there just the same. What he really wanted to do was go back to the thing in the sand that Pocket had taken him to. He wanted one last look before he'd call the RCMP, and then be there for the exclusive.

It was five minutes after four when Rodney heard the crunch of gravel and saw the long black Fairlane pull up to the end of the wharf. Rodney waited for Cuff to get out and approach him, but when he didn't, Rodney began walking towards the car, feeling irritated.

"So?" he asked when he reached the driver's side window.

"So get in," Cuff said. Rodney hesitated. "*Get in.* I won't bitecha."

"What is it?" Reluctantly, Rodney opened the door and climbed in. The detritus at his feet reached his ankles: hamburger wrappers, pop bottles.

Cuff lit a smoke and exhaled into the windshield. Rodney coughed and rolled down the window. With the next draw, Cuff blew sideways through his own window, a conciliatory gesture not lost on Rodney. After a minute, Cuff spoke.

"I got something that's worth something to you. Or worth something to somebody, anyway. Somethin I wanna sell."

"What?"

"Uh, uh. We need to talk uh, *hypothetically* first."

"Okay." Rodney felt, suddenly, as if his whole afternoon since his walk on the beach with Pocket had been hypothetical. He really needed to see the thing again.

"S'pose you had something that would be of *interest.*

Interest to the news guys. Or maybe the military. Somethin they want. How wouldja go about letting them know?"

Rodney stiffened. Did Cuff know about the thing in the sand? It might be just small enough to fit in the Fairlane's trunk, he thought. What if Cuff *did* have it?

"What sort of thing would you be talking about?"

"Say you had something you know someone was lookin for. Say you had proof about somethin. What would you do?"

"I suppose you'd make, uh, general inquiries. Like you're doing now."

"To who?"

"Depends on what you have. I imagine I could, uh, help you with that. If you told me what it is, that is."

Cuff reached under the seat, fumbling. In a rush of relief, Rodney realized it couldn't be the thing in the sand after all. In a moment "What the—" Cuff began. "What the fuck—" he hauled out a sheet of crumpled newspaper, then felt around some more under the seat.

"What are you looking for?" The string of expletives was getting louder and more varied, and Rodney, although fascinated, fought the urge to flee just the same.

Cuff got out and crouched by the car's floor, feeling under both seats. Cigarette packs and other garbage flew over his shoulder, littering the ground around the car.

"It's fuckin gone. Fuckin Ernie. Jesus."

4 Shirley looked around the now-empty store. It was suppertime; most were home at this hour. Normally, Shirley would close for the supper hour, but with all the phoning and store visitors the time had come and gone and now there seemed no point—and besides, she wasn't hungry. Fred was leaving her to herself, and she was grateful for that. She supposed he and Rodney were heating something up in the kitchen. She was grateful, too, that Fred could be fairly self-sufficient, not like some husbands.

She gazed around the empty store, enjoying the absence of voices for the moment. In another hour they'd be back, the usual crowd of men, mostly, sitting in the liar's corner debating what was found, and regretting what was lost. Some, their boats sitting idle and ready for five days, had gone out and would stay out a few days, but some would be back tonight to talk about the day and the catch. Of course, Wilf wouldn't be there, or Scratch, who liked to show up for the talk when he was visiting. She felt a longing, with an almost physical pull, to be with her friend, even though Thelma had been persuasive about respecting the family. But what if the family needed her? She'd only had Wanda's word to go on. She resolved to go over in the morning with a tray of buns. She'd get up early to bake them. And if Wanda tried to stop her coming in—

As if cued, the door opened, and Wanda entered in a rustle of skirts.

"Ain't you gone home yet?" Shirley said.

"We need to talk."

"I don't think so."

"What I said before—"

"Look," Shirley said, placing both hands on the counter that stood between herself and Wanda. "I don't know what you're doing, or what yer playin at," she said, "but if you hurt a soul in that family—"

"Hurt—?"

"It's a hard time, and you're not from here." Shirley's hands were shaking, and she gripped the side of the counter to still them. "You can't know—"

"I—"

But Shirley continued, cutting Wanda off. "You found out somethin about me," she continued. "I dunno how you found out, but ya did. I know it ain't no hocus pocus, yer just pryin so's to get folks thinkin yer something that yer not. Well, it won't work with me."

"No," Wanda said, eyebrows raised. "I can see that."

"So what do ya *really* want?"

"What does any of us want? To find our place in the world. To be loved. It's what you wanted from your sister, and what you gave her."

"That's enough about my sister—"

Wanda continued. "It's what you wanted from your boy and what you gave him, too, for as long as you could."

Shirley gasped as if a needle had entered her body, just above the breastbone.

"Who told you?" She straightened, visibly collecting herself. "Merle knew about my boy. She knew about my sister. She told you."

Wanda looked at Shirley thoughtfully. "She might have. Or you might have, in your own way. There are a million sides to everything. A million ways to look at things."

"And you pick and choose, is that it?"

"Don't you?"

"No," Shirley said, mouth set. "I don't. Things are what they are, and that's the all of it."

Cuff found Ernie and Edie at the Seven Seas, the only sit-down restaurant in the Passage. As the restaurant sat right on the road, Cuff could see them clearly where they sat side by side in the window booth eating cod burgers. He pulled abruptly into one of the four available parking spaces, recognizing the only car, a green Ford station wagon, as belonging to Ernie's father.

"Ernie and Edie," Cuff snarled as he slid into the booth across from them. "Whattarya gonna call yer kids? Emmie, Eddie, Ellie and—what, *Eggbert*?"

"Whassup, Cuff?" Ernie's voice was cold. Edie looked at her plate.

"You tell *me*, Ole Son. Where the fuck is it?"

"Hey! I got Edie, here."

"So ya do. Ya wanna come outside, then, an tell me what ya did with it?"

"What I did with *what*, Cuff? Yer talkin crazy, and yer interruptin my date."

Cuff stood up and grabbed Ernie by the arm. Ernie

was about to protest, but changed his mind. Looking apologetically at Edie, "Sorry. This'll just take a minute," he said. He shook off Cuff's hand and strode to the door ahead of him.

Edie watched through the window while outside, Cuff and Ernie talked animatedly, faces inches from one another. Finally, Cuff threw up his hands and turned, wrenching open the car door and slamming it behind him. Ernie came back in and sunk into the vinyl seat of the booth, the air beneath him escaping in a breathy whistle that echoed his relief.

"He's out to lunch," Ernie said. "Ain't you finished yet? Must be stone cold by now."

At dinner, Cuff interrogated each of his brothers. When he felt sure that nobody had been in his car, he could only surmise one thing: that he'd been seen on the boat, been followed and watched by secret agents, and that he was a victim of theft by official forces of some kind.

There was nothing more to be done. Taking his .22, he went out back, lined up a row of tin cans across the corrugated metal roof of the empty goat-pen, and fired at them until the shed had more holes than roof, and it became too dark to see.

Rodney paced the beach, again. He walked it grid-style, making sure no inch was uncovered. After walking a hundred feet in all directions, he picked up a piece of driftwood and began to meticulously comb the sand, dislodging seaweed and flotsam and with them, a host of sand fleas that hopped ahead like an advancing army. No, he could not have mistaken the location. There was the bank of jutting rocks; here was the broken trap. He could just see the imprint of Pocket's shoes in the sand, his own marks alongside.

He'd called the Halifax paper, introducing himself as a freelance journalist. He was sorry for the other reporter, but maybe—maybe things happen for a reason, he thought, then felt guilty to have thought it at all. Surely if God or destiny or *whatever* exists, it's not to make one benefit from another's misfortune. Still.

He told the editor he had found something significant, something that could be exclusive to the *Herald*.

"It's coincidental you should be offering that story in particular," the editor had told him. "And it just so happens we have a temporary vacancy in the newsroom, as a matter of fact. We're interviewing this week, but we haven't found an appropriate candidate so far. Depending on what you send us, you could have a good shot if you want it." The editor paused, then continued. "There is a…possibility it will become permanent. Where did you say you were from?"

Rodney had hesitated only a heartbeat. "Here," he'd said, leaving the editor to interpret that any way he wished.

In his hand was his duffle bag, its former contents emptied across his bed back at Fred and Shirley's house. He couldn't imagine what he had been thinking, leaving the thing on the beach. What if somebody else came across it?

He took a deep breath and began again: twenty paces, turn, twenty paces. If there were any other footprints, they were now completely obscured by his own.

The light was waning when Rodney finally stopped pacing and sat down on a large, smooth rock, elbows on his knees, fingers on his temples. Spread before him, the Sound, and closer, at the water's edge, the wash of waves across pebbles. On the horizon, a fog bank looming, a dark presence. Above him, a reel of gulls against a pale grey sky.

After a while one landed close to where he sat, a black-backed gull with a beady eye and a white breast. It cocked its head and looked at him sideways as if to say: what did you think you would find?

Near

It didn't matter before. It wasn't something you thought about. It was as if things would always be the same. Now, you wonder how you could have ever felt that way.

Now, it's different. You want to hold the things that matter close to you, as close as you can. If you could, you'd swallow them, absorb them through your skin, wrap yourself around them. There are so many things that matter, suddenly, that it is overwhelming, more than you could swallow in a lifetime, more than if you were a whale. Entire schools of things you would hold safe inside, if only you could.

It's in the remembered smile that swims before you just before sleep, or the laugh that echoes through an empty room. You know that, if you lived to be a hundred, you would still be able to conjure that laugh. And when the black night comes, these are the memories that caress your cheek, and send you softly into sleep.

There are remembered moments that dance in crystal patterns, bright sparks like diamonds on a blanket. Family: your uncle's strong arm around you on a roller coaster; your father's embrace when the dog was run over in the biting cold of a New Year's day; your mother spreading chocolate icing on your birthday cake. You count these moments, hoard them, keep them safe.

But you can't keep everything safe. That's the thing. Uncles, fathers, mothers, even memories. They are gone in an instant or they fade with time, slipping through your hands like water, and when they go they take your heart. You'd think there'd be no heart left, but that's the miracle, your grandmother told you in one brightspark memory on a bluesky afternoon. That's the miracle.

The heart grows back.

If she could, your mother might tell you this: that distance is measured not by miles, but by perception. And yet, perception, too, can be a slippery thing.

When the dog howls in an empty house, is he remembering his master's touch, or is he just lonely, a solitary dog in a vast, unfathomable wilderness?

There is the sky above: pinpoint stars so far away they make you ache. Below, the sea: what if the line you sink never finds bottom? What if there is no sea floor at all? But you have your feet on the land, and this, at least, is something you can be sure about.

Or can you?

You hold close the things that matter, the things you can touch.

You try to wrap them in your own warm skin, and you hope.

Tuesday, October 10

1 The spirit that was Merle Snow sighed into the early morning, ethereal. Only the slightest slip of her floated, soft as a feather, above the bed.

Pocket Snow, who had crept down at daybreak, slept in the chair beside her, bent forward, head resting on the bedclothes. Wilf Snow, who had roused himself from where he lay beside her some hours before and settled himself again in the other chair, sat with his two hands holding Merle's slim one, his eyes on her face, watching her short breaths, holding his own when hers stopped, releasing along with her next shuddering breath. From the kitchen, the low voices of Wanda and Scratch rose and fell like a gentle tide.

The spirit that was Merle Snow danced lightly, briefly, across her lips, her eyes, touched her forehead, a feather kiss. Wilf saw it, and followed it with his own eyes. Then, with the tiniest spark, it was gone.

2 At the Snow house, Shirley looked at Wanda across the threshold while Wanda held the door open. A few days before, Shirley had said to Fred: "Family should be doing for the dead, and if not family, then friends. It's not for strangers." Meaning Wanda.

"It's not right," she said to Wanda, now.

"I know how you feel."

"No, you don't." Shirley's voice was too loud. "No you don't," she whispered. "This isn't your place."

"Look, why don't you come in?"

"Ooh, aren't you lady of the house." But she pushed in and set her handbag on the chair that stood by the bootmat.

"The thing is, this should be done by a woman," Wanda spoke in a low voice. "Women. It will take two."

Shirley set her mouth. "Merle would want a loved one looking after her." Her eyes narrowed, and she lowered her voice to a hiss. "I didn't even get to see her a last time—"

Wilf came out of the kitchen, then, followed by Scratch, and Shirley stopped mid-sentence. "Thanks, Shirl. Thanks to both of ya." His eyes were red-rimmed, his face drawn, clothes rumpled. There was a beer in his hand. It was not yet ten o'clock.

"Oh, Wilf," Shirley said, but he turned and pushed back into the kitchen.

Scratch closed the door with an apologetic smile at

them both. "Doc's come and gone. Finally, just in time to pronounce—anyway, doesn't matter, now. Pocket's up in his room," he said. "We'll stay outta yer way."

Shirley turned to Wanda. "We better get on with it."

"You done a nice job," Shirley told Wanda grudgingly an hour later. Wanda had washed Merle's face and combed her hair, lightly touched her cheeks with rouge. Together they finished washing Merle and dressed her as if for church, and Shirley had placed a string of pearls at her throat. "She looks right pretty," Shirley said, more to the room than to Wanda. Her eyes felt puffy, tears painfully close to the surface. She would not cry until she was alone.

"I'll go up and see Pocket," Shirley said. "Boy needs a mother's touch." The look she gave Wanda dared any objection, but she got none. As she turned to go, a crash was heard from the kitchen, followed by exclamations. There was the sound of hammering.

"S'enough to wake the dead," Shirley shouted towards the kitchen, then clamped her hand over her mouth. "Sorry, Love," she said to Merle, but she was laughing, then all at once crying. "Oh, my dear Lord," she said. Before she could think, she had folded herself into Wanda's embrace. The two stood there for a moment, rocking slightly. "I never got to see her a last time," Shirley whispered.

"I know. I'm sorry. I thought there would be time," Wanda whispered back. "I was wrong."

In the kitchen, the second range of upper shelves was ready to go, Fred wielding a level while Scratch said: "Oh, just wing 'er, it ain't rocket science."

It was into this chaos that Rodney arrived by the back door.

"Look what the cat drug in," Fred commented above the noise. "Yer welcome if ya wanna help," he added, then put his own hammer down, and the others followed suit. "Ya prob'ly didn't hear, since you was sleeping when we left. Mrs. Snow passed this mornin."

Rodney looked at the scene. It wasn't the atmosphere he'd have expected given the situation. "I'm sorry," he said.

Pocket had come downstairs. He stood in the doorway, taking in the room. "What're ya doin, Dad?" he asked.

"Finishing the kitchen, Boy," Wilf said over his shoulder, "What's it look like I'm doin? For yer mother," he added.

"That's right," said Scratch. "For yer mother. She's been wantin a new kitchen forever."

The surface of the kitchen table was completely obscured by pieces of wood, tools, bent nails and beer bottles.

"Wilf, you hold this end. Hold it steady, now," Scratch instructed. "Whoa, Rod, catch that, wouldja?" Wilf shouted, and Rodney caught the corner before the cupboard fell to the floor. "Musta missed the stud. Pocket, could use an extra hand, here."

The cupboards, when they were up, listed at odd angles here and there. Scratch opened and closed the doors, demonstrating that they did, indeed, open and close. The heap of old curtain covers still lay in the corner. Rodney, Wilf, Fred and Pocket were sprawled in the four kitchen chairs, dishevelled but triumphant. Wanda and Shirley came in and stood in the doorway.

"Wilf, ya done good," Shirley said. "Y'all done good. She'd of been some pleased. 'Magin she is, now, wherever she is."

"I'm sure she is," Wanda, standing beside Scratch, smiled.

Against the wall, the contrast of turquoise cupboards on new yellow paint was arresting.

"Cheerful, it is," offered Scratch to murmurs of agreement.

There was a moment during which they all just looked, each of them thinking of Merle where she lay, combed and dressed, in the living room. Then Shirley crossed the floor to the dishes stacked in the corner and picked up a Maritime Rose plate. Wanda opened the cupboard door, and the china settled into the new cupboard like a sigh.

Before leaving, Shirley asked after everyone's needs and then, satisfied for the moment, promised to come back later to talk about plans and slipped out through the back door, Fred by her side. Anyone who had gone by the store in the morning would have found the locked door and known exactly what it meant, but now the store would serve as a place for information and organization: there was a lot to be done.

"S'pose I'll sit with Merle," Wilf said.

"Yep. S'pose ya should," Scratch agreed.

Wanda was in the kitchen washing dust off the dishes and putting them away. Pocket was up in his room.

Scratch took Rodney aside before the long black vehicle was due to arrive.

"Couldja find some reason to get him outta here?" he asked, looking towards the ceiling. "He don't need to see his mum leaving in a hearse."

Rodney felt intrusive walking up the stairs to Pocket's room; he had not even been inside the Snow house before this morning, and, although he had felt wonderfully, magically, a part of something during the installation of the cupboards—the jokes, hands clapped on shoulders, a remarkable equitableness about everything—the spell quickly dissipated as the players returned to their various roles, both familiar and unfamiliar. Nothing, really, was familiar about this time.

The stairs creaked on their risers as he ascended them. He didn't know which room was Pocket's, but felt unwilling to call out. He located it at the end of the hall, where he found Pocket stretched out on the unmade bed, looking at the ceiling.

Rodney stood in the doorway. "Can I come in?"

"Yeah. Okay."

Besides the bed, there was a spindle chair pulled up against a desk, and Rodney pulled it out. The light in the room was a soft grey; outside, the sun tried to break through the fog.

Rodney played with the hem of his rollneck sweater, unsure of what to say. His mouth wanted to form the word *sorry*, but he resisted. "You okay?" he asked instead.

Pocket raised his eyebrows. "My mum's dead," he said. "Whaddaya think?"

"Sorry," Rodney said. "I mean, sorry for asking a stupid

question." He wanted to tell Pocket about the thing in the sand. About how it wasn't there, when he'd gone back. He wanted to ask Pocket who might have taken it, but now didn't seem to be the time. In any case, Pocket had sat up, pulling his legs under him, and was speaking.

"I been lyin here thinkin. You can't help it, you know? It's like, if you're the one left behind, feels like its your responsibility to make somethin of it. You can't just mess around like it doesn't matter. I dunno—" He looked at Rodney. "I'm not sayin it very well."

"No, you're saying it fine," Rodney said quietly.

"My mum wanted me to do all kindsa stuff, like travel, or go to college. Or do art, even, though I can't imagine what I'd do with it. Can't make a livin with pretty pictures."

"I don't think you need to worry about making a living just yet."

"The point is, she wanted me to do *something*," he said. "I'm graduatin this year."

"What do *you* want to do?"

"That's not the point—"

Rodney thought about his own parents. His mother, waiting for that front-page news story. His father, wishing for something more. And yet, if you'd asked them, he was sure they'd have said they just wanted their son to be happy.

"I think," Rodney said, "that more than anything, she wanted you to be happy."

Pocket said nothing, and the two sat for several moments, Pocket looking across the room towards the window, Rodney looking at the corner of a comic book that lay under the bed. *True stories!* it said on the lower right-hand corner he could see,

"What about the thing we found in the sand?" Pocket said at last. "You call someone?"

Rodney told him, then, what had happened.

3 At the shore, they criss-crossed the tumble of seaweed, rocks and damp grey sand on the beach.
"I thought I was looking in the right place, but I wanted to be sure," Rodney said, voice panicked. "I promised them I had evidence."

"Told who?" Pocket's steps traced the same area he had just examined. "See this rock? The split one, here? It was right by it."

"The *Herald*. I told them I had an exclusive. They might even hire me." Rodney stood, hands limp, feet cold in shoes that were damp and sandy. "Might have," he added.

"Can't you just describe it?"

"It was having evidence that made it an exclusive. You want to know the weirdest thing? I can hardly even remember it. It's like...it's like when I try to see it, it's in the fog, so it's not quite—*clear*."

Pocket, facing Rodney, thought hard. "Neither can I," he said at last. "You'd think you'd remember something like that, wouldn'tcha? But ya took a picture, right?"

"No," Rodney admitted. "Camera's uh, broken."

Pocket, numb fingers fumbling, extracted the sketchbook from his coat. "I drew a picture," he said. "I don't s'pose it'd help."

"You *what*?"

"Here."

Pocket pulled the sketchbook from his jacket and flipped to the page. There it was.

"Pocket," grinned Rodney, "you've saved my life."

When he returned home, Pocket found his father in the living room with Pastor Gould. His father sat with his hands on his knees, clearly uncomfortable. In front of him, teapot and cups on an unfamiliar tray, but there was something else, and it took a beat for Pocket to recognize it. Startling for its absence was his mother's bed. The adjustable bed, which had been borrowed from the Yarmouth hospital auxiliary, had already been stripped, picked up, moved out. The furniture had been placed in a semblance of his mother's former arrangement, but not quite; here, a chair was oddly angled; there, a table was placed along the wrong wall. The effect was like the leaning kitchen Pocket remembered from a midway sideshow at the annual fair down in the Passage: everything askew, his balance compromised. A trick of the eyes, a mental confusion, stumbling feet. The angles were all wrong, but you couldn't say how, exactly. He felt dizzy, and sat down on his mother's favourite wingback chair.

"Pocket," his father said looking up. He sounded relieved. "Scratch and Wanda just gone to start rustlin up some food. Now you're here, guess we can eat. Pastor, you won't want to stay——?"

After rising, the pastor shook Wilf's hand and then took Pocket's in both of his, Pocket uncomfortable in their sweaty warmth. "If you need to talk, Son," he said, and Pocket nodded, extracting his fingers. The dizziness had left him, but the living room remained askew. His mother would know exactly how to put it to rights.

"Where ya bin?" Scratch asked when Pocket and his father entered the kitchen. He was sitting with his feet on the table.

"Around," Pocket said. "I thought you were makin somethin to eat."

"Don't need to. Enough food here to choke a horse. Just hadta get outta there," he sighed. "It's good ya got out, got a bit of air. Ya don't want to stay inside all day. Ya need to get away a little. Even Wanda's just gone out fer some air. Don't think her an the pastor got on too well," he chuckled.

"S'pose we should talk," Wilf said, sitting down. There was a deck of cards in the middle of the table and he pulled it towards him and began to shuffle.

"S'pose," Scratch said. "Pocket, get the crib board, wouldja? Thelma's meatloaf's in the oven. Yer dad and I'll play a game while she heats. A game for Merle, eh, Wilf?"

Wilf looked at the ceiling, then back at Scratch. "I do believe she's on my side, Ole Son," he said. "And I'm gonna skunk ya."

Shirley hung up the phone. Her ear felt hot, her mouth dry. But there was a nice satisfaction, there: the funeral was set for Thursday. The women's altar guild was looking after flowers, as well as tea and coffee. She'd rustled up promises for enough squares and brownies to feed three times the residents of Perry's and South Head combined. She hadn't yet talked to Wilf, but she knew he'd need someone to take charge. She knew exactly how Merle would want things.

For most of the day the store had been full of people. People wanting to talk about Merle, people wanting to talk about the goings-on out on the Sound. Funny how the two events should happen at the same time like that, Shirley mused. How Merle would've loved it all. Now, the two events—the crashing of an unidentified flying object into the Sound, and the passing of Merle Snow—would always be inextricably linked.

Later, the Snow kitchen was full of people after an early supper of miscellaneous casseroles no one was much interested in eating. On the wall, the new cupboards hung like unfamiliar visitors, eliciting glances from time to time from everyone assembled. Wanda and Scratch played cribbage at the kitchen table, a game Wanda had only just learned but that Scratch had been playing since he could count.

"Board's been in use more these last few days than if you put all the games together over the last twenty years," Scratch commented. "Thirty-one for two," he added, pegging two holes.

Shirley, looking over Wanda's shoulder, pointed to a card. "Play that one," she said. "Not the other one."

There had emerged an uneasy truce between the two, and Wanda glanced up, recognizing the significance of the gesture. "Thanks," she said, playing the card she hadn't intended to.

"Pair fer two," said Scratch, pegging again.

"Sorry," said Shirley, but Wanda played the last card

for fifteen, and pegged two herself, cancelling out Scratch's advance.

Fred clapped. "Good fer you, Wanda," he said. "High time someone beat th'ole bugger."

Pocket played solitaire, black cards on red. Wilf leaned back, feet on the table.

He poured more whisky into strong tea and stirred the cup with his little finger. "Merle was the best though," he said, and Shirley looked at him, her expression soft. Pocket continued to play, but placed the cards quietly, listening. "'Cept the time she got the hand of twenty-nine," he said. "Donny Drake came over with his Brownie Hawkeye to take a photo to send into the *Southshore News*, you remember?" Shirley nodded. Pocket, who figured he had heard the story a hundred times, set down the cards to listen. He'd lost the game, anyway.

"So anyways there he was. Took a picture with Merle there, holding the hand up along with the jack, grinnin away like the cat got the canary. Who the hell was she playin with, now…?" Wilf paused, and Shirley interjected.

"Me. She was playin with me."

"Right! Anyways, after Donny left, you two finished the game, right? And she lost the game. A hand of twenty-nine, and she still lost the game. Nobody laughed so hard as Merle at that, lemme tell ya."

"She always knew how to laugh, Merle did," Shirley agreed. "Didn't she, Pocket?"

"Yeah. She did," Pocket agreed. Pocket swept the cards from his lost game into a pile.

Wilf regarded his son. "Always said she taught ya to shuffle before you was born," he said, and Pocket smiled.

"S'pose she musta," he said, shuffling, then riffling.

"Y'okay, Boy?"

"Yeah," Pocket said. He set the cards in a neat pile.

Scratch pulled his peg from the winning hole and replaced it, with the others, at the start. "Merle's prob'ly up there right now, playin with Saint Peter," he offered. "Prob'ly skunkin him, too."

Far

When you were young, you thought of space as the blanket of stars in the night sky. They were things to wish on, or to trace patterns among: Orion, Cassiopeia, the Big Dipper. Before, space was a ceiling, like the one in your room.

Sometimes, now, when you stand under a vast sky, land behind and sea ahead, you are overwhelmed by the scope of space around you. If you could find the words to describe such space, perhaps you could control it. But there is no controlling that which spreads before you. It's like controlling a hurricane, a tidal wave, a sunset. Distance is not a thing you can tuck in your pocket, or close in the pages of a book. Space is not something you can hold in your mouth.

Close is the warmth of a stone in your hand, the taste of salt on your tongue, the smell of warm wool as it dries in front of the fire, the sound of laughter. Close is the last breaths of the one who slipped away, when the room becomes all there is, wrapping you in its shrinking walls.

Once, your mother, holding you close, told you a story.

A fisherman, she said, her voice soft, was hauling in his nets one day, and to his surprise a mermaid came up out of the sea holding a beautiful shell. The fisherman couldn't take his eyes off the mermaid, but he saw how she was holding the shell like it held her very heart, so he asked to see it. When he was close, she told him she couldn't lose it, or she wouldn't be able to go home. So when he was close enough he snatched it from her, and began to run back towards his house.

She followed, of course, but he'd hidden it and so there was nothing for her to do but marry him and stay. And she did, and she had three happy children. And then one day the children were out digging and what did they find, but her beautiful shell. When they brought it to her, of course she had to tell them that she must leave them. She hid behind her long hair so she wouldn't see their tears. It nearly broke her heart, but she could not deny what had to be. When she reached the shore with her beautiful shell the other mermaids all rose up, singing like a host of angels, and welcomed her home.

You remember sitting in your mother's lap, her warm breath in your hair, while she told you about the mermaid, leaving her children and going home.

Tucked in your bed, the moon flooded your room like daylight. You felt her soft lips on your cheek as she kissed you. The wool blankets lay heavy, a comforting weight. Alone, you watched the moon. Across the vast night sky, the moon watched back.

You watched and watched, unwilling to close your eyes and lose the moon. You watched until you blinked—just for a moment, just to rest your eyes—and when you opened, them, it was another day.

Wednesday, October 11

1 The day dawned bright and crisp and almost cloudless, save a few white cotton balls scattered like sheep on a hillside. A blue-and-white day, Shirley remembered her mother calling it. She particularly remembered her mother saying it as she hung out laundry, sheets flapping on the line, their brightness mimicked by the whitecaps on the bay. A high wind sent yellow leaves spiralling upwards, while at the shore, rich green marram grass danced as if possessed. How Merle loved a day like this, Shirley thought, and wondered if, in some way, her friend might have sent it.

There was plenty to do and yet there was time. Shirley arrived at the store twenty minutes early just for the luxury of a cup of coffee by herself. She'd set Fred's breakfast in front of him and slipped through the door before he had a chance to say anything, to ask where she might be headed in such a hurry. *Hurryin up to slow down*, that's what she'd have said if Fred had time to ask her what the rush was.

What Shirley wanted to do was spend some time with Merle, or rather, spend some time remembering her. It was easy, in the business of things, to forget that. Folks got together and talked about the deceased, true enough, but that was different from spending time alone. Elbows on the table, coffee poised just under her nose with the steam rising, Shirley closed her eyes and conjured Merle: Merle as a child, a teenager, a young woman.

Shirley remembered, as if it were her own wedding day, when Merle married Wilf. She'd worn Shirley's too-small shoes because she couldn't afford new ones. Then, midway through the service, Merle made an awful face, and kicked them off. Right there at the altar! Wilf was just relieved, he said later: he was sure she'd changed her mind. She did, she told him. She changed her mind about the damn shoes. It was one of the only times Shirley heard Merle swear.

Her eyes closed, Shirley warmed at the thought of this. She could conjure Merle in all of her moods, but most often, with that peculiar smile she had when she was laughing on the inside. That, and the set of her mouth when she was angry or determined. The softness in her eyes when someone was sick or hurt.

And when Pocket was born. Shirley could remember Merle's face, clear as day, the day Pocket was born. She had expected to be envious, but had found herself balmed by her friend's glowing happiness. She let herself float in the memory for a while.

When she heard the door rattle open, "Haven't opened yet," she called out, then saw it was Pocket with her cleaned casserole dish in his hands. She came around the counter to take it from him, then pulled him into a motherly embrace. For a heartbeat she felt as if she was Merle, but just as quickly she was Shirley back in herself and squeezing too hard. She felt Pocket melt against her for an instant, then pull back. *Ah, well, Merle,* she thought. *It's a start.*

"Yer mum loves a day like this," she said, surprised

as she did that she'd used the present tense. "Sun and wind," she added, stating the obvious.

Pocket looked out the back window towards the Sound, where the whitecaps lunged like horses. "S'pose," he said. "Scratch said to say thanks."

"For the casserole?"

"For everythin. He says he'll be over by an' by. Says he's got somethin to tell everyone."

"Maybe he's gonna stick around 'stead of goin back to Yarmouth."

"Hope so."

"Come on, sit. No, you have time, dear. Just sit. How's yer father?"

Reluctantly, Pocket sat down in the chair Shirley had pulled from the table. She took a sip from her cup. "Cold," she said. "I'll start some more."

As Shirley rose from the table Scratch came through the door, closely followed by Wanda. Shirley rolled her eyes. "S'pose ya'll all want coffee," she said, heading for the percolator. "S'pose I'm open after all," she said, looking at the clock.

Scratch scanned the room. "Where's yer boarder?" he asked.

"Busy working on something for the Halifax paper."

"Thought he worked for some paper up in Ottawa."

"I believe things have changed," Wanda offered. She looked at Scratch and smiled. Pocket caught the look that passed between them with a start.

"S'pose yer gonna say you saw it comin," said Shirley over her shoulder as she measured the grounds. "In some tea leaves or some such thing."

Nobody said anything for a minute until Shirley turned around and faced the room. "What?" she said.

"Wilf knows," he said. "Just told 'im. Pocket, I 'spect I shoulda told you sooner, but now'll haveta do. When I head back to Yarmouth—after the funeral, and I won't go 'til you and yer father are all settled again—I'm takin Wanda with me. We're goin together."

Shirley's mouth fell open. "You're *what*?"

"We—"

"She's only been here, what, a coupla days, an yer already—"

"We're goin together, I said. Maybe even, uh, get married. Eventually, I mean."

"*Married?*"

"Congratulations," said Pocket quietly.

Shirley stared at Pocket. "What did you say?"

Pocket looked at her, then away. "I said congratulations."

Scratch put an arm around Wanda. The coffee started perking noisily, and Shirley turned it down.

"Well then," she said when she turned back around. "Well."

"Now, Shirl—" Scratch began, but she held up a hand.

"S'pose if ya was to get married, ya won't be an *illegal* alien, anyway," she said, and Scratch threw back his head and laughed. Shirley smiled in spite of herself. "And I s'pose that means coffee's on the house," she said. "God knows how I manage to make a livin."

The door opened again, and Cuff walked in, bringing

with him the scent of dry leaves, engine oil and gunpowder.

"Ho!" he called. "Did I hear coffee's on the house?" He strode to a chair, pulled it out and sprawled on it expansively, arm over its back.

"You're awfully cheerful this mornin, Cuff," Shirley said, her eyes narrowing. "What're you up to? Oh, never mind. Here: ya might as well have some too." She filled four cups, topped up her own, and pushed the cream bottle forward on the counter.

"Ya mean I haveta come an get it? Man, when Ernie and I get rich, ya'll be servin us, and jumpin to it."

"I doubt it," Shirley said, but brought him his cup. "I was on my way over here anyways," she said, sitting down. "Don't all a you just stand around. Pocket, don't get up, stay sittin here beside me. Scratch, Wanda. I shoulda said it before. Congratulations."

"No, really," Cuff continued. "We're gonna be rich. Well, Ernie don't know it yet, but I'll let him in on it seein as he's my best buddy."

"What are you on about?" Scratch asked him.

"New opportunities, Ole Son. Got plans for a racetrack. Yep, horses." He rubbed two fingers together. "Big money in a racetrack. Just takes a little investment."

"With what? You don't have any money."

"With brains," Cuff said, pointing to his temple. "An I'll sell the Fairlane. Soon as the bets start comin in, I can buy myself whatever I want. A *Lincoln*."

Scratch leaned back in his chair, blowing on his coffee. "How'd you come up with this?"

"Funniest thing. I went and asked Ernie about something over at the Seven Seas an I guess I left in kind of a hurry, like. We'd had words I guess you could say. An I was pissed off about that, and about somethin else. Y'know, s'funny how ya think it's all fallin apart an then somethin else comes up, right outta the blue, like." Cuff shook his head, grinning. "Like it was meant to be or somethin. So anyways I was drivin kinda fast—"

"You was speedin, as usual," Shirley cut in.

"An I saw Charlie Brannen sittin in a bit of a scrub off to the side, waitin fer speeders. Guess with all the UFO stuff over, he's got a lot more time on his hands. Anyways, I passed him at, I dunno, eighty or somethin an I knew he'd be after me soon's he got his car in gear so I went 'round the corner and ducked down that dirt road, y'know, that goes to the point down t'wards Stinky's garage? Haven't been down there since I was a kid, road was some bad, but I kept goin cuz I thought Charlie might be on my tail. Well he wasn't, but I kept goin anyways. An then the land all kinda flattens out an it was like the handa God came down—"

"Don't be blasphemizin," Shirley warned.

"And there it was, all spread out in my mind's eye, like, ya could almost see it in the way the land lies there. There's nothing like that anywheres on the South Shore." He leaned forward. "I already talked to Stinky, he owns that point, an he's all over it. So's I got one partner already. His cousin Pete's got that backhoe. Once the land starts to take shape we'll get backers, no problem." He drained his cup. "Ah," he breathed. "Actually came in here lookin for Ernie. Can't seem ta find him anywheres, and I figure I should let him in on the plan. Ya seen him?" He looked at Pocket.

"Uh-uh," said Pocket.

"Don't matter, I'll find 'im later. Still can't get over it, y'know? Ya follow one thing, and it don't turn out, then it seems like all along it was just leadin you to this other thing—"

"I know what you mean," smiled Wanda.

Cuff continued. "Anyways, cat's in the bag, now."

"Ya think?" Scratch grinned. "S'pose if it didn't work out you could always flood the place an grow cranberries."

Cuff's eyes narrowed. "Fer Chrissakes, ya'd think ya could wish a guy well fer once—"

Wanda leaned forward. "Good luck," she said. "I wish you all the best." There was a beat in which everyone waited for more, but the words were spoken without sarcasm.

"Ya mean it?" Cuff straightened.

Tip Morton came in with a blast of chill air blowing dead grass and leaves across the floor. "Shut the door," Shirley called before he was fully inside.

"It's Ernie," Tip said, sinking into the remaining chair. "You seen him, Cuff?"

Cuff shook his head. "No, matter a fact I—"

"He left a note."

Cuff leaned forward. "He what?"

"He's *eloped*, the little bugger. With Edie Norris. To *Toronto*."

Scratch laughed. "That'll get 'im outta lobsterin."

"Toronto! That's what the note said, left under the salt

shaker on the kitchen table when we got up this mornin. His mother's not laughin let me tell you. Nor's Edie's folks, been on the phone with 'em all morning. Girl's not sixteen."

"Jeezus," Cuff shook his head. "Jeezus," he said again.

Shirley, looking back on that morning at the store, later recalled it as having a peculiar glow. It wasn't that it was so different from other mornings, it was that it was so much the same. There were revelations, of course: Scratch marrying Wanda, Ernie eloping with Edie, and Cuff's newest get-rich-quick plan. And there was the absence of Merle—not just from the store, where, not so long ago, she'd drop in to pick up a package of lard or loaf of bread or just to pass the time—but from Perry's altogether. Gone from the world, in the bigger sense, and the world, Shirley knew, was poorer for it in some subtle way. Over it all, the crash, whatever it was, the wharf closed, the divers, the television crew. The memory was now almost surreal. Had it even happened? It's like when a star falls, she thought. The universe goes on the same, but it's not, quite. And at the same time, Perry's *was* the same, like a quilt you wrapped around yourself. It made you want to go bake something.

After he left the store, Cuff, in the parking lot, put his hand on the door of the Fairlane, the chrome handle so cold it hurt to touch. He couldn't believe Ernie would do this to him. Leave him behind. Not even tell him. He just needed to drive, to think about things.

The note, sticking out of the ashtray, was so obvious now he didn't see how he could have missed it before. He unfolded it, ash falling onto his lap, thinking: he'll explain, say he's sorry he left so fast, tell me where to meet up with him. *Something.* We've been buddies our whole lives, for Chrissake.

Five words, in Ernie's hand.

Stay away from my sister.

2 Rodney found Pocket sitting, once again, on his front step. The wind had died by midday, and the air had warmed slightly as the sun reached its zenith. Now, as the sun began its afternoon descent, the warmth lingered in the surfaces it had touched. As Rodney sat down beside Pocket he felt the heat in the wooden step with its flaking green paint.

"You doing okay?" Rodney asked him.

"Uh huh. Been people comin and goin all day. Half the ladies of Perry's and South Head been over, we got enough food to live fer a month. Hungry?"

Rodney shook his head.

"Tyversons are here, sittin in the kitchen. Wanda keeps fillin plates. All she's been doin all day."

"I heard about Scratch and Wanda."

"Uh huh."

"Surprised?"

"Thought I was at first."

"When are they leaving?"

"Dunno. After the funeral. Longer, maybe."

Rodney played with a broad piece of grass. After a while he stretched it between the two joints of this thumb and blew across it. There was a sound like a soft fart.

"Here," Pocket said, and took it from him. "Ya stretch it really tight, see? And ya make sure you can see a little bit a light showing, here." He blew, a trumpet blat. "Mum could do it best," he said.

"Really?"

"Yeah. I'd bring kids around to show them when I was little. Made her a celebrity, kinda." Pocket smiled and handed the piece of grass back to Rodney, who twirled it between his fingers.

"I sent the story up on the early bus," Rodney said. "I didn't have the courage to take it myself, I guess. Just had a call from the *Herald* over at Fred and Shirley's."

"Already?"

"Yeah. They like the story, they said. And they want me up there tomorrow for an interview. I'll be driving up tonight after supper."

"Thought you had a train ticket home."

"I cancelled it." Rodney had called Mr. Copeland, and got a busy signal. He decided then to call Lorelei, but the voice that answered her line was unfamiliar. "I left a message with my co-worker's secretary," he told Pocket. "I imagine it'll get through."

"Well, good."

"I'll miss your mother's funeral. I'm sorry."

"S'okay. Ya didn't know my mum."

Rodney looked at the grass in his hand. "Feels like I almost did," he said. He recalled Shirley's words. "Someone told me funerals are really for the living. I'm sorry," he said again.

"You'll be back though, right?"

"If I get the job. Definitely. Definitely, I'll be back."

"Well, they took your story. That's good, right?"

"Yeah. And they said they'd use your drawing. Although they did say it looked a bit like a, uh. Like a car muffler." Rodney ducked his head.

"Sorry," he added. "But they're going to run it for sure."

"Cometa think on it, that thing did look kinda like a muffler," Pocket grinned. "Same shape, anyways. 'Magin, seein it in the paper."

"I'll send you a copy. You can use it for your portfolio. You know, for when you decide to become an artist."

Pocket grinned again. He rose, dusting off the seat of his pants. "Ya wanna come in? Mrs. Tyverson brought lemon loaf."

An early supper finished, Shirley Crosbey stood at the counter in the kitchen of her yellow house, six slices of bread spread before her, assembly-line style.

"Ya want ham?" she asked. "What about lobster salad?"

Rodney sat with Fred at the table and made grateful noises while he sipped a cup of tea. Beside the door his duffle bag sat, packed. "I don't want to be any trouble," he said.

"Oh, yer no trouble," Fred winked. "Shirley's happy doin for people. She hates to see anyone go off without food."

"Well, you've been really kind," Rodney said.

Shirley, mashing mayonnaise into lobster, laughed. "Ya haven't got my bill yet!"

"Of course," Rodney stood up, embarrassed. "What do I owe you?"

"Relax, Son," Fred said. "We'll settle up before ya go. S'been quite the week ain't it? After all that, ya feel almost like family. 'Course, ya got yer own family, I expect."

"Um, I—"

Shirley stopped her work at the counter and waited, listening.

"Um, yes. Yes, but we don't talk much." Rodney played with the wet circles from his cup of tea. "I guess I'm a bit of a disappointment. They wanted—they had other plans for me, I guess. It's a long story."

"When did you last see your parents, Son?" Fred asked.

"It's been couple of years, I think. Well, I saw my father. My mother moved out West with her new husband."

Shirley tsked, then returned to making sandwiches, one ear still cocked.

"My father wanted me to do something uh, practical. When he gave up on that, he wanted me to enter the military. He's a retired Major. But I'm not exactly military material..." Rodney's voice trailed off. "Anyway, my mother has another family," Rodney continued after a moment, but Shirley had crossed the kitchen floor to stand beside him, her hand touching his for a moment where it held his cup.

"Ya don't need to say no more," she said. "Family's where ya find it." Fred coughed into the sentimentality of the moment, and Shirley batted the air towards him. "Enough with you," she said.

"What?" Fred protested.

Rodney focused on his cup to hide the feeling of pleasure that crept upon him. "I'll be back to visit," he said into it.

"I 'spect so," said Shirley.

A little later, as Rodney watched the figures in the parking lot recede in his rearview mirror, standing as they were under the lamplight outside the store, he did his best to focus on the interview tomorrow. He imagined walking into the room, extending his hand, shaking with a firm grip.

"Rod Nowland," he said aloud into the hum of the road.

His voice sounded like the sort of man someone would want to hire.

That evening, Pocket sat by the window of his room, looking across the Sound. Scratch and Wanda had gone off for a walk under a clear and starry sky. Walking for its own sake was not normally a habit of Scratch's, and Wilf and Pocket had exchanged glances when he'd announced their intention to walk under the starlight. And sure enough the celestial display was so magnificent that Pocket, peering up from where he stood at the open front door, entertained the thought himself until his father shouted to close the door before the tea froze in his cup. Pocket had gone to his room instead, a place to be alone after an endless day of visitors, but he kept the lamp off, letting the silver cast of starlight wash across the windowsill.

"Ya never got to talk to yer aliens, didja?" Wilf had said to Wanda after supper, before heading for the workshop, before they'd all left to go their separate ways.

"Well, they weren't *my* aliens," Wanda replied.

"What about th'other night—?" Pocket stopped as Wanda gave him a look.

"Oh, I must have gone down to the shore to communicate a dozen times," she said airily. "I know that, one time in particular, a connection was made. Intelligence was exchanged. Of course, they've gone, now. The craft travelled underwater for quite a number of miles before it took off."

"It took off? When? How do you know?" Pocket asked.

"It was Sunday night, I think. Around two in the morning. I felt them leave."

Pocket, in the dark of his room, replayed the night with his mother in the dory. It seemed surreal, now, dreamlike, and yet because of it, something had shifted. His mother's words in the dark. He imagined that, as they'd sat there in the boat, a string had connected them, heart to heart. The thought comforted him.

He stood and leaned into the window, resting his cheek against the cold glass, and felt the moonlight, soft, against his closed lids. Then he walked across his darkened room and descended the stairs. He paused at the living room, where the corner lamp illuminated the new arrangement of chairs. Not new, really. His mother's favourite wingback chair looked as if she had just been sitting there, but had left the room briefly to turn off the kettle or answer the phone. He followed the thought of her into the kitchen, where neither kettle whistled nor phone rang. The dark kitchen was tidy, the dishes done and put away. Although his uncle had once quipped that "see no point in dryin' the dishes with a towel when God'll do it for ya," Merle disliked a pile of dishes left to drain, her will even now trumping Scratch's natural inclination. He moved past the sink to the back door and opened it, breathed the dryleaf smell in the sharp air, and closed it gently behind him, as if to keep from waking someone in the empty house. The yellow light in the workshop window beckoned.

"Hey, Dad," Pocket said. He sat on the stool by the door.

"Just puttin things to rights," Wilf explained. He'd swept up, Pocket could see, and sorted nails and screws into their coffee cans on the workbench, but it looked as if he'd been sitting, not doing anything, for quite some time. A bottle of Scotch stood open on the workbench, a half glass at his elbow. "Thinkin about yer mum, too. Didja know she told me to build this thing out here. Insisted."

"So you'd have a place to work?"

"Nah, I never did much work, tell the truth. But I often wake up middle of the night some peckish. An I come out here."

"You do?" Pocket recalled waking up to the sounds of creaking stairs, the back door shutting quietly. He'd wondered.

"Yeah. When we was first married, I'd make myself a can a soup, some crackers, and bring 'em up to bed with me," he chuckled. "Yer mum was not impressed, I'll tell ya. *You'll not be gettin crackers in my bed, Wilf Snow*, she'd say to me. *That's grounds fer divorce, that is.* So I took to comin downstairs, a little midnight snack in the kitchen. But I guess I'm a loud eater. Said she could hear them crackers all the way upstairs with the pillow over her head."

"So ya had to come all the way out here?"

"Well, I couldn't stop wantin a little something in the wee hours," he said. "An I couldn't do without yer mother. 'T were the only solution." He took a long drink, draining the glass. "Jeesuz, but it's hard to go back in that house with her not inside."

They lapsed into silence. Pocket, a coffee can in one hand, slid the hodgepodge of nails from one side of the can to the other, a restless tide.

"Y'okay?" Wilf said after a bit.

"Yeah."

"That's somethin about Scratch, ain't it? S'pose I'm happy for 'im."

"Me, too."

Wilf picked up the bottle and poured himself a fresh glass. "I'd offer you some, but yer mother wouldn't like it," he said. "Don't expect we'd hear the end of it," he grinned.

Pocket, hands on his knees, smiled back.

"Ya know she really hoped you'd go places. She always thought you was different. Smart in school. Yer drawin."

"Well, I'm right useless in a boat," Pocket offered, but there was no anger in his voice. He thought of telling his father about his drawing in the newspaper, but decided to wait until he had it in his hands, just to be sure it was real.

"It's not for everyone," Wilf continued. "I never thought it was for you, even if I'd've liked some company out there."

"Sorry."

"Don't be sorry, now, Son. She saw ya had lots of talents, now, and she wanted you to make the best of yerself."

"I know."

"Don't s'pose with everythin goin on you've given too much thought to what you'll do after school," Wilf said.

Pocket shrugged his shoulders.

"Well, anyways," Wilf continued, "she was proud a you. And I know there's things she'd've said if she could've. I can't be yer mother, Pocket, but I can guess what she'd've wanted, and I'll try to do my best by you."

"Yeah, Dad. I know."

Wilf drained his glass. "Ya got, what, two more years of school?"

"Just this year, Dad. I graduate this year."

"What, already? Jeez, you was just in diapers last week! How did that happen?"

Pocket smiled and looked at his knees.

"But ya'll be around for a bit yet, wontcha?"

A little while later, the two made their way across the backyard. Behind them, the workshop was in darkness. Ahead, the lamp in the living room, the only light on in the house, cast a dim glow into the kitchen, sending a meagre slant of light through the window above the sink. Pocket reached the door first and opened it, the warmth from inside a balm. In the darkness, he found the switch beside the door and turned on the kitchen light.

The new cupboards, still smelling slightly of paint and sawdust, were festooned with drawings.

"She'd been savin 'em since you could hold a pencil," Wilf said from behind Pocket. "Waitin for her cupboards so she could tape 'em to the doors."

Thursday, October 12

At the top of the church steeple, Pocket pulled out his mother's letter. The paper was warm, the quarter-fold rounded to the shape of his body. He'd been thinking about Rodney's words, about holding onto the heart of something.

Before unfolding it he leaned out, looking down the road below him, catching the tail end of a long black car as it crested the hill past the store and disappeared from view. At the store, here were a half-dozen cars parked outside, more than would generally be there on a Thursday morning, otherwise the road was quiet, as was the wharf, most boats still in dock.

Looking out across the Sound he could see, as always when the fog lifted, the lighthouses of South Head, East Head and Kettle Island, see the full breadth of Perry's Harbour. It looked as it had always looked. It looked as if nothing ever changed.

A sudden wind riffled the corners of the pages. Looking back across the Sound he could see whitecaps: the morning's calm had been the still before the storm, then. There it was, a black presence on the horizon.

You always liked to be up high, high as you could get, he read, then, further down: *Only thing higher is the stars.*

Pocket felt the space around him, the October air surrounding the steeple in which he stood. He felt the expanse of air above him, imagined the highest flight of a gull, above it, clouds, and then the space beyond. The sea floor was a finite thing: deep as it might go, you would eventually reach bottom. But above… His science teacher had told them that space was infinite. That it went on and on, defying human ability to conceive of such a thing.

He looked at the words written in his mother's hand. He wondered where she was, if heaven was up above the stars, the ways the pastor described it, or somewhere in the sea his mother loved. He wondered if heaven was whatever place you loved most. Or were loved most. He felt his mother's love and knew with sudden certainty that it would follow him, wherever he might end up.

He looked at the page in his hand, his eyes resting on her words.

Whatever you do in your life…

He let the first page go, setting it free. As soon as it left his hand he wanted to snatch it back. He imagined it drifting downwards to the road below to find its way beneath the wheels of a passing car or worse, picked up and read by curious eyes, and it might have but for an updraft that caught and tossed it, sending it dancing up, and out. It pulled the remaining pages from his hand and he watched them on their journey until they might have been distant birds themselves, then gone.

As Pocket left the churchyard he felt the absence of the letter. It felt as if he was being lifted off the ground by birds and imagined two white gulls at his shoulders, wings extended.

Her boarder gone, Shirley sat at the window in the back of the quiet store and looked out across the Sound. It was a week ago this morning the store had been full of people talking about the crash of the night before. It seemed like a morning from a very long time ago. Scratch and Wilf had gone into Yarmouth early to see to Merle's arrangements and had caught the headline on the top paper at the newsagent's: *UFO Crash at Perry's Harbour*. They'd bought up three copies to bring back. Shirley looked at the paper now, folded on her lap. Under the headline ran another line: *Locals frustrated by lack of information from Ottawa*, and Shirley smiled at this, even though she'd read the story over twice. Below that: *by Rod Nowland. Exclusive to the* Herald. The illustration had printed well, she thought, the lines sharp despite the fact that it was rendered in pencil.

Her peripheral vision caught a movement, and she adjusted her chair to better see the figure that crossed the beach below the store, moving in the direction of the wharf. It was Pocket Snow, of course. She recognized him from his gangly height, the stoop of his shoulders. She resolved to have Pocket and Wilf over for dinner as soon as the funeral was over, as soon as Scratch and Wanda had left. If the Snow house didn't seem bereft now, it would seem awfully empty then.

She was about to rise and open the window to call out to Pocket, to wave the newspaper and to tell him she was proud of him. Something about him, an air of some sort, made her stop.

Later, she thought.

Ernie, one hand on the steering wheel of his father's green Ford, one hand around Edie Norris, watched the yellow line curve through the gold and red Quebec landscape. Jammed into paper bags and piled on the back seat were the things the two had managed to gather in their pre-dawn flight, each fumbling in the dark of their own houses. The French signs were unfamiliar, but Ernie had already figured a few things out: *Ouest*, he said to Edie with confidence. *West. Sortie*, he told her: *that's our exit.*

Cuff walked the perimeter of what would be the racetrack for the fourth time. In his mind, the pound of hooves, the roar of crowds. He'd have stands built, seats for a hundred. Hell, he'd have seats for five hundred. They'd come from Yarmouth. They'd come from Halifax. Ernie would come back before long, things wouldn't have worked out the way he'd thought they would. He'd show up, see the track and whistle, say: Cuff, it's beautiful, man. It's fuckin beautiful.

Hey, Ole Son, Cuff would say, I got some business to attend right now but maybe we can meet for a beer a little later.

Alone in the tidy workshop, Wilf Snow cried. It was the first time he'd let himself go, and he cried loudly, messily, and unashamedly until his chest and throat ached, and the remaining sawdust shavings were wet with tears. He cried for a long time, and when he had finished he wiped his eyes and blew his nose and folded his handkerchief, placing it in the breast pocket of his workshirt. He walked out and stood on the dry grass, looking at the back of his house where, inside, Scratch and Wanda plotted a future together.

He took a deep breath of salty October air and coughed. Come spring he'd give the old house a fresh coat of paint. He'd still have Pocket around to help him.

The sound of his footfalls on the wharf's planks echoed oddly to Pocket's ears. They sounded the way you might sound crossing a large, empty room, like walking across the floor at the Legion hall after all the chairs had been stacked against the wall. An impossibly lonely sound, it was, and yet here he was outside, with the sea and wind around him, the call of gulls, and his own beating heart. The air was full, and yet it was empty.

At the end of the wharf he stood, looking across the expanse of water. It looked as it had probably always looked, since the very beginning of things, shifting and moody, but fundamentally the same. If it held the secret of what had touched it, and from what distant place, it was giving nothing up. The Sound, to Pocket's mind, looked almost smug.

Kettle Island seemed close, the way it sometimes does, a trick of moisture in the air, an optical illusion. You could almost reach out and touch it, he thought, but his hand went, instead, to his coat pocket, where it closed around something round and smooth. It was cool in his palm, and he drew it out, traced its white line as it encircled the grey granite.

If he could make a wish for anything, what would he wish for?

He could see his life, and the lives of everyone he knew spanning out in intersecting lines, the curves of change, the sharp angles of the unexpected, the steady climbs and the sudden dips. How the shift of one affects the direction of another, alters its course, which alters another, and another. It all seemed impossibly complicated.

In the afternoon sky a daytime moon floated, pale, as if to say that even such things as day and night could not be trusted to stay in their places. You thought you understood something, could just reach out and hold it, and then it could slip from your grasp, just like that.

Pocket heaved the stone with everything he had. He felt the warmth of it leave his hand into the sureness of his pitch, saw its graceful arc towards the deep grey water of the Sound. He watched and watched, across the chop of waves, but he never saw it fall.

Space

Sometimes the things you know are the very things you cannot see.

You didn't see it as it began to move, slowly at first, across the ocean's floor. You didn't see the first orange light or the next, then another and another. You didn't see the row of lights sending beams across the kelp beds, illuminating the bones of sunken fishing boats and lost traps. You didn't see its shape, so unlike anything on the sea bottom, pick up speed as it neared the underwater beacon seen only by itself and the passing schools of fish. You didn't see, later, the lift of water, a pregnant swell birthing into the autumn dark, the sea settling behind like a whisper.

You didn't see, but you know what you felt: a shift. The sudden absence of something. You've felt it before.

You didn't see the soul leave the body like pollen from the flower. You didn't see it, but you know it rose to be carried on the wind, invisible particles lifting to dance on the air currents, kiss treetop leaves, settle on the sun-splashed wings of birds.

You didn't see it, but you know it the way you know where your heart is because of what it holds, know that it's nothing to do with that muscle itself, with veins and arteries, chambers. The push and pull of blood is just a foil for the real reason it beats.

How can you feel something that's not there? How can you see something that's invisible? How can you hear silence? And *how can you move forward through such an absence, and still know the presence of yourself?*

In the cold air, your steady breath: in; out. The fog on your eyelashes makes them heavy; when you blink, water runs down your face, salty in the corners of your lips. Your fingertips are a warm touch against your cheek. Inside your shirt there is the beating of your heart.

Your toes press against the ends of your boots, one size too small for too long, and this, more than anything, puts you firmly where you stand. In your boots, on a beach, in the night's cool embrace, rooted in a way you can't describe beside an ocean that stretches unfathomably long, and wide, and deep.

End

Afterword

In the 1960s and '70s, the only route from Yarmouth to our cottage on Barrington Bay was what is now the Lighthouse Route: the old highway that winds along the shoreline. Some days on this road the fog is so thick that the road could drop into the sea six feet in front of you and you wouldn't know it until you were picking the seaweed out of your teeth—but, of course, a corner leads to another corner, the fog always a short sprint ahead. On fine days, points of light dance off water blue enough to make you cry; every packing shed and boat mast and bell buoy fairly sings in the clear air. It's on this road that laundry flaps a greeting from a turquoise house, while in front of the firehall, a yellow dog smiles as it scratches. Along the road, a woman walks with her head down, thumbing through the mail in her hands.

Driving through Shag Harbour in our old green station wagon, my mother, father or one of my siblings might remark, as we passed through Woods Harbour, that we should start to watch for flying saucers. There were no "Site of 1967 U.F.O. Incident" signs on the highway then, but it was locally known that something mysterious had crashed into the Sound. As the youngest, I might have pressed my face to the window, eyes straining for the spaceship I was sure was just beyond the fog bank.

Unidentified Flying Objects seem like the stuff of storybooks: beside my keyboard, as I write this, is a copy of a comic book called *UFO Encounters*, published by Golden Press in 1978. On page 28: *The UFOs Invade Our Seas!* It's the "true" story of the Shag Harbour UFO crash of October 4, 1967, now comic-book legend a decade later. While it may seem like comic-book fodder, the Shag Harbour incident, sometimes referred to as "Canada's Roswell," is perhaps the most thoroughly documented and certainly the most famous of Canada's UFO sightings.

The Dark Object by Chris Styles and Don Ledger (Dell, 2001) chronicles what many have called "the night of the UFOs," describing eyewitness accounts all along the South Shore, with serious marine investigations in Shag Harbour and Shelburne Harbour happening concurrently. The authors logged hours of interviews, filled out countless "Access to Information" forms, and scrolled through miles of microfilm, in an exhaustive attempt to unravel the mystery. A number of documentaries have been produced on the subject, including segments by The History Channel and Ocean Entertainment. A Google search turns up thousands of hits.

The incident occurred smack in the middle of Cold War paranoia; it's hard to say now if the secrecy that surrounded the investigations stemmed from suspicions that this was Russian spy activity or an alien invasion. One thing is indisputable, captured as it was by CBC television, reflected in the four-inch headline that appeared on the front page of the *Halifax Chronicle Herald*: something crashed into the Sound at Shag Harbour that attracted a lot of official interest. Rumour is that divers pulled something up from the bottom and took it away. Throughout, locals were kept in the dark.

Everyone loves a good mystery, of course, and the Shag Harbour incident is certainly a compelling one. So many aspects of the story are outlandish enough to read like fiction, such as when Halifax reporter Ray MacLeod was suddenly, inexplicably, pulled from the story in the midst of the investigation, or *Dark Object* author Chris Styles' discovery, much later, of abruptly "missing" files.

But writers choose the stories they want to tell, and what interests me most are people, and the mysteries we hold inside our hearts. What I find about people is that, no matter where we live, no matter what our backgrounds, it is the same human emotions that inform the way we experience the things we encounter. Regardless of the experience—be it an unexpected visit of interstellar magnitude, or the passing of a loved one—the way we respond is true to who we are.

Here was a community of people simply going about their lives. When it seemed as if an airplane had crashed into the waters of the Sound, they did what members of any fishing community will do: they got in their boats and went out to see if they could help. Afterwards, while all that interest was focused out there on the water, life in Shag Harbour went on, and yet, in small ways, everyone was touched by the presence of strangers. This is the story I really wanted to tell in *Sounding Line*.

In this novel I took liberties in the interest of storytelling. I renamed the community Perry's Harbour, because of the changes I made to the setting, which I peopled with fictitious characters. I borrowed some local surnames (Snow in particular) and imported others. The characters in *Sounding Line* are not intended to represent anyone living or dead, but are entirely constructs of my imagination. Nicknames are a delightful part of local culture; it was great fun to make up my own, and the reasons behind them.

I randomly moved buildings around; I messed with sightlines and logistics. I played fast and loose with historical facts, hauling in a reporter that was never there and almost doing away with one that was, with apologies to the latter. I even closed the wharf, so as to keep my characters close together and a little more anxious. No doubt the people who live in the area will find a million inconsistencies, and for these, I beg your tolerance; it's fiction, after all.

What the Shag Harbour incident provides for me, as a storyteller, is a backdrop for a human story in the literary plot tradition of "a stranger comes to town, and everything changes." And what a stranger! The event invites both speculation and introspection among the characters, as any good story will.

More than anything, the appearance of an unidentified flying object offers a metaphor for both space and depth. It speaks to the human need to understand what's out there: outside of ourselves, outside the day-to-day familiarity of our communities, outside our World—and at the same time, what lies inside: our own depths.

Anne DeGrace
Nelson, British Columbia
March 5, 2009

Acknowledgments

Thanks to the people who gave me insight into life on the South Shore, people who shared information and anecdotes, local sayings and humour: Viola Nickerson, Ronnie Kenney, Cindy Nickerson, Laurie Wickens, Sharon Greenwood, Darren Perry, Neil Kendrick, and Derek Jones.

Stanley Lamrock suggested "something soft knocking on nothing" to describe a ghost (among other colourful tales), and Cheryl Nickerson gave me the story of the knock-kneed kid and the bowlegged kid who, standing side by side, could spell the word "ox." She made me laugh at a time I needed to, and gave me a story for later. My nephew, Greg Moffatt, dug up the souvenir newspapers that my mother once kept in the bottom drawer of her desk to find the story of Gagarin's space flight.

A great debt of gratitude goes to Dale Nickerson, who let me read the play *The Confusion of Country Living* for local language and colour, filled gaps in my understanding of local life, and acted as ambassador when I needed introductions or to get me onto a fishing boat. I'm especially grateful for her assistance with the first draft of this novel.

For background about the "incident," *The Dark Object* by Don Ledger and Chris Styles was invaluable. For local history, I'm indebted to the writings of Evelyn Richardson, whose beautiful prose provided a clear window into rural Maritime life. Books by authors Hattie Perry, Laurent D'Entremont, Carl D. Smith, and

Lewis J. Poteet offered anecdotes and insights, many of which found their way into the story.

It's interesting to write a story set 5,000 miles away from where you live. Sometimes I felt as if I had one toe in the Atlantic, the other in Kootenay Lake. On the B.C. side, thanks to my writing group: Verna Relkoff, Rita Moir, Jenny Craig, Vangie Bergum, and Antonia Banyard. Other readers of the manuscript were Mary Keirstead, Dale Nickerson, Steve Thornton, Jacquie Cameron, Kathy Witkowsky, and Patricia Rogers. It's no small job to critique a novel, and I'm hugely grateful.

To my smart, creative kids, Alex, Tam, and Annika, and my steadfast partner Phillip: thanks for being my cheering section.

Special thanks to the Canada Council for the Arts and the British Columbia Arts Council for support in the writing of this book.

Finally, thanks go to my agent, Morty Mint, who still pays for lunch most times, bless his heart. To Verna Relkoff (again), who, as a partner in Mint Agency as well as a friend, is always there for me. To Kim McArthur, Taryn Manias, Ann Ledden, Devon Pool, and the rest of the team at McArthur, thanks for having faith in me yet again.